PRAISE FOR TAHOE

"A GRIPPING NARRATIVE...A HERO WHO WALKS CONFIDENTLY IN THE FOOTSTEPS OF SAM SPADE, PHILIP MARLOWE, AND LEW ARCHER" — *Kirkus Reviews*

"A THRILLING MYSTERY THAT IS DIFFICULT TO PUT DOWN ...EDGE OF YOUR SEAT ACTION" — *Elizabeth, Silver's Reviews*

PRAISE FOR TAHOE GHOST BOAT

"THE OLD PULP SAVVY OF (ROSS) MACDONALD...REAL SURPRISE AT THE END" — *Kirkus Reviews*

"NAIL-BITING THRILLER...BOILING POT OF DRAMA"
— *Gloria Sinibaldi, Tahoe Daily Tribune*

"A THRILL RIDE" — *Mary Beth Magee, Examiner.com*

"BORG'S WRITING IS THE STUFF OF A HOLLYWOOD ACTION BLOCKBUSTER" — *Taylor Flynn, Tahoe Mountain News*

"ACTION-PACKED IS PUTTING IT MILDLY. PREPARE FOR FIREWORKS" — *Sunny Solomon, Bookin' With Sunny*

"I LOVED EVERY ROLLER COASTER RIDE IN THIS THRILLER 5+ OUT OF 5" — *Harvee Lau, Book Dilettante*

PRAISE FOR TAHOE CHASE

"EXCITING, EXPLOSIVE, THOUGHTFUL, SOMETIMES FUNNY"
— *Ann Ronald, Bookin' With Sunny*

"THE LANDSCAPE IS BEAUTIFULLY CRAFTED... PACE BUILDS NICELY AND DOESN'T LET UP"
— *Kirkus Reviews*

"BE WARNED. IT MIGHT BE ADDICTING"
— *Gloria Sinibaldi, Tahoe Daily Tribune*

"OWEN McKENNA HAS HIS HANDS FULL IN ANOTHER THRILLING ADVENTURE"
— *Harvee Lau, Book Dilettante*

PRAISE FOR TAHOE TRAP

"AN OPEN-THROTTLE RIDE"
- Wendy Schultz, Placerville Mountain Democrat

"A CONSTANTLY SURPRISING SERIES OF EVENTS INVOLVING MURDER...and the final motivation of the killer comes as a major surprise. (I love when that happens.)"   - Yvette, In So Many Words

"I LOVE TODD BORG'S BOOKS...There is the usual great twist ending in Tahoe Trap that I never would have guessed"   - JBronder Reviews

"THE PLOTS ARE HIGH OCTANE AND THE ACTION IS FASTER THAN A CHEETAH ON SPEED"   - Cathy Cole, Kittling: Books

"A FASCINATING STORY WITH FIRST CLASS WRITING and, of course, my favorite character, Spot, a Great Dane that steals most of the scenes."   - Mary Lignor, Feathered Quill Book Reviews

"SUPER CLEVER... More twists in the plot toward the end of the book turn the mystery into an even more suspenseful thriller."
-Harvee Lau, Book Dilettante

"AN EXCITING MURDER MYSTERY... I watch for the ongoing developments of Jack Reacher, Joanna Brady, Dismas Hardy, Peter and Rina Decker, and Alex Cross to name a few. But these days I look forward most to the next installment of Owen McKenna."
- China Gorman blog

PRAISE FOR TAHOE HIJACK

"BEGINNING TO READ TAHOE HIJACK IS LIKE FLOORBOARDING A RACE CAR... RATING: A+"
- *Cathy Cole, Kittling Books*

"A THRILLING READ... any reader will find the pages of his thrillers impossible to stop turning"
- *Caleb Cage, The Nevada Review*

"THE BOOK CLIMAXES WITH A TWIST THE READER DOESN'T SEE COMING, WORTHY OF MICHAEL CONNELLY"
- *Heather Gould, Tahoe Mountain News*

"I HAD TO HOLD MY BREATH DURING THE LAST PART OF THIS FAST-PACED THRILLER"
- *Harvee Lau, Book Dilettante*

PRAISE FOR TAHOE HEAT

"IN TAHOE HEAT, BORG MASTERFULLY WRITES A SEQUENCE OF EVENTS SO INTENSE THAT IT BELONGS IN AN EARLY TOM CLANCY NOVEL"
- *Caleb Cage, Nevada Review*

"TAHOE HEAT IS A RIVETING THRILLER"
- *John Burroughs, Midwest Book Review*

"WILL KEEP READERS TURNING THE PAGES AS OWEN RACES TO CATCH A VICIOUS KILLER"
- *Barbara Bibel, Booklist*

"THE READER CAN'T HELP BUT ROOT FOR McKENNA AS THE BIG, GENEROUS, IRISH-BLOODED, STREET-WISE-YET-BOOK-SMART FORMER COP"
- *Taylor Flynn, Tahoe Mountain News*

PRAISE FOR TAHOE NIGHT

"BORG HAS WRITTEN ANOTHER WHITE-KNUCKLE THRILLER... A sure bet for mystery buffs waiting for the next Robert B. Parker and Lee Child novels"
- *Jo Ann Vicarel, Library Journal*

"AN ACTION-PACKED THRILLER WITH A NICE-GUY HERO, AN EVEN NICER DOG..."
- *Kirkus Reviews*

"A KILLER PLOT... EVERY ONE OF ITS 350 PAGES WANTS TO GET TURNED... *FAST*"
- *Taylor Flynn, Tahoe Mountain News*

"A FASCINATING STORY OF FORGERY, MURDER..."
- *Nancy Hayden, Tahoe Daily Tribune*

PRAISE FOR TAHOE AVALANCHE

ONE OF THE TOP 5 MYSTERIES OF THE YEAR!
- Gayle Wedgwood, Mystery News

"BORG IS A SUPERB STORYTELLER...A MASTER OF THE GENRE"
- Midwest Book Review

"EXPLODES INTO A COMPLEX PLOT THAT LEADS TO MURDER AND INTRIGUE"
- Nancy Hayden, Tahoe Daily Tribune

PRAISE FOR TAHOE SILENCE

WINNER, BEN FRANKLIN AWARD, BEST MYSTERY OF THE YEAR!

"A HEART-WRENCHING MYSTERY THAT IS ALSO ONE OF THE BEST NOVELS WRITTEN ABOUT AUTISM"
STARRED REVIEW - Jo Ann Vicarel, Library Journal

CHOSEN BY LIBRARY JOURNAL AS ONE OF THE FIVE BEST MYSTERIES OF THE YEAR

"THIS IS ONE ENGROSSING NOVEL...IT IS SUPERB"
- Gayle Wedgwood, Mystery News

"ANOTHER EXCITING ENTRY INTO THIS TOO-LITTLE-KNOWN SERIES"
- Mary Frances Wilkens, Booklist

PRAISE FOR TAHOE KILLSHOT

"BORG BELONGS ON THE BESTSELLER LISTS with Parker, Paretsky and Coben"
- Merry Cutler, Annie's Book Stop, Sharon, Massachusetts

"A GREAT READ!"
-Shelley Glodowski, Midwest Book Review

"A WONDERFUL BOOK"
- Gayle Wedgwood, Mystery News

PRAISE FOR TAHOE ICE GRAVE

"BAFFLING CLUES...CONSISTENTLY ENTERTAINS"
— *Kirkus Reviews*

"A CLEVER PLOT... RECOMMEND THIS MYSTERY"
— *John Rowen, Booklist*

"A BIG THUMBS UP... MR. BORG'S PLOTS ARE SUPER-TWISTERS"
— *Shelley Glodowski, Midwest Book Review*

"GREAT CHARACTERS, LOTS OF ACTION, AND SOME CLEVER PLOT TWISTS...Readers have to figure they are in for a good ride, and Todd Borg does not disappoint."
— *John Orr, San Jose Mercury News*

PRAISE FOR TAHOE BLOWUP

"A COMPELLING TALE OF ARSON ON THE MOUNTAIN"
— *Barbara Peters, The Poisoned Pen Bookstore*

"RIVETING... A MUST READ FOR MYSTERY FANS!"
— *Karen Dini, Addison Public Library, Addison, Illinois*

WINNER! BEST MYSTERY OF THE YEAR
— *Bay Area Independent Publishers Association*

PRAISE FOR TAHOE DEATHFALL

"THRILLING, EXTENDED RESCUE/CHASE"   — *Kirkus Reviews*

"A TREMENDOUS READ FROM A GREAT WRITER"
— *Shelley Glodowski, Midwest Book Review*

"BORG OFFERS A SIMPLY TERRIFIC DOG"
— *Barbara Peters, The Poisoned Pen*

WINNER! BEST THRILLER OF THE YEAR
— *Bay Area Independent Publishers Association*

"A TAUT MYSTERY... A SCREECHING CLIMAX"
— *Karen Dini, Addison Public Library, Addison, Illinois*

Titles by Todd Borg

TAHOE DEATHFALL

TAHOE BLOWUP

TAHOE ICE GRAVE

TAHOE KILLSHOT

TAHOE SILENCE

TAHOE AVALANCHE

TAHOE NIGHT

TAHOE HEAT

TAHOE HIJACK

TAHOE TRAP

TAHOE CHASE

TAHOE GHOST BOAT

TAHOE BLUE FIRE

TAHOE DARK

TAHOE DARK

by

Todd Borg

THRILLER PRESS

Thriller Press First Edition, August 2016

TAHOE DARK
Copyright © 2016 by Todd Borg

All rights reserved under International and Pan-American Copyright Conventions. Published in the United States by Thriller Press, a division of WRST, Inc.

This novel is a work of fiction. Any references to real locales, establishments, organizations, or events are intended only to give the fiction a sense of verisimilitude. All other names, places, characters and incidents portrayed in this book are the product of the author's imagination.

No part of this book may be used or reproduced in any manner whatsoever without written permission from Thriller Press, P.O. Box 551110, South Lake Tahoe, CA 96155.

Library of Congress Control Number: 2016940022

ISBN: 978-1-931296-24-3

Cover design and map by Keith Carlson

Manufactured in the United States of America

For Kit

ACKNOWLEDGMENTS

I used to have a naive view of law enforcement. I thought of it as a romantic profession, the thin blue line between order and chaos.

Since then, I've learned that law enforcement is not a career that most law enforcement officers would describe as romantic!

Nevertheless, that misperception is what drew me to writing about their world. And, romantic notions aside, my law enforcement friends continue to impress me with their dedication and focus. I also benefit from their interest and support of my books.

Last winter, I was asked to participate in another character name auction, this one a benefit for the German Shepherd Rescue of Orange County.

The person who placed the winning bid is Retired Long Beach Police Officer Steve Ditmars. On behalf of rescue organizations everywhere, I thank Steve for his support. As a result, there is a character in Tahoe Dark named Steve Ditmars. I should point out that nothing about the character in the book is based on the real Steve Ditmars.

Once again, I owe huge thanks to my editors, Liz Johnston, Eric Berglund, Christel Hall, and my wife Kit. Turning a manuscript into a finished book is a really big project, and they get all the credit.

For the cover of Tahoe Dark, I asked graphic artist Keith Carlson for a look similar to the dramatic, noirish covers of the era of pulp fiction. Wow, what a great result! I can't thank him enough.

Finally, thanks again to Kit. She's always there for me, and my books wouldn't exist without her support.

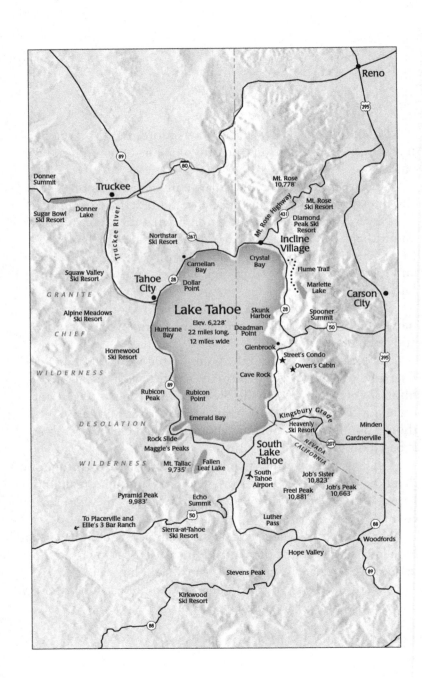

PROLOGUE

"We got your son Jonas," a voice on the phone said. It was a strange, buzzy voice, vaguely feminine, warping like it had been hung in the wind to twist and turn. The words stunned David Montrop and made him freeze in place like a prey animal sensing a deadly threat, unsure of its source.

Until that moment, it had been a good morning. David Montrop had spent an hour on his stand-up paddle board, moving among the huge boulders that dotted the waters of Lake Tahoe just north of Sand Harbor State Park. Eventually, the fatigue from the chemo came back. But Montrop felt less nauseated than normal. The sun was out. Spring snow flurries had given way to the warmer days of June. Tahoe glowed blue as sapphires.

After his paddle, Montrop sat on one of the boulders for a bit to gather his strength. When his breathing slowed, he lifted the 32-pound paddle board, one end at a time, to the roof rack of his Mercedes. The effort made him begin to faint. He leaned against the hood and lowered his head to give his blood pressure a moment to return. Montrop was glad that he could still get the board on and off the car. It was one of those small things that he never used to think about.

Feeling tired but rejuvenated from the exercise and fresh air, he drove north to his home in Incline Village and unloaded the paddle board, leaning it against one of the garage doors. After he changed clothes, Montrop made a shopping list and headed to the supermarket.

He'd just parked and gotten out of the car when his phone rang.

David Montrop fished the phone out of his pocket and was shocked to see his stepson's number. After all the stress, all the drama, it was a major gift to have the boy actually call him. The day was going to be great.

Montrop smiled as he tapped the answer icon. "Hey, Jonas," he said. "Good to hear from you." He wanted to add, 'It's about time,' but he refrained.

Then came the voice sounding diseased and disturbed, claiming to have Jonas.

"I'm sorry, I don't understand," Montrop said, his gut tightening.

"Dad!" a normal voice broke in. "Do what they say! These guys are craz…" Jonas's voice was cut off.

"Jonas?" David said. "Is that you? What's going on?"

The twisted voice came back. "Listen real careful. If you don't do just as I say, we kill the kid. Shoot that bro dead. You unnerstand?"

For a moment, Montrop thought it must be a joke. This was like in the movies, the disguised voice, the dumb speech.

"What do you want?" Montrop asked, his voice cracking, serious fear creeping into him despite the fact that the situation seemed ludicrous. His throat felt like sandpaper.

"We know you're in the parking lot at the grocery store. Walk next door to the bank. There's a path between the parking lots. See it?"

"Yes," Montrop said, barely able to make a sound. The woman on the phone – if it was a woman – was making Montrop shake. He glanced around behind him, looking for a cargo van or someplace where the caller could be hiding. A place where the caller held Jonas against his will. Montrop saw nothing. How did someone know that he had come to the supermarket?

Montrop walked across the asphalt, found the short path, and went through some trees to the bank's parking lot.

"Okay," the voice said, as if the person could see every step that Montrop took. "Go to the left corner of the building. There's some bushes. See 'em?"

"Yes." Montrop's voice wavered. He walked toward the building, feeling dizzy, as if he were about to lose his balance.

"Go over to the bushes," the voice said. "There's two paper grocery bags. One has some dirt in it. The other's empty. Carry the bags by their handles. Keep holding your phone. Keep the phone line open and turn it on speaker. Unnerstand? Go in the bank. Act real normal." The words, spoken in the warped voice, were hard to make out. "Take out twenty-five thousand in cash. You do anything funny, your son dies. Got it? I wanna hear you as you talk to the teller. If you hang up, or if you cover up the phone for even two seconds, he's dead!"

"I don't think the bank keeps that kind of cash," Montrop said, his voice small and weak.

"Yeah, they do. Jonas told us that's where you get your cash for the bands. If they ask what it's for, you say it's for a band. And I want different sizes."

"Sizes?"

"The bills! Some hunnerds and the rest twenties. When they hand it over, put the money in the empty paper bag. That way each bag has something in it. The one with dirt will be the bag to fool people. You got it?"

"Yes, I've got it. The money goes in the empty bag. The one with the dirt is the decoy."

There was a pause. "Right. The decoy." The voice seemed to shift in space. "Then you walk outside and I'll tell you what to do next. The whole time, you hold your phone in your hand. And the phone line stays open, right?"

"Phone line open," Montrop repeated.

"Okay, time to put it on speaker."

Montrop started to panic. "I don't know how to put it on speaker."

"Look on the screen!" The voice was yelling. "There's a button on the bottom. See it?"

"Okay, I found it." Montrop put the phone on speaker.

"Now go!"

Montrop's heart thumped as he walked over to the bushes. A small, sharp pain stabbed at his trachea, constricting his throat.

Behind a row of junipers were two paper grocery bags just as the voice had said. They stood under some branches, easy to miss.

Montrop held his phone in one hand and reached with his other to lift the bags out by their handles. The heavier bag, the one with the dirt, caught on a twig. One of the handles ripped off, and the paper tore down the side. Montrop stopped to breathe. He couldn't get enough air.

Already, things were going wrong. Montrop nearly dropped his phone as he shifted his hands, gripping the torn bag by its top edges. Holding his phone and the bags with one hand, he pulled the bank door open and walked inside. He felt something touch his leg. Montrop looked down and saw a trickle of dirt coming from the torn bag, raining down his leg, into his shoe, and onto the floor. He repositioned the bag, tipping it so the dirt flowed away from the tear in the paper.

There were two men talking to bank tellers, two women in line, one guy over in the waiting area where a bank officer worked at a desk, and a couple at the ATM. The woman pushed the ATM's buttons while the man looked around. The man held a phone in front of him so that he could glance down at the screen. It seemed to Montrop as if the man was watching him even though his eyes weren't directly on him.

When Montrop got to the teller, he tried to sound normal. "Hi, I'm David Montrop of Big Lake Promotions." His voice had a tremor in it. He took a deep breath, trying to stay calm. "I need to make a cash payment to a band, so I'd like to withdraw twenty-five thousand. You can take it out of my business checking account." He lay the phone on the counter, then pulled out his wallet and removed his bank card.

"That's a big payment for cash," the teller said. She made a little frown. Montrop didn't know if he wanted her to figure out that there was a problem or not. If she did, he certainly hoped she wouldn't say anything, because the person on the phone line could probably hear every word they spoke.

"I'll have to get the manager for a cash withdrawal that large," the teller said. She stood up, walked over to the end of the teller counter, and went through a door.

After a moment, she returned with another woman. They came up behind the teller counter, spoke, and looked at the computer screen. The manager gestured dramatically as she asked Montrop for his driver's license, then had him swipe his bank card and enter his passcode. The manager typed on the computer and then said that they'd have to get the money from the safe.

"What denominations would you like?"

"Um…" Montrop felt like his brain went blank. The panic came back. Breath short. Heart thumping. What did the voice on the phone say? Then he remembered. Montrop said, "Half in hundreds and half in twenties."

The two women went through another door.

Montrop waited, trying hard to relax a little. The man who'd been watching him from the ATM was now sitting on a nearby bench. He still had his phone out. He wasn't looking at Montrop, but he was close enough to hear. The woman he'd been with had disappeared.

After a few minutes, the two bank women came back. The manager set down five bundles of twenties and two bundles of one hundreds. Each bundle was held together with a tight paper strip.

"We only had ten thousand worth of twenties. The rest will have to be hundreds. Is that okay?"

"Yes," Montrop said.

While one woman watched, the other broke open one of the packs of hundreds, ran the money through the counting machine, splitting it into two groups of 50 bills, and then rebundled the two groups with rubber bands.

The woman pointed to the paper strips on the other bundles. "Are you okay with the currency straps? One hundred bills per bundle? Or should we break them open and run them through the counting machine?"

"I trust the bundles."

The woman nodded. She went through the bundles of twenties, putting each one down on the counter, their violet-colored paper strips vibrant. "Two, four, six, eight, and ten thousand." She set one of the paper-strapped hundreds next to the twenties. It had a mustard-colored paper strip around it. "A bundle of hundreds is another ten thousand, for a total of twenty thousand. The half bundle of hundreds in the rubber band is five thousand. For a grand total of twenty-five thousand."

The two women each signed a slip, had him sign as well, and then handed him the money. "Will there be anything else, Mr.

Montrop?"

"No, thank you." He put the money in the bottom of the empty paper bag, the one that still had intact handles, and walked out, moving close to the man on the bench. The man seemed not to notice him. He just stared down at his phone.

When Montrop got outside, the voice came from the phone.

"Over by your car in the grocery parking lot is a trash can. Don't slow down. Just walk by the trash can and drop the money bag into it. Hold on to the bag with the dirt. Keep walking to your car, get in, and drive home with the bag of dirt. You got it?"

"Got it."

"We'll be watching you the whole way. You call the cops or anyone, we pop your son. When you get home, you keep quiet 'til we let the kid go. He'll call you when he's free. Unnerstand?"

"Yes."

The phone went dead.

Montrop did as he was told. He walked from the bank lot to the supermarket lot and headed toward his car and the nearby trash can. He dropped the bag with the money into the trash can. Still holding the bag of dirt, he got into his car, started it, and pulled out of the bank lot.

At the first red light, he noticed a vehicle pull up behind him so close he couldn't see its bumper. It was black. The vehicle looked like an Audi, shiny black. The sun reflected off its windshield, so he couldn't see the person driving.

When the light turned, Montrop pulled away. The Audi stayed right on him. Was the driver an accomplice of the kidnapper? Someone else?

Montrop made his way over to 431, the Mt. Rose Highway, and headed up the mountain. When he again looked in the rearview mirror, the Audi was gone. Or was it still back there, several vehicles behind?

Montrop turned off the highway, wound his way up into his neighborhood, and pulled into his drive, which went up at a steep curve. Montrop's home was surrounded by forest, out of view from his neighbors.

As Montrop got out of his car, he sensed movement below. Something dark. Had the black Audi pulled into the entrance of his driveway and stopped? Montrop moved sideways, trying to look through the trees. He saw nothing.

Montrop waited, but nothing appeared. He turned toward his house. Something seemed different. It took him a moment to remember. Earlier, he'd left the paddle board leaning against the garage so that it could dry. Now it was gone.

Montrop turned toward the front door. He heard a noise behind him. He turned fast, which made him dizzy. He felt faint again, so he leaned his hands on the hood of the car. With his head hanging down, his glasses slipped until the bow tips caught his ears.

As his vision returned, he pushed his glasses back up on his nose and looked around. He saw nothing out of the ordinary.

After a minute, he walked to the front door.

Then came another noise. Soft. A whoosh-like air movement. He turned again. Saw movement in his peripheral vision.

A large shape came through the air behind him. Something sharp and hard struck him on the shoulder and glanced off the corner of his jaw just below his ear.

The blow was heavy and shocking. Montrop was thrown several feet to the side. He landed on the drive's paving stones, his chin abrading down to the bone. Montrop was stunned. Panting. His glasses were gone. The world was hopelessly blurry.

He heard the sound of the car door opening on his Mercedes. Then came an angry shout.

"What's this?! Dirt!" The voice seemed vaguely familiar. "Where's the money?! You double-crossing…!"

The car door shut. Another door opened. Then shut. Fast, angry footsteps barely registered to Montrop.

The voice shouted from just behind him. "Where's the money, old man?! Where!"

Montrop had got his palms on the drive and pushed himself up onto hands and knees. His neck was electric with pain. Slowly, he turned his head to the side. There was the vague shape of a person. Nothing recognizable.

"Where's the money!!"

Montrop struggled to speak through his broken jaw. "I did just what you said. I put the money in the trash, and I carried the decoy bag into my car."

"What?!"

Montrop sensed blurred movement. A big dark shape being picked up off the ground. His paddle board. Someone carrying it away.

Montrop tried to turn farther, tried to see. But his neck felt broken. Maybe if he stood up.

He got his hands on his knees and slowly rose, fighting dizziness.

Holding his arms out for balance, he rotated. The person holding the board was some distance away, maybe 10 yards. The person turned and ran toward Montrop. Montrop struggled to focus, but without his glasses it was hopeless. When the person with the board got up to speed, he lifted the board above his head and released it into the air.

As the board arced through the air toward his face, Montrop turned his head. The point of the board hit Montrop's temple, ripping through flesh to his skull bone and knocking him backward. The blow deflected the bow of the board up into the air. The board's stern hit Montrop on the chest, the sharp fin cutting through his shirt and slicing his skin the length of his sternum.

Montrop was slammed down. The back of his head hit the driveway, and he was still.

ONE

Blondie dropped the Frisbee at Street Casey's feet.

"Your dog steals Spot's Frisbee and then brings it to you," I said. "Aren't you worried she's carrying the Yellow Lab Retriever work ethic a little too far?"

Street patted her thighs as Spot ran up to her. He looked down at the Frisbee where it lay at Street's feet. He wagged. Looked at Street, then Blondie. Looked back at the Frisbee with such intensity that it seemed he expected to make it fly by the sheer force of his stare.

"Maybe His Largeness's work ethic isn't quite as robust as Blondie's," Street said as she bent a little and gave Spot a hug.

"No doubt about that," I said. "You know that Great Danes have the lowest work ethic of all the working breeds."

"Unless you consider the couch lounging category," Street said.

"True. On that kind of work, he has no equal." I walked up and gave each dog a pet. "It seems like Blondie's doing well," I said.

"Certainly much better. But she spends a lot of time staring at the front door as if she's waiting for Adam Simms to walk in. I suppose I should expect a range of residual behaviors from a rescue dog. But yesterday at the lab, it was pronounced. When the UPS driver walked in, Blondie kept looking past him as if Adam was just beyond, maybe in the truck or something."

"Anyway," Street said, "overcoming Newton's First Law is a lot easier for a fifty-pound Yellow Lab than a hundred-and-seventy-pound Great Dane," Street said, ever the scientist. "Being small makes it easier to poach Frisbees." She bent down and pet Blondie. "Doesn't it, baby?" As Street spoke to Blondie, her voice sounded dull and gray, as if the normal color was gone. I couldn't tell what it meant.

Blondie picked up the Frisbee, gave it a little chew, dropped it again at Street's feet.

"How does the First Law thing work?" I asked.

"Newton explained how any object in motion continues to move in a straight line unless acted upon by a force. The more mass the moving object has, the more force needed to change its direction or velocity. Because Blondie is so much smaller, she has more horsepower per pound, so to speak, so she can turn faster than this big lunk." As she said it, Street thumped her hands on the side of Spot's chest, playing out a Reggae rhythm. Spot's wagging frequency ratcheted up a notch.

"You're saying that your dog has more horsepower than my dog," I said.

"Per pound, yes. The smaller the animal, the stronger per pound it is. Smaller dogs can leap relatively farther than bigger dogs. A squirrel can leap dozens of times its length."

"Next you're going to tell me that those insects you study have the most horsepower of all."

"Absolutely. A flea can leap hundreds of times its length. The key is power per unit of weight. Remember, an elephant can roll cars over and crush them, but it can't leap at all."

"And you think like this every time you see a dog catching a Frisbee."

"I'm a scientist," she said as if that explained everything.

"What about you and me?" I asked. "Do you have more horsepower per pound than me?"

"Well, I'm half your weight, so that would suggest maybe so. But then, you have the strength advantage that comes with testosterone."

"Whereas you have special girly girl powers," I said.

Street looked at me. "I'm pretty sure no girly girl ever raised maggots as part of her job."

"An unusual mix for sure," I said. "But I can think of at least one activity where you have more horsepower than me."

Street made a small grin. "Would that be per pound?"

"No. Straight up. No pound adjustment necessary."

Street reached up and hugged me. Despite the touch, I sensed a background hum of worry.

Before I could ask about it, my cell rang.

"I'll make it quick," I said to Street. I pressed the answer button. "Hello?"

"Is this Owen McKenna?" A woman's voice.

Street was still hugging me. She heard the woman's voice. Raised her eyebrows.

"Speaking," I said.

"This is Sergeant Lori Lanzen of the Washoe County Sheriff's Office. I hope you don't mind me calling your cell. Sergeant Martinez of Douglas County gave me your number. He also… vouched for you."

"I need vouching for? Regarding what?"

"Let's just say you are a person of interest in a homicide," Lanzen said. "Naturally, the concern is whether or not you're a flight risk. Diamond thought probably not."

Now she had my attention. "Emphasis on 'not' or on 'probably?'" I asked.

Street's eyes were wide.

"Not sure," Lanzen said. "The victim's name is David Montrop. Do you recognize that name?"

"No. What connects me to his murder?" I asked.

"We found a note that names you as his probable killer."

"What?! Any idea who wrote the note?"

"The victim."

"Montrop," I said.

"Right."

It took me a moment to process. "You're saying that David Montrop, who's dead, claims I killed him."

"Yeah."

"Now I know why you wanted Diamond to vouch for me," I said.

The sergeant didn't respond.

"Where would you like me to meet you?" I asked.

"I'm at Montrop's house in Incline. Any chance you could come here soon?"

"Either that or I flee to another country. Let me think about it for a moment."

"I'll give you directions," the sergeant said, ignoring my

attempt at levity.

She gave me an address and some directions, and asked when I'd be there.

"If I'm not there in an hour, send one of your teams to the Air Canada gate at the Reno Tahoe Airport."

When I hung up, Street said, "Quite the conundrum," she said. "A dead guy accusing you of killing him. How do you suppose you did it?"

"I'll know soon." I reached out and touched her cheek. "You okay? You seem stressed."

She made a little frown and shook her head. "I'm fine. I'm just behind on work."

I held her look a bit. It seemed as if there was a shadow across her face even though we were in the sun.

"Really," she said. "I'll be fine as soon as I catch up."

I nodded even though I could tell it was something else.

We hugged goodbye, and Spot and I left.

TWO

Thirty-five minutes later, I turned into a neighborhood above Incline Village on the northeast shore of Lake Tahoe. Up the street were two Washoe County Sheriff's patrol units parked on the shoulder, one of which had its light bar flashing.

In the entrance of a driveway that rose up from the road at a steep angle was a blue unmarked, its multiple antennas a giveaway to anyone closer than fifty yards. I parked in a bit of shade and got out. Spot had his head out the rear window, so I put him in a headlock, gave him a knuckle rub, then walked to the drive, which was made of brick laid in a pattern of overlapping arcs. A uniformed officer stopped me as I approached.

"Sorry, sir, this is a crime scene. I can't let you pass."

"Please tell your sergeant that Owen McKenna is here. She's looking for me."

The man got on his radio, said some words, got a scratchy reply, and then turned to me. "You're right. Go on up." He pointed up the driveway. I walked up.

The house sat behind a row of ornamental Maple trees that were just beginning to bud out in the early June sunshine. The building was made of smooth-cut stone and glass and looked timeless. It had a gabled roof made of copper, with the glass rising to the roof peaks. Where the windows met at a corner was a chimney made of polished granite blocks. To the side were two garages, with double-wide doors constructed to look like broad, modern double gates that would swing out rather than rise up.

A burgundy Mercedes was parked in front of one of the garages. On the brick driveway, 20 feet from the driver's door lay what looked like an expensive Italian loafer. To the side of the car, near the edge of the driveway, half in the shade of a Maple and half in the sun, was the body of a man in his late sixties or early seventies. Although well dressed, his clothes failed to disguise the fact that he was thin to the point of suggesting some kind of health problem. His head was torn open at the temple, a flap of skin hanging amidst a lot of dried blood. The clothes at his chest looked like they'd been sliced up the center with an unsharpened hedge shears. The long rough opening in the fabric was soaked with drying blood.

A cop was taking pictures of the victim from every angle. Another had an evidence kit and was dusting the car for fingerprints.

The house's entry had a large portico to drive under during snow or rain. The portico was held up by stone columns at the corners and had a stone sidewall four feet high. A cop had set a laptop on top of the sidewall. He was typing on it. The sergeant stood in the open entry, talking on her phone.

The sergeant clicked off her phone.

I walked up. "Owen McKenna, your person of interest," I said.

"Thanks for coming," she said. "I'm Lori Lanzen. Sergeant Diamond Martinez of Douglas County explained that you used to be with the San Francisco PD."

I nodded as we shook hands. Her hand was small, but her grip was strong.

I gestured toward the body. "Any idea what killed him?"

She pointed past the body. "Behind those Manzanita bushes is a paddle board. It has blood on the point at the front – what's that called? – and there's also blood on the fin thing on the bottom of the rear."

"The point is the bow," I said.

She frowned. "Oh, right. The bow."

"And the fin thing at the bottom of the stern is just called the fin. Some years back, it was called a skeg when on a sailboard. Now fin is the common nomenclature."

"The fin," she said. "Yes, of course. Well, no wonder the victim thinks you killed him. You have more than a passing familiarity with the murder weapon."

I nodded. "You think it's murder one?"

"Hard to know. It all gets down to intent, right? Clearly, we have malice aforethought. This was not a completely accidental death. At the bare minimum, the person who threw the paddle board intended harm. But first degree murder? If I planned to murder someone, my first choice of weapon wouldn't be a paddle board, even if I were big enough to throw it. So, second degree looks more likely."

I nodded.

"I should start by asking you the basic questions," she said.

"Of course."

"Do you know of or have you ever met the victim, David Montrop?" she asked.

"Never heard of him to my knowledge."

"Have you ever been to this house?"

I shook my head as I looked around at the mountains and the lake in the distance. "I've never even been in this neighborhood."

"Are you associated in any way with the music promotion business?"

"No."

"Do you have anything to do with concerts or bands?"

"No."

"Have you ever heard of a company called Big Lake Promotions?"

"No."

"Can you think of any way that the victim may have known of you?"

"Not in particular. I've been in the news now and then in conjunction with some of my cases. But I'm not that well known. Of course, many local law enforcement officers know of me."

"Do Tahoe LEOs appreciate your presence in the community, or do they resent you?"

"As best as I can tell, most of them don't think of me as too much of a pest. But as you know, cops sometimes have a pejorative attitude toward those of us who go private. Why do you ask?"

"Because David Montrop made a point of mentioning your cop background. It's almost as if he has a thing about cops. But when I initially looked him up, I didn't find a record. Come with me," she said. "I'll show you what we found." She walked across the broad entry, through wide double doors, both open, and into a room with a slate floor. In the center was a pedestal with what looked like a six-foot-tall Remington bronze showing a cowboy on his horse, his arm raised to throw a lasso. I'd never seen a Remington that was that large, so maybe it was just a look-alike.

I followed the sergeant through a grand open living room. On the far side of the room, we went up a step into a study the size of my cabin. The room had one wall of windows that looked up through a Jeffrey Pine forest toward Rose Knob Peak, one of the often-overlooked sister mountains that stretch out to the southwest from Mt. Rose.

The other walls had large bookshelves that held old leather books with embossed gold leaf letters. They were nice decor, but their perfect alignment suggested that they weren't frequently consulted, if ever read at all. Among the bookshelves on one wall was an area devoted to framed certificates and citations with elaborate calligraphy, some with gold award stickers. On a stand was a glass plaque with acid-etched musical notes and lettering no doubt proclaiming some kind of achievement in the music industry.

In the center of the room was a huge desk with a forest green, inset leather top. The desk was relatively clean. It had a banker's lamp, a brass and teak pen-and-pencil holder, and a small brass clock. On the corner of the desk was an 8 x10 photo of an old cruiser-type boat in an easel-back frame. As a boat fancier, I leaned in to get a closer look. It looked like a 1960s cuddy cabin design, maybe a Thompson. It didn't look to be in good shape, but it had probably given Montrop good times at some point in the past. To one side of the desk was a stack of papers. To the other side was a computer printer. On it was a piece of copy paper with printing. The sergeant pointed toward it.

I walked around behind the desk, leaned over, and looked at it without touching it.

The top of the note was dated with the previous day's date and the time of 10:30 p.m., looking very much as if Montrop had typed and printed the note the previous evening.

If something violent should happen to me, it's possible the

perpetrator is an ex-cop named Owen McKenna. He and I go way back, and I have reason to believe he has angry feelings toward me. I wouldn't put it past him to attack me in an attempt to settle an old score.

If someone is reading this note, then that suggests it is too late to do anything other than try to catch him or whoever assaulted me.

I don't want to falsely accuse McKenna, but I will take this information to the police tomorrow. In the meantime, I'm going to bed with a sense of foreboding, so I write this note.

I turned to the sergeant.
"Unusual note," I said to her.
Sergeant Lanzen nodded. "Do you have a comment?"
"No. I have no idea who he is or why he might think I have angry feelings toward him."
Sergeant Lanzen's gaze settled on Montrop's note.
"Have you any idea why he was murdered?" I asked.
Lanzen shook her head. "No. The gardener found him dead when he arrived this morning. He called nine-one-one and indicated in broken English that Mr. Montrop had died."
"The gardener carries a house key," I said.
"Apparently." Lanzen glanced out the window. There was a smallish man sitting on a decorative iron bench in a small garden near the Mercedes. He rocked left and right as if distraught. "His duties include the indoor plants as well," Lanzen said. "He communicated in so many words that the place is as he found it."
"Neat and picked up," I said.
"Yes. Apparently, the housekeeper was here yesterday. It looks like nothing has been touched since then beyond a few dishes in the kitchen, the clothes and bedding in Montrop's bedroom, and…" she paused, then gestured at the desk, "this note."
Lanzen gestured toward the door. "Please come outside and look at the body. You said you don't know him by name, but we should check that you don't recognize him."

"Of course."

I followed her outside. There were two men who had wheeled a gurney and body bag up the driveway and were waiting for her approval before they removed the body.

She spoke to them. "I'll be done in a few minutes."

"You've completed your death scene examination?" I said.

"Yes. And because of the peculiarities, the Medical Examiner already stopped by. We'll know more after the pathologist completes the autopsy, but he said it looks like Montrop died from blunt force trauma to the head."

Lanzen walked me over to the body, then stepped aside so I could see.

The victim's head was turned sideways, the wounded temple facing the sky, the other cheek mashed against driveway brick. I leaned in to get a closer look. From my perspective, he was upside down, not the best angle for recognition. I backed away and walked around to see him from the proper perspective.

When the sergeant had first mentioned the name David Montrop on the phone, I didn't recall the name. But I certainly knew the face.

I turned to Sergeant Lanzen. "I was wrong. I do recognize him. From a long time back. Let me think a moment. It would have been twelve or more years ago. In San Francisco. Probably the reason you didn't find criminal activity is that he went by a different name. I don't recall what it was, but David Montrop doesn't seem familiar. He was a con man who should have spent a decade in San Quentin for voluntary manslaughter. But because of multiple procedural mistakes the prosecution made and some sloppy evidence collection on our part, he got off with just probation."

THREE

"You know David Montrap as a former manslaughter suspect," Sergeant Lanzen repeated as if to be sure she understood correctly.

"Correct. I was a Homicide Inspector when he was charged and prosecuted," I said. "Although I don't think Montrop ever knew my name. I had no direct dealings with him. The cop who brought him in was Bill Riley, a colleague of mine who is still with the SFPD."

Lanzen was frowning. "If Montrop didn't know your name back then, do you think it's a coincidence that Montrop names you as someone threatening him?"

I shook my head. "No. In this business, a good default position is to assume there are no coincidences."

Lanzen said, "You said Montrop was a con man. What do you mean by that?"

"He ran a music scam that began when he discovered a great new band with a great song and a really good demo video. He convinced the band that he was an agent and that he could sell them to a big record company. Of course, the band got excited. Two weeks later, he came back to them with the great news that one of the biggest record companies had made an offer and believed the band was going to become the next big thing. They were supposedly offering a contract that would give the band a little advance money but no royalties until the band became a hit. Of course, he made it all up. Then he told the band that the recording label was also starting a new producing and publishing program where they'd allow certain, special bands to become co-investors. In return for the band putting up a sizable amount of cash, the label would give them a much bigger royalty percentage and a generous sliding scale of bonuses if they hit certain sales targets."

"So the band members coughed up money," Lanzen said, shaking her head.

"Yeah. A lot. Two of the band members had families with money, and Montrop got them to invest two hundred thousand in return for a contract that he said would possibly give them huge returns, potentially ranging into the tens of millions if they became a hit."

"Let me guess," the sergeant said. "He kept the money and never even contacted any record company."

"Worse. He did contact a record company, played them the demo, said it was by a different band, the name of which he made up, and told them that the band was his creation."

"What does that mean?"

"He told them that he created the entire package, hired the band members and the songwriters and even paid for and produced the music video."

"Does that really happen?"

"Often, yes. Famous bands like The Monkees and NSYNC and the Spice Girls were fabricated from scratch by ambitious managers. Montrop got a record company so excited about this fake band of his that they offered a traditional contract with a large signing bonus."

"Which Montrop also kept," Lanzen said.

"Right. But one of the band members suspected the truth and tracked Montrop down and accosted him at Montrop's high-rise apartment by the Embarcadero in San Francisco. They scuffled, and the singer fell off Montrop's balcony to his death. The fight was witnessed by people in an apartment in a high rise across the street."

Sergeant Lanzen looked sad, an unusual expression for a cop.

"I'm sorry to say that we botched the case," I said. "His lawyer knew it, and Montrop was able to plea bargain and get off with parole only. During the case, the music scam came out, which led to multiple civil suits, which Montrop lost. Unfortunately for the fraud victims, Montrop's money appeared to have disappeared."

The men finished tightening the gurney straps and wheeled the body down the driveway.

"You're saying that Montrop claimed to have lost all of the money he stole," Lanzen said.

"Yeah."

"But you don't believe it," she said.

"No one close to the case believed it. He demonstrated financial skill in putting together his scam. Those same skills would have been useful in hiding the money."

Lanzen looked up at the grand house. "You'd need a big bank account to own a place like this. This house must have cost three or four million, don't you think?"

"I'm no real estate expert, but I bet you're in the ballpark. Any idea if he lived with anyone? Did he have family?"

"We just got the search warrant a half hour before you came, so we've made only the briefest search of his things. It appears he has a son named Jonas. In his top desk drawer, we found one of those cartoon birthday cards addressed to Jonas. On the front, it says, 'For my favorite son.' On the inside it says, 'Okay, so you're an only child, but you're still my favorite.' And stuck to the front of the card was a Post-it note that said, 'Remember to get Jonas a birthday present.'"

FOUR

"Have you contacted Jonas?" I asked.

The sergeant said, "I called the number in Montrop's book and got Jonas's voicemail. I left a message asking him to call me about his father. I said it was important."

"Any indication of his son's address?"

Lanzen looked at me. "You're interested in the case." It was a statement, not a question.

"Being accused by the murder victim piques my curiosity. If I'm not actually a suspect, maybe I can help."

"After I called Sergeant Diamond Martinez, I knew you weren't a suspect. I'd be happy to have help. And you would no doubt like to find out why you were mentioned on Montrop's note."

I made a single nod.

Lanzen said, "The son's address wasn't clear. Montrop abbreviated the street in his book and left off the town. I suppose he didn't need it to remember where Jonas lived, so he just wrote down the number. Maybe it will make sense to you."

She led me back inside the house to the study, pulled on latex gloves, and opened the top drawer of the desk. She opened the address book, turned the pages until she found the one she wanted, and pointed to the left side of that page. Montrop had written Jonas's name, a street number, and then the letters TKB.

"Does it give you any ideas?" she said.

"Possibly. One version could be Tahoe Keys Boulevard."

"Oh, very good. South Lake Tahoe, right?"

I nodded.

She got out her cell phone. "I'll Google that address and see what comes up." She tapped on her phone, waited a bit, tapped some more.

After another minute, she showed me the phone.

"Looks like an actual address," I said. "If you like, I can call Commander Mallory of the SLTPD and give him the news. He could send out one of his people to inform Jonas of his father's death. Or I can go myself. My office is on Kingsbury Grade. That's just a few miles away. Now that I've been pulled into the periphery of this case, I'd like to meet the son."

Lanzen thought about it. "You don't belong to a law enforcement agency, but I think that would be okay. Will you let me know if you're able to find him or not?"

"Certainly. One question is, do we know if this house belongs to Montrop?"

Lanzen walked back into the study, put her latex gloves back on, and, careful not to smear any latent prints, opened the file drawers of the desk. She flipped through the folders. "There's nothing here about taxes or utility bills or a house deed, or any of the stuff an owner would typically have. I don't think he has another office because when I looked up Big Lake Promotions, it showed this address."

She pulled out her cell phone, scrolled through her contacts list and pressed a name. While she waited, she turned to me and said, "I know a woman who has a vacation rental company and a real estate broker's license."

I heard a voice from Lanzen's phone.

"Sonia?" the sergeant said. "Lori Lanzen. I wonder if you can do me a favor? Can you please look up a house and see who owns it, where the tax bill is sent, and any related information?"

There was a pause, then Lanzen gave the address. Then she said, "The man living here goes by the name David Montrop." After another pause, "Great. I'll wait for your call."

We went back outside. I pointed to Montrop's car. "Anything of interest in the Mercedes?"

"On the floor on the passenger side was a paper grocery bag," she said.

"Anything in it?" I asked.

"That's the interesting part. The bag has dirt in it. Not much, maybe a half pound or so. The bag was torn, and dirt had spilled out onto the floor."

"Judging by his house, Montrop was neat and clean. I wonder

why he would carry dirt in a torn paper bag?"

"Me too," Lanzen said.

Her cell phone rang.

"Lanzen," she said. After a moment, she said "Really? You're kidding." She listened without speaking for a minute or two, then said, "I see. Very interesting. Thank you very much." She hung up and turned to me.

"The house is owned by a Limited Liability Company called Asset Safety LLC."

"Hard to track ownership of LLCs in Nevada," I said.

Lanzen looked up at the house. "So maybe the money for this house came from Montrop's financial scam, money that came from the multiple victims he defrauded. He put the money into his LLC and used the LLC to buy this house." Lanzen turned and looked at me. "Do you think there is a way to uncover this kind of thing? Find out what that LLC owns and where its money came from?"

"Perhaps," I said. "But it wouldn't be easy. As I understand it, one of the main reasons for having an LLC own your property is to distance yourself from your property and reduce your liability."

Lanzen looked at her watch, made a little start as if she realized she was taking too much time.

I got out my card and handed it to her. "I'll try to contact Montrop's son Jonas. I'll let you know what I learn."

We walked back to the front door. I looked out to where the gardener still sat on the bench. He was still rocking. "The gardener mentioned a housekeeper," I said.

"Right. I haven't yet gotten her contact information. Let's do that."

Lanzen headed out toward the gardener. I followed. "His name is Mr. Kang," she said to me as we walked. "He speaks very little English. We may learn more when we find a Korean translator."

"Mr. Kang?" Lanzen said as we approached.

The man stood up, his head slightly bowed. He wiped the back of his hands across his eyes. Standing, he was shorter than Lanzen, but he looked wiry and strong. His hands gripped each other hard enough to make his knuckles white.

"Mr. Kang, you said that Mr. Montrop had a housekeeper."

He shook his head. "Clean."

"I'm sorry?" Lanzen said. "I don't understand."

"House clean. Thursday. Every week."

"Oh. Not a housekeeper, a house cleaner," Lanzen corrected herself.

Kang nodded.

"Is this house cleaner a man? Woman?"

"Woman."

"Do you know her address or phone number?"

He frowned, held out his hands, and turned them palm up.

"You don't understand," Lanzen muttered. She held her fist up, thumb and little finger extended, and put it to the side of her head. "Phone call?"

Kang nodded. He made a beckoning gesture with his hand, and walked to the house. He went in the door and turned into the kitchen, walked over to a drawer, opened it, and pulled out a small spiral notebook. He flipped a few pages, pointed the tip of his finger to a name and phone number, and handed the notebook to Lanzen.

"Evan Rosen?" she said.

Mr. Kang nodded.

"Thanks. I'll give her a call." She pointed to the notebook. "There's no address, here. Do you know where she lives?"

Kang shook his head, although it wasn't clear if he was communicating that he didn't know or that he didn't understand.

"Tell me, Mr. Kang, do you garden for other homes?"

Kang frowned and shook his head.

Lanzen gestured for him to come with her. She was still carrying the notebook. When we were outside, she walked over to an area with a rose garden and a curving swath of grass. She pointed to Kang, then made digging and raking motions near the roses. She stopped and pointed again at Kang.

He nodded.

Lanzen walked over to the side of the lot, pointed at Kang, then pointed off toward the neighborhood. "Other customers?"

she said.

Kang nodded understanding. He came over, took the notebook from her, flipped pages, then turned the book so Lanzen and I could both see.

At the top of the page, it said, Gardener's Schedule.
Monday, Thursday - Here
Tuesday, Friday - Fernandezes
Wednesday, Saturday - Millers
Sunday - Mows the school fields

There were phone numbers listed for the Fernandezes, the Millers, and the school.

Lanzen made a show of counting each day, then looked at Kang. "You work every day of the week?"

He nodded. "Seven day. Yes."

"That's a heavy workload," Lanzen said.

He nodded again. "Good work." He pointed to the ground. "I still garden Montrop?"

Lanzen nodded. "I think that would be good for the next week or so. Do you have a phone number where I can call you if I have questions?"

Kang turned his palms up again.

Lanzen again made the phone shape with her hand, held it to her head, then pointed to Kang.

He shook his head, and pointed at his schedule in the address book. "Monday, Thursday." Then he pointed at the ground.

"If I want to talk to you, I can come here."

He nodded.

"Okay, thanks," she said.

Kang made a little bow, then backed away.

Lanzen said, "I'd like to talk to the house cleaner." She went through the notebook and found the number. "The prefix is a common one for cell phones. Let me try our reverse directory and see if we can find an address." She tapped on her phone, waited, tapped some more. "It's not listed. Okay, we'll do it the old-fashioned way." She dialed.

"May I please speak to Evan Rosen," she said after a bit. Then, "This is Sergeant Lori Lanzen of the Washoe County Sheriff's Office. I'd like to stop by and talk to you if I may."

A pause.

"Oh?" she said in a professional, non-revealing way. "What is the make and model?" Pause. "I may have information on its whereabouts. May I please have your address?" Pause. "Thanks, I'll be there in ten or fifteen minutes." She hung up.

"Ms. Rosen thought you were calling about a vehicle?"

Lanzen nodded. "She says her car was stolen. A blue Toyota. She assumed that was why I was calling. She's very upset, more than I'd expect with a stolen car."

Lanzen nodded. She turned to one of the deputies. "Isn't there a blue Toyota stuck in the street a block down from here? Consider it potential evidence in the murder investigation. Put it through the full routine."

She turned to me. "You want to join me in interviewing the house cleaner?"

"Sure."

FIVE

Sergeant Lanzen and I walked down the drive, then down the street to the blue Toyota. Its right front wheel had dropped down off the edge of asphalt so that the fender had bottomed out. From the angle of the wheel, it looked broken. There was no key in the ignition.

"Follow me?" Lanzen said.

I nodded.

She turned and walked back to her unmarked Washoe Sheriff's vehicle. She got in and drove. I followed her in my Jeep.

We went around Crystal Bay, past the Cal Neva Resort that was once owned by Frank Sinatra, continued across the California state line and headed through Kings Beach.

Sergeant Lanzen turned off the highway at Tahoe Vista. Like most Tahoe neighborhoods, Tahoe Vista was a mix of old cabins, some of them restored to look charming and attractive. Sprinkled in here and there were newer homes built in the popular Tahoe architectural style with heavy beams and out-sized gable roofs.

Lanzen pulled up at a small, old motel with a sign that said, 'Long-Term Rentals - First Two Weeks Free.'

It was the least appealing building in the area, with peeling olive paint and windows with torn screens. Every other door was labeled with a sign that said, 'Suite' followed by a letter, A through H. Above each sign was a small, antique wall sconce. It appeared that the original 16 motel rooms had been consolidated into 8 two-room apartments.

I parked behind Lanzen. Spot had his head out the window. I gave him a pet as I shut my door.

The motel appeared to sit lower at one end as if the ground below it was subsiding. Near the low end of the motel, a long piece of gutter had become detached and hung down from the eave, almost touching the ground. Lanzen walked down to the low end and knocked on the last door. The door opened. Coming from the apartment was a soft soul track by Earth, Wind & Fire. The vibration and air movement of the opening door made the low-hanging gutter swing back and forth.

"Evan Rosen?" Lanzen said. "I'm Sergeant Lori Lanzen of the Washoe County Sheriff's Office, and this is my colleague Owen McKenna."

Rosen nodded. She had pale white skin that amplified the dark circles under her eyes. Although she was probably in her late twenties, she looked like a child-waif, maybe five-two and ninety-five pounds. She was dressed in loose blue jeans and a green sweatshirt. Her brown hair was cut short. She appeared clean, but without the polished presentation that young women often adopt. No glossy shine in her hair and no careful brushing, no mascara or eyeliner that might enhance eyes that were large and dark. Her hands were small, her skin dry and rough, and her nails were trimmed short where they hadn't broken or torn from labor. She telegraphed a look of fatigue.

The woman motioned for us to follow her, then turned and walked into a dark room that was as dreary as any motel one might imagine.

On a hook just inside the door hung a pair of swim goggles and a tennis racket. It seemed incongruous with the old motel accommodations because I always associated tennis with an upper middle class lifestyle. But I reminded myself not to judge by appearances. The woman might play tennis with the best of them. At second glance, the tennis racket looked quite beat up. At the top of the rim, there was substantial wear as if she struck the court when she made ground shots.

The space was lit by a single ceiling light with a bulbous, frosted-glass diffuser. The vinyl flooring had cracked near the entry door. A tattered couch faced a TV so old it had probably broadcast original episodes of The Rockford Files. On one wall was a stained, laminated counter with a sink, a two-burner stovetop, a miniature fridge, and a microwave with dark rust and corrosion at its edges. In the back corner of the room, across from the entry door, was a small table with two folding chairs. The combination was about the size of my cabin's kitchen nook.

Although my facility, with an oven and a full-sized fridge, was relatively luxurious. From where I stood near the front door, I could see that the floor sloped enough that any vibration from a truck in the street might make the chairs gradually vibrate and shuffle across the floor until they hit the kitchen sink.

The woman picked up a folding chair and set it down so that it faced the couch. She sat on the chair.

As we sat on the couch, I thought that it might be hard to come home to this apartment after cleaning houses like Montrop's.

Evan Rosen looked at the two of us as if to memorize our clothes, our shoes, our demeanor. Her stare didn't seem judgmental, but her face had a melancholy set to it as if she was seeing in just our clothes a lifestyle that she thought would be forever out of reach to her.

"You found my car?" she said. "Where was it?"

"Do you know who took it?" Lanzen said, ignoring her question.

"No. I just woke up and saw it gone. At first, I panicked. Then I realized that, because I haul all my cleaning tools in every night, I hadn't lost everything." She glanced toward a small closet near the front door. "Everybody thinks all you need to clean houses is a rag and some Windex. But I'm like a carpenter. Different tools, but similar in concept. Does my car still run?"

"We don't know, yet," Lanzen said. "At first glance it didn't look like the ignition had been jumped. But the front wheel is off the pavement and looks broken. Did you leave a key in it?"

"No. Not in the ignition, anyway. But I keep one of those hide-a-key containers near the right front wheel well. So maybe the thief found it. Although he'd have to practically lie down on the ground to see it."

Lanzen made a vacant nod. "Do you have a spare key?"

Rosen nodded. "Yeah." She had a key ring hanging off the side of her belt. She threaded one of the keys off it and handed it to Lanzen. Evan looked at her watch. "I missed my morning cleaning appointment. I was hoping I could still make my afternoon house if I could get my car in the next hour. But now that my car is wrecked..."

Lanzen said, "It will take us some time to process it. Then

we'll have it towed to a repair garage. Do you have a mechanic you like to use?"

"No. I don't know what to do. I need that car," Evan said. "Mattie, my older lady friend who helps with babysitting, lives in this building. She can maybe drive me to my customers for a day or two. Without my car, I'm dead in the water. I could lose my accounts."

Lanzen nodded. "It would help me expedite the situation if I had your driver's license number."

Evan got up, fetched a small fanny pack off the kitchen counter, and pulled out a wallet. She removed her driver's license and handed it to Sergeant Lanzen. Lanzen wrote down the number and Evan's date of birth.

"How long have you been cleaning houses, Ms. Rosen?" I said.

"Call me Evan. There's no Ms. Rosen. There used to be. My mother. I've been cleaning houses for three years. It's hard labor, but the best job I ever had. You can make decent money cleaning houses."

"Do you work for a cleaning company, or are you on your own?"

"My own. I worked for a franchise outfit for a few months, but it wasn't for me. Picky rules. No opportunity to make an individual decision, even if it would improve the service. It was more important to follow the rules than to make a customer happy. Mansfield Cleaning is the opposite."

I asked, "Is that your business name?"

"Yeah."

"I like it," I said. "Mansfield Cleaning sounds substantial."

"That's the idea. But cleaning is no one's ideal. So I'll never hire employees to make it substantial. Besides, then I'd have to pay Worker's Comp. Talk about a nightmare." She pulled a business card out of her pocket and handed it to me.

The words 'Mansfield Cleaning' were superimposed over an ink drawing of a large stately building with arched windows, a structure that looked like it was built for an important school or university a century ago. Underneath the building in small letters was the catch phrase 'Your daily mess is our daily mission.'

"Do you clean large buildings?" I asked.

"You mean like the one on the card? No. Houses, mostly. Plus a dental building and a small café."

"Is Mansfield a family name?" I asked, trying to get her to open up.

She glanced out the window, then made a tentative shake of her head. "Just a name I heard."

"Is business good?" Lanzen asked.

"Yeah, when stuff doesn't get in the way."

"What gets in the way?" Lanzen said. I knew she was trying to see what she could learn about Evan before she brought up the subject of Montrop's murder, which would be like a subject trump card and make it impossible to talk or think about anything else.

"When you wake up to no car, that screws things up big time," Evan said. She closed her eyes as if counting to ten.

I said, "You mentioned the woman who helps with babysitting. Do you have a child?"

Evan shook her head. "My sister Mia. She's older than me by two years. But she needs help with most things."

"Mia," I said. "Interesting name."

"Her first name is actually Mira. But she could never make the R sound. So mom just let her say Mia."

"How long has she been with you?"

"Mia always lived with mom in Reno. But when mom died two years ago, she had nowhere to go. I looked into some state services, but Nevada isn't the best state for help. So I moved Mia up the mountain from Reno to live with me. After a year on the California side of the line, she qualified for some better assistance. But it still won't pay for a sitter. So I bring her with me on my jobs."

"Your customers don't mind?"

"Two of them quit me when I first showed up with Mia. Some of the others weren't too happy about it, but they've stayed on. The few new ones I told right up front. You want me, you get Mia. She's quiet, but she's not silent. She's afraid of the dark, so if the power goes out, we're going to have some upset to deal with. And if she sees a spider, she's going to freak out, and there ain't nothing I can do about it. One lady told me that she couldn't have Mia freaking out, no way, so I better be damn sure I clean good enough that no spider ever wants in." Evan rapped her knuckles against the wood arm of the couch.

"Does Mia help with cleaning?"

"No. Her right arm and hand never really worked well. But even if they did, she doesn't track the way other people do. You gotta track to clean houses. Mia's world is Peter Pan and never growing up and learning to fly. It's best for me to park her in front of the TV while I clean. If the TV doesn't have the shows she likes, then I give her my phone and earbuds, and I play the Peter Pan soundtrack."

"Where is Mia now?" I asked.

Evan glanced toward a door that led to what had once been the neighboring motel room. "She's sleeping. Her midday nap is the only way to keep her calm. She wakes up every morning at four-thirty like she's got an onboard alarm clock. I have to get her down from eleven to noon or so, or she'll have a storm fit by midafternoon. The doctor calls it diurnal rhythm deficiency. It goes back to the birth asphyxia. She'll be awake soon." Evan frowned. "This is an awful lot of questions for a stolen car investigation."

"Evan," Lanzen said, "tell us about your relationship with David Montrop."

"What's to say? He's a stuck-up rich guy who acts like he's special. He refers to his Mercedes instead of referring to his car." Evan imitated him, "'Hey, I left the groceries in the Mercedes. Can you put them away, little darlin'?' Gimme a break. I clean his house every week. He lives in a palace. And he feels the need to lord his Mercedes over me like I haven't noticed it. But I try to keep my mouth shut because his house is my easiest job. He never makes a mess, no one else is ever at the house except the gardener, and Mia likes it there. Montrop's got this giant TV that she watches."

"Did you or anyone you know ever have disagreements with him?"

"No, why?"

Sergeant Lanzen answered, "Because he was found murdered this morning."

SIX

I watched Evan Rosen as Sergeant Lanzen informed her of Montrop's murder. Evan made a little jerk, her eyes went wide, and then the hardness in her face softened. Tears pooled in her eyes. She opened her mouth to speak, then swallowed.

"That's terrible," she finally said in a tiny voice. "What kind of person would kill an old man like that? He might not have been the nicest guy, but murder..." She lifted up her hands and put one index finger into the cuff of her other sleeve to wipe the tears from her eyes.

"Now that you know he was murdered," Lanzen said, "does anything about him come to mind? Something that seemed of no account before but may take on significance in light of his death?"

"No. I'm shocked. I don't know what to say." She paused, and then she looked startled. "That's why you called. It was about his murder, wasn't it? It wasn't about my stolen car." Her startled looked morphed into worry. "You must have found my stolen car near his house! Someone told you that I was the house cleaner. Oh, of course, it had to be Kang. He probably told you what my car looked like. Then you found it near Montrop's house. So now it looks like I killed him. I'll be one of those defendants who are convicted on circumstantial evidence. I look good for the crime, right? Maybe it's a frame job. And I can't afford a lawyer." She took a sudden breath and looked away again.

"You thought of something," I said.

She nodded. "I realize that there's something else."

"What's that?" Lanzen asked.

"The last time I was there, Thursday, Montrop and I got into an argument. He said I'd gotten fingerprints on the wine glasses when I took them out of the dishwasher. I said that I didn't know that fingerprints were a special crime with wine glasses. And he said that of course I wouldn't know about wine because it was above my station. So I yelled at him. What did he know about my station?!" Evan made a fist and slammed it down onto the arm of the couch.

After a long silence, she said, "Look, I know I'm kind of a hothead. I get bent out of shape when people downtalk me. If someone heard the way I yelled at Montrop, it wouldn't be a stretch for them to think I might go wacko and cleave that geezer's brain. So arrest me and convict me. At least I won't have to wonder where my next meal is coming from." She turned her head and looked out the window. "But I wouldn't know what to do with Mia."

As she mentioned Mia, her eyes teared up again. If it was for show, she was a good actor.

"Mia's a big responsibility," I said.

Evan shook her head. "It's not that. It's…"

After a long moment, I said, "It's what?"

"It's just that Mia is the only person who ever believed in me."

Lanzen said, "You refer to cleaving Montrop's brain…"

Evan interrupted her. "No! Don't tell me that's how he died! I just meant it as a figure of speech."

Lanzen said, "How did Mr. Kang and Montrop get along?"

"Fine, I think. Montrop would tell Kang if Kang didn't get all the leaves out of a flower bed or something. Montrop could be as rough with Kang as he was with me. But the thing about Kang is that nothing fazes him. Maybe it's a Buddhist thing or something. I don't know. But whenever I saw Montrop raise his voice, Kang would just put his palms together, fingertips under his chin, and do a little bow. He never spoke."

"It seems that he barely understands any English," Lanzen said.

"That's what it seems like. But you can't pass anything by him. I think the non-English thing is an act so that he doesn't have to speak. He can just lose himself in Montrop's gardens." Evan paused, about to speak but hesitating. "So what happened to Montrop?"

Lanzen glanced at me.

I said, "Someone threw his paddle board at him, and it split his head open."

Evan winced.

As I looked at her, I realized that Evan Rosen seemed much too tiny to throw a paddle board. If she was involved in Montrop's murder, she'd need an accomplice. Then again, house cleaning was a lot of work. If the tennis racket and swim goggles were any indication, she probably was in very good shape. I'd heard of petite women who compete in powerlifting tournaments.

"I see your tennis racket by the door," I said. "You play much?"

Evan shook her head. "This guy I met wanted me to take it up. He gave me a racket, and we tried playing a few times. I was pretty good for a newbie. But he was one of those guys who have to slam the ball down your throat to show how much better they are than a girl. I told him he was obviously insecure. So that was the end of my tennis career. He never came back for the racket."

"What about the swim goggles?" I asked.

"I'm…" Evan stopped. She looked embarrassed.

"I didn't mean to pry," I said.

"You're not prying. You're just trying to learn about me so you can decide if you think I'm Montrop's killer."

I didn't respond. Probably, Lanzen was thinking the same thing I was, that Evan kept mentioning the idea that we might be considering her for murder.

"I'm trying to be a night swimmer," Evan finally said.

Lanzen looked interested. "What's that mean?"

"There's a group from the rec center. Seven of us. We play soccer. One day during a break, we found out that we're all afraid of the water. It's not like we can't swim, but we're not good at it. If we were, we wouldn't be afraid." Evan stopped talking.

"So you swim at night?" I said.

Evan made fists on her thighs, her knuckles white. "We found out that we've all had a version of a drowning nightmare. For some, like me, it's about being asleep and then waking up just as someone has tossed you off a ship into the ocean, a thousand miles from land. The thing that frightens us the most is the idea of being dropped into the water at night." Evan made a little shiver as she said it. "You suddenly find yourself in cold, black, bottomless water, and you don't know what's down there, and you're sure that something's going to grab your feet and pull you down into the inky depths." She paused, looking at us. "You're both thinking, 'What is this girl's problem?' But trust me, for us there is no greater fear. And Tahoe is so deep and so cold..." She stopped talking, looked at us, and gritted her teeth, her jaw muscles bulging. "It would be worse than being murdered."

We waited.

Evan resumed, "Nan Trudeau is our group leader. She studied psychology at Sac State. She said that the way you deal with your worst fears is to face them, and force yourself to find out that your fears can't defeat you. So if you can't stand to fly, you get on airplanes and confront the fact that you're still alive after you land. If snakes are your nightmare, you go to one of those places that has snakes, and you handle them. You let them slither all over your body, and it makes you realize that they are just animals without legs. Maybe they're not cuddly like dogs, but they're still animals."

I said, "So you go swimming at night."

"Yeah." Another shiver. "We did it as a group. Six times last summer. We got special permission to turn off all the lights in the pool room at the rec center. Then we went into the pool in the dark. It was terrifying, but we survived."

Sergeant Lanzen said, "I imagine your goal is to do a night swim in Lake Tahoe."

"We already did." Evan shivered yet again, this time violently. "To make it the worst it could be, we went when there wasn't any moon. The night was black. Black as... obsidian. There was a light cloud cover so we didn't even have starlight. We all met at Kings Beach. Just staring out at the black water, cold as ice, created a fear in us that was breathtaking. We could barely see the water. But the black waves crashing in were huge. There was a south wind, so the waves had twenty miles to build from the south end of the lake. None of us would have ever done it alone. But we'd made a pact on a sunny day the week before. We were going to be night swimmers if it was the last thing we'd ever do. We swore on the Goddess Nyx."

"Who's that?" Lanzen asked.

"Gabby Hernandez told us about her. Nyx is the Greek goddess of the night. She lives in the darkness, and she's so scary that all the other gods, even Zeus the king of gods, is afraid of her. So we made a circle and each of us held out a hand in a center stack and swore that we'd take the night swim or let Nyx have our souls."

"And you all made a night swim," I said. "That's impressive."

Evan clenched her teeth, jaw muscles bulging.

"They did," she said. "I couldn't make myself do it."

Lanzen glanced at me. I didn't know what to say.

Evan sounded like she was on some kind of edge, revealing a dark secret.

"It was the scariest thing I've ever contemplated," she said. "We all gathered at the beach in the dark. We stripped down to our swim suits and walked to the water's edge. The waves crashed on the beach, rolled up and splashed over our feet. The water was so cold that just having it on my feet made it hard to breathe. The plan was that on the count of three, we'd all run into the water up to our thighs and then take a deep breath and dive forward into the waves. Then we'd swim underwater as far as we could. Our goal was to make it fifty yards out into the lake while staying at least three feet under."

"You mean, hold your breath and do the entire distance without coming up for air?" Lanzen said.

Evan nodded. "It's actually a regular swimming discipline. It's called Dynamic Apnea. People do it in swimming pools and try to set records for how far you can swim underwater on one breath. But all we wanted to do was to confront the black water. It was an absolutely terrifying concept. Swimming underwater in the freezing lake at night. I had put on my swim goggles like the rest of the women. But when we counted to three and ran to the water, I froze. They all did it. They went out about fifty yards, swimming underwater. Only three of them came up for air just once. The other three kept going on a single breath. Just like in the pool. The whole time they swam, I was imagining that swimming underwater in Tahoe at night would feel like I was a hundred feet down and I'd never find the surface again. My feet burned from the cold of the water, and I had ferocious shivers. When the other women got out there, they treaded water together. They shouted for me, worried that something was wrong. So I lied and shouted out to them that I was okay and just had a leg cramp."

Lanzen and I were silent, not sure how to respond to a confession about a humiliating experience. Even the confession must have been humiliating.

"They all conquered their fear of a night swim. I failed." Evan's lower lip quivered. She reached up and rubbed it. "The hardest thing was when I came home and Mia asked if I did the night swim. I told her I was too afraid. She looked so disappointed. It was like she stopped believing in me that night." Evan's eyes were moist again. "Not the first time I've been an utter failure," she said. "Won't be the last, either."

"It doesn't sound like failure to me," I said. "More like a disappointment, a setback, the kind of thing that makes a person take stock of their goals, then regroup and try again."

"That's your approach," Evan said. "But if enough bad stuff happens, it can drive anybody to the edge. There's been times where if I didn't have Mia to take care of…"

We three sat in silence for a minute.

"Dying by paddle board is ironic for Montrop," Evan said, changing the subject.

"Why?" Lanzen asked.

"Because Montrop was getting rid of stuff. He had a garage sale. He ran ads on Craigslist. He even put stuff down at the bottom of his driveway with a sign that said 'Free.' It was like he'd decided that he was going to clear out the crapola in his life before the cancer could take him down. I guess you have to admire him for that, a man who's looking at death and not turning away. But while he was throwing stuff out, he decided to buy a paddle board. So then the one thing that he does acquire becomes the murder weapon."

"Montrop had cancer?" I said.

"Yeah. He talked about it now and then. Something about his bones, I think. He never mentioned the details, but he was frank about it. I think that when he lost his hair because of the chemo, he decided there was no point in pretending. He said it had advanced too far, and that he was preparing for his end."

"Did he have close friends?" Lanzen asked.

"Not that I know of."

"Did he go out paddle boarding with other people?" I asked.

"Not that I ever sensed. I think he was pretty much a loner."

There was a sound from the next room. The door opened. A woman came out. She was small of frame but still larger than Evan. She rubbed her eyes as she took a few steps into the living room. Then she saw Lanzen and me. She looked worried and brought both of her hands to her mouth. Her right hand came off her wrist at an angle, and her forearm was bent in an unusual way.

Evan jumped up. "Hey, baby, it's okay, these are my friends Lori and Owen." Evan hurried to the woman's side and put her arm around the woman's shoulders. With her other hand, she reached up and touched the woman's face as gently as if she were touching a newborn kitten. "Come meet Lori and Owen. Guys, this is my sister Mia. Mia is my partner and pal, right, Mia? And she's also an expert on afternoon TV. Anything you want to know, and I mean anything, you just ask Mia. Mia, say hi to Lori and Owen."

Mia pulled one hand from her mouth and made a little wave. "Hi." Then she wrapped her arms around Evan and hugged her.

When they stopped hugging, Mia looked at Evan's face, frowned, and touched a fingertip to Evan's cheek just below her red eyes. Mia looked worried, then looked over at Sergeant Lanzen and me.

It seemed a good time to leave. The sergeant told Evan that she'd be in touch about her car. We said goodbye and left.

Lanzen walked over to my Jeep. I introduced her to Spot. She pet him, and he looked rapturous.

I told Lanzen I'd try to find Montrop's son Jonas, and I'd be in touch.

Once again, she looked hesitant. "You're okay with helping me? This isn't your case."

"But it could be."

She nodded.

SEVEN

I drove back down the East Shore. I was hungry, and I knew Spot would be dreaming of lunch, but I decided we could first look in on Montrop's son Jonas.

It was easy to find Jonas's house on Tahoe Keys Boulevard in South Lake Tahoe, the opposite end of the lake from where Evan Rosen lived. Jonas's place was a small, well-kept cabin with brown siding and dark green trim. It sat close to the street, and the house number was displayed with white, metallic numbers nailed to the siding. There was no garage. An ancient, orange VW Microbus was in the middle of the small asphalt parking pad. In front of the house were two fir trees with dense foliage that blocked the view of the front door. I told Spot to be good, got out, and walked along a row of paving stones that curved behind the trees to the door.

There was no doorbell, so I knocked on the door. The tap of my knuckles swung the door in. The doorjamb was splintered. Bits of wood littered the floor.

I could call Mallory and have him send out a patrol unit, but someone could be in trouble, and I didn't want to wait.

I didn't know if I'd find a traumatized victim or a burglar. So I quietly stepped back outside, tiptoed back to the Jeep, and let Spot out of the back seat. I brought him to the house.

As soon as I let go of his collar, he wandered into the living room, his tail high, friendly, inquisitive. He raised his nose toward the dining and kitchen area, turned and sniffed a folding card table with a desktop computer. Then Spot immediately swung his head to the side, pointing toward the little square hallway with three doors that would lead to the bathroom and two bedrooms. Spot's nostrils flexed. He raised his head, still air-scenting, not trail scenting. He walked with purpose to the little hallway as if he knew exactly where he was going and walked into the bedroom on the right. I was directly behind him.

I've learned Spot's body language. I could tell that he wasn't telegraphing that a person was in the room. It was more like he was following a scent that indicated recent human activity.

When I came through the door, I saw Spot sniffing a pillow that lay on the floor. The bed covers were pulled most of the way off the bed. A water glass lay on its side on the floor near the night table. The carpet had a large dark spot curving away from the glass. I bent over and touched it. There was a hint of moisture, but it had mostly dried. There was a chair tipped over. Partially draped over the tipped chair was a pair of jeans and shirt. Two socks lay nearby. A table lamp was lying on the floor a good distance away, the carpet sparkling with bits of glass from the broken bulb.

I took Spot by his collar. "Good boy," I said as I pulled him back out of the room. "Let's not contaminate a crime scene."

After a quick check showed that the other bedroom, the bathroom, and the kitchen were all undisturbed, I pulled out my cell phone. Before I could dial, it rang.

"Owen McKenna," I said.

"Lori Lanzen. Word of Montrop's death travels fast around our Incline Village. I just got a call from the manager of one of our banks, the bank where David Montrop has his checking account. This morning, he withdrew twenty-five thousand dollars and asked for it in cash."

"Did he say what it was for?"

"Yes. He told the teller that he needed the cash to make a payment for a band. His business is booking bands into concert venues across northern Nevada and northern California."

I asked, "Did they say whether or not he often makes cash withdrawals?"

"The manager did say he often makes cash deposits. But cash withdrawals are unusual. Apparently, he usually gets a cashier's check."

"I may have found the real reason for the cash withdrawal," I said. "I just got to Jonas's house. No one's here. The door was broken in. There are signs of a struggle. If I had to guess, I'd say that someone pulled Jonas out of bed while he was sleeping."

Lanzen immediately said, "Someone kidnapped Jonas and demanded ransom from the father?"

"It looks that way."

"So after Montrop delivered the money, they killed him?" Lanzen sounded disbelieving. "Do you think that's what they did with Jonas?"

"I don't know. Often, kidnappers keep the victim alive just long enough to get the money. Then they kill the victim to cover their tracks. So Jonas may be dead as well."

"This all seems unusual," Lanzen said. "Even though kidnappers sometimes kill the kidnap victim, they don't usually kill the person making the ransom payment."

"That's been my experience. Most of the time, they arrange for a payment drop that keeps them physically removed from the person making the payment. It seems strange that the kidnappers would kill Montrop in his driveway. Going to his house would create a substantial risk for them."

"But Montrop's dead, and the cash is gone. It may be a stupid MO, but that could help us."

"Yeah," I said. "Stupid killers are the easiest to catch. I need to call in Jonas's disappearance to Commander Mallory of the SLTPD and Agent Ramos."

"The South Shore FBI office," she said.

"Right."

We hung up. I put Spot in the Jeep and came back with a pair of latex gloves, and, careful not to smear any potential prints, went through the pockets of Jonas's jeans.

He had a key ring with two keys, one for a VW – probably the orange microbus – and another that looked like it would fit the front door. He had a wallet with 17 dollars in it, his California driver's license, a Safeway Club Card, and a Bank of America debit card. I made a note of the license number and date of birth.

I called Mallory.

"Mallory," he said in a loud voice when my call was transferred through.

"McKenna calling to report a potential kidnapping in your fair city."

"Does this have something to do with the action in Incline? I heard that you were a person of interest in a murder. What a kick."

I ignored Mallory's enthusiasm. "The murder victim, David Montrop, was a con artist and defendant in a manslaughter case when I was on the SFPD. That could be why he had written a note that mentioned me. Anyway, I came to inform his son Jonas Montrop, who lives on Tahoe Keys Boulevard. I'm there now. I found the door broken in. The kid is missing. There are signs of a struggle in the bedroom. Sergeant Lori Lanzen of Washoe County just found out that David Montrop withdrew twenty-five thousand in cash from his bank this morning."

"Someone nabbed the kid, nicked the dad for ransom, then killed the dad when he paid the money?"

"Maybe," I said.

"I heard something about how he died, but it didn't make sense. Something about a paddle board?"

"It appears that someone hit him with a paddle board. Or maybe threw it at him. Blunt force trauma to the head and chest."

"There's an unusual murder weapon. So we have to assume that it's connected to the kid's disappearance. What's the kid's address? I'll send a team over."

I gave Mallory the number on Tahoe Keys Boulevard.

"You calling Ramos?" he said.

"Kidnapping is FBI territory," I said.

We said goodbye.

I had the number of the FBI's Tahoe office. I dialed.

"Owen McKenna calling for Agent Ramos, please," I said when the phone was answered. "I need to report a kidnapping." I figured that mentioning a federal crime would make it less likely that Ramos would be out of the office.

"Please hold."

"Mr. McKenna, it is good to talk to you," Ramos said when he picked up, his speech showing his trademark careful diction and precise enunciation. I could picture him at his desk in his sport jacket and pressed trousers and his meticulously-barbered moustache. "You have a kidnapping? We haven't heard."

"I just discovered it. I'm not even certain of it. Tahoe Keys Boulevard. A kid named Jonas Montrop, son of David Montrop who died this morning from a blow by a paddle board in Incline Village."

"I heard of that. Are the death and kidnapping connected?"

"I don't know, but it seems logical. I just got word from Sergeant Lori Lanzen, Washoe County, that Montrop withdrew twenty-five thousand in cash from the bank this morning."

"Ransom?"

"Maybe," I said. "He's a booking agent for bands. He told the bank manager it was a payment to a band. There's no sign of the money."

"You've called Mallory?"

"Yeah. Then you. I'll also let Sergeant Diamond Martinez know. Do you want in on any of this?" I said.

"You know we're here to support all official law enforcement agencies."

I took that as a slam on my non-official, private investigator status.

"But you and I go back a ways," he continued. "So I imagine that you will be working with the officers you mentioned. May I ask who your client is?"

"I don't have a client."

There was a pause. "I see," Ramos said, not sounding happy. "What is the address of the victim?"

I gave it to him.

"Okay, we'll get on it. Let me know if we can help in any other way."

"Thanks," I said. I hung up.

I continued my no-touch search. After the South Lake Tahoe cops got a warrant, they could start opening drawers and be more thorough in gathering evidence.

I walked through the house, looking at everything in sight. Then I went back outside and took note of the layout of the street and drive and the front door. I considered Jonas's bedroom windows on the front, right corner of the house, visible to all, easy to watch from a distance. When he turned off his lights and went to bed, it would be obvious to anyone nearby. I went back to the front door and looked at the damage. Like the cabin, the door was old. It was made of thin wood, and the deadbolt lock, while itself strong, projected into a jamb made of lightweight pine. It would splinter and break with any heavy impact of shoulder against door.

Back in the bedroom, something caught my attention. Near the spilled water was a bit of paper. I reached down and set one of my cards next to it, aligned edge-to-edge to mark its position, then slipped another card under the piece and lifted it up without touching it. The piece of paper was torn, triangular in shape. It was straight cut on two sides at right angles to each other. The hypotenuse of the triangular piece was torn. There was an area with some writing and a portion of a photo. The paper was wavy from the water, and the writing and photo were a bit smudged.

The paper had originally been glossy, as if from a magazine. The photo portion showed the rear half of a runabout speeding across a body of water, its wake a long, low wedge of spreading waves. The adjacent writing had just two words beginning at the torn edge. It said, 'cury sterndrives.' I realized that it had probably said, 'Mercury sterndrives' before it was torn. The reverse side of the paper was white with no printing. Nothing about it offered any clue to the man or men who yanked Jonas out of bed in the night.

I lowered my card so that the torn paper slid off onto the carpet in the exact same position that I'd found it. I picked up the card I'd used as a marker and pocketed it.

I walked back through the little house. It was neat like his dad's house in Incline. But instead of fancy furniture and art, Jonas's living room had only the table with the computer. Jonas had no desk. The only paperwork I found was some mail in a cardboard box next to the desktop computer. Using my pen, I flipped through the envelopes. They were bills addressed to Jonas Montrop.

When I stopped moving the mail in the box, I heard the soft whir of a fan and realized that the desktop computer was on, the cooling fan barely perceptible. But the screen was dark.

I bumped the mouse.

The screen lit up. On it was a note.

'Flynn,
Let me put this in writing so my meaning is perfectly clear. I didn't know about the leak. I swear it. Even though things can be fixed, I'll give you the money back. We didn't transfer title yet, anyway, so it's not like you're stuck with it. You said I was trying to kill you. That's simply not true. I can prove that if you'

The note ended as if he'd been interrupted or had simply stopped writing until he thought of the best words. The police would probably be able to pull prints off the keyboard or see if the keys had been wiped. Every indication in the house suggested that Jonas lived alone. A single toothbrush, one towel in the bathroom, a single glass and plate in the dish rack, one pair of hiking boots by the front door, just a few clothes in the closet.

I saw nothing else revealing, so I went outside to wait for the police.

A South Lake Tahoe black-and-white drove up a moment later. Two men got out.

"Hey, McKenna," one of them said. The other one nodded at me. I'd met both, but I didn't remember their names. "Commander says you've got an abduction."

I took them into the house and showed them what I'd found, then left them to their work.

Back in the Jeep, I dialed the Incline Village Sergeant.

"Lori Lanzen," she answered.

"Owen McKenna. I've got a more thorough report on Jonas."

"Shoot."

So I gave it all to her, the spilled water, stuff knocked over, the computer, the unfinished letter, the little scrap of torn paper.

"Any conclusions?" she said.

"No."

"Let me know what you learn," she said, "and I'll do the same."

We said goodbye.

EIGHT

I called Street. She was at her lab.
"Blondie and I were just about to head home," she said.

"Then perhaps I could interest you in a dinner date?" I said. "Something nice?"

I could almost hear her thinking through her schedule, contemplating whether or not she could meet all of her obligations with the sudden insertion into her schedule of an evening off.

"I'd even take a shower and switch out my hiking boots for shoes," I said to sweeten the deal.

"You really know how to make a girl feel special," she said. "How about picking me up at seven?"

"Will do."

At the appointed hour, Spot and I drove down to Street's condo. When Street opened the door, he trotted inside, greeted Blondie, then made a circuit of Street's kitchen, his nose pausing at the microwave and the toaster oven and then lingering at the stove top, nostrils flexing, divining the details of Street's previous half-dozen meals. Blondie followed him, looking up with a question in her eyes as if to wonder what it was like to be tall enough to reach over counter tops. When it seemed that there was nothing especially vulnerable to a Great Dane's inspection – no defrosting filet mignon on top of the fridge – I turned to Street.

She'd recently had her hair tinted to a very dark auburn and cut in a boyish, asymmetrical bob that curled around her face on both sides. It was parted on the left and combed while still wet so that the coarse comb left faint grooves in her hair, a look that was more casual than what a brush would do. Maybe she sported a hint of auburn eye shadow. Maybe her lip gloss had a touch of matching color. I've never understood the alchemy of makeup, and I've always thought that her attractiveness was intrinsic to her personality and unaffected by the shallower effects of color and hair shape. Street was a scientist, not an actress, and her lack of movie star beauty in no way lessened her appeal to me.

And tonight, Street's allure was riveting. She was wearing a satin black top that ended an inch above the waistband of her thin, skin-tight, black pants. On her feet were black shoes that looked like ballet slippers, revealing ankles so perfect that Michelangelo would have struggled to get them right. Artfully draped across her shoulders was a filmy tie-dyed scarf in purple and magenta with hints of orange. It must have been ten feet long.

"If a breeze comes up and you do a pirouette," I said, "that scarf will flow like an apparition."

"Really?" She held up one end of the scarf, took two fast, long steps across the living room and turned, her hand sweeping the fabric above her head in a large arc. The scarf lofted and traced wave patterns through the air. Street's elegance and grace were mesmerizing. When the scarf had settled, she saw me looking at her legs.

"Do you think these leggings are okay?" She looked down as if to see what I saw.

"Yes, they're definitely okay," I said.

"But you have a look on your face that I can't place."

"I'm just reminded of a Lamborghini we saw in Italy last month. Very sleek but with lots of curves."

"I remind you of a car." Street's eyes narrowed.

I shrugged. "It looked fast. No doubt, it was fast."

"You think I'm a fast girl." She made a little frown.

"Fast with me, anyway," I said.

"And the leggings suggest that? Maybe I should wear harem pants instead."

"No. When someone is as hot as you, leggings make sense."

"That's nice. But I don't want other men to think I'm hot. Only you."

"Not something you have control over. Other men would think you're hot even if you wore a four-man, REI expedition tent."

Street bit the side of her bottom lip. "I've never even tried one on. Is that a new fashion?"

"It will be if you start wearing one."

Street put on her long, black, summer-weight coat. We left Spot and Blondie in her condo and walked outside.

"Like boarding the emperor's chariot," Street said as she got into my dented, bullet hole-ventilated Jeep.

"My thought exactly," I said.

She continued, "Only it's missing the velvet cushions and the silk window coverings and the cello accompanist and the four white stallions rushing us off into the night."

"Is not my Jeep the modern, romantic equivalent?"

She frowned and shook her head.

"Oh," I said.

We drove south, turned up Kingsbury Grade, went past her lab and my office, and climbed up the winding drive to the Chart House Restaurant. They gave us a table by the big windows, and we looked across Lake Tahoe as the sun lowered behind the Sierra Crest. Street had shrimp, and I had salmon, and the Russian River Valley pinot noir was perfect with both.

Of course, Street declined sharing the chocolate lava cake, so I had to eat it all myself.

Through it all, she was my dream date, charming and smart and engaging. And while she always protests my attentions to her beauty, putting an unconscious fingertip to the acne scars, she was gorgeous in every way that I care about.

On the way home, there was a delicious Mozart piece on the NPR station. I pulled off at an overlook on the East Shore. There was a first quarter moon above the lake, its reflective stripe shimmering on the water. The snow fields on the distant peaks were spectacular.

"What is this?" Street said as I came to a stop. "My knight is looking for a nightcap?"

"Would that I shine my armor such that you should want to help me out of it."

"Working on a poem?" she said.

"No. Mere mumblings of a man besotted with love." I put my hand on her thigh.

"You mean lust."

"One leads to the other."

Street didn't respond.

"I sense the trouble is back," I said.

"What do you mean?"

"Over the last few weeks, you've been distracted. This morning, especially, you seemed introspective."

"I'm always introspective."

"This time it's different." I rubbed my hand down her leg to her knee and cupped her kneecap. "I know something's bothering you, but I can't figure out what."

Street was silent, her face staring ahead, at the lake, at the reflected moon stripe. In time, I heard her inhale and then slowly let the air out.

"I haven't talked about it because I haven't known what to say," she said. "Yes, I'm troubled. But just thinking about it makes things worse. It's a subject that worries me at best and terrifies me at worst."

"No pressure," I said. "Anytime you want to talk, I'm here."

Mozart had given way to one of the romantic 19th century composers. Anton Bruckner maybe.

"Three months ago," Street began, "I got an email from the Missouri Department of Corrections. I'm on their victim notification list."

I knew what that meant. "Your father is coming up for parole?"

"Yes." Street took some heavy breaths. "Missouri law allows me to make a statement at the parole hearing. But I couldn't bear the idea of seeing him in person. So I made a video statement on my computer. I hated having to do it. Just thinking about him or talking about him is the essence of misery. Recalling how he beat up my brother…"

She breathed some more.

She continued, "The idea that Tom Casey would eventually be listening and watching my video statement made me sick. I could imagine his snide, mocking grin. I've never forgotten the last words he spoke to me."

"What did he say?"

"It was over two decades ago, so I was very young. Fourteen years old. But the words are chiseled into my brain. After he was pronounced guilty of second degree murder in the beating death of my brother, and they led him out of the courtroom in shackles, they walked him right past where I was sitting. He turned to me and said, 'Someday, you'll be sorry you testified. You have no idea how sorry.' His tone was sinister, a sick, breathy whisper. It was the most threatening thing anyone has ever said to me."

"I can't believe he said that to his daughter. What an evil bastard."

Street paused and sat silent for a time.

I didn't speak. As painful as her thoughts were, it might be better for her to work through them than to have them interrupted.

Eventually, she said, "I didn't tell you when I made the video statement because I couldn't bear to bring those memories into my current life any more than absolutely necessary. You are my safe zone. I'm not a naturally bubbly, happy person, and my time with you has always been the happiest that I've ever experienced. I didn't want to jeopardize that. I know you're okay with such talk. But not me. Now, I've finally brought it up. So I've transformed a wonderful evening into a topic of misery. I'm so sorry."

Street's voice was thick, trying not to cry.

"I'm the one who's sorry for you. What kind of father would be so sick as to want bad things for his daughter?" I said.

"That might be the real issue."

"What do you mean?" I said.

"I suspect I'm not really his daughter."

"Your mother…" I dropped the statement.

"I was born into a lovely situation," Street said, her voice thick with sarcasm. "My brother might not have been his biological kid, either. The moment I first had the thought a few years ago, it explained several things about my childhood. My mother wasn't mean like him, but she was devious and untrustworthy and more than a little promiscuous. Tom Casey probably relished hearing about her death from the overdose."

I squeezed her knee again.

"What's next?" I asked.

"A few weeks ago, I got a letter from my aunt May. She said that the parole board had the hearing as planned. She was at the hearing. She said that when my video statement was played, the hearing room was very focused and quiet. When it came time for her statement, she told the parole board that my father was a twisted man who had played the prison guards like pawns in a chess game and was now playing the parole board. She said his good behavior in prison was just an act so he could get out and seek retribution."

"What did they decide?"

"We don't know, yet. They take eight to twelve weeks to decide. It's been eleven weeks. They will be making their decision any day. I can't sleep, I'm so worried they'll let him out."

"What do you think will happen if they let him out?"

Street didn't hesitate. "I think he will come for us."

"Who is us?"

"The people he thinks put him inside."

"Including you," I said.

Street nodded. "Aunt May. The prosecutor at his trial. Me."

"But even if you're not his biological child, you're still the closest thing he has to a child. I would think that might keep him from a premeditated action against you."

"As a scientist, I know that in the animal world, infanticide is common. Males of many species will kill offspring that are not theirs. If that offspring helped put him in jail for decades, that's only going to make matters worse."

"He'll be aware that if he left the state of Missouri and came to Lake Tahoe, that would no doubt violate the terms of his parole. Won't that temper his actions?"

"I don't think he cares. I think he only wants to punish those of us who testified against him."

"Even if it means they put him back inside," I said.

"Inside, they fed him and gave him a warm place to sleep. There was no insecurity about trying to keep a job and pay the bills and not be homeless. Of course, most people who go to prison think the experience is pure hell. But a few people are well-suited to it. I think Tom Casey is one of them, and he would be happy to go back permanently. Especially if he can exact vengeance first."

We were both breathing hard.

Street reached for my hand and squeezed. The move was sudden and indicated a level of desperation. She turned to me. The tear tracks on her cheek reflected the moonlight. "I need you, Owen. It's like the core of my childhood is a corrosive acid, and it's coming back to torment me. I need your help fending it off, please."

I leaned over, put my arm around her, and hugged her. "I'm here," I said. "Always with you."

"I tried to trade in my past," she said, "and get rid of all the painful memories." Street looked out and up at the night sky, away from the moon, toward the endless stars. "If I could undergo a complete metamorphosis, like a butterfly, I could be free. I would be able to jettison Tom Casey from my mind, my life."

"Anything I can do to help… I'm here for you."

She squeezed my hand.

NINE

The next morning, I pondered Jonas Montrop's kidnapping while I drank coffee. With no clue about the father's killing and no hint of where the ransom money went, I had no lead to follow.

I took Spot and headed south to my office on Kingsbury Grade. The AM station on the Jeep radio began a news squawk about some robbery, the DJ using that excessive sensationalist tone that would only be appropriate if a monster asteroid were about to wipe out the planet. So I again turned the dial to NPR, and the speakers filled with some wonderful orchestral stuff that, a few miles down the road, I learned was Edward Elgar. I turned up the grade and stopped at my office, feeling even more cultured than when I woke up.

Spot pushed past me as I went in the door. He trotted up the stairs to my second-floor digs. When I opened my office door, Spot immediately walked over to the new splotchy black-and-white throw rug that Street had gotten him. She'd put a thick pad under it. The rug was custom designed in a Harlequin Great Dane pattern. Spot sprawled across it with enthusiasm. It was hard to see the outline of his body. Maybe his affinity for the rug wasn't about the comfort of padding but the comfort that there was now one place on Earth where he was hard to see. All creatures, prey and predator alike, like the way camo allows them to hide. Polar Bears on the ice flows. Deer in the sun-dappled forest. Lions on the Serengeti grasslands. Great Danes on a Great Dane rug.

Spot shut his eyes and appeared to instantly sleep while I assessed my coming workload.

I first established that the answering machine wasn't blinking, no UPS or FedEx notices or packages had been pushed through the door slot, and when I dialed up my email, there was nothing in my inbox but spam.

Nobody cared about me and my perspective except a dead guy who thought I'd killed him. I leaned back in my desk chair, which caused it to make a loud screech as if metal were ripping. Spot was flopped on his side. He opened his eyes a moment and lifted his head two inches to look at me, his disdain at my noise obvious. His eyelids drooped, and the jowl on the lower side of his head hung down, exposing the pink of his gums and the white of his out-sized fangs.

"Sorry to interrupt your somnolence, Largeness. The noise to which you object is merely the sound of a perspicacious detective leaning back in his chair and training his weighty and considerable thoughts on the state of the world."

Spot lowered his head to the floor and sighed, the outrush of breath a dismissive punctuation to my statement. Maybe it was because I'd used a big word.

I said to him, "I learned the word perspicacious from Diamond, the man who feeds you Danishes, so you shouldn't be dismissive."

Spot didn't respond. He appeared to be unconscious. The job of riding to the office in the Jeep must be exhausting.

I dialed Diamond's number.

"I appreciate your vouching for me yesterday," I said when he answered. "It turns out I used to know the dead guy back in the day. He was a defendant in a manslaughter case. Now he thinks I killed him."

Diamond sounded amused. "Like a magician, he gets himself croaked and accuses you posthumously."

"Croaked?" I said.

"Been learning more norteamericano slang. I like the word croak. 'If I croak tomorrow' is a lot more real than the breezy, euphemistic 'If I should pass on soon.' Or worse, 'If something should happen to me someday.' Croak says the truth. What did you learn about the croakee?"

So I told Diamond about David Montrop, and how death by paddle board wasn't pretty, and how he left a note suggesting I might be his croaker, and how it appeared that his son Jonas had been abducted in South Lake Tahoe. "Sergeant Lanzen learned that Montrop made a twenty-five-thousand-dollar cash withdrawal from the bank yesterday morning."

"So the perp snatched the kid, then went to dad's house to collect the ransom and killed the dad."

"Yeah," I said.

"If the perp doesn't mind killing the dad, then killing the kid would be no big deal, too. What do you know about this kid?" Diamond asked.

"Nothing. His front door was broken, and he's gone."

"Strange," Diamond muttered. "Did you call because you think any of this is related to the stickup?"

"What stickup?"

Diamond went silent for a moment. "You do a good job at shutting off outside inputs. Here on the South Shore, early this morning. Biggest thing going down in Tahoe in years. I've already spent hours on this, doing the routine just a few blocks from your office. While you were, what, sleeping? Oh, I've got incoming. Gotta go." He hung up.

Just then my phone also rang. I clicked the answer button. "Owen McKenna," I said. Maybe it was Street, or at least one of the few people who'd be sad when I croaked.

"Owen McKenna the private detective?"

"Speaking."

"This is Randy Bosworth, General Manager and Security Director at Reno Armored. You've no doubt heard about our situation. I believe the Douglas County Sheriff's Office is well qualified to handle it. But my boss, Howard Timmens, wants me to get you in on this. He's heard about you and says you'd be a good fit. You probably know how these things go. I do what Mr. Timmens says. He thinks you're the best chance to catch the scum that did this. You are willing to come down and talk to us in Reno, right?"

"Certainly," I said, wondering if I wanted the work. But it sounded like the boss man Timmens might be sad if I croaked, so that was a plus.

"Can't beat a PI with his nose to the pavement," I said. "I have a pretty good scum-catch average." I didn't know what scum or situation he was referring to, so I was just putting words on the line to take up space while my perspicacity struggled to reveal itself. Meanwhile, a little voice in my brain said that if I hadn't gotten all dreamy about Edward Elgar, I would have heard about the scum on the news broadcast that I'd abandoned. Probably, it was the stickup that Diamond just referred to.

"Why don't you give me the rundown from your point of view?"

"Well, it's pretty much like they said on TV. Our number two lockbox got held up at five o'clock this morning. Just as it was getting light."

"Lockbox?"

"What we call our armored trucks. Number two was on its way to make a cash drop at one of the casinos in South Lake Tahoe. Or I guess I should say Stateline, 'cause that's actually the name on the Nevada side of the border. The lockbox was headed down an alley that leads from Highway 50 to the casino loading dock. The alley is narrow with lots of good cover for a robbery. Stupid route choice, I guess. We chose it for ease of access, not security. Anyway, just before they got to the loading dock, a group of robbers stepped out." Bosworth had a faint accent lurking in his speech, like he'd spent his first few years in a Cockney family in London.

"How many robbers?" I asked.

"Four."

"Were the robbers armed?"

"Yeah."

"Your men describe them?"

"They were like gangbangers on TV. They wore black hoodies with the hoods up. What made them creepy was they had on those white hockey goalie masks. They carried AKs, according to Jim who was in Iraq, so he should know. Our driver – that's Matt – stopped when two of the robbers stepped in front of the truck as it was going down the alley. They pointed their weapons at Matt, and at Jim, who was riding shotgun. My guys could see in the mirrors and on the rear-facing video that there were two other men who stepped out at the rear of the lockbox. Our windows are reinforced, but those AKs, well, you don't want to take any chances. In fact, we make our rules clear to our crew. If someone sticks us, we stay in the truck and call it in. No heroes, is our motto. Of course, the trucks have loopholes, but we don't fire through them unless fired upon. We've also got the run-flat tires if someone tries to shoot them out, but if our driver can't step on the gas to get away, we do what the robbers say."

"So your guys played it by the book and stayed put," I said. "Smart."

"Yeah. Jim immediately picked up the radio to call it in, but one of the robbers walked up to the windshield. He put a piece of paper against the glass and tucked it under the wiper. It said, 'No radio, no cell phone.' With his other hand, he held a smartphone against the glass. Then he held up another piece of paper that said, "Remove your weapons and get out of the truck, or we do this." The paper had an arrow drawn on it. The arrow pointed toward the smart phone. Follow me?"

"Yeah," I said.

"The phone played a video that showed a man holding a pack of what looked like three tubes wrapped in silver duct tape. The man on the video tossed the silver pack under a big truck. Then the man stepped behind a building, held up a little remote transmitter, and pushed a button. The duct tape package under the truck blew up in a huge fireball, shredding the truck. My boys said that the video looked like it was copied from a movie. Anyway, the message was clear."

"Not good," I said.

"Right. So, of course, the robber this morning pulled a duct-taped package out of his pack and held it up so that our men could see it was just like the one in the video. He tossed it under the lockbox, held up a remote for our men to see, then pointed to the paper sign that said they should get out of the truck."

"Your men did as instructed?"

"Like I said, right out of our book. Removed their weapons and got out with their hands up."

I thought about it. "Were the handwritten notes used because the men can't hear from inside the truck?"

"Well, the armor makes it pretty soundproof inside. But we have mikes on our video recorders. The ones on the outside of the lockbox record sound with the video. Turns out none of the robbers said a thing. It's like they knew that the hoodies and the hockey masks obscured their visual identity and not speaking obscured their audio identity. That's my idea, anyway."

"Makes sense to me," I said. "What kind of alarm system do you use?"

"We've got the Red Web Alert setup. It includes the system here at our HQ, as well as the mobile communication system on the lockboxes. It's got the full internet connection with the auto-trigger if the connection goes down for more than five seconds. Each guard has a foot switch they can hit without any robber seeing it. Matt and Jim both stomped those babies when those robbers first stepped out. The system is monitored twenty-four-seven and dialed into the police. Cost us thirty-eight grand to buy and nine hundred a month service fee."

"Money well spent?" I said.

"Maybe. Maybe not. The system rang the bells and sent out the auto-messages, but by the time the cops got there, the robbers were gone with the money."

"What happened after your men got out of the truck?"

"The bangers patted them down, took everything out of their pockets. Cell phones, keys, wallets. Larry, who rides in back, was still in there. Matt explained over the intercom about the explosive under the truck, so Larry unlocked the cargo door and came out without his weapon. The robbers cleaned out Larry's pockets, then had them all take a hike."

"Where to?" I said.

"They split them up. Probably a psychological thing, right? They showed Matt a piece of paper that said to walk northwest until he got to Edgewood Golf Course, then wait on the corner for one hour. They showed Jim a piece of paper that said to walk southwest on Lake Tahoe Boulevard until he got to the Heavenly Gondola and wait there for one hour. The paper for Larry, the rear guard, said to walk east until he got to Van Sickle Park and wait there for an hour. The last paper said they had drones and accomplices and would be watching them, and that if any of the guards did anything before they'd been at their assigned places for an hour, their families would be killed. At the bottom of the paper, each of the guard's names was written. Next to Larry's name was his wife's name. And under them, his daughter's name in one of those family-tree drawings. Creepy, if you ask me. They'd obviously been studying our company and had made a careful plan."

"How are your men taking it?"

"Matt and Jim seem to be fine. But then they're single, and they always put up a macho front. So it's hard to know what they really think. But Larry isn't taking it too good. He's stressing about his wife and two-year-old daughter. I told him he could take a week off when this is settled. From the look on his face when he left and went home, I wouldn't be surprised if he decides to give notice he's quitting. I think a job like this seemed reasonable only if the dangers were just, you know, in your mind."

"Abstract dangers, not real dangers," I said.

"Yeah. Abstract dangers. But now that they're obviously real dangers, I think Larry would rather sell shirts at Target."

"Understandable."

"So can you fit us in? I've never hired a private cop before, so I don't really know how it works. Do you charge by the day? Or is it a lump sum contract based on performance?"

"I charge a per diem plus unusual expenses. You can cancel at any time if you're dissatisfied." I explained the details.

"What do you do first?"

"I'll come down and visit your company. I'd like to interview the drivers and look at the truck. Depending on what I find, I may want to talk to your other staff. How soon is good for you?"

"Well, I was told the Douglas County cops will be done with our truck in another couple of hours. So we should have it back at the garage late this afternoon. Would tomorrow morning work? Say, eight a.m.?"

"I'll be there. You and I can talk. Can your drivers be there to talk, say, an hour after that? Nine o'clock?"

"Will do."

"One more question. Have the cops looked at the explosive that was under the truck?"

"No. It wasn't there. The robbers must have taken it when they left with the money."

"Got it," I said. "See you in the morning."
"Yeah." Bosworth hung up.

After I got off the phone, I called Diamond.

I said, "I just talked to Randy Bosworth from Reno Armored, and he told me all about the big stickup. You want to add anything to Bosworth's version? The inside scoop from an official law enforcement officer?"

"Ain't much to tell. Everything went down like you'd expect if the stickup were performed by Navy Seals. The timing was perfect, the method perfect, the result perfect. They left no evidence. We have no clues and thus, as of this moment, nothing to pursue."

"Great. I should be able to bust this case wide open in no time."

"Let me know what you find out."

We said goodbye and hung up.

TEN

I was thinking that a major robbery the day after a kidnapping was very unusual in a relatively unpopulated place like Tahoe. I wondered if there could be a link. Maybe I should find people and ask questions.

I drove up to Tahoe Vista and got to Evan Rosen's motel apartment at five in the afternoon. Evan was out. I took Spot for a walk down to the beach.

After a half hour, we about-faced and headed back.

Evan Rosen was still out. So we waited in the Jeep. Spot hadn't napped for over an hour, so he seized the opportunity to address his enormous sleep needs.

At 6 p.m., an old beige Subaru turned into the lot and parked just down from Evan's apartment. Evan got out of the passenger seat, opened the rear door, and helped Mia get out of the rear seat. A white-haired woman got out of the driver's seat. Evan pulled out what looked like a thick wad of bills. Unless they were ones, it seemed like more money than a house cleaner would carry around. She peeled off some bills and handed them to the woman, then opened the rear hatch of the woman's car and lifted out two five-gallon paint buckets in which were various cleaning supplies. She set them on the ground. Mia picked one of them up with her good hand. They carried the gear to the apartment and went inside. The white-haired woman went to hers, which was four doors down in the same building.

I got out of the Jeep and walked over.

Evan's front door was still open. She saw me. "Mr... Sorry." She paused and set down her bucket.

"Owen McKenna."

"Right, Owen McKenna," she repeated.

"You were able to get a ride today."

"Yes. My neighbor Mattie bailed me out. She's doing it again tomorrow. But she has a doctor's appointment the next day, so I'm stuck. I can't believe the cops still have my car. I checked with a mechanic in Incline and told the sergeant they could have the car towed there. But they haven't done that yet. Do you know when that will happen?"

"I don't know. I could give you a ride the day after tomorrow if you don't have it back."

Evan immediately frowned. She obviously suspected that a favor came with a cost.

"Why would you do that?" she asked.

"You answered our questions yesterday. I might have more questions I'd like to ask you. My schedule is free. It only makes sense that I return the favor."

"You're saying that answering questions to a law enforcement officer is a favor? Questions that I could be required to answer?"

"It's a favor when any person cooperates with law enforcement."

"Just what are you anyway? The sergeant lady didn't say your rank."

"I'm a private investigator. I've been hired by an armored truck company to investigate a robbery."

Evan raised her eyebrows. "The Reno Armored truck robbery? No offense, but what does that have to do with David Montrop's murder?"

"We're not sure, but my cop sense tells me they are connected. In addition, Montrop's son was kidnapped. I think that's connected too."

"Mr. Montrop's stepson was kidnapped?"

"Yeah. Do you know him?"

"No. Mr. Montrop mentioned a stepson a couple of times, but I never met him. I got the sense that there was bad blood between them." Evan looked at me with skepticism. "You said you're a private investigator. I thought PIs weren't actual cops. You don't have the powers of a peace officer, right?"

I was surprised. "You make an astute observation. I often work in conjunction with local law enforcement agencies. I spent twenty years at the San Francisco PD, retiring as Homicide Inspector. You know about peace officer powers?"

Evan shrugged. "Just, you know, basic cop stuff. Not just anyone can be a cop, right? It's like not just anyone can sell insurance. You gotta get the education and the paper that says you have the qualification. It's the power of the state. The state can give, and the state can take away, and if you think you can be a lone wolf and live life any way you want without government involving itself in your life, you can't. The state is still always in control."

"Wow, you could write an essay on the structure of government authority. Do you always think like that? When you're cleaning houses?"

"No. It's just… I don't know. Kind of interesting, I guess. I get a lot of time to think when I'm scrubbing floors."

"I suppose so," I said. I turned and looked toward where the older woman had walked. "Should I plan on giving you a ride two days from now? It's no trouble. But no pressure, either."

She thought about it. I could tell she was weighing the pros and cons.

"Okay. But I'll call you if I have my car back."

I gave her my card. "If I don't hear from you, what time should I plan to be here?"

She thought about it. "The day after tomorrow, my first house is the Olmsteads. They like me there by eight because Mrs. Olmstead heads out to her yoga class shortly after, and she usually has special requests."

"So I should arrive here when?"

"The Olmsteads are on Dollar Point, fifteen minutes from here. So if you could come here at seven-thirty, that would give me time to load up and make sure Mia is comfortable with you and your car."

I pointed to my Jeep. Spot was now awake, and he held his head out the window.

"My dog Spot likes to ride along. Do you think Mia would be okay with that?"

Evan looked over at the Jeep. "She loves dogs, but he's bigger than any dog Mia's ever met. I assume he's friendly?"

"Very."

"Would it be okay if I introduced Mia to him now? Then she

can get used to the idea before you come."

"Of course."

Evan went inside and came back out with Mia.

"You remember meeting Owen?" Evan said, her hand on Mia's shoulder.

Mia looked at me, and made a tentative nod.

I raised my hand in a little wave and said, "Hi, Mia."

"Owen might be giving us a ride the day after tomorrow. He has a big dog named Spot." She pointed toward my Jeep. Mia looked where Evan pointed. Her eyes widened when she saw Spot.

"You know how you like dogs, Mia? Would you like to meet Spot? Let's go meet Spot."

We walked over. When Spot saw us coming, he started wagging, his tail banging back and forth between the front and rear seat backs.

I grabbed Spot's head to show that he was tolerant of any kind of touch. "Spot, meet Mia and Evan. Here, Mia, you can pet Spot. He loves it when you pet him."

Evan knew exactly how to handle it. She stroked Spot's head. "Oh, Mia, Spot loves a pet."

Mia reached out, slowly. Spot's head protruding from the rear window was at the same level as Mia's head. Spot sniffed her hand, which made her pull it back. I put my hand over Spot's muzzle so he couldn't sniff her. She reached forward and pet him. He wagged. Mia made a huge smile.

"Spot likes pets," she said.

"Understatement of the month," I said.

Evan grinned, and I knew that Spot had once again given me entreé into someone else's world.

"I'll see you the day after tomorrow," I said.

ELEVEN

In the morning, I took Spot with me in the Jeep, headed up and over Spooner Summit, cruised down to Carson City and then north to Reno on the freeway. The contrast from cloudy cool Tahoe to hot sunny desert was dramatic.

The Reno Armored company, northeast of the Reno Tahoe airport, was actually in Sparks, Reno's twin city to the east. It didn't seem fair that a Sparks company ignored its home territory and traded on Reno's famous name. But then the Reno Tahoe airport, which itself was nearly in Sparks, traded on the Tahoe name and the allure of a mountain lake that was out of sight almost 2000 feet above and twenty miles southwest of Reno.

I pulled into the parking lot of a new industrial building that housed an auto body shop and a truck detailing store. Reno Armored was on the far right side.

I told Spot to be good, then walked to the entrance under the modern sign that said, 'Reno Armored – Your Security is Why We're Here.'

I pushed through the glass door.

The air conditioning inside was set to sub-zero. The thin young woman behind the counter wore a thick sweater over a long-sleeved blouse. A wool scarf was wrapped around her neck. Her lips were blue and her fingernails were purple underneath clear, glossy polish.

"Good morning," she said, a hint of chatter in her teeth.

"Hi. I'm Owen McKenna, here to see Randy Bosworth."

She looked down at an appointment book. "Yes, of course. I'll let him know you're here." She picked up a phone, dialed three numbers and spoke in a high voice with a tremor of shiver in it. "Mr. McKenna is here to see you."

She hung up and said, "Mr. Bosworth will be out in a minute."

"Thanks." I turned and looked at a wall that had several large, framed poster prints showing a variety of armored trucks, painted with cool-tone grays and blacks. The framed prints were displayed with fancy lighting as if the pictures were of fighter jets. Each poster had a slogan at the bottom. 'We Preserve Your World' and 'We Treat Your Money Like It's Ours.'

I heard the whoosh and click of a pneumatic locking system as a door opened.

"Mr. McKenna," a voice said behind me. "I'm Randy Bosworth."

I turned to see a young man with the skin of someone who'd spent all of his life in the desert sun without a hat and augmented his UV input with a tanning bed. He was only a couple of inches shorter than my six-six, and wide enough that he must have weighed 275 pounds. He wore navy trousers, and a white shirt with a stitched-on Reno Armored logo patch that looked similar to a sheriff's logo. On his left hip was a holstered gun. He had on a narrow navy tie, loosened at the neck. Its presence suggested that Bosworth regularly met with clients or potential clients. Despite the early hour and the frigid indoor climate, his shirt already had sweat stains around his armpits. He contrasted with the frozen, skinny receptionist the way an arctic walrus would with a young fawn trapped out on the frozen tundra.

We shook hands. Up close, the pistol protruding from his holster looked like a .45 Smith & Wesson.

"Thanks for coming down," Bosworth said, not sounding thankful at all. "Where should we begin?"

The man had a metallic, fiery breath that would blister stainless steel. If you mixed hot chili peppers with something radioactive, plutonium maybe, you'd get close. I stepped back. "Let's start with the truck that was robbed. I'd like to look at it."

"Our number two lockbox," he said. "Come with me."

Now that I was talking to Bosworth face-to-face, his faint accent was beginning to sound Australian.

Bosworth turned and walked over to a heavy door set into an unusually heavy frame. He punched a code into a keypad, and I heard a locking bolt slide. He led me through the door out of the office area into a large garage. As he walked, he said, "The

Douglas County cops spent hours going over the truck. But it sounds like all they found were our people's fingerprints."

There were two armored trucks inside the garage. Another man, dressed in multiple, thick layers like the receptionist, was polishing one of the trucks, making it shine like the ones pictured in the lobby. The other truck was somewhat dirty.

"Lockbox number two," Bosworth said, pointing to the dirtier truck.

"How many trucks does your company have?" I asked as I walked up to the truck.

"Three lockboxes. Plus a longer-haul transport, which is out on a trip to the San Francisco Federal Reserve Bank. We also have a pickup for local errands. It doesn't haul money, but it does have our same logo paintjob. Image is everything in the security business. Which is why having a lockbox emptied is such a big deal. Very bad for our image. Insurance covers the loss, but our cred still suffers big time."

I walked along the side wall of the truck. The truck appeared to be like other armored transports I'd seen. Small, thick, bulletproof windows in a large squarish box. Heavy gauge steel body panels and door hinges. Locks that would take a crowbar and a sledge hammer to dent. Loopholes through which occupants could return fire if attacked.

There were video cameras at every corner of the truck and one in the center of the rear, above the rear door.

"You'll notice that the cams are unobtrusive," Bosworth said. "But they're still obvious. Each lockbox also has six hidden cameras, in the body seams, the engine grill, at the inner edge of the wheel wells." He pointed.

"So a naive robber can tape over the obvious cameras but still be a movie star," I said.

"Exactly. Same for our outdoor microphones. You make a sound near our machine, it's recorded for posterity."

"You mentioned that your system is online continuously."

"Right. But we've still got all the feeds recorded by the truck's black box. Every aspect of our security has built-in redundancy. I gave the cops the downloaded copies of our computer log as well as those from the black box. They're going to have their cyber expert look for anything unusual." Bosworth reached into his pocket, pulled out a computer memory stick, and held it up. "The system records on the black box memory and a backup memory simultaneously. In addition to our computers, I've already saved another copy on this stick."

"I will need to look at that."

Bosworth looked irritated. "Whatever Mr. Timmens wants," he said like a petulant child.

I walked to the back of the truck. "After the robbers sent your men walking away, what happened next?"

"The back door was already open from when Larry unlocked it and got out. The camera shows that one of the robbers had a large bolt cutter. He stepped inside and came out with two bags, which is all they had for the delivery."

"How much is each bag?"

"Approximately fifty pounds."

"I mean, how much money was it?"

"Oh," Bosworth said. "Money in multiple denominations for an operation like a casino averages about five thousand dollars a pound."

"So two fifty pound bags is one hundred pounds," I said. "At five thousand dollars a pound, that would be five hundred thousand dollars."

"Right."

"Was the cash marked in any way?"

Bosworth shook his head. "No. And we didn't record serial numbers or put dye packs in the bags. We only do that on what we call our dye-for-distance shipments, which is anything over one million dollars and one hundred miles one way. But this was a relatively small delivery and very routine. Statistically, it's not cost-effective to go to the extra trouble when it's small and close."

"What is Reno Armored's liability in a situation like this?"

Bosworth shook his head. "Nothing. Outside of the damage to our rep, insurance covers it all. As long as we meet all of their security parameters, we're covered."

"When you're carrying cash for a client and it is stolen, how long does the client have to wait to be paid?"

"There's barely any wait at all," Bosworth said. "We belong to a virtual bank network. When a client gives us cash to bring to the bank, the moment we accept the cash, it's like the client already deposited it in the bank. In fact, as we sign for the shipment on the iPad app, the deposit instantly shows up in the client's bank account. It's that immediacy that assures the client. Of course, if it turns out that there is a discrepancy in the deposit, the account balance is later adjusted."

"But this was money going the opposite direction," I said. "Instead of taking money from the casino to the bank, you were taking it from the bank to the casino. What happens then?"

"As soon as the robbery was reported, the virtual bank network worked in reverse. The bank that sent the cash got an immediate credit from the insurance company for the original amount. Then that bank simply sent out a new cash transfer. It went to the casino by a different armored transport company, I'm embarrassed to say. That hurts. But it really doesn't matter to the casino. The replacement cash arrived less than two hours later. The cash is always covered by insurance, and a robbery doesn't really interrupt business much beyond the loss of productivity when employees lose work time talking about it at the water cooler. The only people holding the bag, so to speak, are the insurance companies. But of course, that's their business. They get paid healthy premiums to cover things like robbery or fire or anything else that takes cash out of the system."

I looked around at the garage. "The money you haul. Where do you store it if it's not on your trucks?"

Bosworth turned and pointed to the far corner of the garage. "See that garage door? It's heavy-duty and secure and raises and lowers just like the others. But it doesn't lead to the outside."

"It's a facade," I said.

"Right. Behind it is our vault. It's the same as the vaults banks use. Fireproof, bomb proof, impossible to break into. It has a timed entry system and requires coordinated inputs from two people who each have their own code and key."

I nodded. I walked to the rear door of the truck. "Okay if I look inside?"

"Of course. The door is unlocked. Inside you'll see that there are no windows, just a video screen and microphone. That's the only way the rear guard can communicate with the men in front. There's a touchscreen input so the guard can switch back and forth between any of the camera feeds."

I lifted up on a heavy handle, pulled open the door, grabbed a handle at the side of the truck, and climbed a two-rung ladder into the truck.

The truck's cargo area was spartan in extreme. It had large metal bins at the front wall. On the floor was a locker with a locking lid.

There was a small seat with a seatbelt and near it the monitor screen that was the rear guard's communication port to the rest of the world.

In one corner hung several bags, empty of contents but heavy of fabric. I lifted one off the hook. It was made of a fabric I hadn't seen before. Some kind of mixture of heavy canvas with reinforcement threads of metal. At the top was a folding clasp with a padlock.

I carried the bag to the rear of the truck where Bosworth stood.

"Is this the kind of bag that the money was in?"

He nodded. "Yeah. Two of them. In normal operations, we don't need empty bags in the lockbox. But we carry extra in case a cash pickup instruction changes after the lockbox has left our dock. Never know when a casino loses track of their empties."

"The bags look hard to cut."

He nodded. "It's like chainmail. You'd need a specialty shears designed to cut metal."

"Were the bags padlocked?"

"Yes, again. We have a system that takes the guards out of the loop. We lock the tops of the bags and we also lock them into the truck lockers before the truck leaves our facility. The keys stay here. By prearrangement, the casino or bank or wherever has the only other set of keys."

"That's got to slow the robbers down a lot," I said.

"Yeah. They have to cut the bags out of the locked truck bins, then carry them someplace where they can work on them with a shears or a saw or something."

"The design of the truck and its security features," I said, "is such that a lot of robbers could never even get to the money, right?"

"Yeah. Come at a lockbox with normal weapons, you don't have a chance. The guards can just sit inside. If you fire on them, they can pick you off by shooting out through the loopholes. But explosives, that's a different story. Not much you can do when someone lobs C-Four under your buggy."

I got out of the rear of the truck and walked around to look in the cab. It was similar to other truck cabs but with a smaller windshield and side windows and four small video screens on the dash.

"How do you access the black box info that gets sent over the internet to your computer?" I asked.

"Over here," Bosworth said. He walked over to a desk. "This computer is logged into the system." He sat down, moved the mouse, typed a password, and brought up the software. "When the lockbox is on the road, the video and audio feeds get sent over a secure radio system to the internet. The company that provides the software stores all of the information. We can access it from this computer and also from the one in Howard's office."

"Howard Timmens," I said.

"Right. Armored's President. He works out of an office in downtown Reno."

"Is he the company owner?"

"No. We're owned by a private equity company in San Francisco. There's a bunch of lawyers who own armored transport companies all across the U.S. and Canada. Howard answers to them."

"Can I look at the video feeds from the truck at the time of the robbery?"

Bosworth looked at me like I was wasting his time.

"Sure," he said with false cheeriness. He brought up two different windows on the computer screen. "The main ones are the front and rear cameras, so I can show those simultaneously." He used his finger on the touchscreen to bring up the feeds. "We can search this any way we want, by time, by action, by whichever camera we want to focus on. I've already been through this, so I can show you the robbery sequence without you having to wait forever."

Bosworth dragged his finger here and there, tapped some buttons, and the robbery unfolded.

It was just as he'd described on the phone. Two men walked in front of the truck. They wore hoodies with the hoods up. The hoods came over the top of their heads and partially down over their foreheads. They had on hockey masks so their faces were completely covered. They each carried what looked like a military assault rifle. One stood back while the other held the phone and the papers with written instructions against the windshield.

The other screen showed the two men at the back. They also had on black hoodies and white hockey masks.

"What about the audio?" I said. "I don't hear anything."

"I could turn it up, but all you'll hear is street noise." Bosworth dragged a slider icon on the screen.

I heard some wind in the microphone, a distant horn, some engine noises. "Earlier, you said that the robbers didn't say anything. Any chance they spoke softly to each other? Words that could be pulled out of the background noise by a recording engineer?"

"I don't think so. I listened to the entire recording twice. I paid special attention to those moments when they turned and gestured toward each other. There wasn't even the slightest sense of vocal sounds. I believe that they'd rehearsed so thoroughly that they didn't need to talk. They just communicated by prearranged gestures. When you think about it, it's impressive. We don't know what they look like or sound like."

"Were there any other unusual sounds?" I asked.

"Not that I heard. If you want, I can play the entire audio feed for you."

"No. Maybe later. Right now I'd like to have my dog take a look at the truck if that's okay."

Bosworth looked startled. "You have a dog? Like one of those drug-search dogs the police use?"

"Sort of. My dog isn't a professional search dog, but he's useful. He might notice something I didn't."

"I don't see what good a dog could do." Bosworth glanced

over at the truck as if reassessing a previous plan that hadn't considered what a dog's nose could find.

"I'd still like to have him inspect the truck."

Bosworth's hesitation had turned into resistance. "Between the cops searching and me searching, I can tell you that your dog is unlikely to find anything."

Time to push. "Could you pull the truck outside, please? If I bring my dog in here, the other scents of the building will distract. The cold air will also change his perception. A dog is most useful if ambient smells are similar to where he's been. Then unusual smells stand out."

Maybe Bosworth came to understand that my request was reasonable. Or maybe he realized that resisting made him look suspicious. He walked over to a workbench and lifted a key off a hook on the wall above it.

TWELVE

"We have security garage doors," Randy Bosworth said. He opened a panel on the wall next to the garage door and typed in a code. Then he climbed into the cab and touched the remote on the visor. The garage door went up, letting in a welcoming flood of warm air. Bosworth started the engine, a big diesel that roared in the enclosed space. He backed up slowly, loud warning beeps piercing the air. When the truck was twenty feet outside the building, the garage door went back down. Bosworth shut the engine off and climbed down out of the truck.

"Where's your dog?" he said. "Let's see if he's any good."

"In my Jeep at the front. C'mon, I'll introduce you."

We walked around to the front lot. When we got close, Bosworth stared at the Jeep and said, "Whoa, that boy is..." He stopped walking.

I reached for the rear door.

Bosworth took a step back. "He's friendly, right?"

"Yeah. Name's Spot. Give him a pet, and he'll be your friend forever." I pulled open the rear door of the Jeep. Spot jumped out, wagging. He took two jogging loops around the parking lot, then ran up toward Bosworth. Normally, I step between Spot and other people he doesn't know. It reassures people that they're not about to become doggie lunch. But I decided to let Bosworth grapple with his emotions. Bosworth's hand went to the butt of his gun as Spot did a quick stop in front of him. Bosworth leaned back and his hands levitated into the air as Spot nosed him all over.

"Spot, meet Randy Bosworth," I said. Spot lifted his head high and sniffed toward Bosworth's face, moving slower than normal, probably being cautious about the dangers of the man's breath. Bosworth backed up.

"Just a single pet will satisfy him," I said.

Bosworth reached out a tentative hand and gave Spot a pet, his big meaty hand looking small compared to Spot's head. Spot broke into a pant. "Is he ever... unfriendly?" Bosworth asked. "He could put my head in his mouth."

"He could, but I don't think he will," I said.

"You don't think? That's a joke, right? Tell me that's a joke."

"It's a joke. Okay, Spot, you can run." I gave him a smack on his rear, and he took off across the parking lot.

While Bosworth and I walked back to the truck, Spot cruised past the other parked vehicles, went up and sniffed the front door of the building, charged down the side of the building, and veered off into the vacant lot next door, sniffing out hints of past critter movement through the sagebrush.

"He needs to burn off some energy before he works, huh?" Bosworth said. He looked at Spot, then at the truck.

"Yeah. But mostly I want him to get used to the local smells. When dogs charge around it looks like they're playing, which they are. But they are also acquiring a kind of olfactory acclimatization."

"Like making a smell map of the landscape," Bosworth said, a surprisingly acute observation for someone who still seemed distracted.

"Yeah. That's a good description for what they do."

"Then if they find other smells when they search," Bosworth continued, "they'll know if those smells belong in the landscape or not."

"You'd make a good search dog handler," I said.

After another minute, I whistled, and Spot turned to look at me. He was fifty yards away. Whatever he was investigating was much more interesting than what I had to offer.

"C'mon, boy," I called out.

Spot looked toward me for a moment more, then went back to sniffing the dirt. Next, he trotted over to sniff along a fence.

"Spot, come," I shouted, wishing that just once he'd act like a class valedictorian and do exactly as I asked.

Spot ignored me.

"You want a treat?"

Spot lifted up his head and looked.

I patted the cargo pocket of my pants where I keep treats, pulled one out and held it up.

Spot broke into a run, charged up, then did a quick stop. He sniffed at my hand. I tore off the wrapper and gave him half.

Spot inhaled it, then sniffed at my hand, which was holding the other half of the biscuit.

"It's all about food, huh?" Bosworth said.

"It's always all about food," I said.

"I've got a friend who's a K-nine handler with the Washoe Sheriff's Office. He has a German Shepherd. That dog will do anything my buddy asks." Bosworth sounded boastful. "Never gives the dog a treat until the very end."

"That's the difference between a Great Dane and a German Shepherd," I said. "When it comes to getting paid, Danes are like smart businessmen. They have the sense to demand a fifty percent deposit up front and the balance immediately on completion."

"That's another joke," Bosworth said, sounding unsure.

I turned to Spot. "Okay, boy, you want the rest of your treat, you gotta provide service." I took his collar with my left hand and walked him to the truck. "You and I are just going to do a little look/see on this truck." I walked Spot counterclockwise along the side of the truck, holding his collar with a loose arm so he could move his head. I didn't want to let go because he would probably run away.

Bosworth spoke up. "Is there, like, a command for, 'Inspect the truck for contraband?'"

"Probably your K-nine handler has one. But I doubt it would work on a Great Dane."

"Because of his rigorous business standards," Bosworth said.

"You got it," I said.

We got to the rear corner of the truck and turned to go across the back.

Bosworth followed. "Do German Shepherds have better noses or something?"

"Nope. Same nose. Different work standards."

Spot sniffed here and there but mostly was indifferent. We rounded the next corner and went back up the far side of the truck. When we'd gone around the front, I opened the passenger door. "Look up here, Spot." I tapped the edge of the seat.

Spot looked at me, then looked at the ground.

"Spot." I pointed. "Here." I reached down, picked up one of his paws, and set it on the door sill. Spot raised his other paw to the sill. Looked around. "Now put your paws up here." I patted the seat and lifted one of his paws.

He pushed up and got his paws on the edge of the seat. The truck's cab was high. But when Spot stands on his rear legs, he's seven feet tall. I pointed into the cab. Spot stretched his head out, sniffing the dash, the video screen, the seat, the floor mat.

"Anything in particular you're expecting to find?" Bosworth said from behind me. He sounded concerned.

"No. What I'm looking for is any sense that there is a smell out of the ordinary, in this case meaning smells that don't usually fit with a vehicle, or smells in this general area that don't fit with what he's already learned are the standard smells in this part of Sparks. All dogs automatically pay attention to unusual smells. It's in their nature."

Spot had shown no interest, so we backed down and away from the cab. I shut the door.

"Is he trained at this?" Bosworth asked.

"Actually, the dogs with less training are better at this particular exercise. A really disciplined dog learns to ignore any smell that he's not been specifically scented on. Whereas a less trained dog pays attention to all smells. The untrained dog will do a better job of reacting to all unusual scents, and, if the dog's owner is observant, the owner will notice the dog's reactions. My dog is somewhat trained. But mostly he just wants treats."

I went to the back of the truck, opened the cargo door, and had Spot leap up inside.

He inspected the empty money bags, moved to the video screen, took a sniff or two at the storage bins, then walked to the edge of the opening.

I climbed down. "Okay, Spot, you can jump down."

He jumped down and then took off on another loop around the parking lot. I pulled out a treat and held it up.

It took a moment before he recognized my posture. Then he

swung in, stopped, and looked at me, his tail on medium speed. I gave him the biscuit.

"Okay, boy. One more look." This time I walked him clockwise around the truck, holding his collar with my right hand so he could be next to the truck. We went up the left side, past the driver's door, around the front, down the right side. When we got to the rear corner, Spot made a small alert. He stopped abruptly and sniffed at the sidewall of the right, rear tire.

"What is it boy?"

He sniffed some more, nose almost pressed against the rubber.

I squatted down and looked at the tire.

"Can you see what it is?" Bosworth asked.

"Nothing that seems significant. Something is smeared on the rubber." I leaned in and sniffed. There was a smell of turpentine. "Ah," I said. "Pine pitch. That would certainly catch a dog's attention as a smell that's out of place on a truck or even in this parking lot." I turned to Bosworth. "Where has this truck been driven since it was last washed?"

He thought about it. "We washed it the night before the robbery. Then we sent it out on the casino delivery to the South Shore. Their route was the five-eighty freeway to Carson City, then Highway Fifty up over Spooner Summit, and down to the casino."

"Did your men stop anywhere or turn off on side roads?"

"No, we have strict rules for cash runs. No variation from the scheduled route."

I thought about the route he described. It would be difficult to get pine pitch on the sidewall of a tire on that route. "This is a pretty big smear of pitch," I said. "So it probably got here because someone stepped in some pitch and tried to rub it off on the tire. Any chance your men aren't telling the truth about where they drove?"

"No. No chance at all. The GPS in the truck keeps a constant log of where it's been. It automatically uploads to a map in the computer. I looked at the map after the truck was brought back. This truck hasn't been anywhere else."

"I'd like to take this pitch off the tire to have it analyzed."

"What could you learn from that?" Bosworth asked.

"I have no idea. Do you have a business card?"

Bosworth pulled out his wallet, removed a card, and handed it to me. The card had 'Reno Armored' printed across the top in red letters. Under it, in black, it said, 'Randy Bosworth, General Manager and Security Director.'

I used my pocket knife to carefully slice behind the smear of pitch, trying to keep it from falling apart into little pieces. The pitch was somewhat brittle, but I managed to get a good part of it off the tire without scraping off more than a sliver of tire rubber. Then I scraped the pitch off the knife blade onto the back of the business card.

Once the pitch was highlighted on the white cardstock, I saw a small dark object. It appeared to be a little bug about 1/8th inch long. "Any chance you've got a sandwich bag?" I said. "That would help me protect this."

"Seems like a lot of fuss for some pine pitch."

I looked at Bosworth but didn't say anything.

"We don't keep sandwich bags in the garage," he said. "I suppose I could fish yesterday's lunch bag out of the wastebasket. Would that be acceptable?" He said it with a sneer.

"If it's clean."

"It was pastrami on rye with mayo, mustard, horseradish, the works."

"Maybe you could wash it out."

Bosworth paused as if he thought I was just making busywork for him. But he went back inside. After a couple of minutes, he came back out holding a wet baggie by the corner. I hoped the wash was thorough. If the bag had even a fraction of the chemicals that were on Bosworth's breath, the pine pitch would spontaneously combust.

I took it from him, turned it inside out and shook it repeatedly to get the water drops off. Spot walked up, his nose in the air near the baggie. His nostrils were flexing.

The remaining moistness evaporated fast in the dry desert air. I carefully set the business card with its pitch and bug inside. I didn't want the plastic to touch the sample. I just wanted the bag to enclose it, should any of the pitch fall off the card.

"Was there anything on the video feeds that showed someone kicking the tire?" I asked.

Bosworth shook his head. "No. But I'm not sure that any of the hidden cameras point toward the tire. Maybe that's just out of view." He pointed to the dark area inside the front of the wheel well. "These miniature cameras point up, so if the person rubbed their shoe on the bottom of the tire, it probably wouldn't be in view of the camera. I'll listen to the audio feeds again and see if I hear any kicking sounds."

Bosworth looked at his watch. "The guards will be showing up, soon. Where do you want to talk to them?"

"Do you have an office where we can talk one at a time?"

Bosworth nodded. "We have a small conference room."

THIRTEEN

I put Spot back into the Jeep to hang out.
 Randy Bosworth and I were waiting outside the front door when the three guards showed up together in a 1970s Buick Skylark that had been rebuilt, repainted, and spit polished.

Bosworth introduced me to Matt, the driver of both the armored truck and the Buick, Jim, the guard who rode shotgun in the truck and in the Buick, and Larry, the guard who was locked in the back of the truck with the money and who also occupied the back seat of the Buick. Bosworth explained that I was a private investigator that Mr. Timmens insisted on hiring.

From what Bosworth said, I sensed that Larry was the most sensitive and least likely to put up a facade. So I chose Larry as my first interview, and we went inside and talked in the empty conference room. I had no doubt that, simultaneously, Bosworth and Matt and Jim were discussing me and my irritating presence rather than directing any thoughts toward how to solve the crime.

Larry was slight of build, maybe 6 feet and 140 pounds. His thin, brown hair looked darker than it was because of the contrast with his pale skin. He had a small neat moustache, and small, crooked teeth. His ears stuck out, and he spoke with a soft, uncertain voice.

"I understand you have a family," I said to Larry. "That's got to be the first thing on your mind when you find yourself in a dangerous situation, huh?"

"Yeah. It's really scary. Matt and Jim are all about tough. Tough physically, tough mentally, tough attitude. I'm just, you know, a regular guy. When people stick rifles in my face, I get scared. I'm not ashamed to admit that. But with Matt and Jim, it's like no big deal. On the way back over here, they were debating about how they might have taken all four robbers out. I'm thinking, guys, these robbers had automatic weapons. They were psychos. You don't try to be heroes with psychos. Reno Armored even has a policy about not being heroes. I take that stuff seriously. Better to be an alive coward, able to take care of your family, than a dead hero, worthless to anyone who needs more than a memory of someone."

"I think you're sensible, Larry. And being sensible doesn't mean you're a coward. If someone hurt your family, and you could intervene, I have no doubt you would."

Larry nodded. "Yes, I would. Matt and Jim would probably think I wouldn't be brave enough, but I would. They'd be surprised."

"Tell me, Larry. Is there anything about the robbery that stands out to you?"

"What do you mean?"

"I'm wondering if any aspect of the robbery seemed unusual or unexpected or strange."

Larry frowned, thinking.

I continued, "For example, when the police asked you to give your version of events, was there anything that you might have mentioned but didn't because no one asked about it?"

Larry started to talk, then stopped.

I waited.

"I think what stood out to me was that the robbers didn't act the way I expected."

"In what way?"

"Well, whenever you see robbers on TV and in the movies, they act real tense. Like they're high on some weird drug, and they make mistakes, and they're loud, and they have disagreements. But these guys were more like professionals."

"Like soldiers? Professionals with weapons?"

Larry shook his head. "Well, maybe they were soldiers, but that's not what I was thinking. I meant they had their act together like it was something they rehearsed multiple times. Of course, to pull off a robbery and not talk meant they had to rehearse, right? But even so, these guys seemed like…"

I waited again.

"They seemed like professional actors. I'm not sure how to

describe it."

"You mean, they performed the robbery like it was a play?" I asked.

"Yeah. That's it. That's exactly it. It was like watching a play where everyone knew their lines. Except no one spoke at all."

"Have you wondered if Matt and Jim or anyone else at Reno Armored might have played an inside role?"

Larry went stone-faced, and his skin pinked up a bit. "I have to confess that when I was in the back of the truck, and I first saw the robbers on the video screen, that was what I wondered. One of the robbers held up instructions on pieces of paper. Then he held up a phone with a video of a truck blowing up. The moment I saw that, I thought, this is too perfect. This is too effective. This isn't like stupid convicts making up a plan in prison for some job they'll do when they get out. This was like something a mastermind would plan. And a mastermind would always get inside information, right?"

"Makes sense," I said. "As you think about the potential for an inside job, consider all the people who work here at Reno Armored. Can you imagine that any of them could have worked with the robbers?"

"As I said, I've already thought about it," Larry said. "But I believe the answer is no. I think Mr. Bosworth is too full of himself to play informant to robbers. He'd want to be the boss. But I don't think he'd want to run a robbery operation. Rita the receptionist is too meek to do anything she might perceive as wrong. Harold the mechanic is a straight shooter. It's a big deal to him to play the role of law-abiding citizen. The other guard team are three guys who are – I don't know how to say this – they're not real smart. I don't think they'd have the ability to help robbers in a meaningful way. That leaves Matt and Jim as the only Reno Armored employees with personalities that could fit what you're talking about. Neither of them is focused on a lawful, ethical life, or whatever you want to call it. But they're both smart enough to put together a serious assault on the operations of a company. Give them enough money, they might go along on a robbery scheme. But the problem with that idea is that they're angry that they got robbed. It's like a personal attack. Jim was in Iraq, and

Matt was a jock in high school. He lettered in something like four sports. I didn't even know it was possible to play four sports. They both have a kind of action movie-star fixation. If someone tried to rob an armored truck, guys like them would always want to kick the robbers' asses."

"Except they didn't," I said.

"Right. They did the right thing. They did what they were taught to do. But that means they didn't do what they wanted to do. They let the robbers rob us. And they are still alive as a result. And I know that their mothers are glad for that. But they're not. They feel that they failed in some way."

"Let's go back to the robbers," I said. "Did you get the sense that one of them was the leader?"

Larry thought about it. "It's hard to say. They all looked the same in their hoodies and masks. So as they moved around it was very hard to keep track of any one of them. But, yeah, I do think there was a leader."

"What was the indication?"

"Just one, really. When they got me out of the back of the truck, everyone was standing there. Three of the robbers held their rifles up, watching Matt and Jim, and then me. They looked ready to fire. The fourth had his rifle hanging over his shoulder like you see in war movies. He held the sheets of paper with instructions. The other three kept glancing at that fourth man. It made it seem like he was the leader. But it could be that they were looking simply because he had the papers."

"How did he act when he showed all of you your instructions?"

"He didn't reveal any attitude, if that's what you're wondering. He just held up each sheet of paper with our names and instructions about where we were to walk. Then he held up a sheet that said, 'We have three accomplices following you. If you deviate from these instructions, we will kill someone in your family.'" Larry's Adam's apple bobbed as he swallowed.

"What happened to those pieces of paper?"

"He folded them a couple of times and put them into his pocket."

"Was there anything about that leader that was notable. His

size? His mannerisms?"

"No. He was about the same size as the others. Although I suppose the uniformity of their clothes might add to a sense of uniformity of size."

"Smart observation," I said. "What about Mr. Timmens, Bosworth's boss? Have you met him?"

Larry nodded.

"Do you think he could have been involved?"

Larry frowned with great intensity. He shook his head. "No, I can't imagine it."

"Thanks, Larry. You've been a big help."

I walked Larry out and brought Matt back into the office.

Based on what Larry had told me, I could have predicted everything about Matt. He was big and strong, blond and blue. We hadn't talked more than a minute before Matt managed to change the subject to his high school jock history.

Eventually, he said, "I wanted to kill those guys. One guy, he didn't keep a firm grip on his rifle, and I was really tempted to step in and take that piece from him. But I didn't because Bosworth was real firm on the rules."

After we spoke for fifteen minutes, I asked him the question I asked Larry. "Is there anything about the robbery that struck you as unusual?"

"What do you mean?"

"These guys who robbed you. Was there anything about it that you didn't expect? Anything weird or strange?"

"I don't know. They didn't talk. That was pretty strange. Right there, not talking. How weird is that? Pretty weird, you ask me."

"Okay, thanks," I said. I stood up.

"That's it? That's all you want?"

"For now."

"Hey, let me ask you," Matt said as he stood up. "I'm thinking that driving a lockbox is, you know, a dead end. This PI thing. Is it a pretty good gig? You meet lots of women? Make lots of money? You don't have to go to cop school or anything, right?"

"Sorry to disappoint, Matt. PIs don't make much money, don't meet lots of women, and yes, if you want good prep, you have to go to cop school and then spend twenty years as a cop."

Matt looked up at the ceiling, then at the floor, sighed, and walked out fast.

I followed and came back with Jim.

My interview with him was a repeat of Matt but with his war experience as a substitute for Matt's high school sports. With his dull, curly red hair, Jim wasn't as flashy pretty as Matt. But he made up for it with a steely hardness that probably made him appealing to a wide range of people who liked the idea of the strong, quiet, deadly, soldier type. He was more reticent than Matt, which may have made him seem smarter than he probably was. I didn't doubt that he could help someone plan an armored truck robbery, but like Matt, Jim seemed too upset about getting robbed to be much of a suspect. Maybe both Matt and Jim were acting, but I doubted it.

"Jim, Randy Bosworth said that you recognized the robbers' rifles."

"Sure. I did two tours in Iraq. I carried an M-Sixteen A-Two myself, but I know the AK-Forty-Sevens."

"The robbers all had the same weapon?"

He nodded. "Yeah."

"Anything about them stand out?"

He shrugged. "Just like any other."

"Could they be fakes?"

Jim was shaking his head before I'd finished the question. "No. I know a real AK when I see one."

"Why do you think they used AKs?"

Jim shrugged. "Easy to get," he said. "I've seen some internet chat circles. Guys are selling AKs all the time. The world is awash in AKs."

"Did you come into contact with explosives when you were in the service?"

"I saw some IEDs that military dogs found, but that's it."

"Did you see it when the robber tossed the duct-taped bundle under your truck?"

"Yeah. Not up close, but I saw it."

"Did it look real?"

"No way to know. You wrap something in duct tape, it could be C-Four or pieces of wood."

"Thanks, Jim." I walked Jim out of the office, told them all that I'd call if I had more questions, and he and Matt and Larry all drove off in the shiny Buick.

I told Randy Bosworth that I had everything I needed, and I would be in touch.

"That's all you do?" Bosworth hooked his thumbs into his belt. "I guess I expected a response with more action. You think you're going to find the robbers after what you did here?" Bosworth said.

"I don't know. I'll see."

Bosworth breathed air like he was frustrated. "There's a gang of psycho robbers in hockey masks out there. They carry assault rifles and explosives, and they terrorized our men. Your response is to ask a few questions and drive off with a smear of pine pitch that could have come from anywhere. It seems pretty lame."

I looked at him. "Right. That's what I do. Collect crime scene material that could be evidence and see where it leads me. Like I said on the phone, if you're unhappy, you can dismiss me at any time."

Bosworth was doing a slow, dismissive head shake. "The cops were all about checking the video for hints of the robbers' identities and other profiling-type characteristics. They said they'll be scouring data on past armored truck robberies. They'll be checking gun dealers and gun show promoters. And they're going to have computer technicians analyze the video feeds. They had lots of solid stuff to investigate." He looked at my shirt pocket with the little baggie with the pine pitch as if to emphasize that my approach seemed worthless.

"Cops do all that you mention and more. They do a good job of it. They have more resources than I have. Why would I try to do the same things?"

Bosworth seemed to think about it. "Sure, you have a point. But pine pitch... I don't know."

"You can just pay me for today and I'll walk away."

Bosworth flared his nostrils and spoke with derision in his voice. "No, keep at it. No doubt you'll catch the robbers with that pine pitch. I'll report to Howard and see what he says. Meanwhile, you get to work another day."

FOURTEEN

I put Spot back in the Jeep and drove south toward Carson City. I switched my phone to speaker, slipped it into my shirt pocket, and called Street while I drove. When she answered, I asked how she was doing and where she was and if I could stop by and get a quick bug consult.

"I'm okay. I'm at the lab, but remember that I'm expensive," she said, joking.

I was glad that she sounded cheerful. She must not have heard yet about the outcome of her father's parole hearing.

"I haven't been paid yet," I said, "but I could compensate you with non-cash favors."

"You want me to play hooky from work," she said.

"You're the one who often says that any exercise that's good for the body is also good for the brain."

"Yes, but I was speaking of running. You know, getting your heart really pumping and making your breath really short and breaking a serious sweat."

"Exactly what I was talking about. Anyway, primary function is indicated by primary form. I'm just the lonely drone bee helpless against the draw of the queen's lovely attractions."

"You think I emit all-powerful pheromones?"

"Whatever it is, it's definitely all powerful. So consider my request, please. Light the candles. I'll be there in less than an hour." I hung up.

A long time later, we were sitting on the rug in Street's lab storage room, leaning back against the cot that she keeps for such emergencies. Spot snoozed on the far edge of the same rug. The rug was without Harlequin camo pattern, but he slept just the same.

"I can't believe that I'm sitting in candlelight in my dark

storage room drinking champagne in the middle of a work day." Street held up her glass in front of the candle and looked at the rising bubbles. The candlelight refracted through the glass and liquid and made waves of light and shadow dance across her torso, still moist with sweat.

"Shakespeare's sonnets deal with love, right?" I asked.

"Well," Street said, "he wrote one hundred fifty-four sonnets. Some are more specific than others, but taken together, yes, he deals exhaustively with the subject of love."

"How many of his sonnets do you think he composed in a candlelit storeroom?"

"I suppose some of them might have been penned in this kind of situation. But I don't think he ever had to be careful not to knock over shelves of jars with insects in them."

I glanced around at her samples.

"Speaking of which," Street said, "you had a bug question."

"Which your magic spell caused me to forget. Let me think. Oh, yeah. I found a bit of pine pitch in which was stuck a small bug. I wondered if you might identify it."

"Of course. I love those kinds of mysteries. Where did the bug come from, and does it speak of a murderer's travels?"

"Well, not a murderer that we know of, but maybe of an armored truck robber. Four of them, in fact."

"That's even more exciting. Where is this bug?"

I reached for my shirt and removed the baggie with the business card. I handed it to her.

"Unfortunately, I can't identify bugs in candlelight," she said.

"Does that mean you have to re-cover yourself in all of those pesky clothes?"

"Such are the downsides to work," she said.

"Ah."

FIFTEEN

"Fully clothed and yet still a dream," I said when Street had dressed.

"The power of champagne," she said.

Street turned on the light and slid the business card out of the baggie. She put on her mad-scientist magnifier glasses and looked at the sample.

"Well, it certainly is a bug. But it would be more correct to say that it is a bug part. This is the head and thorax of one of the bugs I deal with all the time. It's a Western Pine Beetle, Dendroctonus brevicomis, scourge of the forest and very effective killer of giant trees."

"How do they do it?"

"The female burrows through the bark. If there aren't too many attacking beetles, and if the tree is healthy and unstressed, the tree will kick out enough pine pitch to overwhelm her attack. But if the attacking army is too large, and the tree is weakened by drought, the beetle gets through the bark. Once under the bark, she tunnels out what we call galleries, and lays her eggs in those galleries. When the larvae hatch, they feed on the tree's phloem, which is the inner layer of bark where the tree transports its nutrients."

"Wow. So this is the little guy who takes down our forest."

"Sort of. There are several notable species that are trouble makers. This one primarily attacks Ponderosa Pines. Although sometimes it expands its diet to include all pines."

"Any idea where one would find both the beetle and the Ponderosa Pine near here?" I asked.

"All over. While our most numerous pine is the Jeffrey Pine, there are Ponderosa scattered all through the forest. And wherever you find Ponderosa, you'll find the Western Pine Beetle."

I reached for a magnifying glass that lay on Street's workshop counter.

"May I?"

"Of course." Street moved back, and I leaned in to look at the piece of insect. Even in the magnifier, it seemed very small.

"You said this is the head and thorax?"

"Right. We're missing the abdomen, the largest part."

"Yes, of course, the abdomen. Hate to lose those abdomens," I said. "It's kind of amazing that this little mini beetle has the audacity to attack such a beautiful giant," I said.

"That's what bugs do. They're audacious by nature. Beetles, especially. If you list all the species of plants and animals on Earth and then sort them into categories, you'd find that most of the species of all living things are beetles."

"I remember you saying something about that in the past. More than all the plants, large and small, and sea creatures and microscopic bacteria and germs and worms in the dirt and no-see-ums that get in your eyes?"

"Way more by species count. Entomologists estimate that the vast majority of all different types of creatures are beetles."

"And they are so numerous because?" I said.

"We don't know. Maybe their success is because they are, as a group, so bold. A tiny critter smaller than the eraser on a pencil goes after a giant tree. The critter is so numerous and effective that it can bring the tree down."

"Because of the bug, we can probably assume that the pitch is Ponderosa Pine pitch, right?"

Street nodded. "That is likely, yes."

"What about Jeffrey Pines you mentioned, Tahoe's most common tree? Does the Western Pine Beetle attack Jeffreys?"

"Not so much. The main parasite of Jeffrey Pines is the Jeffrey Pine Beetle. Similar but not the same."

"How would you imagine that this bug and pine pitch got stuck on the tire of an armored truck that only drove from Reno to Stateline and back?"

"I have no idea." She leaned over the bug once again and then made a little adjustment with her monster glasses. "There's something else stuck in the pitch."

I looked with the magnifying glass. Near the beetle was a

brownish, greenish fleck. "A different bug?" I said. "This one more green?"

"No," Street said. She made another adjustment of her lenses. "It's not a bug part. More like a piece of a plant. Not a leaf. A piece of stem. But it has a specific shape and some distinct markings." She took off the glasses. "I bet if you showed it to a botanist, you might get some more useful information."

"Any botanists hang out in your scientific circle?"

Street frowned. "I know one who teaches at UNR."

"I just came from Reno," I said, not relishing a return trip. "Is there no one at the LTCC?"

"I don't recall the Lake Tahoe Community College having a botanist on staff. But they do have two biology professors. They teach a wide range of biology. They probably know a great deal about botany. It might be worth it to show them this sample."

"Do you have their names?"

"Let me look." Street flipped through an address book. "Here is the one I met. Frankie Blue."

"Sounds like a showgirl's stage name," I said.

"Yeah, except not many showgirls have a masters from UCLA and a doctorate from UC San Diego."

"She must be a very smart Frankie Blue," I said. "A Dr. Frankie."

Street picked up her phone. "I'll see if she's in. Do you have time to run your sample by if she's in?"

"Absolutely."

SIXTEEN

Street got ahold of Dr. Blue and set up an appointment for me the next day at 4 p.m. We said goodbye, and I drove away with the thought that Shakespeare's sonnets would have been even better had he a storeroom companion like Street Casey.

Spot and I had an early dinner of barbecued turkey breast, squash, and green beans followed by vanilla ice cream drizzled with creme de cacao. I knew that chocolate in quantity could be toxic to dogs, but he was a big guy, and our dessert was more about sugary ice cream than the chocolate flavor. Of course, Spot liked the turkey better than the squash, and the squash better than the green beans. But the most focused look he gave me was after he'd finished licking dry the bowl of ice cream and chocolate liqueur.

"Sorry, Largeness, you've already achieved multiples of your full ration of added sugar in your diet."

He looked back at his bowl, then turned and looked at the freezer door with such intensity that it was as if he had x-ray vision and could see the Ben & Jerry's within.

After a walk, we went to bed.

I jerked awake cold and with a disturbing thought. It had been almost 72 hours or more since Jonas Montrop's kidnapping. It's axiomatic in law enforcement that if a kidnap victim isn't released or found within 24 hours, the likelihood of a positive resolution plunges to a very low level.

I fumbled my way to the kitchen nook and turned on the coffee maker.

Spot was sprawled across his bed, head on one corner, hips on the opposite corner, tail three feet onto the floor. Maybe there was still enough residual heat from the wood stove to keep him comfortable without having to curl up, nose under a paw. But it felt cold to me.

I looked at the clock. It was five in the morning. I had to leave in less than two hours to pick up Evan and Mia and take them on their cleaning rounds.

While the coffee brewed, I opened the wood stove, stirred the ash until I saw a bit of red glow, then set two Sugar Pine cones on the mostly spent coals. At 24 inches in length and 7 inches in diameter each, they covered the bottom of the fire box. I set two splits on top of the cones, shut the door and opened the air intake. I wasn't sure that the tiny nuggets of remaining coals were enough to kindle a fire, but it was worth a try.

When the coffee was done, I poured a cup and sat on the rocker next to Spot's bed. I sipped coffee with one hand, and reached down with the other to pet Spot. I thought about this kid I'd never met. The unfortunate odds were that he was probably dead, his body dropped into the lake or cast away into the woods not to be found for months or years, if ever.

I went back through what I'd seen and heard, from Jonas's disappearance to the signs of struggle at his house. I thought about David Montrop's bank withdrawal and the comments the house cleaner Evan Rosen had made about Montrop getting rid of stuff before he died from his cancer.

The Sugar Pine cones burst into flames and made an instant, lively fire with the splits crackling and popping sparks.

As I watched the flames, I remembered the framed photo Montrop had kept on his desk, a picture of an old boat. I also remembered that the unfinished note on Jonas's computer referred to a leak and something about transferring a title.

So I played the game, 'What if?'

What if Montrop had the photo of his boat on his desk because it was an important part of his past rather than his present? What if Montrop had wanted to get rid of his boat? I remembered that it was an older cabin cruiser, a Thompson cuddy, I thought, 17 or 18 feet, what looked like a mid-'60s model. It had what's called a cuddy cabin, a small indoor space large enough to bunk in and cook a simple meal.

So what if he decided to give it to his stepson Jonas?

A young man might think it was a great party boat if only he could figure out an affordable way to moor it or dock it. But as the maintenance bills grew, many kids would consider converting the boat into a bit of cash.

In Jonas's unfinished letter to someone named Flynn, he'd written that he didn't know about the leak and that he'd give him his money back. He referred to Flynn thinking he was trying to kill him. He also said that he hadn't transferred the title.

The meaning of the letter was unclear. But it certainly could be that Jonas was referring to a boat. The tone of the letter intimated that Flynn was unhappy. Jonas said he swore that he didn't know about the leak.

Maybe I was building something out of nothing.

I remembered the little scrap of paper I'd found on Jonas's bedroom floor. It was a bit of a brochure that talked about Mercury sterndrives. I looked on the computer, Googling Mercury sterndrives at Lake Tahoe.

Up popped lots of links that the Google brain thought were relevant. One was Brilliance Marine, a marina on the South Shore, not far from where Jonas lived. I clicked on the link. The website that came up presented itself as a small family marina, west of Stateline, tucked into a neighborhood of homes that occupied a narrow strip between Lake Tahoe Boulevard and the lake. On the first page of the website was the full picture of the boat I'd seen on the scrap of paper at Jonas's house. The caption said, 'All of our boats feature Mercury sterndrives.'

Just like on the scrap of paper.

Maybe I was getting somewhere. But first I had to go give Evan and Mia a ride to their house cleaning appointment.

SEVENTEEN

Spot and I went out to the Jeep, headed down the mountain toward the lake, and were at the Rosens' apartment at 7:30 a.m.

I helped load her cleaning equipment in the back of the Jeep. Evan had Mia sit in the front passenger seat, and Evan shared the back seat with Spot, who was behind Mia.

Spot had taken a special liking for Mia, sniffing her neck and ear, which made Mia giggle. Eventually, Spot leaned over Mia's shoulder and lay his chin down on her chest. Mia leaned her head sideways against his massive head. She reached her arms up and around his neck and seemed to hang on as if he were her lifejacket.

When we got to the Olmstead's, Mia wanted to stay in the seat, Spot's head next to hers. It was only after Evan told her that Spot would be back later that Mia relented.

Evan told me that they would be two and a half hours and that they would then go home for Mia's late morning nap. After that, they would eat lunch, and then head to their afternoon cleaning in Tahoe City, which was a long affair that would last until 8 p.m. Even though I hadn't asked Evan any questions about Montrop, I knew that she saw my presence as part of my investigation into Montrop's murder. Nevertheless, she seemed to appreciate my chauffeur service.

After we unloaded the cleaning gear, and Evan coaxed Mia out of the Jeep and away from Spot, I drove off and found a parking lot where I could make some phone calls.

EIGHTEEN

As Spot snoozed in the back seat, I got busy thinking. Most people think detecting is following people, and eavesdropping on conversations while drinking scotch straight up in dark bars, badgering potential witnesses, and punching out the occasional dirtball who resists reasonable inquiries into his connection to the victim.

But the truth is that the most important part of detecting is just thinking. Marshal the brain cell troops, and force them to perform calculations about every possible arrangement of the current information available.

I'd written down Jonas's driver's license number and birthdate and put it in my wallet. I pulled out the paper. Dialed Mallory at the SLTPD.

Mallory's phone rarely sends you to voicemail. But it does allow you to hold. I held for a long time.

"Mallory," he finally said.

"McKenna calling about the likely kidnap victim Jonas Montrop," I said.

"Yeah," Mallory said. "No word. Nothing. Nada. It looks like a crime, smells like a crime. But that's all we've got."

"I noted his driver's license number at the time. I assumed that the VW microbus in the drive was his. Now I'm wondering if his DMV sheet shows any record of a boat."

"We looked it up, but I forget. Hold on."

So I waited longer.

"I knew it," Mallory suddenly said in my ear. "I remembered that when I pulled the kid's DMV before, there was something else besides the VW. I was thinking it was a motorcycle, which of course is always the second vehicle for a kid in his twenties. But now I see that his second vehicle was a boat. An old Thompson. Nineteen sixty-four. What we used to call a Thompson Camper because of the bow cuddy. A classic in the same way a sixty-four Chevy Impala is a classic. No serious glitz, but a nice ride with good lines." Mallory paused. "You think maybe the kid disappeared on the boat? Like it's out on the lake someplace?"

"I don't know. But it seems worth checking out. I believe the boat used to be owned by his dad."

"The Incline Village murder victim," Mallory said.

"Yeah."

"Good luck," Mallory hung up.

"Next move, McKenna," I mumbled to no one, "is find the boat."

At that, Spot groaned as he got up, in the back seat, turned around, and lay down facing the other direction.

"You could show some approval of my detecting expertise," I said.

He sighed.

In time, my thinking fatigued my brain. I put my head back where the headrest met the side window, and I snoozed like Spot. My stiff limbs woke me up in time to be back at 10:30 a.m. and pick up Evan and Mia. We brought them home to their apartment so Mia could take her nap. Spot and I went and ate grocery store deli sandwiches, and, two hours later, I drove Evan and Mia to a dental office in Tahoe City.

"Makes your life easier, having the dental office close for business at one in the afternoon," I said.

"Yeah. I get to clean uninterrupted while Dr. Millis has to go skiing or boating. But I'm not complaining. The dentist lets Mia sit in one of those pneumatic chairs and watch TV."

"Mansfield Cleaning must have a growing rep," I said.

"Yeah. Too bad the work sucks. Anyway, I talked to Mattie. She'll be back from her doctor's appointment and can give us a ride home when we're done here. And Sergeant Lanzen called yesterday to say they'd gotten my car towed to the mechanic, and he thinks he'll have it fixed tomorrow. So I'm back in business. Thanks for your help. I appreciate it."

"You're welcome."

After I left them at the dental office, I headed to the South

Shore, an hour plus away.

In the Bijou neighborhood in South Lake Tahoe, I found the small road that led back to Brilliance Marine. It consisted of a small building, a dock with a gas pump, and a little lagoon made by a breakwater of rocks. Moored in the lagoon were several boats of varying sizes.

Three of the boats were similar runabouts, probably rentals. Two of them had Mercury sterndrives as featured on their website and, maybe, their brochure, a scrap of which I'd found on Jonas Montrop's bedroom floor.

I walked into the building. It was a rustic shell with exposed and unpainted two-by-four studs and an open ceiling showing two-by-six rafters. All of the wood had weathered to a dark brown. With no insulation, the building was chilly in the early summer afternoon.

The place smelled of motor oil with a hint of gasoline. It was a pleasant combination that brought back memories of when one of my cop uncles took me from Boston up to his cabin on a lake in New Hampshire, there to expose me to the manly art of fishing and all of its miscast-fishing-hook-through-my-earlobe glories.

There was a counter with an old cash register and a glass display case filled with fishing lures. An angled rack held candy bars and small bags of chips. There was a stack of maps of the lake. Next to the wall opposite the counter stood a glass-topped, 1950s cooler that featured a large Coca Cola logo. It was stocked with soda drinks and plastic-wrapped sandwiches.

At the far end of the small building was a rack onto which was mounted an antique Evinrude outboard motor. A man sat perched on a high stool next to it, wrench in hand.

"Help you?" he said.

"Yes, please." I walked over. "I'm looking for an old boat I've seen in a photograph. I believe it's a nineteen-sixty-four cuddy cabin Thompson cruiser. A man in Incline may have given it to his son, who lives here on the South Shore. He might moor it nearby."

"Well, we've got no Thompson here. But any Thompson of that age is going to need regular repairs. The average Joe will be up to scrubbing the brightwork, maybe sanding and varnishing the trim. But real repair needs are going to drive him to the shop. That's how you'll track this old tub down. Check the marinas that offer mechanical repair."

I refrained from pointing out that I was doing precisely that. "Recommendations?" I said.

He shrugged. "There are quite a few marinas around the lake. Most are like me. They do some repairs but avoid the major stuff. I'd visit 'em one-by-one."

"Do you rent boats?" I asked.

"Sure. If you want a perky little number to buzz the lake, we've got a sixteen foot Bayliner with a Mercury outboard. It's only sixty horsepower, but let me tell you, that little guy will blow your cap off. If you want something jazzier, you can upgrade to one of our twenty-four-foot Starcrafts, which, of course, have the bow cuddies and Mercury sterndrives."

The man paused and looked at me. "This is so you can look for the Thompson. No fishing gear needed."

"Correct. I'll just cruise the shore and have a look. I'm sure your Bayliner will do just fine. Assuming I can bring my dog."

He regarded me for a moment. "Sure. Lots of people bring dogs. Dogs like boat rides even better than car rides. We have a four-hour package or the all-day package. Gas not included."

"The four-hour plan will work for me."

So he told me the extravagant price, which included what was probably extravagant insurance, and I pulled out the credit card that I save for just such extravagant moments.

A half hour later, I was instructed in Bayliner runabout basics as well as its nuances. I purchased two prepackaged ham sandwiches, two bags of chips, and a beer. Soon, Spot and I both had life jackets on, were unmoored, and set adrift with engine running.

"Just remember," the man called out to me from the dock. "The water is killer cold in June. You wouldn't want to take an unintended dip."

"Got it," I said. I took him to mean that I shouldn't try any maneuver that might flip his expensive boat. I shifted into Forward and let it idle us ahead at a stately one mile an hour.

NINETEEN

The man at the marina had raised up the Bayliner's center windshield panel, so Spot had already picked out his place, at the bow, in the open passage between the two captains chairs, front paws up on the forward seat, head projecting out over the bow in his best imitation of a 17th century galleon figurehead.

As we cleared the marina's breakwater, I edged the throttle up a bit, but kept the boat slow enough that we didn't get an appreciable bow rise. I had no clue where Jonas might have kept his boat. From the unfinished note to Flynn that was on his computer, his reference to a leak and giving the money back suggested that he'd sold the boat to Flynn. Although he also said that he hadn't transferred the title, it could be that Flynn had already taken the boat out of Lake Tahoe.

But I was hoping that the boat might still be wherever Jonas had been keeping it. Because it was registered with the California DMV, I assumed that meant the boat was moored on the California side. The line between California and Nevada went through the middle of Lake Tahoe. Brilliance Marina was near the state line, so I turned west toward California.

As I motored along the shore, it was hard to distinguish make and model of all the boats. But it was easy to see that nearly all were modern in design, constructed of fiberglass. It was also easy to see that most were bowriders and deck boats and ski boats and runabouts. Very few were small cabin cruisers. It seemed obvious that a '64 Thompson would stand out.

My path took me past El Dorado Beach where dozens of tourists and locals alike were enjoying the new facilities built in the last few years. Next came the Al Tahoe neighborhood and Regan Beach with a sudden density of boats at mooring buoys, tied up at docks, and hidden inside of boat houses.

I couldn't imagine Jonas having the kind of money to rent a boathouse. So I didn't pay attention to those structures. I focused on the buoys and docks. There were lots of boats, but it was easy to see that no old Thompson was among them.

After the Al Tahoe neighborhood, I came to the Truckee River marsh and meadow. This was a protected area with no docks or buoys. Next came the Tahoe Keys. The first canal led to the Tahoe Keys Marina. It contained lots of moorings in a protected lagoon. I knew that their moorings were relatively expensive, so I didn't expect Jonas to have his boat there. Nevertheless, I turned the wheel, slowed to idle, and cruised in at no-wake speed.

It took only fifteen minutes to circle the lagoon and cruise close enough to the docks to see that there was no Thompson cuddy cruiser in the place. Back out on the lake, I went west again. The next passage was the main canal into the Tahoe Keys. There were perhaps a dozen miles of inland canals. With 1500 houses and condos, there could be a thousand boats or even two thousand boats.

I knew several Tahoe locals who boarded their boats at vacation homes owned by people from out of town. The usual relationship was to act as caretaker and routinely check on the property in exchange for a berth at the dock.

So I began a counterclockwise pattern through the main lagoon and then idled my way into the first canal on the right. I'd been to houses in the Keys many times, but I never realized how complex the maze of canals was. I went by countless houses, through intersections with other canals, and when I came to dead ends, I found myself turning around only to go by boats and houses that looked unfamiliar but which must have been on my route heading in. I decided to concentrate on the old maze trick. You don't try to figure out where you've been, you just keep your hand on the right wall and never lift it up. When you come to an intersection, your hand dictates that you turn right. When your passage terminates, your hand requires you to stay attached to the wall and thus come back out the passage but tracking the opposite side from when you came in. If I remembered correctly from the maze puzzles of my youth, the right hand rule would make it so that you explored every part of a maze except – and it was a big "except" – if there was an island to your left. But as I thought about the Keys, I didn't think that any part of it was technically an island.

So I cruised the Keys, in and out and around and back and forth, through every little watery nook.

Two and a half hours later, I came back to the main canal, which led to the main lake. I'd seen only a few older cabin cruisers, none of which was a mid-'60s Thompson. Spot had long since curled up on the back seat and gone to sleep, lifting his head to look out with sleepy eyes only twice. Once when a boat honked and once when teenagers in a yard were playing volleyball and shrieking at each point scored.

When I came back out to the big body of water, I again turned west.

Demoralized, I thought it time for a lunch pick-me-up. So I gently beached the boat at the close end of Pope Beach. Spot and I jumped out, which made the boat more buoyant, and I was able to pull the boat up a bit onto the sand.

We had the east end of the beach to ourselves, no small thing when you're in one of the most beautiful places on the planet. The sun was hot, the air cool, the water was clear as glass. Mt. Tallac and the West Shore mountains loomed close, and a Disney package of squirrels, songbirds, and waterfowl lingered for our viewing pleasure. But Spot ignored all as I opened my pack and pulled out our sandwiches.

He knew he had to maintain a bit of distance until I gave the okay, but his nostrils were flexing as he scented the air nearby. He stared at my pack, and as my hand reached inside, it seemed that his eyes got wider.

I unwrapped his sandwich and broke it into four parcels so that there was less chance of sandwich components falling onto the beach. I set the first on a rock so it wouldn't get sandy.

When I gave him the okay, I heard the clink of fang as he devoured it. By the tone, I couldn't tell if it was a tooth-on-tooth clink or the sound of tooth enamel scraping rock. So I moved to a log for each of the remaining pieces. When he was done, he licked his chops and then looked at my bag of chips.

"Sorry, Largeness. These ain't for them that don't chew."

Spot looked disappointed. He turned and walked over to the lapping waves to satisfy his thirst. I ate my lunch, drank my beer, and we continued on our boat search.

Back in the Bayliner, we continued west past the houses on Jameson Beach Road. After that, it would be a long way to the first houses on the road out to Emerald Bay, and my instinct told me that because they were mostly vacation homes for wealthy people, I'd be unlikely to find the old boat I was looking for.

So I gave up, and we headed back to the marina. I punched the throttle on the way back. The outboard Merc roared, the boat jumped up onto plane, and we were across the southern end of the lake in eight minutes.

As I approached Brilliance Marina and pulled back on the throttle, I looked at the short distance to Edgewood Golf Course, which was on the Nevada side of the stateline.

There were a few houses that came before the state line, California houses in the private Tahoe Meadows area, some of which had boats. I thought I could see them all. But I realized it would be foolish to have done all this searching and then stop before I'd finished. So I cruised past the marina and continued my search.

As with all of the other houses I'd seen, there were docks and buoys and boat houses. Some had no boats, the owners waiting, no doubt, for the warm weather of July. A few had runabouts and sailboats that were much newer than what I'd been looking for. As I got near Edgewood and the last of the houses on the California side, there was a lone cruiser at a dock. It was a big Chris Craft, maybe 36 feet.

So I turned the wheel away from the dock and made a slow curve out toward the open water. When I'd come most of the way around, I glanced back at the cruiser, a beautiful boat that would draw attention wherever it went.

But something else caught my eye. From my perspective farther out in the lake, I could see past the big Chris Craft. There was another, smaller boat nearby, the view of it partially blocked by the bigger boat. From my earlier position, it would have been completely blocked.

So I brought the Bayliner around yet again and idled my way

closer.

As I got closer, it appeared that the other boat was moored to a buoy, but the buoy seemed too close to the shore on the far side of the dock and the big boat. The boat was partially submerged, stern down, and sitting at an angle in front of a vacant portion of beach. It was a sight that many seasoned boaters would recognize. The buoy that held the moored boat was insufficiently anchored. Waves and wind had dragged the boat and buoy toward the shore.

The boat had run aground on the bottom, become damaged enough to spring a leak, and then took on water until it settled into the sand.

The neighbors would have reported it to the Coast Guard or the police, and everyone who saw it would think how lucky they were that it hadn't happened to them.

Meanwhile, the boat owner, whether local or from the Bay Area or from overseas, would be sweating it until the boat could be pumped out and the damage assessed.

When I got closer still, I became much more interested.

It was an old Thompson cuddy, twenty feet long or less, and it looked just like the photo I'd seen on David Montrop's desk.

I dropped the shifter into neutral as I coasted closer, gave it a tiny bit of reverse to slow our approach further, then cut the power. I steered so that the Bayliner was coming alongside the Thompson, approaching from the rear of the partially sunken boat. I leaned over the side and grabbed the gunnel of the Thompson, and pulled us to a stop. There was a coiled line in the Bayliner's side stowage. I used it to lash the boats together, cleat to cleat.

Spot was standing tall, nose in the air, sniffing toward the Thompson.

"Stay here," I said. I stepped on the gunnel of our boat, reached my leg up and over into the Thompson's cockpit, the rear part of which had taken on water. I walked uphill to the companionway that led to the small cabin below.

The companionway door was shut. I grabbed the latch and turned. The door swung open under the force of gravity because of the steep upward angle of the partially-sunken boat.

I peered down into the cuddy cabin, but couldn't see because it was dark inside. The cabin windows must have had the blinds pulled.

Holding onto the edge of the companionway opening, I reached my foot out and down, feeling for the first step, trying to adjust for the boat resting in an uphill position. I found the step, put weight on that foot, then lifted my other foot out and down, stepping into cold water. When I'd descended to the fourth step, I ducked my head, lowered it through the companionway opening and into the dark cabin.

As I waited for my eyes to adjust to the darkness, I became aware of repugnant odors, urine and acrid sweat and the fetid smells of a tropical swamp.

Gradually, I saw light coming in from around the edges of a drape across a window. With another step, I was able to reach the window. I swept the drape to the side. A harsh shaft of sunlight cut through dusty air. What I saw made me inhale.

Hanging by his wrists from ropes that stretched up to the handles of some upper stowage lockers, was a small young man, naked but for his underpants. His head slumped down with unconsciousness or maybe death. Although his eyes were closed, he looked like the picture on Jonas Montrop's driver's license. His knees were slightly bent, lower legs mostly under the water. I stepped uphill toward him, and leaned toward his bent head. There was duct tape over his mouth. I pulled it off.

A whisper of rancid breath washed across my face.

He was alive.

TWENTY

I wrapped one arm around his chest and lifted him up to take the tension out of the lines that were knotted about his wrists. He was very light, like a teenaged boy, and his skin was cold and clammy. While I held him up with one arm, I fumbled with my other hand, grabbing at the knots, catching the cords with my fingernails. I got one untied and then the other before I remembered that I had a pocketknife in my pocket. With the knots untied, his arms flopped down in such a loose manner that it was as if there was no muscle tension at all.

When Jonas's arms were free, I hitched him close to me, still holding him with one arm so that I could reach and hold the edges of the companionway and carry him up the stairs.

When I was back up in the cockpit, I worried that the way I was carrying him was squeezing his chest and making it hard for him to breathe. I shifted his body a bit so that I was holding his weight more by his waist and less by his chest.

I swung one leg over the Thompson's gunnel and made the big step down to the runabout.

Spot immediately sniffed Jonas all over, but he gave me space as I came aboard.

I lay Jonas down on the rear seat. He was unresponsive. But still breathing.

I took off my life jacket and then my shirt and lay the shirt over his body.

Then I pulled out my phone and dialed 911.

"Nine, one, one Emergency," the dispatcher said. "Please state your name and address."

"Owen McKenna calling from a boat near Brilliance Marina in the Bijou area of South Lake Tahoe. I have found kidnapping victim Jonas Montrop. He's unconscious and hypothermic and possibly near death. I'm bringing him into the marina. Please send an ambulance immediately. And inform Commander Mallory." I probably didn't need to state the obvious, but I wanted to make it clear to the dispatcher. "The boat where I found the victim is a crime scene. Mallory will want a team to collect evidence." I hung up and started the runabout. I untied the line that held the boats together, then shifted into Forward and pushed the throttle forward just a touch.

I didn't want a breeze to cool Jonas further. I also knew that it would be a long ten or fifteen minutes before an ambulance arrived at the marina. So I went slowly, hoping that without a breeze caused by our motion, the sun would warm Jonas.

When I pulled up to the marina dock, the man in charge came out. He was smiling until he saw Jonas.

"I called nine-one-one," I said. "An ambulance is on its way. This kid is hypothermic. I want to put him down on the warm dock boards. Maybe you can find a blanket."

The man looked shocked, but he nodded and hurried off.

I lashed the runabout to a dock cleat, lifted Jonas up and laid him on the dock. The man rushed up with several blankets. I laid two of them down, shifted Jonas onto them, and then covered him with two more blankets.

"Does this boy have something to do with the boat you were looking for?" the marina man asked.

"Yeah. He was tied up inside it," I said.

The man looked horrified.

Sirens sounded in the distance. A police patrol unit showed up first. The cop ran out to the dock. We had just exchanged a few words when a giant fire truck arrived followed by the ambulance. There was no room for the fire truck to park, so it just stopped in the middle of the street. Multiple men and one woman trotted out of their vehicles, a show of the silly policy of excess response to a nine-one-one call with no apparent purpose unless spending taxpayer money was the goal.

Paramedics strapped Jonas onto a gurney and wrapped him in more blankets. The medics loaded the gurney into the ambulance and drove away as Mallory showed up.

"Commander," I said.

"Can you show me where you found him?"

I nodded. Mallory turned to the other cop. "Did you grab the evidence kit?"

He pointed to a large toolbox he'd set on the dock.

Mallory turned to me. "Let's go."

They climbed into the runabout, Mallory leaning his hand on Spot's back, and I drove them at speed over to the Thompson cuddy.

I repeated my landing technique and lashed the two boats together.

"There's water to the rear of the cockpit and in the rear of the cabin," I said. "Jonas was tied up in the cabin, facing toward the stern, hanging from a line on each wrist. Both lines are still hanging where I untied them."

"Got it," Mallory said.

He was the first over the gunnel and up into the Thompson. He strapped on his headlamp, turned it on, and looked down into the cabin. The other cop followed, carrying the evidence kit.

Five minutes later, I saw another boat emerge from the shore to the west. It looked like it also came out from Brilliance Marina. The boat raced up to planing speed, then immediately began slowing as it approached. I waved. The boat had two more cops, both in uniform.

I helped them tie their boat to the Thompson. The cops climbed up into the little cabin cruiser and quickly went to work.

Of the four officers, two were still down below in the tiny cuddy cabin. The third man was dusting the cockpit. Mallory was periodically on his radio, keeping track of the rest of the department's activities across South Lake Tahoe. I'd never seen Mallory taking this much interest in the hands-on work of a case, work that was usually handled by a sergeant.

I called out to Mallory. "I have to leave for an appointment. You can all ride back on your other boat, okay?"

"Okay," Mallory called back.

When I was back at the marina, the man looked at the clock. "You went over the four-hour time limit, so I should be charging you the extra time. But it seems like you kind of got stuck with a law enforcement problem, so I feel bad about that."

"You can bill the city for the extra time," I said. "Add it onto the bill for the boat they rented."

"You think so? Really?"

"Really," I said.

I signed my paperwork, and left to go meet a professor at the community college.

TWENTY-ONE

I was at the college off Al Tahoe Boulevard a bit before the appointed time. Spot was so asleep in the back of the Jeep that I don't think he even noticed me leaving.

Because it was early June, just before spring quarter was finished, there was a kind of lightness of step among the collective body of students walking about campus under gorgeous sunny skies.

As I walked through the parking lot, I called Sergeant Lanzen and told her that I'd found Jonas Montrop. She asked for details, and I filled her in.

"Anything on your end?" I said.

"Not much. I sent two men back out to re-canvas Montrop's neighborhood in Incline Village. They found a neighbor who has a filtered view of the opening to Montrop's drive. She said that she saw a car parked in the opening of Montrop's drive the morning of his murder. It was under tree shade, so she wasn't positive of the color, but she thought it was either black or midnight blue or midnight green."

"She get the make?" I said.

"Not specifically, but she said the logo was interlocking rings that reminded her of the Olympics logo. So that pretty much has to be an Audi."

"I would think so."

"Oh, sorry, Owen, gotta go." She hung up.

I couldn't remember which building held the science offices, so I went in the main entrance, asked at the information counter, and was directed to the correct wing.

Dr. Frankie Blue had a small, windowless office filled with bookshelves, which were full. There were two rolling metal carts that held equipment, the purpose of which I couldn't even guess. On the floor, leaning against the wall, was a whiteboard that had scraggy printing in red and blue dry marker. The blue marks were comprised of letters and symbols arranged like three complicated mathematical equations. The red was for the arrows that looped around and connected different parts of the equations.

Blue was sitting on the very edge of her desk chair, hunched over her desk, pen in hand, studying and marking a group of papers that were stapled together.

I paused for a moment to stare at the equations.

"Oh," she said, sensing my presence and looking up. "Can I help you?" she said as she took off her red reading glasses and let them fall to her neck, hanging from a cord.

"If I had to learn and understand the stuff on your whiteboard, I would be in deep trouble."

She glanced at the board, and said, "It looks inscrutable, yes. But it's really just the ATP reaction, Adenosine Tri-Phosphate. Standard metabolic stuff."

"Oh, of course. Standard stuff. I must have had a little brain cramp there."

She smiled.

"Dr. Blue, I'm Owen McKenna. My girlfriend Street Casey called you yesterday."

"Yes, of course." She rotated in her chair, reached up and shook my hand. "You're the detective. I don't know Dr. Casey well, but I know of her work. She's done some groundbreaking stuff with forest ecology. A real brain, that one."

"She says the same about you," I said. "I've brought a bit of plant material that may connect to a case I'm working on. Street said you would be the person to look at it. See if it's anything you recognize."

"Happy to." The woman pushed back her chair and stood up. "Let's go down to one of the labs where I can get a better look at it."

I followed her out of the office, down a hall, through a fire door and into a different, but connected, building. She walked into a room that had four rows of high, narrow tables that students would stand at as they did their work, experiments or whatever. Blue went over to the far wall, which had a workbench running its length. On it were multiple pieces of technical equipment which, like the stuff in her office, I had no idea about.

Blue turned to me. "Do you have the item?"

I pulled the baggie with the Reno Armored business card out of my pocket and held it out. "On the card is a glob of pine pitch. Stuck in the pitch is the head and thorax of a Western Pine Beetle, as Street explained to me. She also saw another bit of material that she thought was plant matter. That is what I'm hoping you can identify."

Dr. Blue slipped her glasses back on, carefully pulled the business card out of the baggie, and held it up to the light. She made a little nod, then walked over to one of the machines on the bench. She flipped on a switch, and a light came on at the bottom of the machine. She pulled out a sliding tray, set the card on it, then slid it back in. There were two eyepieces near the top. It was a microscope, although of a different design than the one in Street's lab. Blue looked in the scope, turned a focus knob, then another, then looked for ten seconds without moving. Then she pulled a three-ring binder off a bookshelf, flipped through the pages, and paused on one, studying it. Then she went back to the microscope.

She finally spoke. "Rorippa subumbellata," she said, still looking into the eyepieces.

"Is that the name of the plant material?"

"Yes." She pulled away from the microscope and looked at me. "I'm not a botanist, but this one is pretty obvious. We've studied it here at the college. You're no doubt familiar with the Mustard family."

"Mustard, the condiment, yes. Mustard, the plant, no."

She nodded. "There are many different kinds of mustard plants, all in the genus Brassica. They grow all over the world. We grind their seeds and mix the material with a carrier like water or vinegar to make the yellow condiment. The oil from the pressed plants has many interesting properties and is even being used as a bio-fuel. And, of course, many people eat mustard greens."

I gestured toward the business card in the microscope. "This pine pitch came off a tire on the armored truck that was robbed. Are there any places along the highway between the South Shore and Reno where this is common?" I asked.

"Not on the highway, anyway. In fact this is very uncommon."

"But you just said it grows all over the world."

"Various mustard plants do, yes. But this is a very unusual variety. In fact, it's on the verge of extinction. It only grows in one place in the entire world."

"Where's that?"

"The common name for this is the Tahoe Yellow Cress. The only place on Earth with Tahoe Yellow Cress habitat consists of a few places along the shore of Lake Tahoe." Dr. Blue paused as if to let me consider the impact of her statement.

She continued, "We believe that this particular mustard plant used to grow in other places. But changes in environment have killed it off everywhere else. Tahoe is the last place where you can find it. It's a low-lying green plant with little yellow flowers. Very pretty in a non-dramatic way. It grows in the beach sand near the water, generally between the low and high water lines. And it's very particular. When we have a drought for a few years, and the water level stays lower, the plants highest up on the shore will often die. The lower plants do better and expand. But when the water levels rise after a heavy winter, those lower plants are inundated and die off. In several places around the lake, we've put up fences around the plant to keep people from trampling it."

"Why has it survived in Tahoe?"

"We don't know. Some combination of high altitude and pure water and granitic sand, and a climate with just the right mix of weather makes it do well here. Beyond that, it's a mystery. But because bio-diversity is precious, it's very important that we save the Tahoe Yellow Cress. Scientists have even grown the plants in a lab and then planted them around the lake, trying to expand the population in hopes that it might survive. Because of its uniqueness, we have our students study it in one of the classes we teach, Plants of the Tahoe Basin."

"Is there any kind of a map that shows which shores one can find it on?"

"Yes. There's even a website devoted to it. I'll write it down for you." Dr. Blue wrote on a pad, tore off the paper, and handed it to me.

http://tahoeyellowcress.org/

"Here, I'll show you." She walked over to a computer and brought up the website. "Here's the map. It has color coding for beach areas with known populations. I'll print it out." She clicked and a nearby printer whirred. She handed me the page.

I pointed to the business card. "The partial bug I mentioned that is stuck in the pine pitch next to the Tahoe Yellow Cress?"

"Yes?"

"Street said it's a Western Pine Beetle. They're the beetles that attack Ponderosa Pines."

"Right," Blue said.

"Can you think of any areas where they grow in close proximity to the Tahoe Yellow Cress?"

"Thus suggesting where this pine pitch might have come from?"

"Right."

Blue frowned. "As you might know, the most common pines near the lake are Jeffrey and Lodgepole with relatively few Ponderosa Pine. Jeffrey Pine occasionally hybridizes with Ponderosa. The hybrids are uncommon, but some of what look like Ponderosa are really half-breeds. Maybe those attract the Western Pine Beetle. I don't know. Dr. Casey would. There isn't much pure Ponderosa near the Tahoe beaches where Tahoe Yellow Cress grows. Nothing comes to mind." She studied the map for a bit.

"Wait," she said. She pointed at the map near the beaches out by Camp Richardson. "Most of the basin was clear-cut back during the heyday of the Comstock Lode, and they used the lumber to shore up the mining tunnels under Virginia City."

"Right," I said.

"But back at the turn of the twentieth century, Lucky Baldwin and D.L. Bliss left some old growth Ponderosa untouched on their land here on the South Shore and on the West Shore. You can tell because they're very big."

"That's right," I said. "Those monster trees over at Valhalla near Camp Rich."

Dr. Blue nodded, then pointed to the map. "And not too far

away is where Taylor Creek flows from Fallen Leaf Lake into Lake Tahoe. There is some Tahoe Yellow Cress nearby."

"Just down from the giant Ponderosa Pines of Valhalla," I said.

Blue looked up at me. "Pine pitch often falls out of trees. It could be that somebody stepped on some pitch that had a bark beetle in it, then walked down to where the Tahoe Yellow Cress grows, and got some of the mustard flower stuck in the pitch on their shoe. Of course, that scenario doesn't get the pitch onto a truck tire."

"That's okay," I said. "Thanks, doctor, very much."

I shook her hand and left.

TWENTY-TWO

I drove north on 89 and headed out past the turnoff to Pope Beach Road. I continued on past Camp Rich, then parked on the shoulder of the road. Late afternoon in June meant that campers had their fires and barbecues going. There were lots of people biking and walking the various paths. I didn't want Spot to startle anyone, so I took his collar, and we walked out the path that led to Valhalla, the public area that comprised the beautiful Heller estate with its grand hall and lawns and beaches, and the Boathouse Theater right on the water. Young couples wandered the beach by the lake. Over at the Beacon Restaurant, laughing groups of people drank beer out on the deck. Out on the lake, a ski boat and water skier took advantage of the calming water that evening brings.

As Dr. Blue had pointed out, most of Tahoe is predominantly treed with Jeffrey Pines. But scattered throughout the Valhalla area near the beach were multiple old growth Ponderosa Pines, giant trees six and even seven feet in diameter and stretching 20 stories tall. Spot and I wandered the grounds, me looking for Tahoe Yellow Cress, Spot enjoying the rock star attention that Harlequin Great Danes draw wherever they go. If he had any regrets in life, it could only be that he wasn't able to sign autographs.

I looked up at the trees, wondering how often they dropped globs of pitch. Street had explained how bark beetles that tried to burrow into healthy pines often got stuck in the pitch that oozed out. But trying to find pitch with stuck beetles did not seem like a reasonable task. Better to just assume that someone stepped in some and then stepped on the rare plant, mashing the two together to be stuck on the person's shoe until they scraped it off on the armored truck tire.

Dr. Blue had said that Tahoe Yellow Cress lives in the beach sand, so I took Spot to the water. I wasn't looking for anything specific, but it seemed appropriate to explore the possible convergence of pitch and pine beetles and mustard plants and armored truck robbers.

We ambled west down the beach, moving away from the giant Ponderosas toward Taylor Creek, where Blue had said that the rare plant grew. We went past the Pope estate and the Baldwin mansion, past the old foundation from Lucky Baldwin's Tallac House Hotel where San Francisco's upper crust congregated during the turn of the 20th century. From there, the narrow beach turned around a point and expanded into the large sweep of Kiva Beach.

The waves were gentle, making lapping sounds on the sand. The nearby trees had substantially shifted toward Jeffrey Pines, and the sound of the breeze through their long needles was mesmerizing. Gulls called out. Spot turned to look as two giggling teenaged girls went by on stand-up paddle boards, racing each other, going the same direction we were but faster. A bald eagle flew by just 20 feet above my head, a large trout in its claws. The bird held the fish so that its head pointed forward, the better to minimize wind resistance and to maximize the photo op for anyone with a ready camera.

Nowhere did I see anything that looked like Tahoe Yellow Cress. But I wasn't yet to Taylor Creek.

Kiva Beach is one of the few where dogs are allowed, but they have to be leashed or under leash-equivalent verbal control.

Spot had never in his life provided any indication that I could control him with nothing more than verbal commands. But my secret weapon was doggie biscuits and my determination to never leave home without them. So I let go of his collar, and he ran with great excitement to the water's edge. Spot has never been big on voluntary swimming, but he loves to race up and down the beach in six inches of water, making great splashing leaps. Then he arcs around and comes back the other way to see how closely he can fly past me. If I can succeed in getting him to stop, he always shakes the water off directly in front of me so that I get the maximum soaking.

When we came to Taylor Creek, the outflow from Fallen Leaf

Lake, the icy runoff of spring was flowing at a robust pace. Because the recent weather had been cold with no rain, the snowpack at high elevations was melting slowly, so it wasn't flooding. I guessed the creek's depth at 4 feet and its width at 25 feet. Such a flow should be considered dangerous. Like a riptide in the ocean, it could carry an unaccomplished swimmer well out into the lake.

The only alternative to fording the creek was to go back to the Jeep, drive down the highway over the Taylor Creek Bridge, and take the Baldwin Beach turnoff. But Baldwin Beach didn't allow dogs. I would have to park on the highway and then hike in through the area outside of the beach jurisdiction, a long hike through wet meadows. The day would be over before I ever saw any Tahoe Yellow Cress.

I turned to Spot. "Care for a cold swim?"

He looked at me with concern.

"Okay, truth be told, a shocking, icy, frigid, freezing swim?"

Spot made a single slow wag.

"I would hold your collar so that if you lost your footing, I could possibly keep you on course. Or you might simply pull me out into the deep lake where we would flounder as we succumbed to hypothermia while waiting for young women on their paddle boards to rescue us."

Another, single, slow wag. Spot knew I was up to something suspicious. He looked at the clear, voluminous, flowing water. Then looked back at me.

A person can walk until wet pants dry and only be mildly uncomfortable. But wet shoes and socks chafe and take forever to dry. I took off my shoes, stuffed my socks inside them, tied the shoes together with their laces, and hung the loop of laces around my neck. I transferred my phone, keys, wallet, dog treats, and other pocket stuff to the two pockets in my flannel shirt and buttoned the flaps.

"Okay, Spot, brace yourself."

I untucked my shirt, lifted up the shirt tails, pulled the rear shirt tail up and over my shoulder, put the shirt tail ends in my mouth, and bit down on them to hold my shirt out of the water.

I took hold of Spot's collar, and we trotted toward the water at a good pace. I didn't want Spot to be tentative. I pulled him into the water. Spot jerked back a bit from the ice shock, but when he realized I wasn't giving him a choice, he charged forward.

As the water rose to my waist, Spot began swimming and I leaned into the current so as not to be pushed over. Spot's legs scraped my legs here and there, but my jeans saved me from the real damage that could have come from the claws on his churning paws.

The cold was spectacular, and I'm pretty sure I made a single, gasping inhalation and then never exhaled until the creek bottom started once again rising. In a few moments, we were to the other side. I let go of Spot's collar, and he once again charged up and down the beach. This time it wasn't so much a frolic of joy as a panicked, clenched-jaw celebration that we'd run the frozen, arctic gauntlet and survived.

I sat down on a log that had floated in on a previous flood and waited several minutes for my pants to drain. When it seemed that anyone close enough to see and get distressed about public nudity had wandered away, I took off my jeans and underpants, wrung them out, and pulled them and my shoes back on.

"C'mon Spot. Are you in the mood to sniff some mustard? I think I see some Tahoe Yellow Cress from here."

I wandered off toward some green plants that hugged the sand. They had little yellow flowers, just forming in the spring sunshine. They looked like the pictures Dr. Blue showed me on the website. In real life, they looked very fragile.

I've never felt much empathy for plants other than beautiful trees being cut down in their prime of life. But I felt a kind of connection to these delicate little green and yellow bits of life. As I glanced around the giant lake, visualizing the relatively tiny scope of where this nearly extinct plant now lived, it was an emotional experience. I stepped away from the plant, not wanting to disturb it, wishing it the best.

Turning back toward Valhalla, I wondered if pine pitch could have been tracked that far down the beach without being caked with sand. The pine pitch sample I'd gotten off the truck tire was free of sand. Maybe there was another source of pine pitch and Western Pine Beetles that was closer to the Tahoe Yellow

Cress plants. I looked around for any sign of Ponderosa Pine. There were many Jeffrey Pines, which would produce similar pine pitch. But Street had said that only Ponderosa would have the Western Pine Beetle.

In the large meadow and wetlands area that stretched back toward the unseen highway a half mile away, there were several sparse groupings of trees. They were tree islands in the meadow, growing on ground that was just high enough above the meadow and regular flood zone to support trees. I couldn't tell from a distance if any of them were Ponderosa Pines, which looked like less lush versions of Jeffrey Pines. But they were the closest trees to my first batch of Tahoe Yellow Cress. There was nothing to lose in checking them out.

I walked through tall grasses, around shrubs. With no advance warning, my feet sunk into mushy marsh, and both of my shoes filled with water. So much for trying to keep one's shoes dry.

As we got close to the trees, I could see that there were a few Aspen, and a few fir, and some bush-like trees I didn't recognize. No Ponderosa. I went through the tree island and looked out the other side. In the distance across the meadow, there was another tree island and then, beyond it, another.

In ten minutes of slogging through wet grass, I got to the next group of trees. It seemed the same as the first, although I had to walk around in the gathering twilight to look at each of the bigger trees to identify their species.

"Shall we keep exploring, Largeness? Or shall we head back to the Jeep?"

Spot looked at me, then turned and looked toward the next island of trees.

"Okay, we'll keep exploring."

I headed on once again. My shoes squished with each footfall and made sucking sounds as I lifted them up. I felt bad disturbing the delicate meadow ecology.

The trees in the distance were definitely bigger, indicating higher ground. As we walked, we moved into an area of moist air that was fast getting very cold. I imagined sitting and drying out in front of my woodstove, Sierra Nevada Pale Ale in my hand.

It seemed crazy tracking plants and trees in the growing

darkness, the unlikely convergence of which had the smallest possible odds of providing any information about an armored truck robbery. My shoes were filled with muddy water. My wet pants pulled on my legs with each marching step. I was cold. Shivering wasn't far off. I had a powerful sense that this was folly.

"What do you think, boy? Movement is good exercise, and suffering in the cold builds character. But we gave it the old college try, right? Time to go home, dry off, warm up, and imbibe a beverage that would brighten the spirit, right?"

I turned toward where I thought Spot was but didn't see him. I stopped and rotated, the muck grabbing at my shoes as if to pull them off. Spot had ranged off to the side of me, looking in a different direction. He was standing still, holding his head high, air scenting. His ears were focused and he looked up a bit. I walked toward him to see what caught his attention.

Spot was looking toward a different tree island. Silhouetted against the still-light sky, this bunch of trees looked similar to the others except that above them flew a group of crows, squawking and circling and making a fuss as if they were arguing over a bag lunch they'd stolen from the beach. Some of them swooped down into the trees. Others flew back out.

"The eternal entertainment of crows," I mumbled to myself as I fought off the depressing cold weight of the misty air, "a group of which is known as a murder of crows. Did you know that, Largeness? One of the world's smartest animal species is, when in a group, called a murder. Imagine that."

Spot ignored me.

I walked a few more steps toward his focus point, stopped, and considered what was grabbing his attention.

"Okay, boy. We'll head on toward those trees instead and see what those birds are about." I walked on past Spot. "But no farther. My mood is in need of a serious application of heat, a full belly, and an awareness that the big bed is but steps away."

After a few more gushy, sucking steps, I turned around again. Spot was hanging back, still watching the crows, still sniffing the air. But something was wrong.

His ears weren't up, but back.

"Okay, Largeness, I'll go ahead and see what's up."

I hiked on toward the trees. As I got close, I looked up to see how the biggest one looked. With the lingering light of the sky behind the tree, I could see that it was a big pine with batches of long needles. But it was easy to see the sky through the needles, so they were sparse. A tall tree with sparse branches and long needles that didn't appear very lush was likely a Ponderosa Pine.

Looking back down toward the ground, my sky-sensitized eyes couldn't see anything in the developing dark. I reached for my penlight. It was still in my pants pocket, soaked. I'd forgotten to take it out before I forded the creek. I turned the switch. Nothing.

So I pulled out my phone and turned it on. The screen light was dim, but it was enough to see where the trees were and step around them. I turned around.

"Spot?" I called out softly. "Are you there?" I couldn't see him. He was somewhere behind. I thought I knew why he was hanging back, and it gave me a sick feeling in my gut.

I shined the phone light around. Moved forward with small, quiet steps.

I came to a kind of makeshift camp. There were two tents, the kind that would just fit two men each. On the ground nearby were a couple of backpacks. A cookstove. A jacket hung on a tree. Something reflected my phone light. An aluminum coffee pot on its side, the top knocked off and coffee grounds spilled out. Something sparkled on the ground. I pointed my phone down. The light reflected off the shiny blade of a knife. There was a pile of beer cans. Bud and Coors Light. The Buds were all crushed, the Coors empty but still round and smooth. Something else caught the light, two pieces of paper stuck in a bush, the kind you rarely see on the ground.

Hundred dollar bills.

I moved forward. Two unseen birds exploded in movement. By the sound of their flapping wings, they barely missed my head. I went toward where I thought they'd come from, holding my phone up to illuminate the campsite.

There was a vague shape several yards in front of me, dark as the tree trunks, but more round. A big pack leaning up against the tree. But as I got closer I thought it maybe wasn't a pack.

I took another step, tried to angle my phone for better vision, then stepped forward again.

It was bigger than a backpack. Longer. Not something natural to the forest. But definitely leaning against a tree.

Another step. In front of the object was something shiny. Silver. Reflective. Obvious even in my dim phone light. Contrasting with the big dark shape behind it.

One more step.

The silver object became clear. It was a spear. It entered the body of the man just below the hollow of his neck and projected down at a steep angle. By leaning to the side, I could see that the pointed tip of the spear emerged from the man's lower back, the point sticking into the bark of the tree as the man fell back in death. I moved my phone forward and up so that I could see the dead man's face.

Now I understood what the crows had been doing.

TWENTY-THREE

My breath was short as I turned and again shined my light around the campsite, certain that no one was there, but checking anyway.

I had two bars of reception. For the second time in one day, I dialed 911.

"Nine, one, one Emergency," a woman said. "Please state your name and address."

I began to explain, but realized that I wasn't getting words out.

"Nine, one, one Emergency," the woman repeated. "Please speak louder."

My jaw was locked, teeth clenched. A spear through a man was a sight I'd never seen. I forced my mouth open. Moved my jaw back and forth. Spoke.

"This is Owen McKenna calling from the marsh just south of Baldwin Beach. I'm north of Highway Eighty-nine approximately a quarter mile and east of Baldwin Beach Road about the same distance. I have found a murder victim, killed by a spear. I suspect there will be others nearby."

"Please stay on the line," the dispatcher said, "and I'll have officers en route immediately."

"I need to conserve my battery as my phone is my light," I said. "So I'm going to disconnect in a moment. If you get a chance, contact Sergeant Bains of the El Dorado County Sheriff's Office. He will want to be here. Tell him that the victim is possibly connected to the armored truck robbery two mornings ago. Also, please contact Sergeant Martinez at Douglas County SO. And one more thing. Tell the men to bring lights."

I hung up.

TWENTY-FOUR

I turned toward the dark meadow where I believed Spot was waiting, hanging back because he'd already seen too much human death, and, as with all dogs, he didn't want to be near it or smell it.

"It's okay, boy," I called out to the darkness. "You were right. Bad stuff, here. But it'll be okay, so just hang in there."

The tree island was the size of a baseball diamond. Using the phone screen as a light, it was relatively easy to navigate the marsh grass at the perimeter. I knew I was leaving footprints and perhaps I'd obscured other footprints. I'd already been leaving prints through part of the camp before I knew it was a crime scene. I decided to step softly on uncompressed grass and those areas where it looked like others hadn't already tread. Even if I could see no evidence of previous tracks, I would walk at the edges of spaces and next to brush and on top of brush so that I didn't mar any more previous tracks. After they'd made casts of the various prints, they could identify which were mine.

When I'd completed the circumference of the tree island and not found anything out of place, I moved back toward the tents.

The door flaps to both tents were hanging down, but they weren't zipped. I approached the first tent from the side, stepping through bushes, and bent down near the corner of its door. I reached my phone through the opening and pushed the door flap aside without leaving prints or disturbing anything.

There was nothing there but two rumpled sleeping bags and a small open pack from which spilled clothes.

Moving over to the second tent, I did the same thing, opening it in such a way that I didn't disturb the dirt in front of it, in case there were identifiable footprints. Shining my phone light, I looked in, realizing at the last minute that there was a buzzing sound coming from within.

I saw a second body. This one, like the other, was speared from his upper front, down and out the middle of his back. He lay facing the tent door, curled on his side. It looked like he'd been lying in the tent, his head toward the wall opposite the door. He likely sat up and was crawling toward the tent door, got himself skewered, then fell over to the side.

It appeared that he hadn't been sleeping in his bag because he was still wearing all of his clothes except his boots. There was money spilling from his right front pocket, like stuffing coming out of a torn mattress.

Unlike the other body, this one still had eyeballs. The tent flaps didn't keep out the flies, but they kept out the crows. My past experience with bodies suggested that a crime victim's eyes relaxed after death and did not reveal the terror of their experience. But this body's eyes still appeared to show shock.

Sirens sounded in the distance.

I left the tent, stepped through brush out of the tree island and back to the marshy grass. I walked toward where I'd last seen Spot.

"Hey, boy," I said softly. "Where are you? C'mere, Spot." I shined my phone, the light from which seemed almost nonexistent out on the open meadow. Something moved off to the side. I turned the light.

Spot stood some distance away, his head hung low, ears back.

"It's okay, boy," I said, walking over.

He didn't move as I pet him. "It's okay," I said again. "Let's walk around the tree island to the other side where the cops will come with their lights. You and me'll answer some questions and then go home and sit by the fire. Okay?"

I pulled on his collar, and Spot came along, slowly, with lethargy that I knew was depression.

When we got to the other side of the tree island, I stopped because I didn't know if the El Dorado men would come from the highway to the south or the beach road to the west. I guessed that the beach road access would be closer and faster. But that would require that they had keys to the gate. The gatekeeper locked everything up at night.

I turned off my phone to conserve battery power, and we waited in the dark. Lights came through the distant trees and then started across the meadow. I heard some men swear as they stepped into the wet, soggy marsh grass. There were several lights in the group, and they bounced and danced toward us but a bit to our side. Flashlight beams shot out across the meadow toward us.

"McKenna?" came a shouted voice.

"Out here," I shouted. "Look for my phone light." I turned it on and held it up.

"He's over there," one of the men shouted. "More to the left."

I saw the lights change direction toward us. Eventually, the group become distinct men in the darkness. They got to us a minute later.

"Hey, McKenna. Sergeant Bains, here. Sounds like you stumbled onto a nightmare. I assume you were looking for it."

"Long story. I found some pine pitch on the tire of the Reno Armored truck that was robbed two days ago. I came out here looking for a connection between a Western Pine Beetle and a piece of Tahoe Yellow Cress that was in the pine pitch. I didn't expect to find the camp of the robbers. And I certainly didn't think I'd find two dead men with spears through their chests."

"Two dead? Whoa. You think two of the robbers killed their companions?"

"Logical guess."

"Hey, Sergeant," one of the men said. "Should we set up a standard perimeter, even way out here in the middle of nowhere?"

"Yeah. McKenna, have you met Dr. Sender? He's our new Medical Examiner." Bains gestured toward a skinny young guy who wasn't wearing an El Dorado sheriff's uniform.

I reached out and shook his hand. "Owen McKenna," I said. "Sorry to meet under such circumstances."

His hand was cold and shook. Maybe he was cold. More likely, he was shaken by the situation. He didn't speak.

Bains said, "You want to say what we're about to find,

McKenna?"

"Borrow a flashlight?" Someone handed me one. I used it to point at the trees. "The little tree island in front of you is where they had their camp. Think of it like a baseball diamond. The tree over there is home plate. There's a body leaning up against its trunk. There are two tents near shortstop. The tent closest to third base has the second body. I tried to step in places they wouldn't. On brush, in the tallest grass. Their footprints should still be mostly untouched. If everyone is careful not to mar the existing prints, we can cast them and figure out which ones match the boots on the bodies. That will tell us which prints don't fit and likely belong to the killers. We can maybe even track them out of here, whether to a car or truck or boat."

"Okay, men, careful where you walk," Bains said. "Only step where these victims wouldn't. Swing from the trees if you have to. We'll do the basics tonight. We can wait until dawn to haul the bodies out. Remember, look, don't touch."

Bains turned to the ME. "Dr. Sender, we'll stay away from the bodies until you're done. The truck robbery was in the early morning two days ago. So, assuming these vics are two of the robbers, these murders happened within the last two-plus days or about sixty hours ago max. Probably less."

Bains turned back to me. "Your girlfriend still doing the insect thing?"

"Forensic entomology? Yeah."

Dr. Sender spoke for the first time. "Are you speaking about Street Casey?"

"Yeah."

"I've heard she is good on time of death analysis," Sender said.

"Would you like a consult?" I asked.

"Yes, please. This may be a clear case, but it never hurts to have as much evidence as possible when it comes to time of death."

"I'll give her a call."

"Sergeant!" a voice called out from the tree island. "There's some money here."

"It goes in an evidence bag!" Bains shouted back.

"I'll join them," Bains said. "You gonna stay here?"

"Yeah. My dog doesn't like death. I'll give Street a call." I had my hand on Spot's back. I rubbed him.

"I remember you telling me that about search-and-rescue dogs," Bains said. "Holler if you need anything." He and Dr. Sender walked into the trees.

I still had 15% of battery power. Enough for a quick call.

Street answered on the second ring.

"I'm almost out of battery, hon, so I'll have to be quick. I'm sorry to tell you that we've got two bodies out on the meadow near Baldwin Beach. The ME is requesting that you do a time-of-death estimate. Any chance you can do a forensic inventory, soon?"

Street was good. No gasping or shocked questions. Just total professionalism. "It's very hard to collect samples in the dark," she said. "Is it okay if I'm there shortly after dawn?"

"I'm sure it would be. Anything I should tell them?"

"Yes. Tell them not to move the bodies. And if by any chance they've got temp data loggers they could set up by each body, that would substantially increase the accuracy of my estimates."

"I'll tell them."

"In the meantime I'll collect past temp data estimates from the NOAA website. How far back do you think I should go?"

"Sixty hours would certainly cover it," I said. "It appears that the bodies are two of the men who robbed the Reno Armored truck two mornings ago."

"Got it," Street said. "I'll get my gear ready. Call me when you're back home?"

"Will do."

"Be careful?" Street said.

"Yeah. You too," I said. We hung up.

"Stay, Spot," I said. "I'll be back in a few."

I left Spot in the dark, where he preferred to be as opposed to on the tree island of death. I used my remaining phone battery power to light my way back toward the men. "Sergeant Bains?" I called out.

"Over here near home plate."

I worked my way around. I saw him and Dr. Sender in the light of one of two big camping lanterns that they'd set up. He was bending down near the body.

"Street needs to wait until daylight to collect samples," I said. "We'll both be back out here at dawn. Will you have someone here?"

"Yes," he said. "Two men for sure."

"She asked that the bodies not be moved."

"I already told the men."

"She also wondered if you've got temp data loggers in your evidence kit?"

"Hey, Don," Bains called out. "Did we ever get those temp data loggers we talked about?"

"Yeah," a voice called back. "We got six of the eighty-hour units with the USB interface. You just plug them into the computer to download them when we're done. You want me to set some up?"

"Yeah," I heard Bains say. "Hey, McKenna, one near each body, right?"

"Right," I called back.

"You hear that, Don?"

"Got it," came his voice.

"Okay, sergeant," I said. "I'll be back with Street at dawn. Dr. Sender, how should Street contact you?"

He handed me his card. In the glow of the lantern, Sender's face looked pale.

"Everything okay?" I said, thinking that for a new medical examiner, this might be the ugliest death he'd seen yet.

"Fine," he said, sounding tense. "The body is past rigor, so we can expect that the deaths happened longer than twenty-four hours ago. Possibly more than thirty-six hours ago. Dr. Casey's estimate will help."

"She'll be here around dawn," I said. "Oh, another question," I said to Bains. "Any chance one of your men could spare a flashlight? I don't have one, and my car's back at Camp Rich. It's a long walk in the dark."

"I've got a spare LED headlamp. Will that work?"

"Perfect."

He handed it to me.

"See you in the morning," I said. I left and rejoined Spot in the dark meadow.

I strapped Bains's headlamp across my forehead.

"Okay, boy, things get better from here on out."

Spot walked with me across the meadow to the beach road, where we turned south toward the highway. Each time a vehicle came, we stepped well off the road. The air was cold, and our proximity to the lake made it humid. Spot usually acted extra alert at night, as if the loss of illuminated inputs made him step up his olfactory awareness. But tonight, he was quiet and restrained. He didn't turn his head to investigate sounds, and he didn't lift his head to sniff the air. He just kept his head low and walked as if life were miserable, and he had no choice but to accept that humans kept dying.

It took a half hour to get back to the Jeep and another forty minutes before we were up the mountain road above the East Shore and pulled into our driveway.

Once in the cabin, Spot immediately lay down on his bed. He didn't go to sleep but was motionless, his eyelids drooping. I fetched a beer, then dialed Street.

"Not a good evening, huh?" she said.

"No. But maybe I don't need to tell you about it now. We can talk when I pick you up in the morning. Let's say four-thirty a.m.?"

"I'll be ready," she said. "I hope you can get some sleep."

"Yeah. Hey, Street?"

"What?"

"Thanks for being so understanding."

"You're welcome. Give His Largeness a hug. Are you going to bring him tomorrow?"

"He wouldn't like that."

"Then maybe he could stay here with Blondie."

"That would be good."

"Okay. See you in a few hours."

We hung up.

I was too tired to cook. I made two peanut butter sandwiches, crumbled one of them up, and stirred it into Spot's chunk-sawdust dog food. He watched from his bed but didn't get up to eat.

I ate mine, drank my beer, and went to bed.

TWENTY-FIVE

When the alarm went off at 4 a.m., I let Spot out for a quick run in the dark while I drank my coffee. I refilled my mug before we drove down the mountain and pulled into the lot at Street's condo. He was glad to trot inside and be with Blondie, but it would take a lot more time away from the dead bodies before he regained his natural enthusiasm.

This time, I'd brought my rubber overshoes and had Street grab hers as well. She also brought her pack with an extra windbreaker and mugs and a thermos. She poured each of us more coffee as we cruised through the Cave Rock tunnel and headed toward the South Shore.

When we got to Stateline, I turned up Kingsbury Grade and pulled into her lab.

Inside, she pointed to a large plastic tool box. "That's my sample case. You could bring that out."

Back in the Jeep, I told her about the previous day, giving Evan and Mia a ride, finding the kidnap victim Jonas Montrop tied up in the boat, learning about Tahoe Yellow Cress from Frankie Blue, and then finding the bodies of what appeared to be two of the robbers.

"Wasn't the murder victim in Incline Village named Montrop? The guy who thought you might kill him?"

"Yeah. Jonas Montrop is his stepson. The kid was still alive, but barely."

Street was silent a moment. "Do you think his kidnapping is connected to the armored truck robbery and the bodies you found?"

"I have no evidence of that, but such violence in Tahoe is rare. First, Jonas Montrop is kidnapped, then his father is murdered, then an armored truck is robbed, then there were two more murders. The confluence of violence makes me think they are likely related."

We drove in silence awhile.

"I should let you know that the bodies are hard to look at," I said. "They were killed brutally, and the crows were feeding on one of them."

"It's okay," she said. "I always know that on any maggot mission, the host bodies are in really rough shape. But thanks for your concern."

"You're a tough woman," I said.

"All women are tough," she said.

I turned off Highway 89 at Baldwin Beach Road, and drove in and parked in the lot before the gatehouse. I carried her sample case, and she carried her pack. We each wore headlamps as we walked through the roadside trees out onto the meadow.

"You weren't kidding about wet marsh," she said as her boots sloshed through watery grass.

Tahoe often gets freezing cold during summer nights, especially in June. There was a frost on the marsh grass, and it made a crinkly, scraping noise as our boots went through it. A fog lit by the approaching dawn hovered over the meadow and wetlands. The tree island emerged from the mist like an apparition from a medieval fantasy. Light from one of the camp lanterns threw shadows through the trees.

I led Street up toward the home plate tree. "Morning," I called out. "Owen McKenna and Street Casey here."

"Oh, hey, Mr. McKenna. We're waiting on you." A man appeared at the edge of the trees. "I'm Deputy Don Jones. We spoke last night. Sergeant Bains had to leave but will be back soon."

"This is Street Casey. She's the entomologist who will be taking samples."

Street and Deputy Don nodded at each other.

"Has Dr. Sender left?"

"A couple of hours ago. He seemed pretty shaken. Not that I blame him. You didn't bring your dog," he said.

"No. He had enough last night."

"Sarge said he doesn't like the smell of death."

"No, he doesn't."

"Me neither," Don said.

"Did the temp data loggers work?" I said.

"Probably," he said. "But we won't know until we plug them into the computer. Should I turn them off, now?"

"No," Street said. "Let's leave them running while I collect samples. The more complete the temp log, the better. We can turn them off when I'm done, which will be a couple of hours or more."

"Right," Don said. "Anything you need? Any way I can help?"

"Sure. Even though it's getting light, it would be good if you could bring one of your bright lights over to each body as I work on it."

"Sure. Where would you like to start?"

"Doesn't matter. You set up the light. When I'm done collecting samples from one body, I'll let you know, and you can move the light to the next. Will that work?"

"Of course." Don turned.

They'd set up crime scene tape to preserve areas of footprints and create paths for law enforcement to walk. Don walked along a tape corridor and over to one of the bright lanterns. He picked it up and carried it over near the home plate body, propping it up near the body's waist so it would illuminate most of the body.

I set Street's sample case near the lantern. "Anything else I can do for you?" I said.

"No. This will be fine. Thanks."

I was grateful to move away. There was nothing about science that was interesting enough to overcome my revulsion of maggots eating their way through bodies.

I wandered over near Don and Jorge, the other deputy who'd spent the night hours with him. The three of us watched as dawn came, the sun rising in the northeast.

As it broke over the ridgeline near Genoa Peak, Don said, "So this woman you brought, the entomologist, what does she do?" he asked.

"She takes insect samples. Insects can reveal a lot about when a person died."

Don looked puzzled. "I understand the abstract concept, but

what exactly is she doing back there?" He moved his head toward the tree island.

"I'm no expert at this, but basically, when an animal dies – and of course that means people, too – flies, especially blowflies can sense it from miles away."

"You mean, they can smell the dead person?" Don said.

Jorge winced at Don's words.

"Yeah," I said. "So they come and they lay their eggs on the body."

Don frowned. Jorge seemed to squirm.

"When blowflies lay their eggs, they focus on any wound where there's an opening in the skin, or on body orifices, the mouth, the nose, the eyes and ears."

Don said, "I don't like the sound of this at all."

"Me neither," I said. "If it's not too cold out, the eggs hatch in maybe eight hours or so. The larval form of a blowfly is a tiny maggot. The maggot's purpose in life is to be a voracious eater. It burrows into the flesh of the dead animal and eats it."

Jorge was clenching his teeth and looking like he was about to be sick.

"You want me to continue?" I said, concerned about Jorge.

Don said, "Yes."

"After a few hours, the maggot has already grown too big for its skin. I don't remember the details well, but I think it molts its skin and begins all over again, growing bigger. The speed at which maggots eat and grow is related to temperature. They grow faster in warm temperatures."

I glanced at Don. He nodded as if I should keep going.

"So what Street does is pluck maggots out of the body. Maggots of different species mature at different rates. The problem is that maggots all look the same. You can't tell which kind you're looking at. So she kills some of them so she can preserve them at whatever size they had grown to. The others she takes back to her lab where she feeds them so that they can mature, pupate, and turn into adult flies. Once the adult flies emerge, she knows what species it is. Entomologists have data on how fast the maggots of different species grow. So once she knows the kind of fly, then she can look at the size of the maggots she killed and that will tell her how old the maggots were."

Don was nodding. "Now I get it. The age of the maggots tells her how long it's been since the fly laid the eggs."

"Right," I said.

Jorge looked pale, and Don looked like he wouldn't be eating any meals for a while.

"What I don't get," Don said, "is knowing how long the maggot has been growing doesn't tell you how long the person has been dead, because we don't know how long it took the fly to find the dead body and lay the eggs, right?"

"Your question makes sense. But it turns out they do know how long it takes for a fly to find a dead body," I said.

"How long is it?"

"Almost immediately."

Don looked confused. Jorge had moved away and was looking out toward the lake and mountains.

I continued, "Street told me that when an animal or person dies, the average length of time before a fly finds it and lays eggs is ten minutes. That's how sensitive a blowfly's sense of smell is. They are out there in large numbers, even if we're not aware of it. When an animal dies, the flies come from all over."

"That's gross," Don said.

"Yeah, it is. The cycle of life has some unsavory aspects to it."

"Is there any time when flies don't come?"

"Sure. Any time the body is inaccessible. A body in a tight car or car trunk. A body indoors in a draft-proof house. A body that's buried right after it dies. Or a body that's wrapped up tightly in plastic or a rug or a body bag."

"How long will it take the entomologist to do her work?"

"A couple of hours."

Don turned and looked back into the trees, which were now lit by blazing sunlight.

"Here comes Sergeant Bains," he said.

Bains walked across the meadow, lifting his feet in that manner that suggested he was walking through water. In the sunlight, the bottom six inches of his dress browns were dark with moisture.

When he got close, he said, "Why didn't I think to stop and

get rubber boots like yours?"

I nodded.

"Your lady doing the dirty work as we speak?"

"Yup."

"How long before she'll have a time of death?"

"I think she can make an educated guess right away, but it's many days before she can make an accurate determination."

"Okay," Bains said. He turned to Don and Jorge. "It's light enough now. It would be good to start your photographs. Err toward thoroughness."

"Got it," Don said. He and Jorge walked back into the trees.

Bains turned to me. "You want to take a look at the scene by daylight?"

I nodded and followed him back into the tree island.

TWENTY-SIX

Street was not in sight. Her sample case was at the door of the tent.

"I'm interested in your thoughts," Bains said. "Maybe you could take a look around and see what you think."

So I walked around and through the campsite. Everything was as I had expected to see it, although the distances in daylight seemed shorter than when I'd slowly stepped my way through in the dark. Scattered through the area was camping equipment that I hadn't seen in the dark of the evening before. The charred remains of some sticks showed that they'd had an illegal campfire, which would have presented a serious risk of discovery had they lit it at night, not so much risk if it was part of an afternoon beer party.

The bodies were far enough from each other that it seemed possible, if unlikely, that the men were unaware as their companion had been killed. The critical aspect would have been how much noise the victims made as they died.

In the daylight, I could now see that the spears were simply ski poles with the handles and baskets removed. These were old ski poles, made of tapered aluminum tubes, no doubt chosen because they had sharp points. Years ago, the point design was changed to circular or squared-off tips with sharp perimeters that would provide grip on slippery ice, but that would be less likely to become a deadly stabbing instrument should someone fall on it.

I wondered how each person could be killed without crying out and alerting the other to the threat. Perhaps a spearing death was so overwhelming that the victim would die silently, any potential vocal reaction smothered in the enormous shock of having multiple organs simultaneously skewered on a cold, metal shaft. Or maybe there were two killers who attacked their victims at the same moment.

The victim at home plate seemed the way I remembered him in the light of my phone, sitting on the ground, leaning against a large tree trunk. His left arm was out behind him, open fingers splayed, revealing a dirty palm. His right arm was in front of him, hand pulled in next to his chest, his knuckles almost touching the ski pole. I squatted down to get a closer look. His hand was clenched into a fist, no doubt his last agonizing spasm from the pain of violent death.

The ME had said that the bodies were past rigor mortis. So the clenched fist was unusual. It was as if he had something precious when he died, something he gripped with such intensity that his hand stayed closed after his body went limp.

I pointed it out to Bains.

"The victim at home plate has his right hand clenched in a fist at his chest. Probably, it's nothing."

"But maybe it's something," Bains said, "or you wouldn't point it out. Let's look."

Bains pulled a pair of latex gloves out of a cardboard dispenser, tugged them on, walked to the dead body, and bent down to look. "I see what you're saying," he said.

Bains put a finger under the body's fingertips. He'd barely begun to open the hand when something shiny fell out.

Bains reached under the pine needles, pulled the object out, and held it up. It was golden and circular.

"A coin?" I said.

"No, a button. A brass button." He rotated it so I could see the other side. Unlike buttons where the stitching holes go through from front to back, this had a little metal arch on the back side. There was an errant thread stuck in the arch as if the button had been ripped from a jacket or shirt. "What's the pattern on the front?" I said.

Bains turned it over. "It's that common eagle symbol."

I leaned in to see it up close. "With the arrows in one claw and an olive branch in the other claw. I forget what it's called. The United States coat of arms or something."

Bains pointed at the body. "You notice the spears?" he said.

I nodded. "Ski poles. Old ones with the sharp points. When

did they start using non-pointed ice tips? Forty years ago?"

"At least," Bains said. "Even so, a lot of houses in Tahoe probably have old ski poles in the corner of the garage. It wouldn't be hard to find ones with the pointed tips."

I thought about ski pole design. "Ski poles have a metal stop ring about four or five inches up from the tip. The basket slides up against that and is held in place with a grip washer. It would be easy to cut the grip washer off with a wire cutter. But the stop ring would be harder."

Bains shrugged. "Maybe. I'm pretty sure the stop ring is just friction fit. It slides onto the pole until the increasing diameter of the pole brings it to a stop. If you cut into it with a hacksaw, I bet it would pop off."

"Without the basket, an old ski pole with the pointed tip would make a good spear. But why take off the handle?"

Bains pointed at the body. "Look at the open end of the pole. It's been filed into a notch, and the edges have been bent out."

"As if to hook onto the heavy rubber banding on a spear gun," I said.

"Or the string on a bow."

"But arrows need fletching to fly straight."

Bains thought about it. "Maybe this pole didn't fly. Maybe it was shot from a foot away."

"Did you notice the sheen?" I said.

Bains took another look. "That explains why they shined in the light of our flashlights last night. It looks like the pole was wiped with oil. I wonder... " Bains stopped for a moment, then said. "A slippery, oiled pole would be a lot easier to run through a body."

"What a wicked image, a killer carefully oiling his weapons. How do you suppose he carried them? If you brought ski poles to the campsite to use as weapons, you'd have to disguise them. So let's say you put them into some kind of tube."

"A rod and reel storage tube like the ones fishermen use," Bains said. "I use one myself."

I held my fingers together to make a circle and visualize. "I don't know how big those are."

Bains shook his head. "They make what they call bulk tubes.

They're a good six inches in diameter."

"That would fit lots of spears," I said, "especially with the handles removed."

"Right. I can see the killer telling his buddies he's bringing fishing gear and he's going to fry them up fresh lake trout for breakfast," Bains said. "When in reality, he's bringing in weapons to kill them so he can take off with all the money. Except that there were four robbers, right? So either there were two killers killing the other two, or only three robbers came to this campsite. From the gear left behind, there is no clear indication of how many men were here."

"And why did they come here?" I asked.

"Good question. It took some work to get to this place. We're close to South Lake Tahoe, and lots of people use Baldwin Beach. But this tree island is like being in the middle of nowhere. So it would give them good cover."

"Makes sense," I said. "Another thing to remember is one of them must have got the pine pitch on his boot and then wiped if off on the truck tire during the robbery. So they were camping here before the robbery."

I looked out at the lake. "Maybe they came by boat. No one would notice them. Or they could come at night and be unseen. Everywhere on the roads, there are traffic cams up on lightposts and at intersections. Vehicles all have license plates. There's no coordinated, real time data logging for vehicles, and you can drive most places in the country and no one knows where you are in real time. But give researchers enough time, they can find traces of you on traffic cams. Even if you turn your cell phone all the way off so the phone companies can't track you, the traffic cams will find you. And when you stop for gas or go into a convenience store, those security cams will record you, too. But there are no traffic cams out on the lake."

"Yes!" Bains said, excited. "You could put in someplace, and once you ride across the lake at night, you could come out someplace where you previously left a vehicle. But there's still a risk, as boats have license numbers."

"Human-powered boats don't," I said. "Kayaks, canoes, and paddle boards. They're not even registered with the state."

Bains frowned. "The armored truck robbers supposedly got off with five hundred thousand. Any idea how much bulk or weight that kind of money takes up?"

"The company's general manager told me that a half million would be in two reinforced bags, fifty pounds each."

"Easy to haul in a kayak or a canoe," Bains said. "But where would the boat be now? Would they have just left it on the beach?" Bains looked out toward the water.

"There's another possibility," I said. "Let's say the robbers got away in a stolen vehicle. They drove it up to the lake to a prearranged location where they knew there were lots of kayaks they could help themselves to. The West Shore, maybe. They could even have stolen a vehicle from an empty vacation home, then brought it back and left it where they found it. No one would know it was borrowed to use in a robbery."

Bains was nodding as I spoke.

I continued. "From there, they could have found two tandem kayaks. Or a single canoe. Lots of people have vacation homes where they keep an extra vehicle and all manner of boats. It's not too difficult to paddle south from the West Shore down to Baldwin Beach." I paused, thinking. "If they wanted to leave here by car, they could have given their borrowed boat a push, and the breeze would have taken it out into the lake. It might be days before it washes up on the opposite side of the lake. It could land in one of the hidden coves south of Sand Harbor."

"We might never find it," Bains said.

"I buy that scenario," Bains said. "It fits with what we have here, and it makes sense from the point of view of the robbers. It leaves them and their money in a hidden, hard-to-track location and near a vehicle they've previously left. They probably parked it across the highway at the Mt. Tallac trailhead parking lot." Bains seemed to think about it. "What doesn't make sense is that the victims were speared from the front. That would give them a chance to see their attackers and call out."

I said, "Maybe both victims were killed at the same time. The two killers could have coordinated their timing. The only other explanation I can think of is that there was one killer, and he wanted his victims to know he was killing them. He wanted them to have that be their last thought."

Bains made a face. "That's really vicious. By definition, first degree murder is always pretty vicious. But spearing a guy to his face is especially so. Let's say there was just one killer. What do you think happened to the fourth robber?"

"No idea. Maybe they sent him out on a food run. Or he could have paddled off in one kayak, towing another so he could ditch it and leave less evidence that the four robbers camped here."

Jorge came over carrying a gym bag. "Found this in the woods," he said. He held the bag open by spreading the two handles, one in each of his latex-gloved hands.

We looked inside and saw two white hockey masks.

"Good find!" Bains said. "There might be some hair on those. Could be a source of DNA."

We heard movement coming from the tent. The tent flap moved, and Street came backing out on her hands and knees. She had a surgical mask over her mouth and nose. She paused, reached out, and set her sample case on the ground outside the tent, then continued to back out. She stood up, walked away from the tent, took off the mask, and took a deep breath. I walked over and put my arm around her shoulders.

"Are you okay?" I asked. "You look pale."

She took another deep breath. It was a moment before she answered. "It's always a bit bracing. The circumstances. The odor. I can see why Spot is so sensitive to death. With a nose that's ten thousand times more sensitive than ours, it must be overwhelming."

"Ready to go?" I said.

She nodded.

"Sergeant?" I said, turning to Bains. "It looks like we're done here."

"Okay. We've got it from this point. Dr. Casey, please send your report directly to Dr. Sender. Thanks for your help."

"You're welcome," she said.

TWENTY-SEVEN

Street and I walked back out onto the meadow and over to the Jeep.

I put my hand on Street's leg as we drove away. "How're you doing?"

"I won't say it isn't hard, but I've been there before. I'm a scientist. It's not the bodies and maggots that bother me. That's just biology. Nature's recycling system."

"Yeah, I have a harder time with that than you."

"What's difficult," Street said, "is thinking about the person who did this. I accept that human deviation goes into some very dark corners. But I wonder what could motivate a killer to be so brutal? What could possibly happen that would turn a person into such a monster? Because in the final analysis, that's what this killer is, right? A monster. A defense attorney may decide to use an insanity defense. And doctors may concur. But he's still a monster."

"I agree," I said.

We were silent a bit, both wrestling with thoughts about the things humans are capable of. To break the tension I said, "You'll want to drop your samples off at your lab, right?"

"Yeah. It will take a little time. I have to sort all the killing vials and the live vials, then measure the maggots, both dead and alive, then feed the live ones."

"You say that like you're feeding the dog. Put out a bowl of maggot kibble, and they'll come crawling, huh?" I tried to make it a joke. But when I glanced at Street, she wasn't smiling.

"I've got beef liver in my freezer," she said. "It'll take a few minutes to defrost it in the microwave."

"How do you feed it to them?" I said, not sure I wanted to know.

"After it's thawed, I just divide it up into small containers, one for each group of homogeneous maggots. There were three different sizes of maggots on the bodies. Which means that they may be different species of flies. Or the bigger ones may have simply grown faster on the body in the tent because it stayed warmer at night. Anyway, each group of maggots gets its own bowl. I put the maggots directly on the liver and set them in the incubator. Maggots love that stuff. They squirm with liver lust."

"Sorry, but that sounds really disgusting," I said.

Street looked at me. "It is."

"Do you have any preliminary sense of time of death?"

Street thought about it. "It's been cool at night, but warm during the day. Blow fly eggs hatch faster when it's warm. If the men were killed in the evening, blowflies would have still been active until it got cold. So they would have laid their eggs. But those eggs might not have hatched until the warmth of the next day."

I said, "So if the men were killed the same day as the robbery, the soonest the eggs could have hatched would be about forty-eight hours ago from now, soon after the sun shined its warmth into those trees."

"Right. Most of the maggots were still in the first instar stage, although a few of the ones from the body in the tent had molted and were in the second instar stage. So my preliminary guess would be that the men were killed roughly in the evening, two days before yesterday evening when you found them. About fifty-six hours before now. I'll have a more accurate analysis in a few weeks."

"In other words, they were probably killed in the evening the same day they robbed the truck."

Street nodded.

I turned up Kingsbury Grade and pulled in front of the building where Street worked.

"Do you need any help in your lab?" I said as I carried her sample case from the Jeep and into her lab.

"No. It's best if I'm alone so I can concentrate and make certain I get everything organized and labeled properly."

"Okay, I'll run across the highway to my office, check messages, and be back in a half hour to take you home."

Street nodded but didn't speak, already focused on the rack of vials she lifted out of the case.

I left.

The answering machine was blinking when I walked into my office. I pressed the button.

"Hey, McKenna, Bains here. I've got IDs on the vics. They had Nevada driver's licenses in their wallets. And the licenses look legit. Give a call when you can." He rattled off a number so fast I had to replay it twice to make my best estimate and write it down.

I dialed back.

"Sergeant Bains."

"McKenna returning your call. The dead guys have names."

"Yeah. I'm still at the campsite, but I thought you'd want to know sooner rather than later. Ready?"

I grabbed a pen and pad. "Ready."

"Carter Remy, age twenty-six, from Fallon, Nevada and Lucas Jordan, age twenty-five, from Reno."

"Both from Nevada," I said as much to myself as to Bains.

"I called Val at the office and asked her to look them up and see if they have sheets," Bains said, "and they do. Both have spent time getting three squares from correctional facilities in the state of Nevada. Between them, they've had two charges for battery, one burglary, two DUIs, one auto theft, one carrying a stolen, unlicensed weapon, one receiving stolen property. Who knows what's in their sealed Juvie records."

"But no armed robbery?" I said sarcastically.

"Right. Taking down an armored truck is good for multiple charges including carjacking. With their records, these guys would have gone away for good. I sure would like to know who their compatriot is. He is some sick piece of work."

"Yeah," I said. "It would take a serious personality glitch to spear someone with a ski pole," I said. "Thanks for the names."

We hung up, and I dialed Diamond.

"McKenna calling," I said when he answered.

"Morning," he said. "I heard you found two bodies that were stabbed with ski poles over by Baldwin Beach. Rumor is they might be my robbers?"

"Looks like it. Bains and his men found some hockey masks in a gym bag, hoodies hanging up on bushes, some cash in the bushes and a wad in one of the victim's pockets," I said. "So it looks like these were the robbers. That leaves two robbers still alive."

"One or both of which is the likely perpetrator," Diamond said.

"Yeah," I said. "Bains just called with the victims' names and records. Choir boys they ain't."

"I'll give him a call," Diamond said.

We hung up, and I went back to Street's lab.

She was almost done.

When we were driving home in the Jeep, Street stayed silent. She would probably need some time in the coming days to process what she'd seen.

We came to the turnoff to Street's condo. I pulled in and parked. She unlocked her door and let Blondie and Spot out, and they charged around with gusto. I could see that Spot's time with Blondie had reset his emotions, and he was back to his normal good attitude. As is typical, he was more interested in playing than in reconnecting with his master who'd been gone for hours.

Street and I walked for an hour while the dogs ran. Then it was time for me to go.

Street said, "If you can learn something about the money at the campsite, I bet that will tell you if these crimes are all connected."

"How is that?" I asked.

"What if there is a way to identify the ransom money the Incline man withdrew from the bank? Or the money from the robbery? You could see if by any chance the money from either or both events was in those bills blowing around the campsite."

"The manager at the armored truck company told me that the money was unmarked."

Street nodded. "Even so, there might be some other qualities about the money that would be useful. For example, was there anything notable about the denominations? Sometimes an assortment of cash will only include twenties and under. Or maybe just hundreds. What if the money that the bank gave Montrop was all hundreds and the armored truck money was all smaller bills? Or maybe one group of bills was newer and the other was quite worn out."

"Street, that's brilliant. There could also be differences in the way the money was bundled. I've seen rubber bands and paper bands. I'll check it out."

Street nodded. She looked very weary. I could tell that her father's parole board decision was weighing on her, and I wanted to cheer her up.

Before I could think of something to say, there was a metallic clunking sound from outside. Both dogs turned and looked at the walls, ears perked up. In the distance, a vehicle accelerated. Street frowned and got up to look out the window.

"That sounded like a fender bender out on the highway," I said. "Or maybe like a pine cone falling and hitting a car roof."

"I don't see anything," she said. She came back to the couch and sat down.

"Before I leave, I have something for you if you've got a moment," I said.

"What is that?"

I pulled out a little gift I'd gotten from the Artifacts store on the South Shore and handed it to Street. She opened it and made a little gasp.

"Owen, it's beautiful! A butterfly in amber!" She lifted the necklace up and set the small oblong of amber in the hollow of her palm. The delicate chain snaked through her fingers, swinging beneath her hand. "This is probably a type of metalmark butterfly."

"What does that mean?"

"The name refers to the metallic markings. See the yellow stripes against the deep blue patches? It looks metallic. And the surrounding coral color is gorgeous. This species is from the Riodinidae family."

"That means butterfly?"

"Actually, lepidoptera is the order of insects we call butterflies. The Riodinidae family is just a small portion of all the butterflies."

She held the amber up to the light and rotated it.

To my eye, the yellow amber was as pretty as the butterfly within.

"Thank you, sweetheart. I love it. I'm going to call it my Metamorphosis necklace. It will be a symbol for how complete transformation is an important aspect of life."

"That's the essence of what butterflies do, right?" I said. "The transformation from caterpillar to butterfly is a metamorphosis."

"Yes. In fact, scientists are currently doing a lot of new research on the process." Street put the necklace over her head, and looked down at the butterfly. "We've always known that when the caterpillar transforms, it pretty much dies by the usual definition of life and death. It ceases all normal functions, and its organs dissolve."

"When that happens to us, we certainly call it death," I said.

"Exactly! It is death, by every traditional measure. Yet somehow, some DNA that was never active in the caterpillar now becomes active and triggers the growth of an entirely new animal, a butterfly, which grows from the proteins that remain after the caterpillar dissolves. We don't understand how it works. And we don't have a precise vocabulary for describing it. One scientist says that the word reincarnation is the best descriptor for what happens."

"Wow, that is pretty cool. I can see how studying bugs could sometimes be interesting."

"Owen!" Street gave me a severe frown. "Studying bugs is always interesting. Many important things that we know about biology and evolution and life itself have come from studying insects."

"Right." I pointed to the amber in her hand. "The butterfly is actually not very perfect," I said. "If you look at the right wing and the right legs, it shows some damage."

"That's great! That indicates that it is the real thing. Perfect specimens are nearly always somewhat artificial. People catch butterflies and pour an amber-like resin over them. In the natural world, when an insect lands on a fresh drop of amber and gets stuck or has amber drip on them from above, they struggle mightily to escape, often damaging themselves. And after they die, the wind and other insects or passing animals may damage them further before more amber can drip down and fully encase them. So this looks to be the real deal. This sample could be tens of millions of years old! It's like a time machine, preserved from eons ago. In fact, this could be from the Eocene Epoch."

I touched the amber. "I thought this baby was probably from the Eocene days. A hot time, the Eocene, right?"

Street's look of tolerance reminded me of how my third grade teacher used to look at me.

It pleased me that her mood had changed. She was now thinking about butterflies from millions of years ago, and thinking about the complexities of biology. It was a great transition from moments before when she was struggling.

"I'm a lucky guy that I can give my girl a bug for a present."

Street gave me a very serious look. "Bugs are very important."

"So I see."

I thought that made it a good note on which to leave.

We kissed, and Spot and I left.

When we walked across the condo lot to the Jeep, I found a ski pole spear plunged through the Jeep's roof. Its open rear end was filed into a notch, with the remaining wings of metal flared out. The flared end stuck up about eight inches above the Jeep's roof. The point of the pole was buried into the rear seat, slightly to the left of center.

I turned a fast rotation looking at the condo parking lot and into the woods and out toward the highway, watching for any movement. There was nothing.

I opened the front passenger door and reclined the seat back as far to the rear as it would go. "Okay, Spot, today you need to squeeze into the front seat."

He jumped in and reached his nose back to sniff the spear that spanned from roof to seat. I held his head away.

"Sorry, Spot. We don't want to smear any prints."

Spot took up an awkward position on the reclined front seat, and we managed to get up the mountain without bumping the spear.

TWENTY-EIGHT

I'm a rational guy, and I'm well into my third decade of chasing bad guys. I've seen every kind of psycho, sicko, and weirdo. It takes a lot to unnerve me.

But the spear through the Jeep roof creeped me out. Partly, it was the boldness, a ski pole that was no doubt the brother of the ones that were thrust through the robbers' bodies.

I called Diamond and told him. He said he could come by in half an hour.

Next, I called Street. I needed time before I decided to reveal the exact nature of a threat that might produce nightmares, but I needed to warn her. So I said, "I just realized that I never said that you should be really careful. This killer probably knows that I'm involved in the case. If so, you could be at risk."

"It's okay. I always know to lock my doors, and I always check the peephole before I open them. I keep Blondie with me, and look outside before I leave home or the lab. Don't worry, Owen, I'm aware of the risk. I never forget the things that have happened because someone's tried to get leverage on you."

"You're kind to just call them 'things,'" I said. "They were horrific events. I want to make certain that nothing like that ever happens again."

"Me, too. So continue with your investigation. Don't worry. If I can deal with the stress of my dad, I can deal with an ordinary psycho, crazy killer who merely sticks spears through people. That's no big deal."

"Like I said earlier, you're tough." We said goodbye.

While I waited for Diamond, I called Washoe County Sergeant Lori Lanzen.

I told her, "I think I told you that Reno Armored called and asked me to investigate their armored truck robbery. So I've been looking into it. Last night, I tracked the robbers to a makeshift campsite on the South Shore near Baldwin Beach. I found two murder victims, who appear to be two of the four Reno Armored robbers."

Lanzen said, "We heard. Everyone is talking about it."

"The victims had been speared by ski poles. Most likely, one of the other robbers was the killer. I just found a similar ski pole slammed through my Jeep roof."

"A warning."

"Yeah. One of the victims had been speared from up high, so the killer was tall and strong. You'd have to be tall and strong to put a spear through a Jeep roof."

Lanzen went silent as if the image took her voice away. I was about to say something when she spoke.

"I'm guessing you suspect this somehow relates to the murder of Montrop."

"Yes. I have no evidence of connection. But the robbery, the murder of the robbers, the murder of Montrop, and the kidnapping of Montrop's son Jonas seem like too many violent crimes in a small area. It would seem an amazing coincidence if they weren't related. So I'm considering that they are connected."

"I agree."

"What did you find out about Evan Rosen's car?"

"It had something broken on the right front wheel, but the mechanic said it would be easy to fix. She's probably got the car back by now. The most interesting thing was that the seat was adjusted to her short stature, and there was dust in the track rail that would have been displaced had someone moved the seat."

"So if someone stole it, either they were short, or they drove it with their knees scrunched up to make it look like Evan drove it. Any prints?"

"None other than Evan's." Lanzen said.

"Someone could have used gloves. If they didn't slide their hands on the wheel, Evan's prints would be preserved."

"Yes. Nothing is clear. And whoever threw the paddle board must have worn gloves. The only prints on it belong to Montrop. Because the car and paddle board were both clean, this killer will be hard to catch. If the killer didn't touch anything at Montrop's house, we're unlikely to find DNA. And if Evan was the killer, well, her DNA is already all over the car and Montrop's house, so that circumstantial evidence is of no value."

Lanzen paused. "What's your next move?"

"There was some money in one of the victim's pockets," I said, "and there were a few scattered bills as if they'd blown around the campsite. I'm exploring how to discover if the money came from the Reno Armored or possibly even from the withdrawal that Montrop made from the bank in Incline. I'm wondering if you could call the bank manager and explain that I'm investigating the kidnapping of Montrop's son, and that you'd like her to answer my questions."

"Sure," Lanzen said.

"Great. Do you remember her name?"

"Hannerty. Jean Hannerty. I'll call her right now. If you don't hear from me, you can assume I contacted her and told her about you. Give me ten minutes."

I thanked her, and we hung up.

Diamond drove up five minutes later. After he looked at the spear in the Jeep, he dusted it for prints. There were no marks on it of any kind.

"Hard to thrust a spear without touching it," Diamond said.

"Yeah."

"Oily, too. I suppose that's to make it easier to stab through bones and organs."

"That's what Bains and I thought."

"Help me remove it? Maybe we can grab it by the rear end." He leaned in close to look at the notched, flared opening. "Looks like a staff of Hades," he said.

"What's that mean?"

"Hades, Greek god of death, had a staff that was forked like a two-prong pitchfork. The prongs flared out. Just like this."

I found a locking pliers. We wrapped the end of the pole with a rag to protect it from damage and improve the pliers' grip, and gradually cranked the pole out of the Jeep.

As we worked, I gave Diamond the details on how I found the dead robbers.

"Two robbers down," Diamond said. "Two to go. Gotta hand it to you on the pine pitch, yellow cress, bug hunt."

After Diamond left with the spear, I called the bank and asked for Jean Hannerty.

After a short wait, a woman said, "Hello, this is Jean."

"Hi, Jean, my name is Owen McKenna."

"I just got off the phone with a Sergeant Lanzen from the Washoe Sheriff's Office. She told me you'd be calling."

"May I stop by in an hour or so and talk to you a bit about David Montrop's withdrawal?"

"Certainly."

"Thanks. See you soon."

An hour later, I walked into the bank in Incline Village and asked for Jean Hannerty. I was directed to a group of three desks. Two were empty. One was occupied by a woman who was speaking on the phone. The woman was a commanding presence, partly because she was large, but mostly because she radiated control and dominance. She held the phone with her left hand. Her right arm was outstretched, making big gestures like a maestro conducting a full orchestra. Hannerty's hair tossed and shivered as her free arm went left and right, her finger pointing at the strings, then the horns, encouraging the basses, admonishing the timpani. She saw me coming and nodded at me. She hung up, made some notes on a pad and then stood and reached out her hand. "I'm guessing that you are Owen McKenna because Sergeant Lanzen said you are very tall."

"Good to meet you," I said as we shook.

"I know you want to ask about David Montrop, but I don't see what I can add. His murder has been a shock to us here at the bank. He was a good customer." She gestured as she spoke, her fingers out, palm up. Then her hand went over her heart as she said that it was a shock. Her gestures were so demonstrative that a deaf person could have understood her without the benefit of lip reading or sign language.

"I was told that he made a withdrawal the morning he was killed. I'd like to ask about the bills that your bank gave him."

"You're hoping that we have the serial numbers, but we don't record them as a general rule." Her right arm was conducting again. "Mr. Montrop generally had us write a cashier's check for his band payments. This time he asked for cash, which, although unusual, was not the first time. Some of the bands he books don't have a band checking account. They like cash because then they can divvy up the money to each member."

"Sergeant Lanzen said he withdrew twenty-five thousand. What denominations did you give him?"

"I double-checked with Mary this morning – she was at the teller window the morning Montrop came in – and she and I both remember that he asked for half in twenties and half in hundreds. But we only had ten thousand in twenties, so we gave him the other fifteen thousand in hundreds. We note the denominations so we can go back and verify if needed."

"You said you don't record the serial numbers as a general rule. That implies that you sometimes do?"

"I meant that as a generic statement about most banks. A few banks have bill counters that also scan for serial numbers. But they're expensive, and we've never felt the need. We're just a little small-town bank."

Her small-town bank line sounded well-rehearsed as if she regularly tried to downplay the bank's role in a town with enough Silicon Valley billionaires to be one of the richest towns of its size in the world.

"When do you record serial numbers?" I asked.

"Unless we have a special request, we only record our robbery packs."

"What's that mean?"

"Come, I'll show you." She brought me across the bank lobby and through a locked door that opened to the area behind the counter. There were two tellers working at one end of the counter. Hannerty walked to the other end. She typed a code onto the computer keyboard, put a key into a cash drawer, and pulled it open.

"This is a robbery pack." She pulled out two bundles of twenties. "Every teller's cash drawer has them. If a robber comes in, we make sure that he goes out with this. The first bundle are bills where we've recorded the serial numbers. The second bundle is a dye pack."

"Which can explode and blow dye all over the money and the robber, right? How are yours triggered? A timer?"

"At the door of the bank, there is a transmitter. If the dye pack is carried through the door, the transmitter starts the timer in the pack. Thirty seconds later, it blows. They're very effective in catching robbers, as you no doubt know."

"And if any of the bills escape the dye, you have their serial numbers."

"Right."

Hannerty escorted me back to the front of the bank.

I said, "The money you gave to David Montrop, were there any other descriptive aspects to it?"

"What do you mean?" Hannerty asked.

"New bills? Old bills? A mix?"

"They were all old bills."

"Were they in rough shape or pretty smooth?"

She thought about it. "In our bank, we use the standard currency strap, a bill count of one hundred for every denomination above the one dollar bill. The bundles we gave Montrop were pretty flat on the hundreds, so the bills weren't too worn. But the twenties were more worn. Those bundles had more volume."

"From what you're saying, if I found a stash of cash with twenties and hundreds, there's no way I could identify whether or not it came from the money David Montrop withdrew from your bank."

Hannerty was nodding and gesturing before I finished my sentence. "Correct. Unless the bills are marked or recorded in some way, cash in the form of mixed bills is almost impossible to trace. But of course, that still gives you some useful information."

"What would that be?"

"If you find money you're wondering about and it contains bills other than twenties and hundreds, you know that those other bills didn't come from the withdrawal that David Montrop made."

"One, fives, tens, and fifties," I said. I reached out to shake her hand. "That is useful information. Thanks." I said goodbye and left.

TWENTY-NINE

Mama Nature was showing off the beauty of high-altitude weather, so I decided to drive north and head to Reno by way of the Mt. Rose highway, and see just how hot the sun can be at 9000 feet when the air is only 48 degrees. Because Spot had been confined to the Jeep while I was in the bank, he was eager to stick his head out the window and inhale the cold wind blast as we cruised up the mountain.

We crested the pass and followed the twisty road past the Mt. Rose ski area and down 4500 vertical feet. The pines gave way to sagebrush as we came to the broad, angled slope that drops down from the mountains on Reno's west side to the urban center of the valley.

Twenty minutes later, I walked through the front door of Reno Armored and into the arctic blast.

This time, Rita, the receptionist, was wearing a quilted, goose down coat that was colored a deep purple. Probably, it took the color edge off her unpainted-yet-purple fingernails. She told me that Randy Bosworth was in. Whether the vibration in her voice was her vocal characteristics or shivering, I couldn't tell. She buzzed Bosworth and said he would be out in a minute.

The heavy door made a whoosh as Bosworth pushed through. He'd switched from his long sleeves of two days before to a short-sleeved shirt, the better to keep from baking to death in the event the cooling system couldn't keep it below 50 degrees.

"Hey, McKenna," he said as he pumped my hand up and down about three times too many. He grinned at me. "When I didn't hear from you yesterday, I wondered if you were maybe taking one of those staycations, you know, where you stay at home to enjoy what the local area has to offer. Your job's got to be one of the great ways to scam some bucks, right? You walk the beach and hike the woods, then bill for your time. No one can actually prove whether you were working or playing. And, of course, you can always claim that you were thinking, puzzling out a complicated case. But then I got a call from a cop who knows me. He said that the El Dorado County cops brought in two of the robbers' bodies." Bosworth made a little chuckle.

My lack of sleep had made me impatient. I wanted to walk out, but I took a deep breath and counted to five.

"I need to ask about the cash your men were bringing to the casino," I said. "I'd like to know the denominations, the way it was bundled, and any other details you can remember."

"I guess that would save you more legwork, huh?" Bosworth said in a mocking tone. "I'm not going to give you details about the cash or anything else, because you'll just detail it in your report as if you'd done yet more work, but it's all just a Sherlock Holmes charade." Bosworth was now sneering. "You might be able to fool Mr. Timmens, but you don't fool me."

I pulled out my phone and dialed the number I'd entered in my contacts list. I put it on speaker as it rang.

"Who're you calling?" Bosworth said. "I've got work to do, and I can't waste time while you continue this act."

A young male voice answered, "Reno Armored. How may I direct your call?" he said loud enough for both Bosworth and me to hear.

Bosworth stared at my phone, frowning.

"Owen McKenna calling for Mr. Timmens," I said.

"Hey, you can't do that," Bosworth said. He took a step toward me and raised his arm as if he might try to snatch my phone from my grip. "You try to spin some tale to my boss, I'll kick your ass."

I lifted my phone high so that Bosworth couldn't reach it without jumping, which, given his girth, he probably couldn't do. "Hey, Owen McKenna!" an enthusiastic voice came out of the phone. "My God, I can't believe what you've done! I got a call from the El Dorado Sheriff's Office, and they told me about how you and your dog found the bodies of two of the robbers all because of some pine pitch you got off the tire of our truck! That is a fantastic bit of detection! I already called our casino client and gave them the news. Earlier they had told me that they were going to cancel our contract. But now that two out of four robbers have been found dead, they're acting like we're clearing the streets of scum. They said they're going to have us take over their cash needs for their Vegas casino. Not only have you saved us, McKenna, we're going to substantially increase our business because of you. Whatever your fee is, I'm going to double it!"

"Thanks, Mr. Timmens. I appreciate the feedback. I'm actually here at your Sparks facility, and Randy Bosworth is stonewalling me. He said that I was taking a…" I turned toward Bosworth and spoke loudly enough that Timmens could hear over the phone. "What did you call it, Bosworth? You accused me of taking a staycation and passing it off as billable hours? What was the other thing? Oh, yeah. Something about me taking credit for what the cops did." I turned to speak directly toward the phone. "Bosworth thinks I'm faking my work." Behind Bosworth, I saw the receptionist's eyes get very wide.

"What?!" Timmens was shouting. "Bosworth, is this true? Are you screwing up again? Not only have you gotten this backward, you've slandered McKenna. If anyone else heard you, we'll be in serious hot water! I want you in my office, Bosworth. One hour."

"Mr. Timmens, I was given false information by the police. I got the impression that McKenna didn't do anything to find the bodies. I was just responding to what I'd been told." Bosworth's voice had risen an octave.

"Bosworth, did the police specifically tell you that the El Dorado Sheriff's Office found those bodies without any help? Did you call the El Dorado Sheriff's Office and ask them about McKenna? Tell the truth, because you know I'm going to call them and ask."

"Well they didn't exactly say that, but…"

"One hour, Bosworth. In my office in one hour. Do you understand?"

"Yes, sir," Bosworth said, his voice low.

"And Bosworth?"

"Yes?"

"Before you come over here, tell McKenna anything and everything he wants to know."

"Yes, sir."

"McKenna?" Timmens said.

"Yeah."

"I'm going to make this up to you."

"No sweat," I said, and hung up.

Bosworth looked like a dog, hanging his head, looking defeated. But I could tell that he was already scheming about his revenge.

"Details about the money?" I said for the second time.

Bosworth took several heavy breaths. "The money was our standard assortment, ones, fives, tens, twenties, fifties, and hundreds. Everything bundled with currency straps, one hundred bills per denomination."

"How many bundles of each?"

"I don't know. It varies from casino to casino. We have their requested proportions in the vault along with the iPad where we keep notes on the cash disbursement app and a physical log sheet we keep for redundancy." He looked at the clock. "I can't get in there, now. It's a timed vault, impossible to break into outside of predetermined times. That way no one can just pop in here and rob us. They have to know the times for each day and week, and that information is encrypted. We can only learn the times for a given day each morning at ten a.m. And it changes each day, so no one can make advance plans."

"If you don't know the proportion for each denomination, give me your best estimate."

He thought about it. "I think that particular casino goes heavier than normal on hundreds and twenties."

I nodded. "What's the condition of the money you deliver?"

"Used, but not real worn. We have a policy of pulling the limp bills. It makes a big difference to the casino to get money with snap and stiffness."

"Your currency bundles," I said. "Do they sit pretty flat?"

"Yeah. Flat and thin."

He looked at the clock again. "I better go." He waited for me to precede him out the door. It seemed like he was about to say something like a parting shot, but he thought better of it and stayed silent.

I turned to leave. Bosworth looked at the time. "When Rita's on her lunch break, she locks the door. So I'll let you out."

He escorted me to the front door, pushed the release bar and opened it up. I figured he might try to hit me, so I kept my eye on him as I left.

I walked out to my Jeep and left.

As I drove out of the parking lot and turned down the street, I realized that I'd turned the wrong way. I had come from the other direction. The industrial area was confusing. Maybe I could get out a different way, but I'd be a lot less likely to get lost if I turned around. So I pulled into a different parking lot, made a U-turn, and headed back the way I'd originally come.

Then I made one of those belated realizations. In the parking lot where I'd turned around, I'd passed a parked silver car. A man was sitting in the driver's seat. A woman was standing outside the car at the open passenger window, leaning down talking to the driver. I hadn't gotten a good look at them, but something about them seemed familiar. I hit my brakes and came to a stop, trying to visualize the people. As I pictured them, I realized that the woman looked like Rita the receptionist. That made sense, as Bosworth had said she was on her lunch break.

But the driver of the silver car, the man, was also someone I thought I'd seen before. I couldn't place his face in my memory. Sensing a vague recognition of a person in a place I'd never been was nothing unusual. But why, when I saw the Reno Armored receptionist near a car, would I recognize another person with her? That would be an unlikely coincidence.

I turned around yet again to drive back and have a second look. Then I remembered where I'd seen the male driver. It was the Korean gardener at David Montrop's house in Incline Village. A man named Kang who couldn't speak English.

Now I was very curious. The gardener was connected to a man who'd been murdered up at the lake, and the receptionist was connected to a company that had a truck robbed at the lake.

Obviously, Rita and Kang needed to explain how they knew each other and what, if anything, they knew about the crimes. And if she wasn't speaking Korean, he must have been speaking English. Yet he'd presented himself to me and Washoe County

Sergeant Lanzen as not speaking English. But I recalled that the house cleaner Evan Rosen thought he was faking his inability to speak English.

I sped up toward the parking lot and made a hard turn into its entrance.

The silver car was gone.

I looked around. There were exits at both the front and back of the lot, multiple ways to escape. Maybe Rita had gone with him. Or maybe she'd simply walked somewhere.

Thinking that Kang may have spotted me and wanted to get away fast, I picked the main road and drove in the opposite direction from where I'd come.

It turned in leisurely S-curves, an attempt to make the industrial park more esthetic. I careened around them, looking into every lot and side alley. When I came to intersections, I looked for a silver car, but had no luck.

After ten minutes of searching, I gave up, pulled over, and dialed Sergeant Lanzen. I got her voicemail.

"Hey sergeant, Owen McKenna here. I thought I should tell you what I just saw. I came down to Sparks to talk to the manager of Reno Armored. As I was leaving, I saw the Reno Armored receptionist outside talking to a man in a car. I'm not certain, but I think the man was Mr. Kang, Montrop's gardener who supposedly doesn't speak English. I have no idea what it means. But it's an unlikely coincidence. The car was a silver sedan, but I didn't notice make, model, or license plate because the man's identity didn't come to me until I'd driven away. When I realized who it was, I went back, but they were gone. I made a search of the local roads and found nothing."

I hung up and drove back toward Reno Armored. I wanted to talk to Randy Bosworth and see if I could shake any information about Rita or Kang out of him. I pulled back into the Reno Armored lot and parked. But the front door was still locked, and no one responded to my knocks. I walked around back and pounded on the garage doors, but got the same result. Maybe he'd already left to go visit his boss Mr. Timmens. Or maybe he was staying out of sight inside the building, plotting his revenge on me for revealing his behavior to his boss.

THIRTY

As I drove away from Reno Armored, I thought about the dead robbers. One was from Reno. The other was from Fallon, a town to the east.

I pulled into a Home Depot parking lot, parked in the far corner, and called Sergeant Bains. He was out, but I left a voicemail. As I considered my next move, I saw a food truck at the curb. Unlike the popular new gourmet food trucks where one can buy barbecued, stuffed poblanos with scallions, spice-rubbed pork, and black rice, this truck just had the words 'OLD-FASHIONED, FOOT-LONG HOTDOGS' painted in bold red letters along the top of the truck. Written above the red letters was the word 'ORGANIC' in black script.

I turned in my seat and said, "Hey, Largeness, what would you say to a foot-long hotdog?"

Spot had been snoozing in the back seat. He lifted his head and looked at me with sleepy eyes.

"It says 'Organic,' so that means it's healthy. Probably has as many vitamins as broccoli? Are you game?"

It could have been my enthusiasm, but probably it was the word broccoli. He got up fast, trying to stand on the back seat. Which meant his legs were bent, his backbone was pushed against the Jeep's headliner, and his tail was on high speed, smacking the right, rear window. The excitement of a healthful lunch was manifest.

"I'll be right back," I said.

Five minutes later, I returned with a fiberboard tray holding two beers and two foot-long hotdogs in toasted buns and drenched with bacon-mango salsa.

I set the tray on the center of the hood. I lifted one hotdog out of its wrapper and set it on the hood just above the right headlight. I let Spot out of the back. He knew he couldn't have any treat without permission, but he reached his nose over the headlight, toward the food, nostrils flexing, tail on slow speed, the sign, I've learned, of doggie self-hypnosis brought on by anticipation of Heaven. I opened the hotdog bun, letting the aromatic dog and salsa tempt the canine gods.

Spot glanced up at me for a fraction of a moment, then looked back at the hotdog. His stare was so intense that if that hotdog tried to go anywhere, I knew there would be mayhem.

"Ready," I said.

Twin streams of drool flowed from Spot's jowls, landing on the Jeep's hood.

"Set," I said.

Spot tensed his legs, made a little jerk of anticipation, and the drool streams jiggled, tracing twin, liquid, calligraphic signatures, cursive for food passion.

"Go."

He lunged. It was fast and probably painless for the hotdog. I know Spot bit down at least once, and he had to have swallowed at least once, unless he'd developed a new food-vac technique that I hadn't yet witnessed. But I wouldn't swear that there was more than one bite or swallow.

Spot never let up focus. As he licked his chops, he transferred his laser gaze to the other hotdog in the center of the hood.

"No, that one's mine," I said.

Spot looked up at me for another moment then turned back to study the remaining hotdog. The drool had stopped, which was a clear signal that he understood the next hotdog wasn't his. But his continuing focus showed that he hadn't given up hope that I might change my mind.

I was hungry as well. I picked up my hotdog and ate it fast. Spot watched me, maybe wondering how it could possibly take a human most of two minutes to eat a giant hotdog. He licked his chops again.

I fetched the bowl I keep in the back of the Jeep and poured Spot's beer into it. The Pet Police might disapprove, but I'd learned that a single beer for a 170-pound Great Dane was like a single beer for me. A taste, a tease, a hint of good things to possibly come. But nothing more.

Spot lapped fast. I sipped mine. Spot got to the bottom of the bowl and proceeded to lick the metal down six or eight parking spaces before he decided he'd gotten every last drop.

My phone rang.

"Owen McKenna," I answered.

"Am I interrupting?" Sergeant Bains said.

"No, perfect timing. Spot just finished his organic food-truck hotdog and beer, one of the many impressive offerings to be found in the lovely town of Sparks. Meanwhile, I'm taking my time with my lunch, lingering and savoring."

"I knew you were a man of delicate sensibilities," Bains said. "You called."

"Yeah. Earlier, you said that one of our robber stiffs was from the Reno/Sparks area. So I thought maybe I could learn more about this guy. I could canvas the neighborhood. Visit the local bars. See what I can learn. It occurred to me that first I should see if you've learned anything useful."

"Actually, I have. In the wallet of Lucas Jordan, there was an old newspaper clipping with a photo of a football game. The caption said, 'Big Bears receiver Lucas Jordan making the game-winning catch.' It looks like Jordan was trying to preserve the memory of the biggest moment in his life. Anyway, I poked around and found out that the name of the football team at Wilson High School in Reno is The Big Bears."

"That's great," I said. "Didn't you say earlier that the vics were both about twenty-six years old?"

"Right."

"So that would mean Jordan graduated about eight years ago."

"If he graduated." Bains sounded derisive. "As you know, a lot of these kinds of guys are showing substantial skills if they learn how to dress themselves and pull a drive-by with a stolen piece."

"Thanks. I'll see what I can find out."

"Oh, one more thing."

"What's that?" I said.

"The sheen of oil on the spears?"

"Yeah?"

"I wondered if we could find out what it was without waiting two weeks to get a lab test. So I asked this woman at the office who's got a killer sniffer. You know, the kind who can smell a scent and say it's a Lady Slipper orchid or the cleaning solution they use on the floor at the main Post Office in Bakersfield. So I had her sniff one of the poles and she said that she has an aluminum cookpot she sometimes uses for boiling pasta. But first, she puts olive oil in the pot. She said that's what the spear smelled like."

"Olive oil," I said.

"Olive oil on aluminum," is what she said. "The poles are aluminum, so I'm guessing she's accurate."

"Good info," I said. "I'll keep my eye out for olive oil."

We said goodbye and hung up.

I searched for Wilson High School on my new smart phone. When the website appeared on the screen, I felt very smart.

From what I could tell, Reno's Wilson High School had only a one-page website. At the top of the page it said,

Wilson High School, Home of The Big Bears

Where Excellence Is Our Business

There was a picture showing studious-looking kids sitting in a circle on lush green grass, notebooks and textbooks on their laps. When I scrolled down, another picture showed a classroom with desks in perfect rows. The photo below that was at graduation, the students wearing pressed gowns. One of the students was giving a speech at the podium on the stage. Clearly, the excellence on display had not been sufficiently assimilated by Lucas Jordan the armored truck robber.

Below the photos was the school's address and phone number.

I dialed the number. After a half dozen rings, a computerized voice told me I could leave a message after the beep. But no beep ever came. Eventually, I hung up.

I found Wilson High School on the map, in an area that used to feature windowless buildings with neon signs advertising naked dancers. I knew that most of Reno's few seedy neighborhoods had been gentrifying in the last couple of decades. Wilson High looked to be a centerpiece of the improvements, even if their phone system had some glitches.

When I got to the Wilson High School neighborhood. I watched for the lush lawns and neat grounds featured on their website. Instead, I found a gray, featureless concrete block building in the center of a large expanse of crumbling asphalt with a broken spider web of weeds crisscrossing the area. The building had once been painted ivory, but most of the paint had peeled off. The walls were now covered with frenetic, aggressive graffiti that didn't pause as it went from concrete to window glass and back to concrete. The entire school area was surrounded by chain link fence, broken here and there. At first, I assumed that the fence was to keep out any lowlifes who might be prowling the neighborhood. But when I took another look at the school, which looked less inviting than most prisons, I thought maybe the purpose of the fence was to keep people in.

As I approached the entrance, I saw a police patrol unit parked next to the gate. A Reno cop was stopping each vehicle entering the school property.

When I got to the cop, I rolled down the window.

"Afternoon, officer," I said as I showed him my license. "I'm Owen McKenna, in the employ of Reno Armored, looking to talk to school officials about one of the armored truck robbers who may have been a student here years back."

"Do you have an appointment?"

"No. This case is developing fast. We've got two bodies run through with spears and a killer who also has automatic weapons. I didn't want to take the time to set up appointments."

He frowned, thinking, then looked into the backseat at Spot, who was sprawled from left armrest to right armrest, snoring. "This your K-nine patrol unit?"

"Kinda," I said. "He's not certified, but he can devour a hotdog with the best of the professional dogs."

"That's a joke," the cop said, his face very serious. "Funny," he added, his frown intense. "The administration lot is on the east side of the building," he said. He handed me a blue placard. "Put this on your dash and park in the visitor's section."

"Are you here for a special event?" I asked.

"According to Wilson High officials, every day is a potential special event. So the school board put it in the budget to have an off-duty cop at the gate every day."

"Anything special happen today?"

"Not yet."

"Thanks," I said. I put the plastic sheet on my dash, drove away, and parked where he said.

The nearby door was a single glass panel with vinyl letters that said 'Wilson High Administration.' It too was covered in graffiti. I pulled it open and walked into a passage that smelled like Margaritas mixed with sweat. There was a sign that hung down from the ceiling. It said 'Information.' To the side was a counter. Behind the counter, a short woman with bright red hair pulled back into a bun worked at a computer.

I walked up and gave her my most charismatic smile.

She immediately looked happy. Charisma rules.

As with the cop at the gate, I pulled out my license and gave her a short elevator pitch about a man named Lucas Jordan who was of interest in a crime I was working on, and I explained that he may have been a past student. I left out any mention of robbery or bodies.

I said, "I'd like to look at the school records for the student in question. He would have graduated about eight years ago," I said.

She made a little nod. Then a phone rang. A buzzer buzzed. She looked away from me and picked up the phone.

"This is Cheryl," she said.

A tinny voice came through the speaker, loud enough that I could hear the tension.

"Oh, no," Cheryl said.

The tin voice continued.

"It just happened?! Oh, no," Cheryl said again. Then, "What should I do?"

I listened as someone yelled or berated or pleaded. I couldn't tell which.

Cheryl hung up. Her face had paled.

"Is everything okay?" I asked, knowing it wasn't.

"We've just had a bomb threat," she said. "We're going on lockdown." Cheryl looked scared. "I don't even know what that means, lockdown. I'm new on this job." Her voice quivered, and her eyes did a fast, imploring search of mine.

In my most reassuring voice, I said, "Not to worry. This isn't unusual for some schools. You can provide valuable documentation. What you should do is stay at your post, stay calm, and make notes of what happens. Who comes in, who goes out, what time it is. What people say. Anything else that happens. You'll be responsible for documenting the events as they happen. Does that make sense?"

She nodded. "Yes, but I'm scared."

I reached over the counter and patted the back of her hand. "You'll be a huge help," I said as I turned and left.

When I got out the Administration door, I used a fast-casual walk to hustle out to the Jeep in a manner that wouldn't look strange on the security cameras. I got in, started the engine, and again drove away at a fast-casual speed. They might make notes about the private investigator whose timing coincided with the bomb threat, but I didn't want to become an object of special attention. Nor did I want to be stuck at the school for five hours while the Reno cops went through their laborious interviews with everyone before letting them leave.

When I got to the gate, the cop had left his post and was over looking through the window of a parked Chevy Malibu. He was talking on his radio and looked stressed. Then he turned to look out at the street as he talked, looking east, then west, rising up on tiptoes, leaning his head sideways to get a better view. I gave him a short wave, coasted out the gate, and drove away.

THIRTY-ONE

I headed toward downtown and turned into the parking lot at the main library. Inside the library, I found another information desk, this one staffed by a young man who wore black pants and a black long-sleeved shirt with the buttons buttoned all the way up to his collar. He had a chubby neck to match his chubby body, and as the tight collar edge pressed into his neck flesh, I wondered if he was getting enough oxygen.

"Any chance you keep yearbooks of high schools in Reno?" I said.

"Well, of course," he said in a haughty tone as if to suggest that I was a fool to consider that it might not be so. "I can think of lots of them off the top of my head. Damonte Ranch, North Valleys, Wooster, Galena, Spanish Springs, Reno High, Washoe Wolf, and others." He paused.

"Wilson High?" I asked.

He wrinkled his nose. "Well, that's more of a maybe," he said. "Are you a Wilson High alumnus?"

"No."

"Oh. Well you should know that Wilson has problems to say the least." He rolled his eyes. "In the last ten years, they've only done three or four yearbooks. They're the black sheep of Reno Sparks schools. Of course, I went to one of our finer schools, so I know what those poor students are missing. I suppose they do as well as they can with such limited resources, both financial and intellectual. For most schools, doing a yearbook every year is standard stuff. Get a group of kids together to play with Adobe Illustrator, and out comes a yearbook. But at Wilson High, trying to find a group of kids who are computer-fluent enough to produce a yearbook is pretty much out of their league. For all I know, they might not even have a computer with a graphics program. Just my take, of course."

"Can I look at what you have?" I said.

He nodded and came out from around the counter.

I followed him as he walked down the stacks. He made a left turn, then a right, moving with incisive purpose and obvious skill, paused, his forefinger out, tracing the spines of books, his hand position just so. He moved a yard to the side, scanned the shelves, moved another foot, then said, "Here we are. Five books. One, two, three, four, five. Wilson High's total yearbook production from the last – let's see – twenty years. Are you looking for a particular year?"

"About eight years ago," I said.

The young man touched a book, turned his head as if to see the spine better in the dim light, then pulled out a volume. "This one is nine years ago. That's the closest we have. I don't know for certain, but it appears that Wilson High didn't produce a yearbook for the year you want."

I took the volume from him. "Thanks. I'd like to look this one over, if I may."

He pointed to the big library tables. "Have at it," he said.

I walked over, sat down, and opened the book. Maybe Wilson High wasn't producing gold-embossed volumes to make the alumni proud, but the book did the job. It had all the usual features, articles on the year's great moments, pictures of the kings and queens and princes and princesses of the various festivals, and photos of the football players and other sports jocks.

I turned to the pages where all, or at least many, of the students had provided their picture along with their name and nickname and membership in sports and clubs. Because this book was a year before the time the robber would have likely finished school, I turned to the pages that showed the students who were juniors.

I pulled out the slip of paper on which I'd written the robber's names. I flipped through the book to the Js. Lucas Jordan was partway down the page. He had short brown hair, swept up and cut in a flat top like from the 1950s. He wore a sweatshirt with a camouflage pattern. Unlike the other students in the yearbook, Lucas wasn't smiling. He looked angry and mean. Maybe his juvenile parole officer required him to sit for the class picture.

Under Lucas Jordan's photo, where most of the students listed sports and clubs and favorite activities that they participated in, it said 'Hunting' and 'Target Practice.'

A high school photo is hard to connect to a murder victim nine years later, especially one whose eyes had been eaten by crows, but I guessed that Lucas Jordan was the man I'd found at the home plate position on the tree island near Baldwin Beach.

I turned more pages in the yearbook and, as I suspected, came to the other victim.

Carter Remy was dressed like a prep student. His shirt had thin blue vertical stripes and a button-down collar. There were two pens in his shirt pocket. His thin hair was parted far down on the right side and neatly combed. While Lucas radiated a malevolent personality, Carter's face was vapid, and his eyes looked dead. I'd seen those eyes on a serial killer. There were no activities listed. The photo of Carter Remy looked vaguely like the body in the tent albeit with the tent body having gained about forty pounds of additional weight since the yearbook photo was taken.

I studied each picture again, looking for similarities. It seemed there were none. Yet the robbers were bonded in some way that brought them together for a major crime nine years after the yearbook was produced.

Of the two, Carter Remy looked the most dangerous because he exhibited no emotion at all.

The robbery had involved four men. Because these two had gone to the same school, it seemed there was a good possibility that the other robbers would also be in their class. But because these two were so unlike each other, I couldn't imagine how I might identify the others, one or both of whom possibly killed the other two.

I started at the beginning of the book, flipping through one page at a time, looking at every photo for sophomores, juniors, and seniors. I looked for any possible connection to Lucas and Carter. I saw students of a dozen ethnicities, wearing all kinds of clothes and listing every imaginable activity. But nothing seemed notable. No one else listed hunting and target practice as activities. No one else had a flat top haircut. No one else had dead eyes.

Judging by which subjects had the most number of pages in the book devoted to them, football and basketball loomed as the most important part of the high school experience. By contrast, the lack of pages focused on educational activities suggested that academics was of no account in this high school. But of course, on reflection, and from personal experience, it seemed that academic learning was of little account in many high schools.

Near the end of the book was a collection of casual photos taken at various events throughout the year. I scanned them fast, turning pages in a desire to be done. I'd just turned a page when I had the thought that maybe I'd seen something. I turned back.

There were several photos from what looked like a costume party. Kids were dressed in superhero costumes, laughing and holding up clear plastic glasses with colored drinks. One photo showed a boy standing next to a girl. He had his arm around her neck, the crook of his elbow bent at her throat, pulling her sideways and a bit off balance. The boy was thin and tall, the girl thin and short. The boy radiated confidence, the girl insecurity. The boy looked happy and dumb. The girl looked intelligent but frightened.

Under the photo was a caption that said, 'Flynn and Evan chillin.' If the words matched the people above them, Flynn was the boy, and Evan was the girl.

I looked closer. Two things stood out.

The first was that the girl was Evan Rosen, the house cleaner who cleaned for David Montrop, the murdered man in Incline Village.

The second thing that jumped out was the style of buttons on Evan's shirt. They were hard to see in detail. But they weren't the standard, simple plastic buttons. They appeared to be made of metal, and they had some kind of intricate pattern on them.

I leaned in closer, squinting my eyes to see more detail. The photo wasn't sufficiently detailed enough to be sure, but the buttons looked like the one we'd found in the hand of one of the murder victims. The symbol of an eagle with arrows and an olive branch.

THIRTY-TWO

I went back through the yearbook, checking every photo and name to see what class Flynn was in. I was careful not to go too fast. I determined that his photo was nowhere else in the book.

Evan's official photo was in with the sophomores. The caption said 'Evan Rosen.' The Activities section was blank.

I asked the librarian to direct me toward a copier.

He said they'd been having problems.

I said, no problem, I'd just check the yearbook out.

He said yearbooks were reference books that didn't circulate.

I said that I respected his concern and his allegiance to library protocol, but that the yearbook was important evidence in a murder case.

"I'm sorry. We have these rules for a reason. I can't make an exception for you. If I did, what would I say to everyone else?"

"Please understand that this is an important case, and I need you to make an exception. I will bring the book back soon."

The man stood up just a bit taller, puffed out his chest, and said, "No. What don't you understand about no?!"

I knew I could pull out the fake sheriff's badge I'd purchased years before in a Virginia City tourist shop. I knew I could lean over the counter and intimidate him by telling him a story that would suggest that he'd be on the receiving end of legal action and civil lawsuits if he didn't cooperate. I knew I could make it so he didn't sleep at night if he didn't acquiesce.

Instead, I said, "Okay. I'm sorry to hear that." I turned and walked out with the book.

Behind me, I heard him huff and puff and call out that I was breaking the law. But I was gone before any gendarmes came. I'd return the book when I was done with it, and perhaps include a nice donation to the Reno Friends of the Library.

THIRTY-THREE

I arrived at Evan's motel apartment just as she came back from her house cleaning.

"I've got a question for you, if you can spare a minute." I held the yearbook at my side so that it wasn't obvious.

"Let me set this stuff inside." She opened the door, set the buckets by the closet, then came back out on the little walkway that stretched across the front of the motel apartment building.

"I've learned that you went to Wilson High School in Reno," I said.

Her eyes widened with fear. "What does that have to do with my car getting stolen?"

"I'm not sure. But it might be connected. At least two of the suspects in the armored truck robbery also went to Wilson High. Those suspects are now dead. It's quite the coincidence that you also went there."

Evan tried to hide her fear behind a facade of toughness. "Wilson was a bad school in a bad neighborhood. I told you how Montrop said I came from a low station. Well, everyone at that school was from a low station. Kids without intact families. Kids with abusive guardians. Probably, you could find a hundred major crimes in the last ten years that were committed by kids who went to Wilson. Of course, most of them just started at Wilson and then dropped out."

"You mentioned kids with abusive guardians. Interesting choice of words."

Evan looked at me like I was dense. "It's a catchall term. Some kids had actual parents, usually just one who was off at a job all day. Some kids were orphans being raised in foster families. Some kids lived on the street, bouncing from a friend's couch to a shelter to sleeping in a car. Some guardians were great. They should get a medal. But you don't want to know how often kids were abused. Evil stepdads. Evil foster dads. Evil real dads. Evil boyfriends of drug-addicted moms. And sometimes, evil moms. Women can be as bad as men. But the hard truth is that most abusers are men. And the victims, both girls and boys, grow up in a warped world. They don't know what's normal. So they get into situations where they become repeat victims. Worse, some of them go on to abuse others."

"I'm sorry," I said, realizing that Evan was probably talking about herself and was likely a victim of abuse. "I'd like to show you some pictures," I said.

Her look of fear became more pronounced.

I opened the yearbook to the picture of Evan and Flynn.

"Where'd you get this?" she said, her tension obvious.

"It's the Wilson High School yearbook. Nine years ago. You went there?"

"Yes. Worst time of my life."

"This photo of you," I said. "The shirt you're wearing has unusual buttons. Do you remember the shirt?"

"Sure. In fact, I still have the shirt. But I should get rid of it because I never wear it. I wore it back then because my mother told me it belonged to my dad when he was a boy. So I used to wear it to feel closer to the idea of my dad. The dad I never met. The dad who was a deadbeat who abandoned us when Mia and I were very little. Why would I hang onto his shirt? I guess it's just another way that I don't have courage. I can't even throw out a connection to my loser dad. I'm as bad as Mia, living in a Neverland world of silly hopes and dreams."

"May I see the shirt?"

"Sure. What do I care?" She opened the apartment door, held it open for me, then walked over to the clothes rod in the corner, pushed some clothes back and forth. She found the shirt, lifted it off the rod, and carried it over. She handed it to me. "You can have it if you know someone that size."

I took the shirt and held it up. It had metallic buttons like in the photo and just like the one I'd seen gripped in the dead man's hand. The second button from the bottom was missing.

"Any idea where this button went?" I said, pointing.

"No." She frowned. "It wasn't missing the last time I looked at that shirt." She leaned over and fingered the fabric where torn threads dangled.

"When was the last time you wore this shirt?"

"Probably when that yearbook picture was taken."

"When was the last time you pulled this shirt out, a time when you might have noticed that the button was missing?"

"Years and years ago. I can't remember. I've just kept it with my clothes, moved my clothes when I moved, hung onto it simply because I never made the decision to throw it out. When you're poor, you just don't throw things away without making a conscious decision about it."

I nodded.

"Why are you asking about the missing button? How did you suspect it was missing?"

"We found two of the robbers from the armored truck robbery. They were dead, murdered. One of the dead robbers was clutching it in his hand."

Evan jerked as if she'd been slapped. She turned red. Her eyes took on a look of shock.

"Someone is framing me for the murder of the robbers! Just like framing me for the murder of David Montrop!"

"Let's say that's true," I said. "How do you imagine that this person, or these people, got into your apartment to steal the button and steal your car?"

"The car is easy to explain. The hide-a-key that I zip-tied under the fender was gone. Whoever took my car must have found it and cut it off. But I don't know how someone got into my closet and found that shirt. It's like… It's like someone was very careful about breaking in so that I didn't realize it had ever happened."

"You never noticed anything strange? There was never an indication that you'd been burglarized?"

"No. Nothing."

I didn't say anything.

In time, Evan calmed herself. "You said you found the truck robbers dead?"

"Two of them, yeah. I'd like to show you their pictures and see if you remember them."

"Okay."

I opened the book and showed her Lucas Jordan's photo. Evan inhaled and stared at it.

I waited a bit, then turned to the photo of Carter Remy. This time she gasped. "You said they were murdered?"

"Yes."

"Are you sure it was them? You saw their bodies?" The book in her hand shook so hard that the pages made a crinkling sound.

"Yeah. I found their bodies. They had driver's licenses. The photos matched."

She thought about it, then said, "Good."

"Good? You're glad they were murdered?"

She was quiet a long moment. "Yes."

"Why?"

She hesitated as if she wanted to say something and then reconsidered. "They were bad. They didn't deserve to live."

"What did they do that was so bad?"

She looked away. Her eyes were moist.

"Please tell me, Evan. It could help us find the other robbers."

Eventually, she said, "Bad stuff."

"There were two other robbers," I said. "But we haven't caught them. Can you think of any kids who spent time with these two?"

"I don't think these two were that close, but..." she stopped. She began turning pages. She flipped from one to the next, faster than a person could study the photos. It seemed that she was looking at the names, which were in alphabetical order. When she got to the Ps, she slowed and ran her finger down the page. She came to a picture labeled Gavin Pellman and tapped her finger on it.

"This guy," she said. Her voice was tense, monotone, spoken through locked teeth. Her fingertip vibrated. The knuckles on the hand that gripped the book were white.

"Gavin Pellman hung out with the other robbers?" I said.

Evan was staring as if she could see through the book. "At least some," she said. Then she spoke in a small voice that was mostly a hiss. "Maybe you'll find him dead, too."

THIRTY-FOUR

"You say that like you wouldn't mind if Gavin Pellman is dead."

Evan spoke in a whisper. "He didn't deserve to live, either."

"Did you ever see these three with a fourth person?"

Evan seemed in a kind of nightmare trance. Gradually, some of the tension went out of her face. It was several moments before she answered. "You know how high school is. There are some tight little groups, kids who are always together. These guys weren't like that. You'd see them individually in the halls between classes. They were loners, mostly. But when there are lots of kids in the halls, you can never tell who's in a group."

I asked, "What did these guys care about?"

"Not school, I can tell you that. Gavin was a hustler. Three card shuffle, poker, any trick that he could rig and get other kids to bet on. Lucas was into guns and knives. He always brought them to school."

"There's a rule against that, isn't there?"

Evan stared at me as if I were unimaginably dense. "No one paid any attention to the rules at Wilson High."

"Right," I said. "The third guy, Carter, what was he into?"

"Nothing. He was a total loner. All the kids in school could tell he was a psycho."

I reached for the book, and she thrust it into my hands, glad to be rid of it. "I'd like you to think about whether anyone else hung around with these kids."

Evan shook her head. "No one that I can remember."

"I want you to look at this other photo again." I flipped back to the photo of her and the boy named Flynn.

"Can you tell me about Flynn?" As I asked the question, I noticed that if you added a hundred pounds to the person in the picture, he'd look vaguely like Randy Bosworth at Reno

Armored.

"Not really. He was from another school. But he sometimes hung out at Wilson. I think he lived right on the other side of the boundary between different schools. His neighbor friends went to Wilson, but he had to go to another school."

"Did you know him well?"

"No. He was just around. Someone took a picture of us, that's all."

"What was his last name?"

Evan shook her head. "He was just Flynn. I don't remember him or anyone else ever saying his last name."

"Was he friends with the robbers, Lucas and Carter?"

"I don't know."

"If Gavin was the third robber, could Flynn have been the fourth robber?"

"I don't know. Maybe. But probably not. The other three were… bad. Flynn was more normal."

"More normal. Not totally normal?"

Evan looked at me. "A totally normal kid would not hang out at Wilson High."

"Why?"

"Because Wilson was a center of bad kids doing bad things. The Wilson neighborhood was full of scum. Any good kid who could avoid Wilson would stay a long way away. The only good kids at Wilson were there because they had no choice."

"Any idea where Flynn is now?"

She shook her head.

"Can you think of anyone who knew him well enough that they might have kept in touch with him?"

"No."

I thought about Bosworth's accent, which I'd first thought was originally Cockney and then wondered if it was Australian. "Was Flynn American, or from a different country?"

Evan frowned. "I assume he's American. But now that you mention it, he did have a little bit of an accent of some kind. Since I moved up to the lake, I've met some skiers who come to Tahoe on an exchange program from Australia. Flynn sort of sounded like them. But it was a long time ago, so I might be way off."

"You say that good kids would never hang around Wilson High. What about you?"

"I wasn't that good of a kid. I did some bad stuff. I should have stayed by myself at home or gone to the library and read books. But I was too stupid to leave."

"What bad stuff did you do?"

"Nothing like the real bad kids. But I cultivated a hard personality. I picked on kids who were smaller or younger than me. I'm very ashamed of that."

I closed the yearbook and thanked Evan for her time.

As I walked away, she called out my name.

"Owen?"

I turned around. "Yeah?"

"I'm sorry those pictures made me so tense. I forgot to thank you for the rides you gave me. You probably kept me from losing some customers."

"You're welcome." I got into the Jeep to leave.

The motel parking lot could be accessed from both ends. This time I was close to the far end. So I drove out, turned onto the street. There was a ski and sport shop that I hadn't known about. It backed up to the back side of the motel apartment. The shop was closed, but it gave me an idea to check on later.

THIRTY-FIVE

It was late when Spot and I got home. I checked in with Street. She seemed okay. I still didn't tell her about the ski pole spear through the Jeep. I wanted to give more thought to potential repercussions.

The next morning, I called Sergeant Lanzen and arranged to meet her at the Incline Village Substation.

We stood outside in a parking lot and talked next to the Jeep. She rubbed Spot's head.

I said, "Yesterday, when I was in Reno, I talked to El Dorado Sergeant Bains. He said that one of the murdered truck robbers had an old newspaper clipping in his wallet. The clipping was about a football game. I tracked it to Wilson High. Just as I got there, they had a bomb scare. I got out before they locked it down."

"Wilson High drives the Reno police crazy. Some crank caller does this every month or two. Nothing ever happens, so they wonder if it's a student who's just trying to disrupt class. But, of course, they have to treat it seriously."

"I ended up going to the Reno Library and looked at Wilson High School yearbooks. I found photos of the two murdered robbers. I also found a picture of Evan Rosen with another boy."

"They all went to the same school?" Lanzen said. "There's an interesting bit of information."

"Evan was a year or two behind the boys," I said. "So I drove up to Evan's place and asked her about it. When I told her about the robbers and showed her their pictures from the yearbook, she got visibly upset."

"Upset that they died?"

"No, upset at just seeing their photos. She has some traumatic memory associated with the robbers. She was glad they died."

"Being glad they're dead is a strong emotion," Lanzen said.

"She gave you no indication of what this memory was?"

"No."

"Do you think it could have been strong and bad enough to give her motive for killing them?"

"Maybe. But as I've gotten to know her a bit, she doesn't seem like the killing type. Aside from my belief that the killer would have to have much more size and strength than a petite woman."

"Okay, let me know if anything else turns up." We said goodbye, and she drove off in her unmarked.

I drove to Tahoe Vista and went into the ski shop I'd seen behind Evan's motel apartment the evening before.

"Hey," the young salesman said.

"I've got an unusual question about the history of ski poles," I said.

"Try me."

"Do you know when manufacturers stopped making sharp ski pole points and switched to the square and circular ice tips that are less dangerous if one were to fall on the sharp end?"

"That would require knowledge of ancient history. Let me get our resident ancient history expert." He walked behind a counter, leaned in through an open door and called out. "Hey, Michael, do you know when they stopped making sharp ski pole points?"

I heard movement, a chair being slid, a filing cabinet drawer sliding shut. A man in his sixties emerged from the doorway.

"You mean the pointy version of sharp?" he said. "Because new ski pole tips are very sharp. They grip ice better than the pointy ones ever did."

"Right," I said. "I'm curious about the pointy ones, the ones that are dangerous if you fall on the point."

"Well, it's funny you ask. I was actually thinking about that very question a couple of weeks ago because we decided to clean out the storeroom before summer gets into full swing. And in the way back, where it's so dark you can't even see, there are these bins. And in the bins were a bunch of old, used ski poles. These would have been from our rental program back when I was a kid. And sure enough, those poles had the old pointy tips. So I was thinking about how long the industry used such points. We're talking fifty years ago."

"What did the poles look like?"

He looked puzzled. "Like regular ski poles, absent the fancy colors and graphics of today. Silvery aluminum. All scratched and bent here and there."

"Could I look at them?"

"Sorry, we tossed them. Later, I thought maybe I should have found a recycling company to take them. I don't know that they could be reformed into beer cans or anything like that, but I'm hoping the trash company didn't just toss them into a landfill. Why the curiosity?"

"Sorry for all the questions. I'm an investigator on an El Dorado County crime, and we found some ski poles at the scene. Do you know how long your poles sat in the dumpster?"

He frowned. "I hope I'm not in trouble for tossing poles."

"Not at all."

"We get a pickup each Tuesday and Friday, and we were doing our spring cleaning on Sunday. So a couple of days."

"Could someone other than the trash company have taken them out of the dumpster?"

"Well, sure. But why? People care about style and things looking new. It would be a rare person who'd want a fifty-year-old ski pole. Now, if you wanted to barbecue a goat on a spit or something, I suppose you could use a pole for that. Of course, you'd have to cut off the basket."

"How many poles do you think you tossed?"

"Lots. Several dozen."

"Where is your dumpster?"

The man swung his arm around and vaguely pointed at the back wall. "It's just behind the shop, right near the back of the motel apartments."

"Thanks. I appreciate your time."

"Either that or I go back to paying bills," he said.

THIRTY-SIX

Spot and I headed to the South Shore, where I drove to the hospital.

The woman at the hospital reception counter was in her mid sixties. She was plump and white haired and wore silver reading glasses that matched her spare, dangly, silver earrings. She emanated comfort and professionalism.

"Good afternoon," I said. "I've come to visit Jonas Montrop, a young man who is a crime victim and apparently has a police officer guarding his door."

"Right here in this very hospital?" She widened her eyes as if in surprise, yet I was certain that she was aware of it.

"Right here, indeed," I said. I pulled out my investigator's license. "And I'm involved in the case."

"Oh, my," she said, raising her eyebrows as she looked at my license. "I was an accountant in my past life, and I never thought there could be an occupation more exciting than that. But a real-life detective must come close!"

"I don't know. If I even think about doing the books or taxes, my heartrate goes up, my breathing goes short, and my fight-or-flight impulse kicks in. Intentionally going into battle with numbers? Wow, you'd have to be made of strong stuff."

"Well, of course, that's how I always thought about it. You want me to do an audit? How thrilling! Let me get my sword and shield!" She looked at her computer screen, clicked the mouse, tapped some keys. "Please give me a moment to check on one little thing." She reached for my ID, then picked up the phone, and pressed some buttons. "Officer Cronin? Betty Jean at the reception desk." She angled my ID so she could better read the tiny print. "I have a Mr. Owen McKenna here. He's an investigator and wants to visit Mr. Montrop." She paused. "That's okay? All right, I'll send him up." Like a well-trained hotel receptionist, she didn't say Jonas's room number out loud. Probably, discretion about patient privacy is even more important than discretion about hotel guest privacy. More so for someone who is under armed guard. She wrote a room number on a pad, tore the sheet off, and handed it to me. "This is his room, and the elevators are over there." She pointed. "If you need anything else, please let me know."

"Thank you very much."

She grinned as I left. Personable. Understated. Elegant, if not beautiful. If Street ever took her youthful, vibrant, sexy, vivacious, irresistible self off to a life without me, I might call this kind, older woman and plan a lifetime of fireside chats with her. She could even help with my taxes.

I could tell where Jonas Montrop's room was when I got off the elevator and turned down the hall because there was a uniformed cop dressed in city blues standing by a door.

"Owen McKenna?" he said as I approached.

"Yes. Have we met?"

"Nope. But I've heard Commander Mallory say stuff about you."

"That sounds intimidating," I said.

"No, it's not bad. I mean, I'm not saying he was, you know, crooning your virtues. But I sensed some respect."

It was a decent recovery. "Ah," I said. "Is Jonas up for having a visitor?"

The cop shrugged. "He's pretty out of it. And I have to stay in the room while you're in there."

"Mallory say that in case I showed up?"

The cop grinned. "That's Mallory's rule for any visitor." Then he lowered his voice and turned so that no one, Jonas or otherwise, could hear. "Maybe you know this, but the kidnapper strung the kid up expecting that he would die. So now Mallory's worried that the kidnapper might come into the hospital to finish the job."

I nodded. "I think Mallory's caution is smart."

"You should also know that Jonas Montrop isn't what you'd call communicative. I heard a doc say he wasn't in a coma, but let me tell you, he is one sleepy kid."

"Got it," I said.

I turned and walked into the room.

Jonas looked more like a dead body under the white covers than a vital young man. His slight build looked even scrawnier than when I'd pulled him out of the boat. The only parts of him that were exposed were his right arm and head. His right wrist had a nasty burn ring from where the rope had chafed. An IV was taped at the inside of his elbow.

Jonas's eyes were closed. His eyelids made a dramatic bulge over what seemed like large eyeballs. The appearance was probably created from losing weight over the three days he was tied up. Beneath his eyes, the skin was dark gray-blue.

"Mr. Montrop," the cop said to the motionless form. "You have a visitor. A man named Owen McKenna is here to talk to you."

"Hi Jonas," I said to the motionless form. "Sorry to bother you. I'm hoping you can answer some questions. Can you hear me?"

I sensed movement. A foot twitched. A leg bent at the knee. The left arm flexed, a hand emerged from under the covers. Fingers gripped the edge of the sheet and blanket. He didn't tug at the blanket, just held it.

He didn't open his eyes, but his eyeballs moved beneath the lids, left and right, like he was having an intense dream. It was similar to what I'd seen with dying people, movement in response to spoken words, but the stimulus wasn't enough to bring them to consciousness.

"Can you hear me, Jonas?" I said again. I reached out and touched the fingers gripping the blankets.

His hand jerked, and his grip intensified, knuckle skin going whiter than before.

"They're coming!" His voice was high and frightened. His eyes were now clenched tight, a frown creasing his forehead.

"It's okay, Jonas," I said. "You're safe now."

He turned his head sideways on the pillow, the frown more intense. His eyes started to open, wavered, closed again. His left arm started to reach up toward his face, then stopped.

"Ow! My shoulder..."

The rope burn on the left wrist was even more pronounced, with areas of crusted scabs. He'd have scars after it healed.

He opened his eyes, stared at me for a moment as if I were a monster, then looked past me, elsewhere around the room. "Who are you?" he said, his voice shaky with fear.

"Owen McKenna. I'm the guy who found you tied up on the boat." In my peripheral vision, I saw the cop at the door turn his head toward me.

"What? How did you find me?" His voice was less worried as if fear was replaced by curiosity.

"I'm an investigator helping the cops. I found you three days after your kidnapping." I didn't want to immediately tell him about his stepfather's death for the same reason that Sergeant Lanzen didn't want to give the news to Evan until after we'd asked most of our other questions.

Jonas reached up his other arm, stopped as before, then moved the side of his face against his pillow as if to wipe away an invisible spider web filament that was tickling him. Or maybe he was trying to clear the fog from his brain. He blinked hard several times, like a person waking up.

"A nurse told me I was tied up," he said, his voice clearer. "I can see pictures in my mind. But I can't tell what are memories and what are the things she said. I was in my boat. I remember that."

"Where did you get the boat?"

"My stepdad gave it to me. I just sold it to a friend. But the boat got a leak, and he didn't want it anymore."

"Who's your friend?"

"Flynn."

"What is Flynn's last name?"

"I never knew. He just went by Flynn. Like Prince or Sting. It was always just Flynn.

"How did you know Flynn?" I asked.

"I've always known Flynn. He goes all the way back in my memory." Jonas frowned. "He was a kid in the neighborhood. We were both outcasts, so we kind of hung together."

"What neighborhood?"

"We lived in the projects."

The reference didn't fit for where his stepfather David Montrop lived in Incline Village, because the entire town was upper middle class or richer.

"What city?" I asked.

Jonas had turned his face to rub his cheek on the pillow again, up and down like a horse scratching its cheek on a fence post.

"Incline Village. That was my stepdad's joke. We were up off Mt. Rose Highway. There was a townhouse project that went in. Smallish units. My stepdad thought it was funny to call it the projects."

"Why were you and Flynn outcasts?"

"The usual reasons. We're skinny, awkward kids who don't know how to talk to girls. We always got pushed around by the bigger kids."

"How old are you, Jonas?"

"Twenty-three."

"And Flynn?"

"I don't know. Older than me. Twenty-seven, maybe."

"I was told that Flynn lived in Reno during high school."

"Yeah. His mom moved down there for some job."

"Where does Flynn live now?"

Another frown. "I don't know. Someplace on the West Shore, I think. He's never told me where. Flynn keeps getting more secretive as he gets older, like he's turned into a spy or something."

"Why did you sell him your boat?"

"Because he asked me to. He said he'd always wanted a boat. And I needed the money. My stepdad said I could have the boat. The house where it was moored was owned by one of his bands."

"You refer to the bands like they were your dad's bands," I said.

"Well, they weren't really his bands. He just managed them. Booked their venues. Watched over their houses. He told them he was like a caretaker, making sure everything stayed in good shape. But the reality was that he used their houses for his own purposes."

"How many are there?"

"Why don't you ask him? Three that I know of. West Shore, South Shore, and East Shore. He parties at those houses. Uses their cars. Goes out on their boats. That's why he got sick of his own boat. Why hassle with a boat that was old and leaked when you have use of a new cruiser?"

"These bands that own the houses and boats, they must be really successful."

Jonas's eyes got wide, and he nodded. "You have no idea. But I can never tell anyone the names of the bands because then their houses would be vulnerable. My stepdad says that if people knew about the houses in Tahoe and then they saw the band on TV performing a concert in London or something, they might break into the houses. So everything was designed to obfuscate. That's my stepdad's buzzword. He always says obfuscation is fortification."

I asked, "When did you move to the South Shore?"

"When my stepdad kicked me out of his place in Incline."

"You say that like you're still angry at him."

"Of course I'm angry. I hate him. He's the biggest jerk I've ever met. When I was little, we lived in San Francisco for a year. Then he got in trouble with the cops. You know what he did? He blamed me. He said that having me around made it impossible to be a businessman, that I tied him down. How was I responsible for him breaking the law or whatever he did? He was always a cheat. I knew it from the time I was a young kid. All my life I've been trying to distance myself from him." Jonas frowned. "Why are you asking me all these questions about my stepdad? And why am I saying all of this private stuff? It must be these drugs they've got me on."

I said, "Can you tell me what happened when you were kidnapped?"

Jonas jerked as if the memory were searing.

THIRTY-SEVEN

"I don't remember much about the kidnapping," he said. "I was sleeping. There was a crash. Somebody grabbed me and pulled me out of bed. There were two guys. They were wearing hoodies and hockey masks. That was the scariest moment of my life. They didn't say anything. I tried to grab at the bed and the chair I keep nearby, but I couldn't get a grip. They were really strong. Of course, probably any guy would be strong compared to me. They put duct tape over my mouth and dragged me outside. I had my underwear on, but nothing else."

Jonas was breathing hard. He turned and reached for a plastic cup by his hospital bed, groaning at what I assumed was shoulder pain. The cup had a lid and a straw. As he picked it up, he shook so hard, I worried he'd drop the cup. But he managed a sip.

"What else do you remember about your kidnapping? They took you away in a vehicle?"

Jonas nodded. "They had an old van. A third guy got out of the van. He wore a mask, too. They threw me inside the back door, and two of them sat on me. Then they taped my wrists and ankles together. One of them leaned down and whispered in my ear. He said he'd cut my throat open if I made another noise. So I went silent. I just lay there and shivered. It was really cold. I felt like I would freeze to death. The van started up. So I guess the third guy must have gotten in the driver's seat. They drove awhile. I couldn't see anything. After a few minutes, I realized that I should have been paying attention to their turns. But I didn't have the focus to notice. They looked like aliens with their hockey masks. It was terrifying. And I was shivering. Lying on the metal floor of the van was like lying on ice."

Jonas paused to breathe. It seemed like the memory had him shivering now.

I asked, "When the guy spoke to you, did his voice sound

familiar?"

"No. He whispered. You can't tell a person by a whisper. Right? At least, I can't."

"What happened next?"

"After a while, the van stopped."

"How long had it been driving?"

"I don't know. Ten minutes. Fifteen. The back door opened. They put a tarp next to me on the floor of the van and pushed me onto it. One of them whispered again, telling me that if I struggled or made a noise, they were going to drown me in the ice cold lake. So I didn't do anything. They rolled me up in the tarp. I freaked out even though I was trying not to move or say anything. It was just like when I was little, and some bullies at the Judgment Sunday School in San Francisco rolled me up in the church's stage rug and left me there. I would've died if Father Duncan hadn't forgotten his briefcase and come back late that night to retrieve it. And this time it was you. That makes twice somebody saved my life. I guess I should say thanks."

"You're welcome. What happened next?"

"They picked me up, and one of them put me over his shoulder and started walking. It was like I weighed nothing to him. The next thing I knew, the guy carrying me started swaying, and I realized I was on a boat. After a while, they moved me to another boat, and I thought it was my boat – the boat I sold to Flynn – because I smelled kerosene. I'd broken a kerosene lamp in the cuddy cabin right after I'd agreed to sell the boat. No matter how I washed the flooring, I couldn't get the smell out.

"Anyway, they carried me down into the cuddy. Then they unwrapped me. They still had on the masks. They took the tape off my wrists and tied lines to me, yanking up my arms and stringing the lines to stowage lockers on either side. I felt like I was crucified like Jesus, only without the cross. By then it was getting light out. They stayed there drinking this disgusting smelling liquor. Some kind of whiskey, I think. I don't know. I've barely had a beer in my life.

"My shoulders were starting to scream with pain. Then they took the tape off my mouth. They said I might need to talk to my father to convince him I was still alive. So one of them called my stepdad. That person had a second phone. I don't know how it worked, but it was like he had an app on the second phone that disguised his voice and made him sound like a woman. When he talked softly into the first phone, the woman's voice came out loud and went into the second phone which was connected to my stepdad. Even though I was close, I couldn't hear his normal voice, just the louder, fake, woman's voice. So I leaned my head forward and shouted into the phone that was dialed to my dad. But two of the guys jerked me away and put tape back on my mouth. Meanwhile, the third person kept using the two phones, making it sound like a woman, telling my stepdad to get money from the bank and where to put the money. After a while I began to think that the third person really was a woman behind the hockey mask, and the second phone was just to disguise her voice."

"Where did he or she tell your stepdad to put the money?"

"In a trash can in a parking lot. At first, I couldn't understand what was happening. They were talking to my stepdad like they could see what he was doing, like they were there at the bank. But we were on the South Shore, and my stepdad lives in Incline on the North Shore. At least, that's where I thought he was. Then I saw that the phone guy – that's how I thought of him – the guy holding the phones had a third phone propped up on one of the stowage lockers. That phone had a moving picture on it of where my stepdad was."

"Do you think there was a fourth person taking video of your dad and feeding it into the phone guy's phone?"

"That's what I thought at the time. But later, when I was alone on the boat, I started to fall asleep. My legs would collapse as I drifted off, and I'd drop down until the lines on my arms jerked tight. It felt like my arms were going to pull out of their sockets. Anyway, I had these visions. One was like I was looking out from inside the grill on my stepdad's Mercedes. I realized they might have put a webcam or two on my stepdad's car. Then they could watch wherever he was and see where he was going."

"What happened after they made the call?"

"They left. They put another piece of tape on my mouth just to be sure I couldn't push it off with my tongue. Then they took their whiskey bottle, climbed out of the cuddy cabin, and shut the door, leaving me tied up by my arms. I was all alone in the boat, unable to scream. My arms felt like they were being ripped off."

"That would be scary," I said.

"The thing is, I'm a classics major. I've read about all kinds of terrible stuff, but I don't do stuff. Having someone torture me was so far out of my experience, I felt helpless. I cried for hours. Then things got foggy. All I can remember was struggling to keep standing so my arms wouldn't be yanked off. But I kept falling asleep and dropping down."

Jonas looked stressed and worried. I wondered if he was about to cry.

I said, "If someone knew your stepfather had money, he or she might single you out for kidnapping. But that doesn't explain why someone would tie you up to die in a boat. Like you just said, that's torture. It suggests a motive much different than money, almost as if the money were an afterthought. Can you think of anyone that might apply to? Someone whose primary goal was to inflict pain on you?"

Jonas was shaking his head. "I'm totally, like, no threat to anyone. There's no reason why someone would torture me! I couldn't be a threat if I wanted to. I have no enemies, just like I have no friends. I'm a nobody. I live alone, I go to community college. I don't get together with anyone. I don't even know anyone to play video games with except my internet group. So there's no reason why someone would target me for any reason other than to get money from my stepdad. I think they just tortured me because they're sick. They wanted to punish me for being the stepson of money." Jonas was shaking his head. "All they had to do was look at my little rented cabin and my VW bus that doesn't run. It's obvious that I have no money. My stepdad never gave me anything beyond my school allowance of a thousand dollars a month. You can't do anything on a thousand dollars a month! I'm having to take out school loans just to eat!"

"Where is your mother? Could she help out?"

"She died when I was little." Jonas was breathing hard.

I waited a minute for him to calm down. "Where do you

normally keep your boat? Flynn's boat."

"At the house that belonged to the band. On the South Shore."

I asked, "Has the doctor said how long you need to be in the hospital?"

"She said I can go as soon as my shoulders heal enough that I can take care of myself. I don't know when that will be. I still can't reach my hands up to my face. I have to be able to take care of myself because there's no one to help. You'll probably find this hard to believe, but my stepdad has never visited me here. He hasn't even called. That tells you what a close family he and I are."

"Jonas, do you have siblings?"

"No, why?"

"I'm sorry to tell you this, but your stepfather was found dead four days ago, the day you were kidnapped."

"What?!" Jonas was shocked. His eyes moistened. "I knew his cancer was… terminal. But I didn't know he was that close to death."

"He didn't die from the cancer. He was killed in his driveway. Someone threw his paddle board at him. The board struck him in the head."

Jonas stared, his face a mix of confusion and horror. "I don't understand. He was murdered? Why?"

"We don't know."

Jonas's eyes went back and forth, focused on some distant idea outside of the hospital room. Tears filled his lower lids. Jonas turned his head again, trying to wipe the tears on the pillow. He turned away from me, embarrassed at his emotion.

"I'm sorry about the news, Jonas. It's a hard thing to absorb."

"Who did it?" Jonas said, angry. "He was a miserable jerk. But he didn't deserve to die like that. Who killed him?"

"We have no idea."

"Do you think that his murder was somehow connected to my kidnapping?"

"We don't know that, either. We learned that your kidnapper ransomed you for twenty-five thousand dollars. David Montrop withdrew that amount from his bank in Incline Village. After that, we have no idea what happened. Some time later, Montrop's gardener found him dead in his driveway. The money was gone."

"I never trusted Kang," Jonas said.

"Why?"

"I don't know. It's just a feeling I get from him."

I took out my card and set it on the table next to Jonas's bed. "When you're ready to go home, call me. Maybe I can help."

"What do I do next?" Jonas was pleading.

"Rest. Heal. Then we'll talk some more."

Jonas's face changed. I couldn't identify his look exactly. Wonderment, maybe. After I said goodbye, nodded at the cop, and walked away down the hall, I had the sense that Jonas had rarely if ever experienced someone being nice to him.

THIRTY-EIGHT

Back in the Jeep, I thought about what I'd learned. I couldn't make a clear picture out of the case or even convincingly connect David Montrop's murder to the robbers' murders. Complicating the case were the multiple jurisdictions involved. Montrop was murdered in Washoe County, Sergeant Lanzen's territory. The armored truck robbery was in the county where Street and I live, Douglas County, which is Sergeant Diamond Martinez's turf. Jonas Montrop had been kidnapped and tied up in the city of South Lake Tahoe, SLT Commander Mallory's grounds. I'd found the murdered robbers in Sergeant Bains' El Dorado County. The only person I'd found with connections to all of the murder victims was Evan Rosen, and she lived in Placer County.

I knew I'd be talking to Diamond soon, so I first called Sergeant Lanzen and told her about my conversation with Jonas Montrop. My next call was to the SLT police, and I said nearly the same words to Mallory. After that, I dialed the El Dorado Sheriff's Office and got put through to Sergeant Bains's voicemail. I left a message saying I had some things to go over. He called back in a minute.

"I've got a meeting in five minutes at D.L. Bliss State Park," Bains said. "It won't take long."

"I'm on the South Shore. How 'bout I come out there?"

"That works. Meet me at the trailhead to Rubicon Trail. Twenty minutes or so."

Twenty minutes later, I pulled into the park, drove out near the trailhead, and parked.

Spot and I walked over to an overlook and stared down at the water. Just out from the Rubicon Trail, the water hides a cliff over 1200 feet straight down, one of the grander underwater drop-offs in the world. The result of such deep water is a mesmerizing indigo blue. Even Spot seemed entranced.

"McKenna," a voice called out. Sergeant Bains walked over, shook my hand, pet Spot. "You want to find a place to sit? Or we could make it a walk-and-talk and let your hound run."

"The park has a leash law like every other place in Tahoe."

Bains pointed to his sheriff's badge. "Somebody complains, I'll assure them that law enforcement is going to find the responsible culprit and exact an appropriate punishment."

So we headed out the Rubicon Trail, the beginning of which follows a cliff ledge with vertical dropoffs straight down to the water. Spot never seemed to be respectful enough of the dangers, but he'd been here before, as well as on many cliffs, so I wasn't worried.

"What you got?" Bains said as we walked.

"You recall the murder of the man in Incline Village."

"Right," Bains said.

"I have evidence linking the man's house cleaner to the robbery suspects. The evidence is circumstantial. And my gut instinct tells me that it is misleading. But I told you I'd report whatever I learned about the case."

"Ready to be misled," Bains said.

"The house cleaner, Evan Rosen, lives in Tahoe Vista. Nine years ago, she went to Wilson High School in Reno, the same high school as the two dead armored truck robbers. I cannot directly connect her to the robbery, however I recently saw her pay her neighbor for rides. She peeled the bills off what looked like a large wad of cash. And I saw her picture in a Wilson High School yearbook. In the photo, she's wearing a shirt with buttons on it very much like the one we found in the robber's hand. She still has the shirt, and she showed it to me. It has a button missing."

"That's certainly compelling."

"Unfortunately, there's more. When I showed Evan the pictures of the dead robbers, she got upset just seeing them. She said she was glad they were dead."

"Whoa," Bains said.

"I asked her why. She wouldn't explain, but she said they didn't deserve to live. She wouldn't say why. It seems obvious that these guys did something to make her hate them."

"Like..." Bains broke off.

"No idea. Maybe they hurt her sister Mia or something."

"Yet, despite this circumstantial evidence, you think it's misleading," Bains said. "All because of your gut instinct. Perhaps you can elaborate?"

"I don't think she committed those murders."

"Why?"

"She doesn't seem like the type. I will say that she admitted that she is a bit of a hothead. That can lead to impulsiveness, and some people who murder exhibit impulsiveness. But you know that it takes more than that for a person to murder. Murderers are amoral or stupid or devious or mean, or all of the above. Evan doesn't seem like any of those things. Also, the paddle board murder as well as the ski pole murders would require a lot of strength, and she is a diminutive person."

"But the evidence points to her," Bains said.

"'Points to her' is too strong a phrase for this situation. Nevertheless, this information is what I wanted to tell you. Doing my duty against my desire. I believe that after you investigate, you will agree with me."

"Do you have an address?"

I gave it to him. "End unit on a converted motel. I should let you know that she takes care of her sister Mia, who has some kind of disability. So if you question her, maybe be gentle, okay?"

"Gentle? Wow, you must have been a tough cop back in the day."

"Yeah. That's me. Tough."

THIRTY-NINE

After Bains and I finished talking, I was thinking about Montrop's gardener Kang, the man who supposedly didn't speak English but whom I'd seen talking to the Reno Armored receptionist Rita.

I drove north around the lake and parked on a side street a half mile down from Montrop's house. I left Spot in the Jeep and walked up toward Montrop's neighborhood. I didn't turn up the street that led to his driveway. Instead, I walked along the next street down. When I thought I was nearest to Montrop's house, I turned into the forest and made my way up toward his street. When Montrop's house came into partial view through the trees, I shifted to the side until I could get a glimpse of the steep driveway.

As I got close, I realized that I couldn't remember if this was one of the days when Kang was scheduled at Montrop's house. Might as well wait and find out.

Evan had said that she thought he knew more English than he revealed. If that were true, and I tried to talk to him, he would play the same role as before. But if I waited until he left and followed him, maybe I'd witness him going someplace where he might speak to someone else. If I caught him in that contradiction, I might be able to pressure him into telling me what he knew about Montrop or Rita and the Reno Armored company.

I knew that if I went up to the house, he might see me before I saw him. So I waited in the trees down below, hoping that I would see him when he left.

Kang came walking down the drive 45 minutes later. At the street, he turned left. I waited until he was 30 yards away, then stepped out of the trees and followed him. If Kang turned, he'd see me. But at this distance, I thought he probably wouldn't recognize me.

Kang went up over a rise, then down out of my sight. I jogged up the same rise. When I got to the top, Kang was nowhere in sight. I strode down fast, looking into the woods. Nothing.

There was an intersection ahead, where a road came from below and made a T with the street I was on. I heard the whine of a starter motor. The engine fired, the small, soft sound of a 4 cylinder. The sound appeared to come from the side street. The engine made just the slightest revving sound, then went silent, consistent with a driver giving a car enough gas to get it off the shoulder but then taking his foot off the gas as he turned downslope and let the car accelerate on its own under the force of gravity.

I turned back the way I'd come, sprinting back over the small rise, turning into the woods, and running as fast as I could for the Jeep.

I had my key out as I got close. In a practiced motion, I was inside the Jeep, got it running, and drove away fast.

The road I was on went vaguely toward the road Kang was on, but how or if it connected was not clear. There was an intersection ahead. I guessed that turning down the mountain would be the likeliest direction Kang was going. I cranked the wheel and skidded around the corner, barely slowing. The road made an S-turn through the forest and went by scattered homes. I came to another intersection and again turned down, figuring that it was unlikely that Kang, a gardener, lived in such a luxurious neighborhood. All of the roads out of the neighborhood went down.

At the next intersection, I went straight, then came to the Mt. Rose Highway. I took a right and headed down toward the lake, accelerating to a high speed.

A quarter mile ahead was a small silver car with the dull finish of an older vehicle. As I got close, I could see that it was a Kia. Closer still, I could see that the driver appeared to be a male about the size of Kang. I couldn't tell if it was Kang for certain, but I was reasonably sure, so I dropped back.

The silver Kia turned west on Highway 28. I followed it around Crystal Bay and through Kings Beach. It turned right on

267. I stayed back several car lengths as I followed it up and over Brockway Summit. The man drove fast, and as the traffic in front of him turned off into Northstar, the Kia accelerated and flew through the Martis Valley and on into Truckee.

Kang went through the old railroad town at high speed, worked his way over to Donner Pass Road, turned off on Northwoods Boulevard, and drove up into the Tahoe Donner subdivision.

I had to stay farther back to avoid being seen, and I nearly lost Kang as he wound around the arc of houses that front the circular golf course. When I came to a section with more visibility, he was gone. I didn't want to slow dramatically and make myself more obvious, so I continued on, following the large loop of Northwoods Boulevard all the way around and eventually retracing my steps. This time I drove a bit slower, but still kept up a pace that would not look suspicious to anyone. I also tried to look in opposite directions from my earlier loop, paying special attention to the side roads.

After several intersections, I glimpsed a silver car down a road to the left. There was no way I could drive by it without being obvious, so I pulled over and parked in front of a house.

No doubt it was obvious that I didn't belong in the neighborhood. So I put two clip pens in my shirt pocket, and I grabbed my clipboard with the pad of paper that has several paragraphs of boilerplate legalese in a small font and short descriptions in a larger font with check boxes to the side. From the glove box, I pulled out my official bureaucrat's clip-on name tag with an insert I'd made on my computer. It showed my name in red with words underneath in black that identified me as a certified county inspector, badge #69834, my commission expiration date listed as the following February 19th, and, in the really fine print beneath that, two sentences that broadly defined liability limits and two sentences that outlined complaint procedures along with the county website address and toll free phone number to call with further questions.

I got out in full view of the world. I opened the rear hatch and pulled out my white hard hat with the reflective orange hazard tape and put it on.

I turned around slowly as if to survey the neighborhood, then held my phone up in the air as if I were taking a Geiger Counter reading. I made several notations on my pad, walked across the nearest intersection, repeated the dance with my phone and pen and paper, then pocketed my phone. Any observant neighbors would never bother me, having seen first hand that I was just another self-important, officious, government didact who was wasting tax dollars while searching out minor civic infractions and code violations by people doing much more important work. Those people would not engage with me for fear that I would pay them even more attention as I wrote them multiple citations.

I walked with purpose down the road where I'd glimpsed the silver Kia. It was parked on the street between two houses, giving no clear indication as to which house Kang might have gone. I strode on past as if I had no interest in the car.

Twenty yards farther down, I sensed movement in my peripheral vision. Turning my head a minimal amount, I could see Kang in the back yard of one of the houses. He was standing at the corner of a broad, square patio, putting his key into the lock of an adjacent shed.

I continued on as if not noticing him. As I walked, I wondered about the house. It wasn't grand, but it was far nicer than anything a gardener could typically afford.

When I came to a landscaped area with heavy plantings of manzanita and fir trees that fronted a small forest of young Lodgepole Pine, I took off my hard hat and ducked into the cover. I lowered my head to go beneath branches and walked back away from the street, weaving through the closely-spaced pines.

Ahead was a large group of boulders, one nearly the size of a house. I went around it, and on the far side found a group of bushes, Chinquapin, I think, that gave me good cover as I sneaked up on Kang's patio.

Except that it wasn't a patio. It was a mat of some kind, square-shaped, about twenty feet on a side. The shed door was open. Kang came out of the door. He was barefoot and wearing sweat pants and a hoodie. He began doing stretches. After five minutes, Kang started making a series of martial arts moves, slow and methodical, his arm and leg positions seemingly more about the art and esthetics of martial arts than exercise. Where other men came home after work, popped open a Budweiser, opened a bag of chips, put their feet up, and turned on the TV, Kang came home and exercised.

Next, Kang reached into the shed and pulled out a brown staff three or four feet long, close to the length of a ski pole. It seemed about an inch and a half in diameter, possibly made of rattan. He held it out in front of him and spun it the way a baton twirler spins a silver baton, but using both hands flipping the pole over and over at high speed. The stick blurred like an airplane propeller, and he made it jump to his side and behind him and then to his other side. Periodically, he would stop the spinning and thrust the stick like a sword or swing it in elaborate ways as he began to do physical moves like a gymnast.

I'd only been exposed to formal stick fighting a few times, but as I watched Kang, it struck me that an accomplished stick fighter might have an advantage over an equally accomplished sword fighter because the stick fighter can grab the stick from either end or in the middle. The stick fighter can stab and lunge and block. A stick fighter can wield his weapon with two hands much more easily than can a sword fighter.

Kang was clearly an expert, and he built his workout to a frenzy of explosive moves that would make me want the protection of an Army tank should I be his foe in a conflict.

I heard a phone chirp. Fortunately, it wasn't mine.

Kang stopped his workout, stuck his stick in a small hole in the ground so that it stood, easy to pick up without bending over. Kang walked into the shed, and came back out with his phone in his hand. He was breathing hard, and he took several quick breaths before pressing the answer button.

"Hello?" he said.

There was a pause.

"No," he said, "I told you I'll have the money soon."

From my place in the bushes, I could hear him clearly. Gone was any pretense of a struggle with language. His English was perfect, his accent standard American English as if he'd grown up in any of a hundred cities across the country.

He continued, "It's practically foolproof. The money is untraceable. Better still, when I take it from the person who has it, there will be no protest. They will not be able to utter a word. Untraceable cash is like bearer bonds. Whoever possesses it, owns it." He paused, then said, "Okay. Bye." Hi clicked the phone off.

I thought it might be a good time to make an appearance.

Kang was facing away from me.

I stepped out onto the mat and cleared my throat.

Kang spun around. I expected him to recognize me, realize that he'd been caught in a compromising situation, and possibly flee.

Instead, he stuck his phone in his pocket, got into a fighting stance, and advanced on me.

His stick was close to me, not him. I pulled it out of its holder.

He came toward me like a cat making little sideways steps. His reaction disturbed me. I'm a fit, sizable guy, halfway between six and seven feet. I held a sturdy fighting stick, and I had the moral high ground on my side. Kang was a fraction my size.

But I felt like I was facing an alien being who considered me a troublesome bug that would need to be squished.

I raised the stick and held it like a baseball bat, ready to put one far into left field.

Kang took a running step, then launched himself toward me.

Whatever happens, hang onto the stick, I told myself.

I swung at him. It was an awkward move, probably the kind of thing his martial arts buddies would joke about. His foot shot out and struck the stick in the middle. Behind the loud smack of foot flesh on rattan, I heard the splintering of fibers. Fortunately, the rattan split its sides, but didn't snap in half.

Despite the severe blow, I could still swing the stick even if it was now a bendy weapon.

He came at me again, and I swung it again. He blocked the stick with his forearm, deflecting it up into the air.

The fractured stick flexed in an unpredictable way, moving in a wobbly arc, the bendy end coming down like a knuckleball in an improbable drop, making a loud smack against Kang's cheek.

He staggered backward, more stunned than hurt. I took advantage and lunged forward with a well-aimed gut punch, my left elbow going back as I rotated my upper body, which helped to propel my right arm forward, fist clenched.

Hitting Kang's abs was like hitting a leather-padded board. My knuckles didn't shatter from the blow, but it felt like they could have. Kang bounced back hard, going down on his butt. He rolled sideways, came to his feet as if by levitation, and sprinted away, still barefoot. He went around the side of the house and out toward the street. I ran after him, jumping over a low fence and scraping turf as I careened around a grouping of Aspen trees. As I got to the street side of the house, I angled hard, thinking that his silver Kia was to the left.

A car door slammed to my right. I turned and saw that I'd misjudged. His car was to the right. The starter cranked. I didn't think that his sweats had pockets, so he must have kept the key in the car. The engine fired. It was obvious that I couldn't get to him. He revved the engine as he shifted into Drive. The tires squealed, and the car raced away.

I turned the other direction and sprinted back toward my Jeep. But it was a quarter mile away. By the time I got there, Kang could have been well on his way to Reno or heading up Donner Summit on his way down to Sacramento or cruising up Highway 89 next to the Truckee River as it flowed down from Lake Tahoe, or even going the other direction and heading north out of Truckee toward Graeagle and Quincy and on toward the wilderness around Mt. Lassen. There was no way I could catch him except by unusual luck.

I thought of getting on the phone and alerting local law enforcement, but Kang had committed no crime.

Instead of getting into the Jeep, I walked back to his house. It was probably empty. But one never knows. I knocked on the door. I heard sounds of movement. The door opened. An old man with white hair that stood up as if under permanent electric shock looked out at me, frowning hard. He wore a baby blue terry cloth robe. His legs were bare, his varicose veins like river tributaries against white skin, and he wore leather slippers over his sockless feet.

"Yeah?" he said.

"I was hoping to speak to Mr. Kang," I said.

He made a fist with his thumb sticking out and pointed the thumb over his shoulder, gesturing toward the wall behind him. "Lives in back. You can go around the side of the house."

"You mean I should knock on your back door?"

"No." The man shook his head vigorously. "Kang lives in the shed out back. He has a key to get into my bathroom. But the shed is his domain."

"Oh, I see. Can you tell me if he's around much? I don't see his car."

"What, he owes you money, too?"

"Not much," I said.

"Well, you better get in line. The last guys who were looking for him would kick your butt if you tried to collect before them. I used to be a dealer in Reno. Twenty-five years. So I recognize those kind of guys, and I know how it works. I told Kang, you want to gamble beyond your means, you're gonna get involved with some mean-ass men."

"And they came to your door?"

The man looked at me. "I told them that Kang was my renter, not my buddy, and to leave me the hell alone."

"Did they?"

"Yeah. The thing is with sharks, if you owe them and you don't pay up, they'll cut your wife into pieces if they think it will motivate you to pay. If they don't think you're ever going to pay, they'll cut you into pieces. But if they can't see how to use another person like me to get their debts paid, they'll leave me alone. I won't say it's like a code of ethics. More like a matter of practicality. Saves time sharpening their knives if they minimize their butchering."

"Mind if I go back to the shed and leave Kang a note?"

"Be my guest. But if the door's locked and you bust it down, I'll get a picture of you doing it, and I'll call the cops."

"Got it," I said.

I walked back around the house and entered the shed. It was like any other shed, small and stuffy, with a barn door to make it easier to get lawnmowers and snowblowers in and out. But this shed had no yard equipment. The walls of the shed were lined with insulation. In one wall was a single window. There was a bed made from a piece of plywood on two-by-four legs. It had a thin mat on top. A sleeping bag had been rolled up and secured with a belt. A rod held some clothes on hangers. There was a single plastic chair and a wide shelf that served as a table. On the shelf was a single-burner propane cook stove and a cookpot. Next to the cook stove was an open coffee can that served as a holder for a few pieces of tableware, a can opener, a tin of black pepper, a tall, narrow jar of spicy Szechuan sauce. Under the table was a flat of plastic water bottles. Above were two shelves loaded with canned goods.

In the middle of the single room hung a lightbulb that was plugged into a thick, black extension cord that went out through a hole at the top of the wall. It must have been plugged into an outlet on the main house. On the floor was a space heater, also plugged into the extension cord. There was no plumbing or other amenities. In one corner was a small porta potty designed for primitive RVs. In another corner was a footlocker made of metal. I opened the lid. Inside were various food stores. Dried goods, pasta, rice, cereal. Things that didn't need refrigeration but that would be vulnerable to mice if they weren't in the locker. I lifted several items to the side to see if anything had been hidden at the bottom. There was a stack of plastic bags of rice filling one end of the locker, four five-pound bags. I lifted the corners of them up.

Underneath was a bit of white plastic. I moved the rice. It was a hockey goalie mask like what the truck robbers wore. Even in such a benign hiding place, the mask, with its angry eyes and sneering mouth, looked wicked.

I covered it back up, putting the food items roughly back the way I'd found them.

The shed seemed to me like refugee housing in a third-world country, a huge step up from being homeless, but very primitive. I couldn't imagine that the rent Kang paid the old man was worth it. More likely, the main value the old man provided was that Kang was able to live off the grid, hiding in plain sight. Kang's name wouldn't be on any utility bills or IRS computer records or Post Office box. He could pay the old man with cash received from his gardening customers. Kang could communicate using burner phones bought from Walmart, no phone company account necessary.

There were millions of people like Kang across the country, living a cash existence. In that sense, Kang and Evan and Mia were all similar. Maybe the robbers, too.

Did Kang run from me because he was undocumented, or because he worked for a man who'd recently been murdered, or because I now knew that he'd made an elaborate charade of not knowing English, which, like the hidden hockey mask, suggested that he might be hiding many other things?

There were several possible reasons. But as I drove away, the lasting image I had was the skill and strength with which he manipulated and thrust the stick that was about the length of a ski pole.

FORTY

The next morning, I remembered the San Francisco psychologist who'd given me valuable information a few years before when an arsonist was murdering people by setting the forests of Tahoe afire. The psychologist was a former consultant for the FBI, his name was George Morrell, and he was the uncle of my favorite waitress at The Red Hut Café. I looked up George's number and dialed.

I got an answering machine and was leaving a message when he picked up.

"George Morrell," he said. He was winded, panting hard. "Sorry, I was just coming in the front door when I heard the ringing. Give me a moment to catch my breath."

"Hello, George. Owen McKenna calling. I'm an investigator in Tahoe. We've spoken in the past."

He was still blowing air, trying to catch his breath.

I continued, "I came to your house, and I recall trotting several hundred steps up Russian Hill to get to your gate, and I was more winded than you are now."

"Yes. Yes, of course," Morrell said. "You wanted to know about the psychological profile of a firestarter. We spoke of the homicidal trinity."

"Wow, you have quite the memory," I said.

"A quirk of us shrinks. The twisted, the perturbed, and the disturbed stay with us. Maybe I should say, haunt us."

"Haunt us investigators, as well."

"No doubt it is another case that brings your call," he said, puffing a little less.

"Yes. Would you have a few minutes to talk?"

Morrell chuckled. "You forget that I'm retired."

"As you were the last time we spoke," I said.

"Ah, now you are the one demonstrating feats of memory."

"If you won't charge me a fee for services rendered, I can simply return the favor with a case of your favorite wine."

"Okay, sold. I'm now sitting down, feet up, looking out the window at the Coit Tower and the Bay Bridge in the background. The Bay, in case you're wondering, is about as blue as Lake Tahoe. So this crime you're dealing with... You've got a bad guy who doesn't fit the typical mold."

"You are already perceptive about him and I haven't said a word."

"My business," George said. "The fact that you called me suggests that he's not your everyday dirtball, blaming his constant stupid decisions on bad parents, or no parents, or his sexual abuse as a child. Of course, many bad guys are morons. But I know that this one isn't so stupid for the simple reason that you haven't yet found him. A bad guy who isn't easily caught is often smart. Because of that mystery, he's got you struggling to figure out what turns the gears on his clock. You're hoping that if you can learn something of the mechanism, you might find a clue to his identity."

"You are correct. I should let you know that the crimes are a bit gritty."

"Wonderful!" George said with what seemed like too much enthusiasm, a trait I remembered from our previous conversations.

I said, "It began with a kidnapping of a young man and a twenty-five thousand dollar ransom demand made to his con artist stepfather. The stepfather withdrew the money from his bank, and presumably paid the kidnapper. Then the stepfather, who was already dying of cancer, was murdered at his home in Incline Village by a blow to the head with a stand-up paddle board. Most likely, someone threw it at him. Three days later, I found the kidnap victim. He was tied up in a boat and near death, but he survived."

"A very good beginning," he said. "Go on."

"The morning after the kidnapping, just before dawn, there was an armored truck heist on the South Shore. Four men in black hoodies and white hockey masks held up the truck on its way to deliver cash to a casino. The men relieved the armed guards of their burden, which was five hundred thousand in unmarked, untraceable cash."

"Even more promising," George said.

"I was brought in by the armored truck company. On the armored truck's tire, my dog found some pine pitch. It turned out that the pitch contained a bit of pine bark beetle and a piece of an endangered plant called the Tahoe Yellow Cress, which only grows in Tahoe. Neither the pitch nor beetle nor plant could have easily been acquired on the truck's route to the casino. So it seemed that one of the robbers may have had the pitch on his boot and scraped it off onto the tire. With the help of a biology prof, we correlated those components together onto a map and found a campsite here on the South Shore of Tahoe near where one would find pine pitch and bark beetles and Tahoe Yellow Cress. That campsite also featured a bit of cash blowing in the bushes, along with two of the four robbers. Both had been murdered with spears made from old ski poles from which the baskets and handles had been removed. Each victim had been thrust through from front to back."

"Nothing more exciting than a new murder method, right?"

"Well, excitement isn't the way I think of it."

"Owen, I'm a shrink. Never forget what motivates us to go into this profession."

"Got it. Because of the rarity of such crimes in Tahoe, I'm assuming some kind of connection exists between the kidnapping and murder of the man who paid the ransom and the ski pole murders of the armored truck robbers. But I haven't found a breakthrough. Perhaps if I knew what you know, I'd be better at finding the perpetrator." I paused.

George spoke. "First, let me say that the robbery and the kidnapping and the murders could, as you suspect, all be connected. I believe they very likely are. Why? The answer lies in the twisted maze of the psychopath's mind. You see, psychopaths are very unlike the rest of us in that they have no empathy, no ability to feel someone else's pain. If they accidentally step on a kitten and hear it scream, they are interested in how much pain the kitty has experienced, but they don't feel it themselves. There is no emotional distress for them in stepping on kittens. They may even step down harder just out of curiosity about how loud the kitty can scream or at what point its bones crush."

I remembered back to when I talked to George about firestarters. He seemed a little too eager to talk about their mental peculiarities. I sensed the same thing now.

George continued, "So the key to knowing and understanding the psychopath is to remember that singular characteristic. No empathy. And with no empathy comes no remorse. Those two things are cousins, and we find them in all psychopaths. Psychopaths are also very good at planning crimes. And because of their careful planning, they often get away with them. So, based on this aspect of these crimes – the fact that you haven't caught the perpetrator or perpetrators – I suspect they were all committed by a psychopath."

"What about sociopaths," I said. "Isn't that another word for the same thing?"

"No, they are very different. Where the psychopath has no empathy, the sociopath has a little bit of it. The sociopath is more like a normal person but much more impulsive and without the ethical constraints on his behavior. The sociopath is perfectly capable of committing serious crimes because he doesn't have a governor on his behavior. Sociopaths primarily commit crimes of opportunity, crimes of passion."

George stopped. I didn't interrupt his thoughts.

"It's quite easy to diagnose," he continued. "If you see a crime, ask yourself if it looks like a crime of passion or a crime that was carefully planned out. The former will lead you to a sociopath, the latter to a psychopath."

"Because the psychopath does so much planning, he probably doesn't leave many clues," I said.

"You've got it," George said. "And if he does leave clues, they are often designed to mislead. All is in service to his ultimate goal, the money, or world domination, or whatever it is. If it suits his plan to kill two men with ski poles or a paddle board, he will do it without pause. All that matters is his end game."

"How would you suggest I look for this killer?" I asked.

George paused again. "Years ago, I told you about the homicidal trinity, a fascinating set of characteristics that often come together in serial killers."

"I remember," I said. "If you find a boy who tortures animals and also wets the bed and also commits arson, look out when he grows up."

"Right. Boys with those three behaviors often grow up to be thrill killers. And if you look at it in reverse, it's creepy how often a known serial killer exhibited those behaviors as a boy. But now I want to tell you about something that we psychologists call the dark triad," George said.

"Just the name sounds bleak," I said.

"It is. The dark triad is another set of three traits. It is in some ways, a great darkness, so to speak, nearly as dark as the homicidal trinity. The first trait is psychopathy, the second is Machiavellianism, and the third is narcissism."

"I think I know what you mean by Machiavellianism, but why don't you clarify it," I said.

"Of course. During the Renaissance, around the time of the Medici Pope Clement the Seventh, Niccolò Machiavelli lived in Florence, and he wrote a political treatise called The Prince. This would be in the early fifteen hundreds. In The Prince, he discussed forms of government and rule and the way that rulers acquire power and keep it. Much of his focus was on the manipulative aspects of how those in power operated at the time. And, of course, it applies to the way those in power today still operate. Thus the adjective machiavellian is pejorative and describes all of those cunning and subversive techniques used by politicians then as well as now. You see machiavellianism everywhere you look, from Shakespeare's tragedies to the U.S. Congress. We can all think of people we know who are manipulative and manipulate in a cunning way. That is machiavellianism."

"You said the dark triad was psychopathy, Machiavellianism and narcissism," I said. "Machiavellian psychopaths would clearly be people to avoid. But why would narcissism be such an evil personality trait?"

"The term of course came from the Greek myth about the young man Narcissus who fell in love with his own image that he saw reflected in water. By itself, narcissism just produces vain, self-important, self-aggrandizing, arrogant, irritating people."

"Is that all," I said.

"Right, that's all. The problem with narcissism is when you combine it with psychopathy and Machiavellianism."

"The dark triad," I said.

"Exactly. When you find that combination in an individual, you often see a whole range of predictable results. Such dark triad men – and they are mostly men – are usually sadistic. They enjoy watching others suffer. They are bullies. They push around other people to get what they want. They can bully to the point of destroying another person, whether it be emotional destruction or financial destruction or physical destruction. They can torture, and they can murder. They use whatever tools they can find to achieve their desires, regardless of who they have to step on."

"Is it easy to spot the three characteristics of the dark triad?"

"Yes and no. Our gut sense about them is pretty accurate. You see someone who is vain and self-absorbed and arrogant, and they exude a sense of entitlement, you know they're narcissistic. You see someone who is manipulative and nasty, lying and cheating their way through life, you know you're witnessing what Machiavelli described. And in addition to your visceral sense of these things, there are a host of psychological tests that easily reveal these characteristics as well. Psychologists are always studying these things for their predictive possibilities."

I said, "So you can easily tell about narcissism and Machiavellianism. What about psychopaths?"

"The third part of the dark triad, psychopathy, is much harder to diagnose. The reason is that psychopaths are good students. They may not have any empathy, but they can pretend that they do. They may not care about you or your wishes, but they can say the appropriate things to make you think they care. This characteristic makes them better able to plan and commit heinous crimes. They may have no remorse about committing terrible crimes, but they know what it takes to make other members of society think they would never do something horrible. They may be sexually promiscuous, but they won't reveal it. They may fail to take responsibility for their actions, but they will pretend otherwise. And because they are often very bright, they can play the psychologist interviewing them, which of course, is another aspect of Machiavellianism. Manipulating the shrink is just another fun pastime for a smart psychopath."

"You're saying they're good actors," I said.

"Absolutely. They can play a role with the best."

"Are psychopaths common?"

"Very. And because they have a single-minded determination to get what they want, they are often very successful. You'd be surprised how many CEOs of major corporations are psychopaths."

"That implies that other people believe in them," I said. "You can't get to be CEO without the people on the corporate board considering you to be a compelling person, someone who they'd be proud to have lead their company."

"True. Psychopaths are also risk takers. That combined with staying cool under stress and exhibiting a great deal of confidence bordering on arrogance, makes them often seem charismatic. In fact, there have been studies that show that women are more attracted to men who exhibit dark triad characteristics. They've even studied men with dark triad characteristics and found that dark triad men have many more sex partners than other men. And they are more likely to have casual sex."

"Getting back to my original question," I said, "do you think it is reasonable to consider the truck robbery and the murders and the kidnapping as the work of a single man?"

It was a moment before George spoke. "Yes. Except for the killing by throwing a paddle board. That seems impulsive, the crime of a sociopath. Of course, that, too, could be acting. The psychopath may have purposely committed a crime that would look like a crime of passion rather than a crime that was carefully planned. The other crimes all required careful, advance planning. The robbers took meticulous steps to succeed at taking down an armored truck, and they took pains to disguise themselves. While some of the robbers may just be foot soldiers, the crime shows the planning of a psychopath. Committing murders with a ski pole and getting away with it shows equal planning. And pulling off a kidnapping demonstrates yet more complex planning. I can easily see one man behind it all."

"Does it make sense that his motive was the money?"

George thought about it. "Yes, I think so. A half mil is a big piece of change. The murders were no doubt to cover it up and make it so the mastermind didn't have to split the money."

"As best as we can tell, the kidnapping only netted twenty-five thousand," I said. "By comparison to the truck robbery, the kidnapping hardly seems worth it."

"Perhaps the wildly divergent amounts of money were intended to make the crimes appear to have been committed by different individuals. But they could be connected in some unforseen way. They could have been planned concurrently."

"Why would this guy kill the other robbers and not kill the kidnap victim?"

"That's right," George said. "You said the kidnap victim was tied up and left to die, but he survived. That indicates punishment. The kidnapper may have wanted the relatively small ransom fee. But it seems that the primary motive was to torture the kidnap victim. A classic crime of a psychopath. Torture is as dark as the human psyche can get. No empathy at all."

We were silent for a bit. I said, "Here's a thought. If I could find someone who hated the kidnap victim and also exhibited dark triad characteristics, I might have a good suspect?"

"Indeed," George said.

We spoke some more, I thanked him, we said goodbye, and I made a mental note to send him a case of wine.

FORTY-ONE

My cell phone rang while I was out walking Spot and drinking my third cup of coffee.

"Hey McKenna, Bains here. Courtesy call."

"It should be a hallmark of cops, right, sergeant?"

"Yeah. Protect and serve and be courteous. Anyway, after you told me about Evan Rosen and the evidence connecting her to the robbers who were murdered, I drove up to Tahoe Vista yesterday afternoon after we spoke. Because she lives in Placer County, I'd informed Sergeant Jack Santiago of Placer County. He had me meet one of his deputies, Deputy Russo, to accompany me when I spoke with Evan Rosen. She was not especially forthcoming."

"She didn't answer your questions?"

"She did. Reluctantly. Lots of anger. But to be fair, I think the anger was because I caused her to miss a cleaning appointment. She claimed to be worried about losing the client on account of she really needed the money. But I think that was probably a false representation."

"Why?" I said.

"Wait 'til I explain. Her answers to my questions didn't all add up. When I said that she'd been seen with a lot of cash, she got all bent out of shape and started yelling that I didn't have a clue what it was like to live on the margin of society, having to pay everything with cash. When she raised her arms and stomped around in a circle, Deputy Russo put his hand on her elbow to try to calm her down."

"No, don't tell me," I said, knowing where he was going.

"Sorry. She struck him on the shoulder, closed fist. That girl can pack a real punch. So he arrested her."

"You and the deputy didn't see that as unnecessary escalation?" I said.

"You know how it works. In a situation like that, a cop has

to rely on his gut instinct. In fact, it seems to me that you talked about the whole gut instinct thing just yesterday."

Bains didn't say it like a barb, but it felt like it anyway.

"Anyway," he said, "it was her reaction, to use your words, that was an unnecessary escalation. Before he arrested her, Mike asked me what I thought. The truth is that her actions made me think that there was something else going on. So I told him that he knew the rules. He nodded and arrested for her for assaulting a police officer. We put her in the back of the Placer County patrol unit. Of course, that arrest allowed us to do a protective sweep and warrantless search of her residence. It didn't take long for us to find two thousand-plus dollars hidden behind her garbage under the kitchen sink. That gave us probable cause that a crime had been committed. So we had to seize those assets."

I was breathing hard. When I'd originally told Bains what I knew about Evan, I knew it could come to this, but I hadn't wanted it, nor did I expect it.

"Are you there?" Bains said.

"Yeah. Go on."

"Her closet has one of those shelves across the top. The shelf was stacked with pants and sweatshirts. At the back, under the clothes, was a ski pole. No basket, no handle. The open end was notched and flared just like the murder weapons. It had been wiped down, but it was still a bit slippery."

"Olive oil?" I said.

"Smells like it. Considering the hidden ski pole spear and cash, and what you said about Ms. Rosen having substantial animosity toward the murder victims as well as the shirt with the missing button that matches the one found in the robber vic's hand, and we've got a good case against her."

"Where is Evan now?" I said, even though I guessed the answer.

"We requested her transfer from Placer County to El Dorado County. At this point, I don't know if Placer County is charging her with resisting arrest. We're now holding her in the South Lake Tahoe Jail. The El Dorado Assistant DA was informed about what we found, and he's charged her with two counts of first degree murder."

When I got off the phone with Bains, I had to sit and think a minute. I hadn't moved, yet I was breathing hard.

It had been the information I provided Bains that led to Evan's murder charge. The evidence was mostly circumstantial, although the shirt button found in the victim's hand would maybe turn out to be direct evidence, compelling enough to convince a jury to convict her.

In providing the information to Bains, I hadn't done anything technically wrong. But I felt like I'd made a grave mistake, and I'd just been too dense to have seen a better approach. It gave me a giant discomfort, a hollow feeling that felt like a precursor to a heart attack.

I imagined what Evan must be thinking. Either she'd been guilty and was caught or she'd been wrongly charged. If the charge was wrong, then either she'd been the victim of an extraordinary set of coincidences or she'd been elaborately framed.

Regardless of the seriousness of the charge, Evan's main concern would be Mia. It seemed that Mia could handle the basics of taking care of herself for at least a day or two. But I didn't know what her state of mind would be. Would Evan's sudden absence be incapacitating? Would she fall apart or just be worried and scared? I was pretty sure that Mia didn't drive, but would she walk to the store for food? Did she have money? Evan would have been given a phone call. Would she have called a lawyer? Or Mia?

I felt at least partially responsible for Mia. Someone should at least reassure her. I would visit Evan as soon as possible, but it would be best if I could tell her that Mia was okay.

I took Spot, and we drove up to Tahoe Vista. I parked in front of the motel apartments. Mia would recognize and feel friendly with Spot much faster than with me. So I took Spot with me, and we walked up to the end unit.

I knocked and then stood back so that Spot and I wouldn't intimidate whoever opened the door.

There was no response, so I knocked again.

I heard the sound of a door down the walk. A white-haired woman looked out. The babysitter I'd seen before.

"Hi, Mattie, I'm Owen McKenna. I'm sorry, I don't mean to sound disrespectful, but I don't know your last name. You may have seen me giving Evan and Mia rides when her car was stolen. I'm looking for Mia. Any idea where she is?"

The woman thought about it. She turned and leaned into her apartment but left her hand on the doorjamb. In a moment, she came out, shut the door behind her, and walked down to me, moving slower as she got close, her eyes on Spot. She came to a stop several feet away. She stared at Spot.

"Don't worry, he's friendly," I said.

"Do you know where Evan is?" She tried to make the question sound straightforward, but I could sense the fear and worry in her voice.

"Yes. As Evan may have told you, I'm an investigator, and I've been in contact with the police regarding the murder of one of her customers, David Montrop. I don't want to alarm Mia or you, but Evan has been arrested and charged with murder." I didn't bother to explain that the charge was for the murder of the robbers and not the murder of Montrop.

The woman raised her hand to her mouth, her open palm against her lips. Her eyes were wide and terrified.

I said, "Evan is currently being held at the South Lake Tahoe jail. I'm going there to visit her as soon as visiting hours open. In the meantime, I wanted to check on Mia and make sure she's okay."

The woman didn't speak.

"I don't think we should tell Mia that Evan's in jail," I said. "At least not right away. Maybe we could just say that Evan's talking to the police and she'll be back as soon as she can. Mia likes my dog. Petting him might reassure her."

Eventually, the woman spoke. "Mia's with me. When the cops came to their apartment and took Evan away, Mia became very upset. Very upset," she repeated. "Let me think," she added. After a bit, she said, "How long do you think it will take to get Evan out of jail?"

"I don't know." I didn't want to say that it might not happen. "Could you take care of Mia for a few days? Or at least look in on her or whatever would help? You know better than I do what

Mia needs."

"She can stay with me," the woman said. "I have some things coming up that I'm supposed to do, but I can cancel them."

"Thank you. Do you need money or anything?"

She shook her head. "I think you're right about your dog. I'll bring Mia out, and you can tell her that Evan will be gone for a bit."

The woman went back to her apartment and went inside. A minute later, she came back out with Mia. She'd put Mia's hand around the back of her elbow so that it appeared that Mia was helping Mattie walk. It seemed a smart move, giving Mia a sense of purpose that would distract from Evan's absence.

"Hi Mia," I said. "Remember me, Owen McKenna? I wanted to stop by so you could visit Spot."

Mia's eyes and cheeks were red from crying. Seeing Spot seemed to immediately distract her. She didn't smile, but she let go of Mattie and walked to Spot. She bent over to hug him.

Like a trained therapy dog, he wagged but didn't move. He was happy to have her weight on his back.

"Mia," I said, "Spot and I came to tell you that Evan will be gone for a day or two. Mattie said you can stay with her. If there's anything you need from me, Mattie can call me. Will that be okay?"

Mia didn't respond to me. She kept hugging Spot.

"Mia, I'm going to be seeing Evan. Is there anything you want me to tell her from you?"

Mia's eyes were shut. She didn't appear to hear me.

I looked at Mattie. She made a little nod. She pointed down at Spot's head and mouthed the words, 'This is good.'

We waited a bit, then Mattie tapped Mia on the shoulder. "Come, Mia, we have to let Owen go back to work."

Gradually, Mia released Spot and stood. She pet Spot on his head, making precise careful strokes between his ears.

Mattie spoke, "Mia, Owen wants to know if you have a message for Evan."

Mia seemed to chew on her cheek. "I'm going to ask TB for fairy dust, and I'll sprinkle it for Evan."

"Okay," I said. "I'll tell her."

"Say goodbye to Spot," Mattie said. Mattie took Mia's hand, placed it inside of her elbow, and had Mia walk her back to her apartment. After they were inside, Mattie came back out. She handed me a piece of paper.

"Here's my phone number. Call when you learn something?"

"Will do." I handed Mattie my card. "Thanks," I said. "Evan will really appreciate that you're looking after Mia."

Mattie nodded.

"One question about Mia's message," I said. "What does TB refer to?"

"Tinkerbell."

"Ah." I gave Mattie a smile, and Spot and I left.

FORTY-TWO

When I got home, I called the El Dorado County Jail in South Lake Tahoe.

"My name is Owen McKenna," I said when a young-sounding man came on the line. "I'm a private investigator working on the case of one of your inmates, Evan Rosen."

"I know about you," the jail commander said.

"Evan Rosen is charged with murder. The District Attorney's case against her is largely based on information I provided to El Dorado County Sergeant Bains. I have new questions I need to ask her that are critical to the case. But I assume I'm not on her active visitor list."

"I've got it here," the jail commander said. "No one's on her list. But if you want access, I can change that," the jail commander said. "When do you want to come in?"

"You've got evening visiting hours. I was hoping I could come this evening at seven."

"Okay. I'll put you down."

"Thanks."

Spot and I had an early dinner, then drove down to South Lake Tahoe. I pulled into the parking lot off Al Tahoe Boulevard, left Spot in the Jeep, and walked into the jail. I went through the security protocol, signature on the form, boxes checked, statement of intent, questions answered, keys and pocket knife and all of my dangerous pennies and dimes in the storage tray.

"Gun?" the guard said as he opened one of the gun locker doors.

"I don't carry," I said.

"I thought you were an ex-cop."

"I am. I probably should carry. But I don't."

The man frowned as he looked at me. "Whatever," he said.

He gestured toward the metal detector, and I walked between the vertical detector posts.

"Come with me." He turned and walked through a heavy door with a lock that could only be opened when a video observer hit the buzzer. I followed him into the visiting area. He pointed to a chair. I sat.

"Give us a few minutes," he said.

I nodded and waited among other visitors and inmates.

It was an eye-opener to see this facility with 150 bunks for criminals set in the midst of the Tahoe Basin. It was hard to reconcile the beauty of the lake and mountains with life inside these jail cells.

A guard brought Evan in. Her hands were cuffed in front, locked to a chain around her waist. Her feet were shackled. She might be a petite woman, but they were playing by the book. We sat on opposite sides of a counter with a heavy plexi divider. We could see each other and talk.

"Owen McKenna," Evan said. Her voice was lifeless.

"How are you doing?" I said.

She looked down at her handcuffs. "Not good." Her voice sounded lifeless.

"I'm sorry about this," I said.

"You don't need to be sorry," she said.

The words were painful to hear. At some point in the future I might tell her that I was the person most responsible for putting her in jail. But I didn't think it would be helpful to tell her now.

"When I heard you were in jail, I drove to your apartment to reassure Mia."

"You saw her?" Evan's words were a bit more alive than before.

"Yes, a few hours ago. She was at Mattie's apartment. I told Mattie what had happened, and she's clearing her schedule to look after Mia."

"How was Mia?"

"She was sad and worried about you being gone, but otherwise she's okay. She said to tell you that she's going to ask Tinkerbell for fairy dust so she can sprinkle it for you."

Even closed her eyes for a moment. "What did you tell

her?"

"I just told her that you'd be gone a few days, and that you were coming back home as soon as possible."

Evan frowned. "It ripped my heart out to see Mia's face when they hauled me away. I never should have touched that cop. It was just a slap on his shoulder. But it was wrong. I have no impulse control. He pushed all my buttons and I snapped."

She looked at me as if I might comment, but I didn't know what to say.

"What's going to happen next?"

"Have you talked to a lawyer?"

"No. It's not like I can afford a lawyer."

"Have you been arraigned, yet?"

"No. They say that happens tomorrow morning. What should I expect?"

"You will be assigned a public defender. That person may be coming to see you yet this evening or early in the morning. He or she will discuss your options. At the arraignment, the judge will inform you of the charges against you and ask how you plead, guilty or innocent. The judge will then deny bail because the charges will be murder with special circumstances. That's a term that means you were…"

"Lying in wait for the victims," she interrupted.

"Right," I said, surprised. "It's considered the most serious kind of murder, so they won't let you out. The public defender will consult with you and prepare to defend you in court."

"Which doesn't make for a good prognosis," she said.

Once again, she was using a word I wouldn't have expected.

I continued, "My guess is that the prosecutor will attempt to find out what you know about the other robbers or the robbery. If they believe you have valuable information, they may offer you a plea bargain in exchange for giving up that information."

"But I don't have any information about them."

"Then there'll be no plea bargain."

"I wouldn't plead guilty to lesser charges anyway because I'm innocent."

"Right. In answer to your question about how long you'll be held, it will be until you're acquitted."

"If I'm acquitted," Evan said.

"Correct."

"Is there no other option?" Evan asked. Her eyes seemed heavy and dull with what seemed like depression.

"The only other way out would be if the District Attorney decided to drop the charges."

"What would that take?"

"If we can prove you are innocent, then we may get him to consider dropping the charges. Although I won't mislead you. It doesn't look good."

"I don't understand. If you could demonstrate my innocence, they would still prosecute me?" Evan was appalled.

"The unfortunate reality is that the justice system isn't especially good at identifying every innocent person and then freeing them quickly. They generally leave that decision to the jury. I've never met a District Attorney or prosecutor whose primary career driver is a Mother Teresa-like sense of charity and fairness."

"But what's fair should always come first!"

I shrugged. "In most states, District Attorneys are elected. That makes them politicians even though they'll dispute the characterization. As an elected official, a DA works for the public, and a DA rarely suffers in the public eye for appearing hard on criminals."

Evan looked off to the side, toward a wall. "And of course, I'm an evil, wicked criminal."

"Are you innocent?" I asked.

"Of course. It's a stupid case."

"Stupid in your eyes, no doubt. But the button in one of the victim's hands matched the missing button on your shirt. The robbers were killed with spears made from ski poles. Sergeant Bains and Deputy Russo found a matching ski pole spear in the back of your closet."

"What?! That's what they brought out in the plastic bag and put in the trunk? That couldn't be! They must have planted it there. They…" she paused. "Someone else planted it there. The real murderer. To frame me!"

"The ski poles were originally taken from a dumpster behind

the ski shop the next street over. The dumpster is directly behind your apartment."

"My God! This is a perfect frame. Someone's been planning to set me up all along! But almost for sure I have an alibi. I'm always working. Or else I'm home taking care of Mia. If you can find out when the murders took place, I can go through my calendar and find out where I was."

"That probably won't help," I said. "The bodies were found a long time after they were killed. We've established their approximate time of death, but it's not accurate enough for an alibi defense. The prosecutor will claim that the victims were murdered at night. He or she will pick the night closest to the time-of-death estimate and claim that you drove to the South Shore in the middle of the night and found the men where they were camping. So an alibi is out unless you could prove you were out of the country for a period of days near the time of the murders."

Evan looked devastated.

"When the cops searched your house," I said, "they found two thousand in cash hidden under your kitchen garbage. Where did you get it?"

Evan looked desperate, like anyone would whose life was unraveling.

"If you want even a slight chance at being acquitted, you will have to answer all questions they put to you. And if you entertain any dream that the murder charges could be dropped, you will have to be more than forthcoming. You'll have to be cheerfully helpful to everyone."

Evan looked away.

"That starts with this question about the source of your cash. Or consider the possibility that you'll spend the rest of your life in jail. If they take Mia away and put her in a home of some kind far away, you might never see her again."

Tears formed in Evan's eyes. "There's no law that says you can't have cash. My mother always told me to keep a little stash tucked away. That way if everything goes south, you've always got that cushion. So every now and then, I add a hundred dollar bill to my stash. I think of it as insurance for Mia. If I were to break my arm or something so I can't clean houses, I could still provide for Mia, at least in the short term. And in case they're wondering, I report all my cash income." Evan's eyes were wide. "They left the money there, right?"

"No. The law allows officers to seize assets if they suspect it might have been acquired through unlawful means."

"No! No! That's not fair!" Evan shouted. "That money is for Mia!"

The nearby guard gave me a stern look. "Keep it down, or the meeting is over!"

I nodded at him, then spoke to Evan. "They can't keep assets worth less than twenty-five thousand unless you're convicted," I said. "If we can get you acquitted, you will eventually get the money back."

"What else is there besides the money?"

"The ski pole spear is very compelling. A person can't just go out and find an easy source for such poles that are so old they have sharp points. They haven't been manufactured for almost fifty years. The ski shop behind your apartment threw a bunch of old poles out not long ago. The poles match those that were used as murder weapons. They sat in the dumpster for several days. The fact that they all came from near your door is compelling. The ski shop owner will no doubt identify the pole found in your closet as coming from the batch of poles he threw away."

I continued. "More circumstantial evidence comes from the fact that you went to the same high school and at the same time as the two dead robbers. You demonstrated fear and animosity when I showed you their high school yearbook photos."

Evan was shaking her head in what looked like shock and disbelief.

"I'm sorry, Evan, but even Mia's presence works against you."

"How could that possibly be? Mia would bring out the sympathy in anybody."

"Right. A caring jury would easily see how you loved her and would do anything to secure her future. In the jury's mind, Mia becomes your motive, the reason you killed robbers to get money for Mia."

Evan frowned so hard that it wrinkled her entire young face. "And once I killed the robbers and took their money, what did I supposedly do with it?"

"The jurors will be wondering that as they convict you. They will assume that you stashed the money someplace and are waiting until things calm down before you do anything with it. The prosecutor won't be looking for boats or diamonds that you bought with the robbery money. He'll just be presenting you as someone who needed to work a little less and have a little more money, all so you can better provide for Mia. As the prosecutor paints you as someone who murdered to get money to help support her sister, he will also paint the murder victims as evil robbers. That will make it easier for the jury to buy the story that you killed them. Once they think there were good reasons attached to what you did, they will convict you of murder."

Evan looked so stressed that I expected her to cry. But her eyes remained dry. She shook her head. "Everything's gone."

"What's gone?"

"Everything I ever hoped for." She stared at the floor. "I had some plans that..." Evan paused and clenched her teeth. "I've never had anyone but Mia. She's sweet and kind, and I love her to death. But I have to hold her up, and now I can't."

"She really believes in you," I said. "She thinks you are everything and can do anything."

"She's the only one who does," Evan said.

I wanted to protest, but that would sound hollow.

"Sometimes belief is everything, don't you think?" Evan said. "And I don't mean religious belief. I mean the belief another person has in you. If you've got one of those people, you can do anything. But if you don't, life can be... Pretty hard. Mia's belief is all I've got. And if that shatters when she realizes what's happening to me, then she and I will both be destroyed."

"Do you have any other family who can help with Mia? Cousins or aunts or uncles?"

Evan shook her head. "If I do, I don't know who they are. Mom rarely talked about her family. I understood that it was painful to her. She mentioned a brother and a few cousins, all of whom are in jail. That left me with no names in my address book."

"Close friends?"

"Mr. McKenna, you should understand that all I do is work. All I've ever done is work. My plan was to change the way I work, but I've still got Mia to take care of. If I ever get a spare minute, I'm not going to leave Mia someplace while I go out and meet people and hope to find a friend. I'll either spend the time with Mia, or I'll take her with me wherever I go. And I'm not making judgments when I say that it's pretty much impossible to meet people and develop friends when you're with Mia. It's just the fact of the matter."

"You said that everything you hoped for is gone," I said. "What did you hope for?"

FORTY-THREE

Evan took several breaths. "My plan was a longshot, but I thought it was at least possible. I had to make several things come together, but I believed I could pull it off. At least, I believed it on the good days. Now, the plan is a distant memory. A flight of fancy."

I didn't speak.

"I've been taking classes at the university in Reno. Most of them at night."

"UNR's a good school," I said. "What classes?"

Evan paused before answering. "Just basic stuff to fulfill my distribution requirements before I can graduate. This quarter, it's humanities and math. Trigonometry. I hate trigonometry."

"When will you graduate?"

"Owen, I'm in jail."

"Sorry. I was just interested."

Evan didn't speak.

"Do you have a major?"

She shook her head.

"A future career focus?"

"I'm just considering possibilities," she said.

"The main thing is to get a college degree?"

She shrugged.

I remembered the card she'd given me. "On your Mansfield Cleaning business card is a picture of a building. I thought it looked like a classic old university building. Is that part of UNR?"

"No."

"But it's significant in some way because you put it on your card."

"Look, this is like you're my shrink or something. I'm probably going to be behind bars permanently. What's the point?"

"I'm trying to get a better sense of you. I'm curious about your interests. I'm impressed that you're going to school at night instead of sitting at home watching TV or drinking in a bar. You're putting a large part of your life on hold because you're taking care of your sister. Your business card doesn't just have a picture of a mop and bucket. The building on your card, the name of your business. It's all an unusual combination." I still had her card in my wallet. I took it out and set it on the counter in front of me.

"It's all a stupid combination. It's a set of hopes that were never going to go anywhere."

She paused.

I waited.

She sighed.

"The building on my business card is the Union Block building in Mount Pleasant, Iowa. In eighteen forty-six, a woman named Belle Babb was born in Iowa. She and her older brother were raised by their mother after their father deserted the family." Evan took a deep breath.

"So far, her life is similar to yours. Your father abandoned your family, too, right?"

Evan nodded.

"Was she one of your ancestors?"

"I wish. At that time, most women couldn't get accepted into colleges. What was the point in letting a woman into school when all women were good for was cooking and making babies? But because so many men were going off to fight in the Civil War, Belle Babb got into Iowa Wesleyan College. She graduated in three years and was valedictorian of her class."

Evan seemed to look past me as if she were seeing a woman of achievement 150 years ago.

She continued, "Belle Babb married a young professor named John Mansfield. When she took his name, she changed her first name to Arabella. Arabella Mansfield wanted to be a lawyer, but no state in the country allowed women to be lawyers. So, of course, law school for a woman wasn't an option. Nevertheless, her professor husband gave her his blessing to pursue learning about the law. Talk about an amazing man.

"So Arabella Mansfield studied the law on her own. She read all the law books she could find. When she felt ready to take the bar exam, Iowa law only allowed men to take the test. But she somehow managed to take the test. Maybe the examiner was a man like Arabella's husband, open minded to what women could achieve. Or maybe the examiner wondered just how badly she would fail, and so he let her in so he could gloat. Whatever the reason, she passed with good scores.

"Even so, it was still against the law for a woman to be a lawyer. But Arabella Mansfield was tough and stubborn. She challenged the law in court, and the court eventually ruled that a woman could be allowed into the bar." Evan pointed her finger at the building on her business card. "She took her oath at the Union Block building in Mount Pleasant Iowa." Evan took a deep breath. "Arabella Mansfield became the first woman lawyer in the United States."

Evan's chained hands were clenched into fists in front of her. Her eyes were teary but they were the tears of determination not sadness.

"Arabella Mansfield is your role model," I said.

"So that's why I put that building on my card. That building is a sacred place. And Arabella Mansfield is a goddess. I always thought that if she could come from a fatherless household and fight the system that made it illegal for a woman to do practically anything..." Evan broke off.

Eventually, she spoke in a very small voice, "I thought maybe I could do some little version of that. Maybe I could get past my family and my circumstances and get a college degree and then go to law school and make something of myself."

I looked at Evan, taking in the depth of her passion, but stayed silent. I didn't dare disrupt the situation that had gotten her talking.

Evan took several deep breaths. She had a small look of wonder in her eyes, a look that reminded me of Mia when Mia spoke about fairy dust.

Evan continued, "The percentage of legal professions that are made up of women is growing fast. Women in corporate law, private practice, teaching law, working as judges, all of these have undergone enormous changes. Women now make up over half of all law students, and over half of all law degrees go to women. This is a profession that used to be run by men for men, the same men who made it illegal for a woman to be a lawyer. It's all different now, and Arabella Mansfield started it all."

"I'm impressed," I said.

"With Arabella?"

"No, with you."

Evan looked away.

"Has anyone else in your family gone into one of the professions?" I asked.

"No one else in my family has even graduated from high school."

"I don't want to sound judgemental, but when you finished high school, did your mother ever consider ways you might have gone to college?"

"We were broke. Mom was not real together. Our whole life was just about the logistics of making sure that someone was always home to take care of Mia."

I felt at a loss. Maybe the woman across from me was a murderer, or maybe not. But she was impressive in her focus. I'd certainly never met another murder suspect remotely like her.

FORTY-FOUR

"Here's a little thought experiment," I said, trying to keep Evan's thinking in her world of dreams for just a bit longer.

"Let's say you beat this rap," I said. "Let's say you continue your classes and graduate from UNR. Have you thought about law school? Are your grades good enough to get in?"

"I've done enough extra credit that my GPA is better than four-O. But that doesn't matter much. I have to take the LSAT, at which I'll probably do okay. But the problem is that law schools don't want someone like me. There are exceptions, but in general they prefer younger applicants who went to college in four years, not cleaning women who've been squeezing in classes at night. Law schools prefer people who fit their picture of the kind of person who will do well as a lawyer. A person who's well connected in their community, a person who's fluent with the contemporary world, a person who will easily get hired by companies who need lawyers. They also want legacy admissions."

"What's that?"

"A legacy admission is when they admit someone who has a family member who graduated from the same law school."

"Nepotism?" I said.

"Sort of, but with a specific financial aspect. If mom or dad was successful in a law school and went on to be a successful attorney, that suggests that their kid might do well, too. However, what they don't talk about is that law schools, like all other schools, need as much money as they can get. If they admit the offspring of their successful former students, those parents are very likely to give more money."

"Are you saying that admissions officers are in bed with the people soliciting financial support for the law school?"

"Not directly. But studies have shown a huge connection

between donations from wealthy patrons and the admission of their kids into the school."

"Surely, law schools must have some openings for kids from less advantaged backgrounds," I said.

"Yes, and they always talk about those students when they get a chance. And they mention those students in their brochures. But the relatives of those students mostly don't donate to the school at all. And those students as a group never do as well in school or out in the business community as do those students who came in under the legacy umbrella, students who have a huge support network from day one."

It was a lot to absorb. I now understood that Evan Rosen had a great deal more intellect and ambition and knowledge than I'd previously thought.

"You said Arabella Mansfield was raised by her mother, that her father abandoned the family. Your father abandoned your family, and you were raised by your mother."

Evan nodded. "Yes to both."

"You're currently taking college classes, so you must have done well in high school."

Evan's voice was so soft I could barely hear it. "I was valedictorian of my class. But that's not saying much when forty-five percent of my classmates dropped out before graduation."

"It's still a major accomplishment. But you didn't immediately go off to college because..." I stopped.

"My mother had Type Two diabetes. At that point she was almost constantly under medical care." Evan's voice was a low monotone, without emotion, like a person in some kind of hypnotic state. "I had to stay home to take care of Mia."

"I thought you said that Mia lived with your mother while you were cleaning houses up here in Tahoe. So your mother took care of her at a later point."

Evan nodded. "Mom had a kind of remission for a few years. When she first got the diagnosis about the seriousness of her situation, she started walking every day. Mia and her together. A half mile at first. Then one, then two, three, and four. It was like a born-again religious fervor. She changed her diet. No more sugar, no more refined foods with high fructose corn syrup. She went weird for spinach and carrots and kale. She said she felt like a cow, eating nothing but greens and veggies. But she lost sixty pounds, and her diabetes nearly went away. Then Mia tripped and broke her ankle. She had to have it pinned. She was down for over six months. Mom had to stay home with her. She fell off the wagon. No more walking, and back to her old eating habits. She put the weight back on, and the diabetes came back. She got a foot infection that wouldn't heal. They amputated, but the infections had spread elsewhere. She died not long after. That's when I had Mia move in with me. Now I'm in jail, worthless to Mia. I've failed in every way." She gave me a hard look. "Why are you even here? What's in it for you?"

"I was hired by the armored truck company to look into the robbery. From there I've segued into concerned-citizen territory. I'm concerned about your case. It must be scary being in jail."

"Yeah. But it's not as bad as some things."

I didn't expect that answer. "What could be scarier?"

"The Night Swim."

"The swim you wanted to do in Lake Tahoe," I said.

"At night, yeah. I think I told you I couldn't do it. I still have nightmares about it. I'd rather sleep in this noisy jail than do a Night Swim."

"McKenna," a loud male voice said. "Time's up."

I looked at Evan. Her brow was furrowed with worry. I felt I hadn't done anything helpful. "Your situation may not look good," I said. "But there are some possible ways out of this."

She made a tentative nod. "When Mia is in a bad way, she believes she will find some fairy dust that will make everything better. That doesn't work for me. Nevertheless, whenever I begin to have doubts, I remind myself of what J.M. Barrie, the author of Peter Pan, said. 'The moment you doubt whether you can fly, you cease to ever be able to do it.'"

"A good rule," I said. "I'll be in touch."

She made a small nod, and I gave her a little wave as I turned to leave. As I was going out of the room, I glanced back.

Evan had lifted her elbows to the counter and dropped her head to her hands.

A guard came and tapped his fingers against her shoulder.

FORTY-FIVE

As I drove home, I thought about what Evan looked like as I left the jail, her elbows on the counter and her head in her hands. Her last words to me were brave. But her posture was a picture of despair.

I couldn't get the image out of my mind. It reminded me of a Van Gogh painting. I remembered it as an old man sitting on a chair, elbows on his thighs, his head lowered into his hands. I didn't remember the title, nor did I remember any information about when Van Gogh painted it. But I recalled that the man was rendered in blue pants and blue shirt, and the painting had always stood out to me as a masterful depiction of depression and despair.

After I got home, fed Spot, and got a fire going in the wood stove, I fetched a couple of Sierra Nevada Pale Ales from the fridge, went over to my shelves of art books, and pulled out my monograph on Van Gogh. I scooted the rocker up to the wood stove, set the beers on the floor next to it, and flipped through the book until I saw the painting.

It was called Sorrowing Old Man (At Eternity's Gate). Van Gogh painted it in 1890, two months before he committed suicide.

I stared at the painting as I drank one of the beers. The subject's face was not visible, just his head in his hands. The impact of the image was almost as potent and undeniable and heartbreaking as my memory of Evan at the jail, her head in her hands.

I took a long pull of beer as if to bring myself back to the here and now, as if to force a redirection of emotion, a negation of the pain of depression. But the painting still seared. And as I drank beer and stared at the painting, the Sorrowing Old Man morphed in my mind into Evan Rosen at the jail, despondent at a situation that offered no escape.

I closed the book, sat, and finished the beer.

Spot was sprawled sideways on his bed nearby. For some reason, he wasn't snoozing. He rolled up onto his chest, elbows spread wide, right front paw crossed over the left, and looked at me with droopy eyes.

"Sorry if I'm telegraphing stress, Largeness," I said. "That girl you met is in big trouble. I'm worried about her, and I'm powerless to make it better. Worst of all, I put the trouble onto her. Probably, some bad guy somewhere set it up for her to take the fall on a couple of murders. But I brought in the cops and pointed them at her like I was aiming artillery at a helpless child. Now she's in a place with no cover and no serious hope of defense. They're going to come and tie her to the stake and light the torches while they call for her to confess her witchcraft. It won't matter whether she professes her alliance to evil or refuses to acknowledge any wrongdoing. When they touch the torches to the pyre, she'll go up in flames. At the last moment, I'll probably try to intervene. But it won't be like in the grand stories, Lancelot riding in on his steed to rescue Guinevere while the rejected King Arthur secretly hopes for his success. No, I'll fall off my mount, and the king's knights will throw a line around my neck and drag me off behind galloping horses. The girl's going to burn, and there's nothing I can do."

Spot shifted forward, doing a little two-step elbow shift toward me so that he was now within reaching distance. I pulled the opener out of my pocket, opened the next bottle, and drank deeply. Spot and I both stared at the flames through the wood stove window. I reached out and pet him while I drank.

"She's no Guinevere," I said. "She doesn't scintillate. There's no gorgeous sparkle. She's like Street was as a runaway trying to escape the abusive, deadly father. But unlike Street, who could blast through the multiple barriers with sheer force of intelligence and will and no responsibilities slowing her down, this girl has a sister to take care of. The sister is sweet and loving and deserving of all the girl can give her, but it still sucks up the girl's mental and physical resources. The girl has no one to help. There's no fairy dust to make it all better."

Spot, with new frontal exposure to the heat of the wood

stove, started panting. But he was somber. He understood that my tone wasn't happy.

I drank more beer, guzzling it down harder now. I got to the end, drained the last drops, and set the bottle down on the floor, a hard impact, not unlike the way Evan had dropped her head to her hands.

"Even still," I said, "the girl's got her own fire down in there, tamped down, half-starved of oxygen, but a fire nonetheless. From the outside, she appears to be an ordinary kid trying to make her way through life and doing a lackluster job of it. But when you get in up close, you see she's someone who never really had a break, never got to stand at the round table and make her pitch, never got to show the knights what she could do if someone would just help get the wind in there to fan her desires."

FORTY-SIX

It took two calls to get the name of the Assistant DA who was handling cases in South Lake Tahoe. I called his office.

"Steve Ditmars's office," a man said.

"Owen McKenna calling for Mr. Ditmars."

"I'm sorry, Mr. Ditmars is unavailable. Would you like to leave a message?"

"Please. I'm the private investigator who provided most of the information that led to the indictment of Evan Rosen. I have new information about the case that Mr. Ditmars will want."

"Hold on, please."

I waited to music that had been designed as torture. This particular selection featured a male singer trying to sing with a baby girl voice and then channeling it through an echo chamber. The song had no discernable melody and unintelligible lyrics. It was an effective technique that would make most callers on hold give up. I, too, had almost succumbed when a voice came on.

"This is Steve Ditmars."

"Owen McKenna. Thanks for taking my call, which is about Evan Rosen, a woman you have in custody. I have new information on the case. As you probably know, the search of Evan Rosen's apartment revealed two thousand plus dollars in cash hidden under her garbage. The assumption was that it may have come from the armored truck robbers who were murdered. I've since learned that the money appears to be legitimate."

"Why don't you come to my office and we'll talk. I also have a development you'll want to know. Something serious. Can you meet me today? Eleven a.m.?"

"Sure."

The man told me where to find him in the El Dorado County government center on Johnson Boulevard, just around the corner from the jail in South Lake Tahoe. I told him I'd be there.

At the appropriate time, Spot and I parked in the lot off Johnson. I went in and found Assistant DA Ditmars's office. A secretary took my name and waved me in.

Ditmars and I shook hands, said our how-do-you-dos, and made a little small talk about the weather. The man was maybe 28 years old at the outside. From just his first few words, he telegraphed an obvious, razor-sharp intelligence and substantial education. His youth might be a handicap in court. But his appearance would possibly scare jurors into doing his bidding. Ditmars was a thin, well-dressed man with a countenance so severe it would frighten children. His eyes were close set, his eyebrows angry black slashes not unlike the shape of the fright marks on the hockey masks. Ditmars had thick black hair combed up into a spiky look that had been set in place with so much goo that a saber-toothed tiger would rather take a chance on the La Brea Tar Pits than wander too close to Ditmars's head.

He pointed me toward a chair, sat down at his desk, and gave me a long and very serious look before he spoke.

"You said you had information about the cash found in Ms. Rosen's apartment."

I made a single nod. "Yes. I visited her at the jail last evening. She explained that she learned from her mother to always keep an emergency stash of cash, just in case things go bad. She's a house cleaner by trade, a job that doesn't produce a lot of income. Yet she has periodically added one hundred dollars to the kitty and built it up to over two thousand. The woman takes care of her sister Mia, a woman with a disability, and she considers the cash an insurance policy for Mia, to help her in the event that something should interfere with her house cleaning income."

Ditmars made the kind of nod that suggested he'd heard such explanations a thousand times over his long career in the legal profession. "Yes, I understand that this is possible. The specificity of the details make the story quite believable. But our main evidence is the button you and Sergeant Bains found in the hand of one of the victims."

"A button that could have come from any number of places," I said. "However, it very likely came from Evan Rosen's shirt. It increasingly appears that someone is trying to frame Evan for murder. I believe that the frame was carefully planned, and the real murderer chose Evan because she knew the robbers back in high school. Then he broke into Evan's apartment, took the button from her shirt, and planted the ski pole under her clothes, all before the murders took place."

Ditmars rested his hands on the desk, the fingers of his left hand twisting a heavy ring, perhaps a class ring, on the ring finger of his right hand. "I understand that is a remote possibility. However, Ms. Rosen has withheld other important information, information that suggests a strong motive for the killings."

"And what is that?" I asked.

"Nine years ago, when Evan Rosen was nineteen, she claimed she was sexually assaulted, possibly by multiple men. We've obtained a police report from the Reno Police."

"You're saying she was gang raped?"

"So she believed. She had gone to a dance rave in a warehouse area of Reno. She remembered having some drinks, dancing, and seeing some people she knew. Then she remembered nothing further until she woke up early the next morning lying on a couch at an abandoned apartment. Ms. Rosen had a shirt on, but her pants and underwear were off, the underwear torn. She was horrified and frightened. So she put on her pants and left, running two miles home to the apartment where she lived with her mother and sister. There, she took a long bath to calm herself and tried to remember what happened. She called a friend, and the friend came over and convinced her to report the crime to the Reno Police. The police took her to the hospital emergency room where they have a rape kit. Unfortunately, there was little to find. Because the woman had bathed and urinated and brushed her teeth and changed her clothes, direct evidence of any rape was gone. However, the hospital was able to get enough of a urine sample to test, and they found in her urine a drug called Rohypnol. It's illegal in this country but legal in many other countries, where it is commonly prescribed as a sleeping pill. It is also commonly used as a date rape drug because it has little to no odor or taste and it easily dissolves in drinks. Newer supplies have had dye added because of this very problem. But the non-dye version is still available in some places. And even the version with dye can't be seen if it's put into dark beer or other dark drinks."

I said, "I assume this stuff knocks you out like other date rape drugs?"

Ditmars nodded. "If someone drops it in your drink, it dissolves fast and renders you pretty helpless or even unconscious within fifteen minutes of consuming it. And of course, when the drug is combined with alcohol, it has an even more intense effect. When you awaken hours later, you feel like you've got a major hangover. And you generally can't remember anything that happened during the time the drug was in your system."

"A terrible situation," I said. "But what does it have to do with your current case against Ms. Rosen?"

"As you might imagine, Evan Rosen had no memory of any assault. But in addition to waking up with her pants off, she reported feeling very hung over and with a sickening feeling that she'd had sex that she couldn't remember. Nor could she remember anyone who'd been at the apartment with her or even how she'd gotten there."

I stayed silent, waiting for the punch line that Ditmars had been working toward.

He said, "In the police report, she stated that she clearly remembered the earlier part of the evening at the rave. She said that three guys from her high school class had shown up at the dance. She didn't dance with them, as she had always thought them disgusting, but as she was dancing somewhat provocatively – her words on the police report – with another young man, the kids from her high school catcalled her and made lewd suggestions. Later, they hung around her in a kind of triangle so that no matter which way she turned, one of them was always behind her. She said they were drunk and rude, and they scared her dance companion away. She said that she was distracted when they frightened her dance partner, and she believes it was probably at that moment that one of them dropped a pill in her drink. From that point on, she remembered nothing until she woke up in the abandoned apartment."

"Did the police charge anyone?" I asked.

"No. There was no evidence and no witnesses."

"So there was no case to bring," I said.

"Right."

"Did she remember the names of the three guys from her high school who were catcalling her?"

Ditmars nodded. "Yes. Lucas Jordan and Carter Remy, the two men who were killed by the ski pole spears out by Baldwin Beach. The third was another student named Gavin Pellman."

It was the name of the person in the other photo Rosen had pointed to in the yearbook, the third person who, in her words, didn't deserve to live.

Ditmars said, "Because she believes they raped her, that gives her substantial motive for wanting them dead even if money weren't involved."

"The third name you mentioned," I said. "Any idea what happened to Pellman?"

"No."

"You said it was nine years ago. That's a long time to nurse a motive," I said.

"Maybe it took that long for her to get brave enough or hardened enough to murder."

"It would take a great deal of strength to stab someone clear through with a ski pole. And from the angle of the thrust, it appears that the murderer was quite tall."

"Such are appearances," Ditmars said. "But that doesn't prove anything. Someone as devious as Evan Rosen would take that into account and try to arrange the crime to make the situation look like it doesn't fit her well."

"But my other explanation makes even more sense now that you've found a possible motive. It gives the real murderer even more reason to frame her."

Ditmars shook his head. "I think you should face the facts. It's common for people like her to end up like this, in a jail cell, at the end of a long history of bad choices." Ditmars said it in a way that sounded like he was being philosophical. But it merely sounded petty and vicious.

"We all make bad choices at times," I said. "When I was young, I went to bars that I would now think were stupid places to hang out. Going to a rave and dancing provocatively may not be as safe as going to Sunday school, but it doesn't mean you deserve to be raped."

Ditmars flipped his hand through the air in a dismissive wave. His spiked hair wobbled from the motion. "Of course not. But she probably did those kinds of things often, going to the wrong places, hanging out with the wrong crowd. Because people in my line of work talk shop, I know of that Reno neighborhood, and I've heard of Wilson High School. Kids from that part of town are notorious for getting into trouble. They know what the right thing is, but they actively choose the wrong thing."

"You never made bad choices?"

"No." Ditmars sounded affronted. "I could have. Where I grew up in the industrial part of South San Francisco, kids often got into trouble. But I decided early on to be a good kid. I got grief for it. But I had the sense to stick to my principles."

"How do you know that Evan Rosen didn't do the same thing?"

"Because she went to a rave and drank. Probably lots of times. And this time it caught up to her."

"Let me ask a related question," I said.

Ditmars frowned.

"Did you do well in school?"

"Of course. I was in the top five percent of my high school class. I graduated from Sac State with honors. I went to California Western School of Law in San Diego and graduated in the top half of my class. I passed the bar exam on my first try."

"Did you have two parents growing up?"

"Sure. What does that have to do with anything?"

"Did both of your parents participate in your life, help you with homework, take you to events, take you traveling, take you up to The City to see a play or visit a museum? Did they take you on family vacations?"

Ditmars looked shocked.

I continued, "Did your parents have enough money that you never worried about food on the table? Did you ever want for a doctor or dentist when you needed one?"

Ditmars's ears had turned red. His eyes were even narrower than before.

"Listen, McKenna, I don't know what you're trying to do here, but…"

"I'm pointing out that you had a host of advantages that pre-selected you for success. For you to sit here and judge Evan Rosen with your sanctimonious attitude is the height of callous indifference. Maybe she made some bad choices, but she was raised in a crappy neighborhood by a mom whose husband abandoned the family. As long as she can remember, she's had to help take care of her disabled older sister. Her mom had significant health problems and died a few years back. Now the sister lives with Evan. Evan cleans houses, which is back-breaking work. She has to bring her sister along on her jobs. She never had anyone dedicated to giving her a full life with an intellectually-engaging childhood. Nevertheless, Evan was valedictorian of her high school class. And she has a four point O average at UNR."

Ditmars shook his head. "Anyone could be valedictorian at that high school."

I continued as if he hadn't spoken. "But she couldn't go to college after she got out of high school, partly because she had to stay home to help take care of her sister, partly because they had no money, but mostly because she didn't have anyone giving her positive feedback and showing her the way. She has a dream of someday going to law school and joining you in your profession, but her circumstances have so far precluded that from even being a remote possibility."

Ditmars stood up. He was shaking with anger. "McKenna, you are so far out of line, you'd better be careful. Yes, I had decent parents who tried to do well by me, but I bootstrapped my way all the way up through school, studying my ass off, taking out student loans, which I'll be paying off for the next twenty years. I didn't have a rich daddy who paid all my bills. I'm covering it all myself. So you can leave this office right now."

I stood up to go. "Just one more question. Did either of your parents or aunts or uncles go to law school, let's say California Western School of Law where you went?"

Ditmars hesitated. "What if one of them did? So what? I earned every accolade I've been given."

"No further questions, counselor," I said, and walked out.

FORTY-SEVEN

Because I was in South Lake Tahoe, I decided to stop by the hospital and see how Jonas Montrop was doing.

There was a different woman at the reception desk. After inspecting my credentials, she consulted her computer and told me that he'd been released that morning.

"Does your record show where he went? Do you know who picked him up?"

"No, I'm sorry. He probably went home, right? I remember him waiting here for a bit. I noticed him because he looked worried. Then a cab arrived, and he left. We have a phone number on file. I can't give it to you, but it's a local prefix if that helps."

I pulled out my note of his home number and read it off.

"Yes, that's what we have," she said.

"Thanks."

I left and drove over to Tahoe Keys Boulevard and pulled into Jonas's drive, parking next to the old VW microbus.

When I knocked on the door, a frightened voice said, "Who is it?"

"It's Detective Owen McKenna, Jonas. I went to the hospital, and they said you'd been released. I thought I'd stop by and see how you are doing."

The door opened an inch until chains stopped its movement. Jonas looked out at me, then carefully peered past me and to the sides. He shut the door. I heard two chains being slid. I knew that no number of chains would secure the door because it was set into such a lightweight frame. But if it gave him comfort, that was good.

The door opened. Jonas motioned me inside, then quickly shut the door behind me, rehooking the chains.

"The cops had someone replace the broken lock," he said, pointing. "He put metal straps up to hold the door frame back together. And he added two chains. So at least I'm a little safer."

"Are you worried the kidnappers will come back?"

"I shouldn't be, if only because my stepdad is now dead. Who would they ransom?" He glanced at the windows. "But I admit I'm afraid. I used to like this cabin. Now I just see how the door is flimsy, a couple of the window locks don't work, and the back door is completely hidden by trees so none of the neighbors would notice if someone broke in. I'm going to move to an apartment building as soon as I can find one for a similar rent. That will be safer."

"How are your wounds?" I pointed toward his wrists.

He held his wrists out as if to look at them. "Better. Still scabby. But that'll go away. I still can't lift my arms up to my forehead."

"Are you able to go back to school?"

"Yes, but spring quarter is almost over. I was going to take classes over summer session, but I have to figure out how to pay for it now that my school allowance died with my stepdad. One of the nurses said I might be able to get some kind of restitution if the kidnappers could be caught. But I wouldn't know where to begin on that. I'd probably have to call a lawyer, right? I have no money for that."

"What happens to your stepfather's assets? Did he have a will?"

"I have no idea. I doubt it primarily because I doubt he had any assets to worry about. He was always trying to work a deal, and as a result, he never saved or did anything sensible. If he needed money, he saw the solution as working another scam, not working like everyone else."

"I learned that his house in Incline is actually owned by an LLC out of Vegas," I said.

"Oh, that's perfect. That's classic David Montrop. One more part of a scam, no doubt."

"Have you thought any more about the kidnapping? Have you remembered anything else that might help us track the kidnappers?"

"I wish. It's very scary to think of them out there. I keep having nightmares about men in hockey masks, tying me up, whispering threats in my ear. I wake up calling out, soaked with sweat."

"I don't mean to sound like I'm downplaying it, but it will get better with time."

Jonas nodded.

"Anything else you need?"

"No. Just catch those guys, please."

I didn't want to tell him that it had already been long enough that it was unlikely we ever would. "We'll keep trying," I said. "One more question. You said you didn't know where Flynn lives. Can you think of anyone who might? Or any way I might try to find him?"

Jonas shook his head. "No, sorry. He used to stop by all the time. We had good times together on my boat. That's why he wanted to buy it. But after the boat started leaking, Flynn got so mad at me, I haven't seen or heard from him in weeks." Jonas paused, then said, "I'm no help to you at all, am I?"

"Don't worry about that. But if you think of anything, give me a call right away, okay?" I gave him my card.

FORTY-EIGHT

After I left, I went over what I knew about the man known only as Flynn.

He was a contemporary of Evan as well as the robbers who'd been killed. He hadn't gone to Wilson High in Reno, but he hung out there. He must have been about the same age, which would put him in his mid-to-late twenties. I also remembered thinking that if you took the man called Flynn in the yearbook and had him put on 130 pounds, he'd look something like Randy Bosworth of Reno Armored. Evan thought Flynn had spoken with an accent, possibly Australian. I'd thought the same about Randy Bosworth.

The logical next step would be to ask Bosworth about his past, find out if he had gained a lot of weight since high school or if he had a skinny brother. But after getting him in trouble with his boss, I knew I'd never get any information out of him.

Finding someone when you didn't know anything about them other than a first name and a location where'd they'd been seen nine years earlier was not an easy task.

When I got home, I called Street.

"You're pretty savvy with the whole social media thing, right?" I said when she answered.

"Not at all."

"But you said you do Facebook."

"I use Facebook in just a rudimentary way. It just allows people to have a vague sense of what I'm up to so I don't have to send out Christmas cards. And it takes less time than checking in with people by telephone or email. My use of Facebook is sporadic and somewhat ineffectual."

"Like I said, you're savvy with social media."

"You're thinking of joining Facebook?"

"No. But I'm wondering if you could show me how to do

something on it. I think I told you about a guy who used to hang out at Wilson High in Reno nine years ago. All I know is that he went by Flynn and he knew Evan and the two robbers who were murdered."

"But you're a detective. It's your business to find missing people."

"Sure. I could use the old skip tracing tricks. Often the gumshoe technique of going door-to-door with a photo will produce results. But in this case, the information about this guy is so lean, it might take ten years. I'm thinking that new technology might speed things up. I've heard that people find long-lost relatives and friends on Facebook."

Street was silent for moment. "What you're saying is that despite your skip tracing skills, you haven't a clue about this guy's whereabouts."

"Busted. What say you? Would you help me?"

Over the phone, I could hear Street shaking her head. "Owen, I'm a scientist. My contacts are other entomologists in insect paradises like Hawaii and sub-saharan Africa and Indonesia. People who study bugs are by definition introverts. Why else would we spend so much time with little creepy crawlies? How are entomologists scattered around the world going to know a guy named Flynn who was last seen in Reno nine years ago?"

"I guess I had a vague idea that Facebook had an enormous reach."

"Okay, come over and I'll show you the limitations. And bring His Largeness. Blondie could use a run in the forest. I haven't let her off the leash for a while because my neighbor saw a mountain lion the other day. But if Blondie's with Spot, she'll be safe."

Spot and I drove down the mountain and showed up at Street's condo door 15 minutes later. Blondie was so excited, she started leaping at Spot, who kept turning and giving her shoulder blocks. Then they bolted into the forest, Blondie darting at random through the trees, Spot trying without much luck to keep up.

Street and I went inside, and I pulled a dining chair over to her desk so we could both sit at her computer. Street brought up her Facebook page.

"Basically, think of this as a bulletin board," she said. "I can stick stuff on the board. Other people who pay attention to my board and have my permission to look at it will see what I put on it." She stopped and looked at me to see if I comprehended.

"That's what Facebook is?" I said.

"Well, it's more than that, but that's the main thing I know how to do. Did you think it was something else?"

"I… I guess I assumed it was a book of faces."

Street started giggling. "Oh, that's rich. Tell me you're joking." She laughed so hard her face turned red. "Maybe I could post that on Facebook. My boyfriend, the brilliant detective Owen McKenna, is wondering where to find the book of faces."

"Sure, humiliate me across the internet universe."

She was still giggling. "Were you hoping to search through the book of faces and see if Flynn was in there?"

"Something like that." I pulled out the Wilson High yearbook and showed her Flynn's picture.

"Here's what we'll do," Street said, still making little laugh hiccups. She opened her scanner, set the photo on it, and hit the button. The scanner light moved under the photo. In a moment, Street used her trackpad and tapped keys, and Flynn's nine-year-old photo appeared on her screen.

"So," Street said, "if you like I can post this photo on my Facebook page with a little explanation. Then my limited group of nerdy science friends can look and see if they recognize his picture and his name. If they are incredibly bored and have nothing to do, they could also send the picture to their circle of friends. Although I should warn you that scientists have a limitless curiosity, so they are never incredibly bored. As you can imagine, the chances that someone I know happens to also remember a Flynn from years ago in Reno are very small."

"I can see the futility," I said. "Plus, if you posted Flynn's picture, your Facebook friends would probably think you're a bit strange, as if you were incredibly bored and had nothing to do."

"Then I'll word it so they know that you are behind it," Street said. "Okay, how about this." Street began to type as she spoke. "'Hi all. My private investigator boyfriend Owen McKenna is trying to locate an important witness in a case that goes back years. The man's name is Flynn, last name unknown, and Flynn was last seen at Wilson High School in Reno nine years ago. I don't imagine that any of you know Flynn or were at Wilson High nine years ago. But some of you might know someone who was in that area, and you could put the question to them. Long shot, right? But hey, that's what Facebook is good for.'"

Street clicked and dragged with her track pad and then tapped a few more keys. "Now I'll upload the picture we just scanned and put it on my page above what I just wrote."

"Got it," I said.

She clicked again. The picture of Flynn appeared on the screen just above what she'd written. "There, you're live on the Street Casey Entomologist Facebook page. Something like twenty-seven people in the universe can now see it."

"I really appreciate your help."

"No sweat," she said.

"Some of your colleagues might think you've gone around the bend. If so, I'd feel bad about…"

"Hold on," Street said. She pointed at the screen. "We've got incoming. We couldn't get a reply that fast, could we? But we did. This is from Candy Cane Cloutier, an entomologist in Miami."

"Candy Cane?"

"She studies certain ants and uses a particular brand of candy canes for bait. When she got written up in one of the journals, the writer used the moniker, and it's stuck ever since. Here's what she wrote."

Street read. "'Hi, Street. I've never heard of Wilson High and I've only been to Reno once. But remember when I was vacationing in Tahoe three months ago and your schedule was too busy for us to get together? Anyway I got talking to a restaurant waitress who works as a ski instructor in the winter. She got her master's degree in sociology, and we got into the whole thing about the similarities between groups of people and groups of social insects, especially bees. I know, sounds like a riot, doesn't it! Anyway, we were trying to quantify the male's place in a world where all the worker bees are female. Remind you of people? Ha! Other than fertilizing the queen, the drones, i.e., the males, are pretty much worthless, right?'"

Street turned to me, grinned like the Cheshire Cat, then went back to reading.

"'So this waitress was using male ski bums as comparisons. She said they're just like drone bees, good for nothing except sex. And then she joked about how they mostly weren't even good at that. But her example was a ski bum named Flynn. I remember the name because she said he was flaky. Flaky Flynn, she called him, and she said she could have really used him as a role model of uselessness back when she was writing her sociology thesis. Anyway, I'm pretty sure that Flynn basically hangs out at the ski area where she is a ski instructor. He's probably not the guy your guy wants. But how many Flynns can there be?'"

Street paused.

"Is that the end of Candy Cane's note?"

"Yeah," Street said, nodding as she typed. "I'm asking her if she remembers the name of the waitress or the ski resort or the restaurant."

"Just what I was thinking," I said.

"Here it comes back. 'No on the waitress name or the ski area name. But the restaurant was right on Lake Tahoe on the West Shore. A good sized place. Outdoor tables on the water where we had beers even though it was snowing! We huddled under the overhead warmers, and it was great. I got the feeling the ski area was close by.'"

"Sunnyside Restaurant," I said. "And Homewood Ski Resort is just down the road. Perfect."

"Okay, let me thank Candy Cane Cloutier and sign off." Street typed.

"I'm really impressed," I said when she was done.

"You're welcome."

"I just have one question," I said.

"What's that?"

"Are men really like male bees, good for nothing except sex?"

"I suppose some men aren't even good for that. But regardless of your value, you can rejoice that you don't have the sex life of a drone bee."

"Really? Why?"

Street made a hint of a grin. "Because a drone bee has to be very lucky to get accepted by the queen. Only the tiniest percentage of drone bees get that honor."

"You say that like it's a problem."

Street nodded. "From the perspective of the male bee, probably yes. Glorious as it may seem, sex for the lucky drone is a one-time event. Because when the drone and the queen are done, and the drone tries to separate, the queen's grip is so tight that the drone's genitals rip off and stay inside the queen."

"Oh! Major ouch. What happens then?"

"The drone dies immediately."

"Okay, I changed my mind. The life of a monk looks better and better."

An hour and a half later, I was on the West Shore at Sunnyside Restaurant.

Spot was unconscious in the rear seat. I cracked the windows an inch, and went inside.

"Table for one?" the host asked.

"Actully, I'm looking for someone. A friend said she knew a waitress here who is a ski instructor in the winter. Does that sound familiar?"

He looked off at a blank wall. His fingers made counting motions. "Four. Four of our female wait staff are ski instructors. Well, actually, one is a snowboard instructor. And three of our male wait staff are ski instructors. Let me think. We represent Squaw, Alpine, Northstar, and, of course, Homewood just down the road."

"This instructor is a sociologist."

"Heck, yes, I know her. Sophie Gaines. A sociologist by education. Never underestimate the wait staff at Tahoe restaurants. I, for example, am a screenwriter."

"Hey, that's great. Is Sophie around?"

"Her shift was over twenty minutes ago. She lit out of here like a Nascar driver in the pole position."

"Any idea of where I could find her?"

He shook his head.

At a nearby table were three teenagers with their wallets out, counting their money.

"Phone number?" I said.

Another head shake. "Privacy laws. But I could leave her a message."

"That would be great." I handed him my card. "If you would, please tell her that my name is Owen McKenna, and I'm a private investigator looking for a ski bum named Flynn. Tell her I learned about her from an entomologist in Florida."

"Are you serious? A PI? An entomologist in Florida? That's, like, right out of a screenplay."

"Yeah. Maybe I'll let you write the story."

He regarded me for a moment, then pulled out his phone and dialed.

"Sophie? I've got a private investigator here who is looking for you. Says he wants to know about a ski bum named Flynn. He heard about you from an entomologist in Florida. Is that…" Pause. "Okay."

The man clicked off his phone and put it in his pocket. "She's heading to the Tahoma Market. She'll meet you there in twenty minutes. She drives a white Toyota Highlander. Do you know where the Tahoma Market is?"

"Yes. Thanks. I'll meet her there."

Spot barely opened an eye when I got into the Jeep. "Coulda had a burger for you, Largeness, but it didn't work out." I pulled out of the parking lot and turned south. In several minutes, I was at the Tahoma Market, a small, cute general store inside an old Tahoe cabin-style building. I pulled over to the side of the road and stopped.

Five minutes later, a white Toyota Highlander pulled into a space near the market's front door. I got out and trotted across the highway.

"Sophie Gaines?"

The woman who looked up at me was in her thirties and had the frown of the reluctant intellectual. Her hiking boots and jeans and flannel shirt and Carhartt vest revealed the rugged Tahoe outdoors woman. But the master's in sociology, which she probably kept secret from most locals, produced the tension frown. I'd seen it many times. It's hard to pursue a profession that requires a university in the big city, when the heart wants to put some snacks and craft brews in the pack, strap climbing skins onto the back-country skis, and bag another Sierra Crest peak. Once there, the body and soul can look down across the vast snowfields, munch some sharp cheddar and whole grain crackers, and drink a fermented celebration to a late-spring sunset, the big reddish orb lowering into the Pacific 170 miles to the west.

"I'm Owen McKenna," I said, reaching out my hand.

She shook my hand, but said nothing.

"Sorry for the interruption in your afternoon. I'm an investigator looking into a crime, and my current case has me searching out a man whose first name is Flynn. Through a question posted on my girlfriend's Facebook page, your name came up as someone who knew a ski bum named Flynn. I don't know if this is the Flynn I want, but I'm hoping you can help me."

She hesitated. Maybe she wasn't suspicious. But she was cautious.

"Who's your girlfriend? Do I know her?"

"Street Casey. She's an entomologist who lives near me across the lake."

The woman thought about it.

I waited.

Eventually, she said, "What is this crime you're investigating?"

"There have been three murders, one in Incline Village, and two on the South Shore near Baldwin Beach. We don't have many leads. But two of the victims were suspects in an armored truck robbery. Those two men went to Wilson High School in Reno. Flynn, who's in his late twenties, spent at least some of his high school years in Reno and spent time with the victims. I have indications that he's recently spent time in the Tahoe Basin."

Another pause. "This man named Flynn," she said. "Is he a murder suspect or a witness or…"

"He may be a suspect. But my best guess is that he's a potential victim. He apparently knew two of the murder victims, and he was friends with a person who has connections to the third victim. My guess is that he has some kind of past relationship with the murderer, but he may not know that the person is a killer. If Flynn doesn't pay attention to the news, he also may not yet know that anyone has died. If I could speak with him, I could alert him to the potential danger. Is there any chance you could give me his contact info or tell me where to find him?"

"I don't know enough to be of much help. All I recall was a guy who skied almost daily at Homewood."

I pulled out the photo of Flynn and showed her. "Is this the man?"

"Yes. Although now he's a lot heavier."

"Do you have a phone number or address?"

"No, nothing like that. I don't even know his last name."

"Did he ever say where he worked?"

Sophie shook her head. "I got the impression he didn't work. He just played."

"Is he a trust fund baby?"

"Oh, no, nothing like that. More like a bum."

"How did you meet him?"

"He was just always around, eating his lunch outside at the busiest deck on Homewood mountain, chatting with anybody who would listen. A few times he maneuvered himself in the ski lift line so that he could ride with me on the chairlift. That was excruciating. I don't think he ever showered. He smelled of patchouli. It was awful."

"Do you know any of his friends?"

"I don't think he has any friends. Who would want to be around someone who doesn't bathe and smells like that?"

"Any idea where he lives?"

"No. Oh, wait. Perhaps one could deduce a general location. I once was teaching a mogul class up on Bonanza when Flynn showed up. He kind of hung around as if to check out my teaching moves. He struck up a conversation with two young guys who were in the class, totally interrupting my teaching. I heard him say that he was a true backwoods man who skied every day and lived in a converted garage just walking distance to the lifts. He was talking to the young men, but I think his real motive was to impress me. What a joke."

"So I should look for a converted garage near the mountain.

That's a good tip. Thanks. Anything else you can think of?"

"Not unless you can convince him to move to another ski area."

"You have some animosity for Flynn."

Sophie gave me a look of disgust. "I believe in live and let live. In other words, don't move into my space, literally or metaphorically, unless I invite you, and I won't move in on you, either. But people who dip themselves in patchouli or, for that matter, women who douse themselves in heavy amounts of perfume, are like people who bring their music to a public area and play it loud. These are the fringes of humanity who have no capacity for self-critique."

"Flynn was like that," I said.

"More than I can say."

I handed Sophie my card. "If you think of anything else useful, please let me know. Thank you very much for your time."

She nodded, turned, and walked into the Tahoma Market.

FORTY-NINE

I got back in the Jeep. Spot was sprawled across the back seat. I should have him run with Blondie every evening before bed. Maybe then he wouldn't wake me in the early morning, cold nose to my face, tail thwacking the bedside table like a drum, demanding attention from the impossibly somnolent human.

I motored north a couple of miles to Homewood and turned into one of the neighborhood roads closest to the base of the ski area. Crawling along, I looked at every garage for signs of human habitation, not sure of what would be the best indicators. Perhaps lights on inside, a barbecue out the garage's side door, a garage door that had been replaced with a picture window and siding, a wood stove smoke stack protruding from the garage roof.

There weren't many streets that were adjacent to or even very close to the ski area, but it took a surprising amount of time to cruise them all. There was nothing that fit my imagination of a converted garage. I realized that the garage where Flynn lived could look ordinary in every way. If so, the only way to find out if a garage was actually a lodging room would be to knock on the house and speak to whoever was inside. Even that would be unsatisfactory, because most of the houses were vacation homes, empty much of the year, with no one to answer the door. If Flynn left no indication of his presence, I wouldn't be able to find it.

When I'd finished with the streets that were closest to the ski lifts and ski runs, I moved out to the next tier of roads. After another fifteen minutes of slow driving, I came to a dead end and was backing around to reverse direction when something caught my eye. There was a single story house with an attached garage on its right side. Everything about it looked vacant. Its windows were dark. There was a phone book lying on the side of the drive, moist, wavy pages flipping in the wind as if it had been delivered there weeks before. Just another typical vacation home waiting for its owners to come up in July, the average start of the Tahoe summer.

Yet on the far side of the garage was a plastic garbage can. The lid was slightly crooked as though just one side had snapped into place. Near the bottom of the can were three aluminum beer cans. Maybe a bear had pried the other side of the lid loose only to find that it was full of recycles, and in the process three of the cans had fallen out.

What struck me was that most homeowners keep their recyclables inside their garages instead of outside for the simple reason that recyclables are worth money, and people don't want the trash pickup service hauling them away.

But if someone were living in the garage, he might, on the days when the trash service doesn't come, leave the recyclables outside for convenience and more space inside the garage.

I pulled over, parked, and walked over to the garage. There were windows in the garage door, but they were dark. Leaning up close and using my hand to shade the glass, I saw that there was some type of dark curtain or shade pulled over the glass. I moved around to the side door near the recyclables can and knocked.

There was no response. After a second knock and 30 seconds wait, I pulled out my shirt tail and gently used it to try the doorknob. The knob was locked, but the pressure of my touch made the door flex a bit. I gave it a light push. The door moved. I saw some folded paper fall to the floor, and then the door swung in with no added pressure.

I reached in and swiped my hand at the wall, catching a light switch.

An old fluorescent fixture on the ceiling flickered, then came on, bright and harsh and buzzing like a trapped hornet.

The garage apartment reminded me of Jonas Montrop's cabin. At my feet were scattered remnants of the broken door frame along with the tightly folded copy paper that had been wedged between the door and jam to temporarily hold the door shut with friction.

Everything was a mess, furniture askew, a small wooden table tipped over. There was a counter with a two-burner stove top and microwave. Next to it was a sink that was similar to what

Evan had in her motel apartment, only this sink was full of dirty dishes. Above it was a set of cabinets. One of the cabinet doors had been mostly pulled off and was hanging, upside down, from its bottom hinge.

On the rear wall of the garage was a bed, unmade, the top sheet pulled much farther to one side than typical for a person sliding out of bed. A heavy metal cooking pot lay next to the pillow. In the middle of the bed was a man lying face down, a ski pole protruding from his back near his left kidney. The bloody point projected three feet into the air.

Perhaps his assailant had struck him hard enough to drive the spear all the way through until the flared end was at his chest. Or maybe the spear hadn't gotten its final thrust until the victim fell face down and the bed drove it flush to his chest.

The man was small in stature. He had a thick crop of black hair. His face was turned sideways, one cheek mashed down into the bedding. The one eye I could see was wide open, as was his mouth, frozen in shock and surprise.

Although I couldn't see his whole face, I thought I knew who he was.

It was the person who was in the third photo in the Wilson High yearbook, the one where Evan Rosen could barely point at it because her finger shook so violently. Evan's third attacker from nine years ago as described by the Assistant DA.

Gavin Pellman.

FIFTY

I pulled out my phone to dial 911, but realized I didn't even know the address. So I walked out and around to the front of the house and got the number off the wall by the front door. Then I headed down the street past the Jeep. Spot was now awake and staring at me from the back seat.

Once I had the street name from the sign at the nearest intersection, I got through to the 911 dispatcher. I went through with the routine and then explained that I thought Placer County Sergeant Santiago would want to know about the crime. As always, the dispatcher asked me to stay on the line. But I said I was certain that enough time had elapsed that the murderer would not be in the area. I told the dispatcher that I would wait at the scene, and I hung up.

I went back to the garage and did another visual search of the apartment.

In the corner of the garage was a compact bathroom, its door open. In another corner was a closet of sorts, formed by a curved bar that held up a drape. I eased the fabric aside and saw some clothes on hangers and more piled on the floor. I flipped through the hangers, sliding them from one end to the other. When the clothes were moved, the end of the clothes rod became visible. Up against the wall, hanging from the rod by one of its straps, was a hockey goalie mask. Although the face openings had different shapes from the other masks, it looked equally hostile and venomous.

On the floor near the wall with the garage door lay some kind of wooden paddle about four feet long. I squatted down to look at it. Half its length was handle and the other half a paddle blade that was formed into a shallow scoop reminiscent of a shovel. The paddle was carved and inked with designs, swirls made of dots and a writhing snake pattern up one side. The wood was sanded and oiled smooth and looked a hundred years old. Or maybe hundreds of years old.

At the bottom center of the paddle blade was a nub of wood about the diameter of a carpenter's pencil. It was pointed and stuck out half an inch from the surface of the blade. It was a peculiar design that could be approximated by imagining one's palm and outstretched fingers as a paddle blade and then bending the last joint of the middle finger to represent the nub.

The nub was worn and abraded as if the paddle was designed to be displayed on a wall, hung up by poking the nub into a hole in the wall.

I left it where it lay and stood up.

It seemed clear that there had been a struggle, people grappling, knocking furniture around, throwing things. I imagined a home invasion similar to what happened when Jonas was kidnapped. Maybe Gavin Pellman kicked in the door and surprised Flynn, possibly in bed as had been the case with Jonas. But this time, Flynn had gotten the upper hand and killed his intruder with a spear.

As they fought, they bumped into nearly everything in the one-room space. It appeared that the only items that were untouched were three wooden boomerangs that hung together on one wall. Like the strange paddle, they too were decorated with patterns. The designs looked, to my naive eye, like aboriginal art, so maybe the items were Australian as well.

I looked again at the strange, carved wooden paddle. The little pointed nub at the end of the blade was a darker wood than the rest of the paddle.

Most of the paddle was the color of teak or cherry, its grain imbued with oil from back when it was first carved and finished. The nub point was as dark as black walnut. At first, it seemed apparent that the difference in color was just a natural variation in the wood, as if from sapwood to heartwood. But as I bent down to look closer, I thought I saw moisture on the dark nub. After time, water will seep into wood and darken it. I looked around for tipped water glasses or leaky plumbing, and saw none. Which made the moisture on the paddle nub especially curious.

Placer County law enforcement had yet to make an

appearance, so I dialed Diamond. In a dark situation, he can usually distract me.

It rang four times. I thought it switched over to voicemail, but suddenly he was on the line.

"Busy?" I asked.

"Always," he said.

I said, "Too busy to apply your intellect and never-ending curiosity to a conundrum at another murder scene while I wait for the local coppers?"

"Who died this time?" he asked.

"A guy named Gavin Pellman, as seen in a nine-year-old yearbook from Wilson High School in Reno. I was looking for the domicile of the missing Flynn, a young man who shared a photo op with Evan Rosen in the same yearbook. A tip about Flynn led me to a garage over by Homewood Ski Area. It's been converted into a one-room apartment. But instead of finding Flynn, I found Gavin Pellman."

"Another ski pole assault?"

"Yeah," I said.

"What's the conundrum?"

"On the wall of the garage are three boomerangs that appear old and hand-carved and painted with Australian aboriginal designs, dots and circles and writhing snakes."

"Australian decor," Diamond said. "Always liked that stuff."

I continued, "Flynn was possibly Australian, so it makes sense he would have them. Anyway, on the floor is an unusual paddle of sorts, about three feet long. Half the length is a handle like on a regular paddle, the other half is a narrow blade that is scooped enough that it would really grab the water as you paddled. Or you could pour soup into it and use it to eat your dinner. It looks like it was hand carved a long time ago, and it too has the same kind of decorations."

"An aboriginal canoe paddle?" Diamond said.

"Maybe."

"Then what's the conundrum?"

I tried to describe the little pointed nub of wood at the end of the paddle blade. "I figure it was something to hang the paddle with. Or maybe it made the blade a much nastier weapon. If someone were to swing the blade at an enemy, that would make a mean club. But with the nub, it would tear away flesh."

"Still no conundrum from my perspective."

"The nub is wet," I said. "Shiny and dark, but it doesn't look like blood. I've looked around, and there is no spilled water in the garage. If I knew something about the canoe paddle..." I heard a siren. I looked outside. A Placer County patrol unit pulled to a stop.

"Your Placer County colleagues have just arrived," I said to Diamond, "so I gotta go. But it would be fun to have you call and solve the paddle mystery while I'm still talking to Sergeant Santiago. Not that you county boys have any rivalry, of course." I hung up.

Two deputies got out of the patrol unit, one in her late thirties and one in his late twenties.

We introduced each other. He was Sergei, and she was Pam. Sergei was a big guy, and just the way he walked telegraphed self-importance in front of the much smaller, slightly older Pam. Without any evidence beyond gut instinct, I guessed that his chest puffing implied that she had more seniority and he didn't like it. I thought I should help him deal with it. So when Sergei asked a few questions, I spoke to Pam as I answered.

A fire department rescue truck rushed down the road and behind it was a fire truck, once again the overblown emergency response.

Four firemen jumped out of their vehicles looking intense and focused.

I called out, "Sorry guys, no EMT services needed. We've got a murder victim, nothing more. Maybe you guys would like to wait around and carry out the body after the ME looks at it. But it's going to be a while before they process the scene."

They nodded.

I brought the two cops into the garage. Two of the firemen followed us while two stayed back.

Sergei made a show of looking as solid as a Sierra boulder when he saw the body, but I could see that it shook him. Pam was tense but didn't posture. The firemen looked in from the door. They'd maybe seen burnt bodies, but a spear takes disturbing to another level.

All of them were respectful of routine and didn't touch or move anything. Pam started taking pictures of the crime scene.

Another patrol unit showed up ten minutes later. I went outside. Sergeant Jack Santiago got out of the passenger side door, and a deputy got out of the driver's seat.

Santiago nodded at the firemen, and he and I shook hands, and he said, "Victim in the garage?"

"Yup," I said.

"Any thoughts about the crime scene?" Santiago said.

"From the side of the victim's face, I'm guessing it's a man known as Gavin Pellman, who was a high school companion to the truck robbers. He may have been one of the robbers, too. The likely renter of this garage is a man known as Flynn, who was also one of their school mates."

"And you came upon this scene because…"

"The name Flynn and a photo of him during high school came up a few times in connection with my investigation of the South Shore spear murders and the Incline Village paddle board murder. A series of tips and hints had me looking for a converted garage near Homewood."

Santiago made a little nod. "Let's have a look at the victim."

I led him into the garage.

As Santiago looked at the body, he turned to Pam. "You take pictures?"

"Couple hundred, yeah. But we haven't touched him. So I don't have pics of anything you can't see from where we're standing."

"Establish rigor?"

"Like I said, we haven't touched him."

Santiago pulled on latex gloves, reached out and lifted on the body's arm. "He's in full rigor mortis. You check his ID?"

"We haven't touched the body," she said for the third time, weariness in her voice.

"Just checking." Santiago said. He reached into the victim's pocket and pulled out a wallet. He flipped through it. "One hundred, twenty, forty, forty-five, forty-six bucks. Guess our spear man wasn't after money." Santiago pulled out some cards, held up a Nevada driver's license. "Here we are. Gavin Pellman, just like you thought, McKenna."

Santiago was feeling in the man's other pockets. He got a grip on something and pulled it out. "Hello," he said. "A roll of cash."

The roll had a thick rubber band around it, blue like what they put around bundles of asparagus at the supermarket.

Santiago hefted it. "This is a fair piece of bank." He thumbed the corners. "Mostly hundreds. This might be eight, ten thousand. Why would spear man walk away from that kind of cash?" He turned to Pam. "Evidence bag?"

She pulled out a plastic zipper bag and held it open. Santiago dropped the money roll into it.

"So now that we know this isn't Flynn," Santiago said, "maybe Flynn is our spear man." He turned to Pam and Sergei. "I'd like you to do a thorough inventory and document all, notes and photos. I don't have a warrant, yet, but I'm pretty sure most of this guy's stuff is visible, and you can do a look-see search without touching." He walked over to a small dresser and used a tissue to pull open the drawers. "And these drawers were open, so it's easy to look inside and see the contents."

They both nodded. Pam pulled a small notebook out of her pocket. She handed her camera to Sergei. "I'll write, you shoot and describe."

Santiago got on his radio and said some words about the Medical Examiner. A woman's voice told him to hold on. Santiago said, "The ME is down on the West Slope, and our local coroner can't make it. But it's not like we don't know what killed the victim."

"Who takes the body?" I said, when he clicked off the radio.

"The county has a contract with a mortuary in Truckee. They'll make the pickup." He looked at the firemen. "So you guys can go back to the station and resume your card game."

With not even a hint of a grin, they turned and walked back to their trucks.

Santiago saw the unusual paddle on the floor. He pulled up on the front of his trousers and squatted down to look at it. "Do you know what this is?" he asked.

"Nope. It looks like some kind of Australian Aboriginal canoe paddle."

My phone rang.

"Been spending some time researching on Google," Diamond said in my ear. "The paddle you asked about? It's called a woomera."

I saw Santiago look at me. I pointed at the paddle on the floor. "I'm putting this on speaker so Santiago can hear you," I said as I switched the phone. For Santiago's benefit, I said, "It's Sergeant Martinez, Douglas County. I had called him about the paddle. Diamond, you said it's called a woomera."

Diamond's voice was clear. "Right. Like you thought, it's an aboriginal tool that goes back thousands of years. You can dig with it, dip water with it, fight with it, display your art on it. Does that sound right based on what it looks like?"

"Yeah," I said, staring at the paddle and envisioning everything Diamond said.

"But if you wanted to kill with it," Diamond said, "a woomera is hard to beat. Because their main use is as a spear thrower. They make it so you can propel a spear four times faster than with your arm alone."

"You're saying the whole point of a woomera is to throw spears?" I said as I stared at the carved wooden paddle.

"Yeah," Diamond said. "The wooden nub you mentioned. There's two ways to use it. You can hook it into a leather loop at the tail end of the spear. Or you can carve a cavity in the tail end of a spear, and the nub fits into the cavity."

"So a ski pole spear works perfect because the rear end is hollow," I said.

"Right. You hook the spear onto the little nub, then hold the spear flat against the woomera so that your hand wraps around both the woomera handle and the spear at the same time. When it comes time to launch, you swing the woomera like a tennis racket. At just the right time, you open your fingers a bit so the point of the spear shaft comes free. The spear tilts out as you swing the woomera through the air. As you finish your swing with the woomera, the spear shoots away like a tennis ball off a racket. Apparently, bushmen are so skillful with a woomera that they can kill nearly any game, piercing their prey with a wooden spear at some distance."

As Diamond said it, I thought of Evan's tennis racket. It had excessive wear on the top of the rim. I thought the wear was from striking the court. But the flared end of the spear would hook onto the top rim of a tennis racket just as well as it would hook onto the nub of the woomera. With repeated use, the flared end of the ski pole spears would abrade the tennis racket rim.

I was looking at the dark, pointed nub of wood. "Any idea why the nub would be wet? Oh, wait, never mind. I just realized that it's not water on the nub. It's olive oil from off the ski pole."

"Santiago there?" Diamond asked.

Santiago spoke up. "I'm listening in."

"My regards," Diamond said.

"Thanks for the research," I said, but he'd already hung up.

FIFTY-ONE

Santiago sent Sergei and Pam out to canvas the neighborhood, which consisted of just a few houses. He asked his other deputy to fetch his recorder. The man ran out, came back, and handed the recorder to Santiago.

"No ME means I do the honors for the time being," Santiago said. He turned on the recorder and began talking. He began by stating the time and date, the house address, his own name and rank, and the names of us present, and the victim's name and driver's license number.

"The victim is in full rigor mortis. This garage is heated and thus has provided conditions for an accelerated pace of rigor mortis. The onset of rigor mortis usually occurs within three or four hours of death. Because of the warm ambient temperature, my estimation is that rigor for this victim began earlier than normal. It also appears that the victim and his assailant struggled. Exercise also accelerates onset of rigor mortis, sometimes creating a cadaveric spasm, or immediate rigor mortis. Because of the combination of temperature and exertion, I estimate that the onset of rigor mortis began within three hours from time of death, probably much sooner, and possibly almost immediately after death.

"Temperature and exercise also accelerate the pace of rigor mortis, which usually lasts twenty-four to thirty-six hours. Because of the temperature and exertion aspects, I estimate that rigor mortis will pass within twenty-four hours from onset, or twenty-four to twenty-seven hours from time of death. Thus the victim likely died..." Santiago looked at his watch, "after two p.m. yesterday, and perhaps much more recently."

He turned off the recorder.

The two deputies came back from canvassing the neighborhood.

"Learn anything?" Santiago said.

"Not much," one said. "Only one house had anyone inside. An older woman. She says she's home all day long and doesn't miss much. But she never saw anyone come down the road that leads to this garage."

I left the scene shortly after that. I sat in the car and called Sergeant Bains. He wasn't answering. I was impatient, so instead of leaving a message, I called the South Lake Tahoe Jail, identified myself and spoke to the jail commander.

"I'm hoping you can do a favor for me. Could you please look at your log and tell me what time Evan Rosen was signed into your jail?"

"This isn't a good time," he said. "We're pretty jammed up. Maybe call back later, okay?"

"I'm sorry to bother you. This is very critical. Can you please check now. It won't take you long. I'll make it up to you."

He seemed to huff with displeasure, but he didn't speak.

I waited.

"Three o'clock yesterday afternoon, Evan Rosen was released from Placer County custody and signed into our custody."

"Thanks very much."

FIFTY-TWO

As I drove away, I went counter clockwise around the lake, heading south to South Lake Tahoe. I wanted to talk to Assistant DA Steve Ditmars, the man who'd charged Evan Rosen with murder. After our last bit of tension, I was confident he would not agree to see me. I thought it best just to surprise him, which, of course, would only work if he was in.

Ditmars's secretary was visible in the reception area outside his office, but his office door was shut. If I went in and spoke to the secretary, she might use her secret decoder ring to let him know who it was, and then he'd escape out the back.

So I went down the hall, found a small waiting area with two chairs and a table covered with magazines. I immersed myself in a Sports Illustrated. When I heard people talking down the hall, I made a surreptitious sideways glance and saw Assistant DA Steve Ditmars ushering a woman out of the office. As he turned and walked back into the office, I was behind him.

"Mr. Ditmars, so glad to find you in," I said.

He turned and made a face as if he'd just bit into a rotten banana.

"I don't have a spare moment." He turned, walked around his secretary's desk, which had been shifted to better block access to his door. As he pushed on his door to shut it, I put my hand on the door edge, opened it back up, and stepped inside behind him.

Ditmars was immediately exasperated. His jaw was set, and I could see that he was about to call security, when he had second thoughts. If I could look inside his brain, I knew I would see him forming little mental pictures of the people I was connected to, at least tangentially. He would immediately run calculations about whether those potential connections could make his life difficult. I hoped that he would decide I was a pest that he had to accommodate.

Ditmars made a show of looking at the clock on the wall. "Five minutes," he said. "Five minutes max." He sounded very firm.

"I don't need five minutes. I just left the crime scene of a third murder victim near Homewood, killed in the same manner as the first two, stabbed by an olive oil-lubricated ski pole spear. The victim is the third man we spoke about, Gavin Pellman, one of the boys Evan Rosen said may have assaulted her in Reno nine years ago. Pellman had a substantial roll of cash in his pocket. I don't yet know for certain, but the odds are great that he is a third member of the Reno Armored truck robbery gang. His possible murderer is an Australian man named Flynn, whose garage apartment is where the murder took place. Flynn owns a woomera, an aboriginal spear-throwing device. On it is some olive oil that no doubt matches the olive oil on the spear. It is clear that the same person who committed the murders for which you've charged Evan committed this murder."

Ditmars made a slow, disdainful shake of his head. "And why do you think this has any bearing on my case against Evan Rosen?"

"Because this victim is in full rigor mortis. The ME was not at the scene, but Placer County Sergeant Jack Santiago is quite expert in rigor mortis science, and he estimates the victim died after two p.m. yesterday. Evan Rosen was transferred from the custody of Placer County to the custody of El Dorado County at three p.m. yesterday. Placer County had held Ms. Rosen since the prior afternoon. That means Evan Rosen has been in custody for approximately forty-eight hours. Even if Sergeant Santiago is wildly inaccurate in his time-of-death estimate, this most recent murder took place during the time Rosen has been in custody. Therefore, the only reasonable conclusion is that you have charged the wrong person." I tossed my card onto his desk. "When you decide Evan Rosen is innocent, let me know, and I can give her a ride home."

"We'll let a jury decide if she's innocent."

I was thinking about how I might play into his possible worries about whether I could make trouble for him.

As I was about to walk out his door, I turned and said, "You ever play golf?" I said. "You and I should hit the links sometime. You'd probably like it because I'm a really lousy golfer. I make every member of any foursome I'm with feel better about their own game. As a result, guys like to play with me. I bet I've done eighteen holes with all of the bigshots at my favorite course, which is Sierra View in the foothills near Placerville. Of course, I'd do better if I chose an easier course. But I keep playing at Sierra View because I like the greens. But those doglegs are impossible. Anyway, let me know."

I turned and walked out.

I didn't know if my gambit would work. But the only man any Assistant DA is ever afraid of is the big man himself, the District Attorney. And it was widely known that the El Dorado County DA's favorite course was Sierra View.

I left and went back out to the Jeep. I didn't drive away but reached around into the back seat and pet Spot. "I'll bet you a steak-and-fries dinner that I'm going to get some action out of the El Dorado County bureaucracy within the next hour." Spot stuck his cold nose against my neck. I assumed that meant the bet was on. I dialed up NPR and listened to a Ted Talk that had just started. A half hour later, my phone rang.

"Hello?"

"Mr. McKenna? This is the Jail Commander at the El Dorado County Jail in South Lake Tahoe. I have an inmate named Evan Rosen who is being released. I was told to call you to give her a ride."

"When will she be ready to go?" I asked.

"She's ready now."

"Thanks. I'll be in soon." I clicked off the phone and turned to Spot. "You lost the bet, but how 'bout we do the steak and fries anyway?"

He wagged.

FIFTY-THREE

Evan seemed in a daze. She looked shocked, moved mechanically, didn't speak. I knew that being released from a murder charge, while a huge positive change, was nevertheless traumatic. The human psyche gears itself up for anticipated stresses. When the stress is suddenly removed, it takes time to recover.

She seemed to need help as I brought her out to the Jeep. I opened the passenger door and then shut it after she was inside. Once I got in and started the engine, I realized she was having trouble with her seatbelt, so I helped her with the latch.

As we drove, I explained the basics of what had happened, how I'd found another victim who died by spear, and that I'd demonstrated to the Deputy DA that the time of death indicated that she could not have been the murderer. Thus her sudden release.

We were halfway around the lake before she spoke.

"Is Mia okay?"

"She doesn't know you are released yet."

Evan didn't respond.

When we got to the motel apartment, Evan was even more sluggish in her movements. While Mia jumped around with excitement, I took Mattie aside and explained the situation. She told me she would stay near them both for the next day.

I drove home and called Street. She was too busy for dinner but was very glad to hear the news about Evan's release. After a short talk, I asked if she'd heard anything about her father's parole. She hadn't, which I thought was a good sign. We agreed to talk the next day, then said goodbye.

I also called Diamond, thanked him for the woomera research, and told him about Evan's release.

"I'm surprised the Deputy DA would release her that easy,"

Diamond said.

"I wouldn't say it was easy."

"You didn't imply a threat to his job or anything?"

"Me? Threaten an important government official? I'm shocked you would wonder that. You know my ethics are gold-plated."

"What I thought," Diamond said. It sounded like he might have been chuckling as he hung up.

The next morning I drove down to Sparks to see what I could pry out of Bosworth about his accent, and his similarity in looks to the picture of Flynn from nine years ago, and maybe his knowledge of Montrop's gardener Kang.

"Hi, Rita," I said as I walked into Reno Armored. I was halfway to her desk when I realized that the temperature was no longer frigid, and Rita was no longer dressed for the Arctic. She wore pants and shirt with no overcoat or scarf. Her fingers weren't blue, her fingernails weren't purple, and she wasn't shivering. "Maybe you remember me," I said.

She made an exaggerated nod. "I'm sorry if you came here to see Mr. Bosworth."

"He's out, and by the looks of you, the excessive air conditioning mandate is out as well."

"I'm… I can set the thermostat higher now. At least, I can for the time being."

"Is Bosworth on vacation?"

"He no longer works here."

"Did he quit, or was he fired?"

She said, "That's, you know, private information." She seemed to think about it for a bit. "But since you were sort of involved, I guess I can say it. It's interesting that you think he might have been let go. Yes, he was fired."

"It seemed," I said, "that the well-being of the business and the other employees was not at the top of his priority list."

She frowned an unspoken question.

I explained, "From the freezing temperature in here, to Bosworth's lack of desire to do what Mr. Timmens wanted in hiring me, he wasn't very considerate."

"Um, no, maybe not. And I should probably tell you that

your well-being wasn't at the top of his list, either."

"What did he say?"

Rita squirmed in her chair. "I don't believe I am allowed to reveal things that get said here. You know, private, company things. But I would be careful."

I gave her a polite smile. "As you know, Mr. Timmens asked me to investigate the robbery. He was upset that Bosworth withheld pertinent information from me. He might also be upset if you withheld information."

She made a little nod. Reassessing. "It's just that when Mr. Timmens came and fired Mr. Bosworth, Mr. Bosworth started yelling. He said he knew it was the detective who got him fired. And he said that the detective would pay. Only those weren't all his exact words."

"Bosworth made threats about me," I said.

"Yes. Now maybe it was just words. Like, you know, when a person is really angry."

"Did he say any details about what he might do to make me pay?"

"What do you mean?"

"Did he say, 'I'm going to go to McKenna's house and shoot him?' Or 'poison his dog?' Like that?"

Rita was shaking her head vigorously. "No. It was more general. Like you, um, messed with him, so he was going to mess with you. But he didn't use the word 'mess.'"

"Has Mr. Timmens hired a replacement yet?"

"No. It's just me for the time being. I'm to answer the phones, help keep the schedule."

I said, "I have a question for you. The other day I saw you at the window of a silver car talking to a man named Kang. Is he a friend of yours?"

"Oh, no. He was a potential customer. He wanted to know about our services. I never knew his name. Did you say Kang?"

"Yes. You don't know him personally?"

"No. Of course not." Rita seemed affronted by the idea.

"Don't potential customers speak to Mr. Timmens to learn about your services?"

"Yes. The man said he did that. He said that Mr. Timmens

suggested he come here to see our facility. I was coming back from lunch just as the man pulled up at the back parking lot. He rolled down his window and said he had talked to Mr. Timmens and he was doing some initial research on armored truck services for the company he worked for."

I held up my finger. "Let's just check on that." I got out my phone.

Rita looked worried.

"Don't worry. You've done nothing improper." I dialed. While it rang, I said to Rita, "Did the man speak good English?"

"Sure. Normal. Just like us."

I got Timmens on the phone, told him who was calling, and said, "I'm at your Sparks facility talking to Rita, and a question came up. Have you had any contact with a man named Kang? It's possible that he used a different name. If he visited you in person, he's Asian American and small in stature, although very strong. "

"No, nothing like that. Why?" he said in my ear.

"He's loosely connected to the Montrop murder case in Incline, and I saw him in his car near your Sparks facility. I wondered if he had tried to get information out of you."

"No. But Rita's very observant. Maybe she's seen something. Oh, and McKenna, Bosworth is no longer with us."

"Got it," I said. I told Timmens I'd keep in touch, and we hung up.

I turned back to Rita. "Timmens told me to ask you. So you can feel comfortable saying anything. What were Kang's questions?"

"He said he was doing quality control and security research on armored carrier firms because his company was thinking of switching providers. He wanted to know what personnel he should interview to learn how our schedules and deliveries and priorities were set. He also wanted to interview some of our guards and drivers."

"Did you give him names?"

"Well, sure. Mr. Bosworth. And Matt and Jim. Was that not the right thing to do?" Rita looked very concerned.

"No, that's fine. Was there anything else that Kang wanted

to know?"

"No. He wrote down the names I gave him. Then he saw someone drive by where we were talking, and he got real tense. He said he had to go, and he sped off."

"Where did you go after that?"

"Nowhere. I just went in the back door here and got back to work."

"If you see him again, give me a call, okay?" I set my card on her desk.

"Sure."

"One more question," I said.

Her worried look came back.

"I witnessed stress between Bosworth and Timmens," I said.

Rita made the slightest of nods.

"There is a question about whether or not Bosworth might have been involved in the robbery in some way." I didn't see any need to tell her that the question was mine. If she inferred from my statement that the question was Timmens', that might make her feel more comfortable in revealing what she thought.

"Are you asking me if I thought Mr. Bosworth was, you know, doing bad things behind Mr. Timmens's back?"

"Yeah."

She thought about it for a long time. "I never saw, you know, evidence of wrongdoing. But Mr. Bosworth had a bad attitude. I sometimes wondered about that. Like, if his attitude would make it easier for him to do bad things. When Mr. Timmens fired him, Bosworth just stomped out of here. He tried to slam the door, but it's got one of those dampers that won't let you do that. So that just made him madder."

"Didn't he take his things from his desk or wherever he had stuff?"

"Not at first. He forgot to clear out his coat locker, so he came back later to get that stuff."

"He liked it freezing in here. Why would he keep a coat?"

"Not a coat, but his skates and stuff."

"He's a skater?"

Rita nodded. "He belongs to a hockey club. They meet at a rink someplace near here, two mornings a week. I always thought he was, you know, too big to be a hockey player. Those guys have to move really fast."

"Do you know anything about the group he plays with? The other players? Or where they meet?"

She shook her head. "No, he never mentioned anything more about it. Just that he played two mornings a week."

"Thanks, Rita. I appreciate your help."

She nodded.

I turned to leave. Before I walked out the door, I turned back and said, "I'm glad for you that you no longer have to work in a freezer."

Rita gave me a big grin and a little wave.

When I got out to the Jeep, I dialed Timmens again. After his secretary put me through, I said, "I wanted to tell you that I found another one of the robbers, a man who went to high school with the other two. He was killed over on the West Shore, the same way they were."

"Really? Wow. You're doing a great job, McKenna. I'm not sorry to hear the man died. So you've got one more robber left. He's probably the one who killed the others, right? That would make him an especially nasty piece of work. Be careful, McKenna."

"I will."

We hung up.

FIFTY-FOUR

I stopped at Street's condo on my way home from Sparks. I knocked. I heard Blondie make a little bark from inside. As Street opened her door, I could see that she was shaky. Her voice wavered. She seemed unsteady on her feet.

Spot normally greets her with enthusiasm. This time he stopped and looked at Street, his brow furrowed.

I put my hand on her arm. "You got news about your father."

She nodded. Her skin was pale. She looked like she might be sick. "Aunt May called. They released him this morning."

"I'm so sorry. Did your aunt have any information about where he was going? The name of the place where he'll stay?"

"She said he's going to a halfway house in St. Louis called Liberty Pathways. I'm supposed to get an email tomorrow with the contact info for his parole officer."

"That's good. Anytime you're uncomfortable, you can contact that officer and reassure yourself that everything is okay."

Street nodded.

"You want to sit in front of the fire?"

She nodded again.

I shut the door behind me, then steered her over to her couch. I turned the dial on the fireplace thermostat control, and warm flames grew behind the fake logs.

"Wine?" I said.

She nodded.

Street's wine rack had three bottles in the lower row. All had dust on them. I pulled one out. Found the corkscrew. Pulled out the glasses. Poured.

I handed one to Street as I sat next to her on the couch. Spot and Blondie had already taken up strategic positions in front of the fire, he, with his short hair, close to the flames, and she, with her thick fur, off to the side.

The firelight reflected in Street's eyes. She looked weary and tired and fearful. I'd been paying attention to another weary, tired, fearful woman. I worried that I'd missed my primary focus.

"I want to help, but I would first need to know your desires," I said.

"Aunt May will be in contact with his probation officer. Tom Casey has to meet with the officer once a week, and the officer told Aunt May that he will be making unannounced visits to the halfway house."

I saw that Street's eyes were directed at the fire, even though I knew that she was seeing something else.

"I keep thinking about our justice system," she said. "It can't guarantee rehabilitation. It can't guarantee our safety. All it can do is sometimes find a perpetrator and sometimes take him off the streets and sometimes give us a respite from our fears."

"The cliché that there is no justice probably comes from that 'sometimes' aspect. Nothing is certain except for the sometimes. And sometimes we let the wrong guy out. But when it happens, we can prepare for it."

"How?" Street said, her voice tiny and vulnerable.

"There are several ways. Unfortunately, they all require continual focus on the problem, an ongoing awareness of threat, a plan for response, and regular practice of the moves."

"That's what I hate. If I want to prepare, I lose the innocence of free time. I can no longer just let a day unfold. Instead, I have to be on constant guard. Each day, I have to rehearse what to do if the enemy launches an attack. To be prepared, I have to assume that the worst can happen at any time. That's not living free. That's living under siege."

I made a small nod.

Street drank wine.

"I don't want you to have to live like that," I said. "But I want you safe. I'll take my cues from you. Once you decide how you want to proceed, I'm in one hundred percent."

"Give me an example," Street said.

"If you decide to continue life as normal, with no changes unless you get a change of information, then I make no changes either, except to possibly be more vigilant. If on the other hand, you want to put up full security and make it very hard for Tom Casey to get to you, or to send someone else to get to you in his place, then I'll turn your home into a bunker, your activities into an inscrutable maze, and I'll turn you into a warrior that no one could attack without a potentially deadly response. If you choose a middle-ground approach, then we'll work out a combination plan, alarm at your condo and lab, increased awareness, general security measures, escape routes, some defensive moves."

Street didn't respond. We drank wine and watched the fire.

"The girl named Evan," she finally said. "She hasn't found justice, either."

"No, I don't think so."

"Men assaulted her and went free."

"I believe so," I said.

"And she's got the responsibility of caring for her sister. But she has to do it with very little money."

"Yeah."

Street drank more wine. "If her situation were to get critical, I'd want you to call me."

"Because you could help me help her?" I said.

"Yeah."

"And that would maybe help you," I said.

"It could."

I drank the last of my wine. "Do you want me to stay here with you tonight?"

Street shook her head. "No. I need to think through this situation alone."

"You want His Largeness for protection?"

"No. You two go. I'll be okay."

So Spot and I left.

Thinking about Street's evil father made me deeply sad for Street and intensely mad at Tom Casey.

Maybe it was that building anger that fueled me when I parked at my cabin, got out, shut the driver's door, and, before I could turn to let Spot out of the back, saw the ghostly hockey mask charging toward me from the dark forest.

FIFTY-FIVE

The thick growth of trees to the side of my cabin form a heavy canopy, ensuring the darkest of cover even when the moon is bright. But the mask, with its angry dark slots, made a face as evil as one could imagine on a dark mountainside.

I had no weapon to defend myself from attack. From the speed of the rushing apparition, I instinctively knew that if I turned around to reach for the rear door handle, I would be dead before I could let Spot out. Instead, I dove to the side, my hands out as I slid to a stop on the dirt.

There was a heavy thud in the dirt near my head, a vicious strike of some kind of stick. It was clear that the attacker intended to kill me.

I scrambled up onto hands and knees and leaped back and to the side, launching myself toward my attacker. I could not see anything but the grotesque mask floating in the dark, but I sensed the movement of another swing of the stick. I raised my arms to protect my head as I sprinted into the attack. His invisible dark stick hit my outstretched fingers, bending them back as it crashed through and struck my shoulder.

My instinct was to spin away from the pain. Instead, I leaped toward it, catching the stick across my abdomen as I went down to the ground. The attacker tried to jerk the stick out from under me. I felt the motion and got a hand on the stick handle, a hard rectangular shape like a hockey stick. I held on and kicked my foot out into the darkness.

Maybe I hit his knee. He grunted and went down. I swung out with the stick, putting serious effort into it. The stick hit a tree, a blow that shattered the stick into multiple pieces.

I kept hold of the short piece in my hand and leaped through the dark toward the glowing mask. The mask disappeared, then reappeared to my right. I charged. His fist came from my left.

The blow to my ribs was like that from a battering ram. As I went down, I realized that he'd taken the mask off and held it out to his side for misdirection.

I rolled over twice, hitting a tree trunk. Got up, still holding the broken end of the stick.

The mask was floating in the darkness, taunting me. I knew it wasn't on his head, but I couldn't tell if he was holding it out with his left hand or right hand.

I threw the piece of stick to the ground far to his side. He spun at the sound. From the motion of the mask, I guessed his location. I took two running steps and dove through the air, turning to make a horizontal blocking motion, my legs and arms stretched out for maximum reach.

My right upper arm and back caught his shin bones, made him trip and fall over me. He went down with a loud exhalation.

I jumped up, saw the mask on the ground, and made my best guess as to his position in the dark.

My leap was foolish, driven by rage. I launched into the air, arcing down to land on my knees rather than feet, a move that might have hobbled me for the rest of my life if I'd been wrong about his position. But my knees never struck the rocks and logs of the forest floor. One hit his sternum, the other his throat.

My assailant made a gagging, choking sound and then stopped moving.

I pushed myself up, pulled out my phone, and pushed the button to turn on its light.

In the dim glow of phone light, I could see Randy Bosworth, the former manager at Reno Armored, staring up at the night sky, his lifeless eyes reflecting the moonlight.

Two hours later, Diamond came into my cabin. As he opened the door, I could see the harsh flood lights they'd set up in the woods. "They're hauling the body away" he said as he pet Spot. "The medical examiner said that a knee drop to the chest and neck can kill a man in several ways. But based on your report of nearly instant death, he's guessing the blow ruptured the man's aorta."

I nodded.

Diamond continued. "Quite the mess out there. Pieces of hockey stick strewn about. Fresh-broken branches. Forest duff scraped off the dirt like someone was doing some random digging with a hoe."

I nodded again.

"And that boy is one big piece of beef. Armed with a hockey stick and protected with a hockey mask. Yet you took him down without any help from your hound." Diamond said it like a question.

"I'd been down at Street's. She told me that the parole board just released her father. That news had me already upset. So when Bosworth attacked, I got pretty mad."

Diamond said, "Do you think that Bosworth is the fourth robber? Is he the guy who killed the other three?"

"I doubt it. If he were, I would have thought he'd come after me with a woomera or tennis racket and a ski pole spear. I think this was him blaming me for losing his job."

"So we've still got a killer out there?"

"I think so," I said. "Maybe two. The fourth robber killing his comrades and Jonas Montrop's kidnapper killing David Montrop."

After a bit, I said, "Beer or coffee?"

"I'm working. Coffee."

I filled the drip pot and turned it on. When it finished, I poured two mugs.

"You want me to call Street and tell her what happened?" Diamond said.

"No. I'll do it after I'm calm."

As we drank coffee, Diamond asked questions about both cases, his focus on any possible link between the two.

He said, "The main connection between Montrop's murder and the truck robbers is the girl, right? Evan Rosen?"

"Yeah. She worked for Montrop and went to school with the robbers."

"And she had animosity for all of them," Diamond said.

"Maybe a little for Montrop, but definitely a lot for the robbers. They assaulted her."

"So she is the most logical suspect," he said.

"Most logical person to frame, too."

"Why do you think she didn't do it?"

"Lots of little reasons," I said. "But mostly, my gut instinct."

Diamond nodded. "You got a suspect for framing her?"

"Yeah," I said. "The one other person connected to both cases. Flynn. Mystery man from Australia. He knew Montrop's son Jonas from way back. There may have been many reasons why Flynn didn't like Montrop. Maybe he didn't like that Montrop referred to where he lived as 'the projects' in Incline Village. Flynn was also unhappy that Jonas sold him a leaky boat. And Flynn hung out with Evan and the robbers at Wilson High School. The third robber's body, Gavin Pellman, was found dead in Flynn's bed. At least, I believe it was Flynn's bed."

"But you have no clues to Flynn's whereabouts."

"No. So I'm examining all the extraneous stuff I haven't been able to track down. Montrop's gardener, Mr. Kang, who pretends he doesn't speak English but is actually fluent. I'm looking for any possible reason that Jonas Montrop was tied up in a boat instead of being killed outright like everyone else. How the truck robbers got inside details about Reno Armored's operation. Why there was a black Audi parked in Montrop's driveway the morning he was killed. How come..."

"Wait," Diamond interrupted, "what about a black Audi?"

"When Washoe County Sergeant Lanzen had two of her deputies canvas David Montrop's neighborhood after he was killed, the neighbor across the road said that on the morning of Montrop's murder, she saw a very dark car drive partway into his drive and then stop. She noticed because the tail end of the car was just visible when it stopped, and she thought it wasn't up the drive enough that it could even be seen from Montrop's house."

"And it was a black Audi?"

"Maybe. The car was parked in the shade, so she thought it could have been black or midnight blue or midnight green. She didn't say it was an Audi, but she said the logo reminded her of the Olympics."

"Interlocking rings," Diamond said. "Not that there's any connection, but we got a call this morning from a man who lives on the East Shore, across from Hidden Woods."

"South of Cave Rock," I said.

"Right. He said his neighbor is out of town in winter and won't be back until July. But he thought he saw his neighbor's car going down the drive at twilight. The reason it made an impression was that its lights were off and its brake lights never flashed. The guy said the car driver must have used the parking brake to stop. He called the phone number he had for the owner but didn't get an answer."

"And the neighbor's car is a black Audi?"

"Sì. So the neighbor gave me the address and gate code, and I sent out two deputies, and they found a dark house. No answer at the door. At the top of the over-sized garage doors are horizontal rows of little square windows. So they backed up their patrol unit and used the bumper to boost themselves up. Inside was a black Audi and a red Lexus. There was also an alarm sign, so I called the company, and they had no intrusion code on their computer."

"Did their computer show if anyone had entered the property in the proper way using the key code?"

"I asked that, and the guy launched into a sales pitch about new alarm systems and how he'd tried to convince the owner to upgrade. But the owner wouldn't. So they don't have data on when anyone enters the house as long as that person has the code."

"Who's the homeowner?"

"He said he couldn't reveal that without a warrant. Of course, property ownership is a matter of public record, but I haven't pursued that. I asked if he could forward a request to the owner to have him call the Douglas County Sheriff's Office. He said he would. But we haven't heard anything yet."

"Maybe I should go out and have a look. Talk to the neighbor."

"You think you can find something my deputies can't?"

"I doubt it."

My phone rang. I held up my index finger to Diamond. "Hello" I answered.

"This is Evan." She sounded panicked. "I had to clear my head, so I went to the store. I just got back, and Mia's gone! Something is very wrong!"

FIFTY-SIX

"Take a deep breath," I said. "We'll figure this out. What's the norm when you go to the store?"

"Sometimes I take her with me. But Mia was tired. She just wanted to sit and watch the Peter Pan DVD in my computer. When I got home, the DVD was still playing, but she's gone!"

"Was the door locked?"

"I locked it when I left. But it was unlocked when I got home." I heard Evan's breath catch.

I spoke slowly and softly, trying to sound calm. "Let's not jump to conclusions. There could be an innocent answer. If she went out for a walk or something, where would she normally go?"

"She wouldn't. She never goes out alone at night. She's even more afraid of the dark than I am."

"Did you check with Mattie?"

"Yes. She hasn't seen or heard anything."

"Has she given you a fright like this before?"

"No! You've got to help me!" Evan said.

Diamond had stopped petting Spot as he listened to my side of the conversation. His frown was intense.

I asked, "Has she ever gone out during the day?"

"I don't remember. During the day. Let me think. Once, she saw a cat outside the window. She went out to try and find it. She said she thought it might have been a cat from Neverland."

"Did she get lost, or did she come back?"

"She got lost, way down by the shore. It was terrifying."

"But she was okay," I said, trying to reassure her.

"Can you come here now and help me look? Please?!" Evan was pleading. "It's so dark out!"

"Okay," I said. "It will take me most of an hour to get there."

"Hurry! I'm scared. I know something terrible has happened!"

"Don't go far, Evan. And remember that Mia has always been okay before. She's probably okay now, too. See you soon," I said, and hung up the phone.

I stood up. Spot jumped to his feet. I gave Diamond the basics as I grabbed my jacket.

"Do you suspect a crime?" Diamond asked.

"There is no evidence for it," I said. "Evan said that Mia's gone missing before during the day and turned up okay."

"But…" Diamond said, prompting me as I opened the door of my cabin.

"But Jonas Montrop was kidnapped, tied up, and left to die. And Mia isn't that many steps removed from Jonas."

I pushed out the door. Spot ran ahead to the Jeep.

"Let's take the patrol unit," Diamond said. "The light bar will get us there faster."

I ran to his patrol. I jerked open the rear door and let Spot inside, then climbed in the front passenger seat.

Diamond started the engine, turned on the light bar. The forest flashed blue and red as he raced down the mountain.

I got Street on my cell.

"Sorry it's so late," I said. "But you said I should call you if something critical happens with Evan. It just happened. I'm in Diamond's patrol unit, coming down the mountain."

"I'll be ready," Street said.

"We're stopping at Street's?" Diamond said.

"Yeah. She can help with Evan."

Diamond drove faster, hard on his acceleration, steering, brakes. Street opened her door and ran out as Diamond pulled up. She got in back with Spot.

Diamond raced out onto the highway. I kept my hand on the door handle as he pulled G-forces on the curves.

I explained to Street what had happened. She asked very few questions, no doubt thinking about Evan.

Diamond maybe sensed me looking as we shot past the sign that said we were entering Carson City County rural area, the narrow strip of territory that extended from Carson City up to the lake.

"Tahoe Vista is Placer County, out of your jurisdiction," I said in answer to what I thought was his unspoken thought.

"The Fresh Pursuit doctrine allows us to operate in other jurisdictions," he said. "Law enforcement officers like to cooperate with each other."

"Even if there's no pursuit?"

"Maybe the bad guy got away from me." I saw Diamond in the lights of the dashboard. His dark skin glistened. His intensity would frighten anyone who didn't know the circumstances.

We raced through Incline Village, around Crystal Bay, through Kings Beach, and over to Tahoe Vista. A few times, Diamond got on the radio, talking in low tones, probably explaining to other LEOs what he was doing in their territory.

I pointed where to go, and Diamond braked to a fast stop in the narrow lot in front of the converted motel. The door opened in the end unit, and Evan peeked out. When she saw Spot jump out, she knew it was me.

"Did you find Mia?" I asked.

"No! I ran around the block calling her name! I ran down to the beach! She's gone!"

The woman shook with fear. "We'll find her," I said.

I saw Evan looking at Diamond. "This is Sergeant Diamond Martinez of the Douglas County Sheriff's Office."

Street had gotten out of the patrol vehicle. "And this is my girlfriend Street Casey. She came along to help. Can we go inside and talk?"

Evan made a rushed, half-nod and ran in through her open door.

We followed. Spot raised his head, nostrils flexing, maybe smelling hints of his friend Mia.

"How does Mia contact you if she wants?" I asked.

"She knows to call me. She has a phone just for that purpose, and I buy her those pants with the special phone pocket to keep it in. She's good at taking it out of the drawer whenever she leaves and putting it in that pocket." Evan pointed at a kitchen drawer. She walked over and pulled out the drawer as if to show us.

Then she melted, sagging forward, leaning one of her arms

on the counter to catch her weight.

"She didn't take it! Her phone is here!" Evan pulled a phone out of the drawer. "Something terrible has happened. I know it!"

There was a chime. It took a moment for Evan to reach into her pocket and pull out her own phone. She glanced at it, tapped at the screen, dragged her finger. "It's just an email. Mia doesn't do email. She always calls." Evan was about to put her phone back into her pocket, when she looked at it again. She dragged her finger on the screen, then frowned.

"This is weird," she said. "This is scary. I don't know this email address. But the subject line says, 'Tell Owen McKenna.' Let me open it."

She tapped on the screen, then read aloud, "'Evan, Since McKenna managed to convince the cops that you weren't the murderer, he and you leave me no choice. Tell him you're guilty and to bring you back into custody. This is your only chance to save what's left of your world. If not, I won't go so easy as you wanted me to with Jonas Montrop. We agreed that he was supposed to suffer, not escape. I won't make the mistake of listening to you again.'"

Evan frowned and stuttered, "It's lies! All lies! I don't know who's sending this. I never knew Jonas Montrop was kidnapped. I didn't…" She stopped in mid-sentence as she dragged her finger to scroll further down the email.

Her sudden gasp was so gut-wrenching, it froze part of me, and I had trouble breathing. A guttural, moaning wail came from her mouth and rose to a full scream.

She held her phone out like it was on fire. Her eyes were fixated on the screen with such horror that I couldn't imagine what she was seeing.

I reached out, took the phone from Evan, and turned it so that Street, Diamond, and I could all see. The screen showed a close-up picture of Mia's face, a wide piece of duct tape over her mouth. The fear and terror in Mia's red, weeping eyes was like a gut punch.

FIFTY-SEVEN

I handed the phone to Diamond. "Evan's sister Mia," I said.

He took the phone. Anger shone in his dark eyes.

Evan's scream had died down to a terrified whimper. Her hands went to her mouth, and she sobbed and shook and gasped and choked.

I reached out and took Evan's hand. She was quivering as if being electrocuted.

Street stepped forward and gently put her arm around Evan.

"Come sit down," she said in her calmest voice.

She led Evan over to the couch, easing her down. I sat next to her, still holding her hand, trying desperately to think of a plan as I grappled with the statements in the email, the accusations of Evan's involvement in the murders and the reference to the kidnapping of Jonas Montrop. Maybe the statements were true. I couldn't tell. Either way, Evan's shock and distress were real.

Diamond set Evan's phone down on the kitchen counter where Evan couldn't see it.

Evan was gasping, her head and upper body jerking with each choking breath.

"Breathe," Street said. "Deep breaths. Again. Good." Street rubbed Evan's back.

Evan didn't move beyond her labored crying sobs and efforts to breathe.

I said, "I have some questions, Evan. Would Mia have kept the door locked when she was here alone?"

"Yes. We rehearsed it. The door stays locked unless it's me or a friend that she knows."

"What friends are in that category?"

"The night swimmers. Nan and Gabby. Mia's met them several times. She would probably open the door to them. Maybe there's others, but I can't think of any right now. I don't really have friends other than my swim group."

"What about Mia's friends?"

"Her only friends are imaginary. Peter Pan, Tinker Bell, Wendy."

"If someone knocked and said their name was Nan or someone else Mia knows, she would probably open the door, right?"

Evan frowned, wiped tears off her face. "I don't know. I never thought of that. Maybe. Oh, God, I've screwed up so bad."

"The person who murdered David Montrop was probably connected to the kidnapping of his son Jonas Montrop. Evan, you and Mia were both regularly at Montrop's house. Can you think of anyone you saw there who knew about Mia, anyone who paid her any attention?"

Evan tried to inhale, her breath catching. "No. Just Montrop. And his gardener, Kang. But they paid Mia no attention. I parked her in front of the TV, and they went about their business without regard to either of us."

"Kang didn't pay her attention?"

"No."

"If Kang had come to your door, here, would Mia have opened it to him?"

Evan looked into space, her eyes looking horrified. "I once found him sitting on the couch with her in front of Montrop's TV. He was speaking softly and pointing at the TV, and she was giggling. I don't know what he said. But it made me realize that he knows English much better than he reveals to the rest of us. So yes, she probably would open the door to him."

"You don't know what he said to her?"

Evan shook her head.

"Did you ask her?"

"Mia doesn't track like that. If you ask her about something that happened, she won't remember. If you show her a face, she can tell you if she's seen that person or not. But she won't be able to tell you where or when."

Looking at me, Diamond said, "You mentioned the black Audi at Montrop's the day he was killed. I told you about the call we got. A vacation homeowner's black Audi seen coming and going when the owner is nowhere around."

"That could be it. Montrop's son Jonas said that Montrop looked after three houses that belonged to bands he represented. One each on the West Shore, South Shore, and East Shore. Kang probably knew about them. Maybe knew where they were. It wouldn't be impossible for him to get the alarm codes."

I turned to Evan. "It's a long shot. But it's possible that someone has been using these bands' vacation houses and their vehicles, both boats and cars. If that person has taken Mia, it's possible he has her at one of those locations. Does that possibility fit with what you know of Kang? And if Montrop had written down the alarm codes to the vacation houses, would it have been possible for Kang to find them?"

Evan was shaking her head, not in denial, but in confusion. "I don't know. He was the gardener, mostly outside. But sometimes he'd come inside to ask a question. I once found him in Montrop's bedroom. When he saw me, he said Montrop's name as a question, as if he was looking for him. So I guess anything is possible."

I turned to Diamond. "You want to go to the house with the black Audi and look for Mia?"

Diamond nodded. "It's a long shot."

"Evan," I said. "Can you think of anywhere that would be a more likely place for someone to take Mia?"

"No."

"Then let's go," I said.

FIFTY-EIGHT

Evan and Street squeezed into the back seat with Spot. Diamond turned the light bar on and raced back around the lake the way we'd come.

A mile south of Cave Rock, Diamond slowed, shut off the light bar, then pulled off the highway on a no-see-um drive that was shared by several houses. He drove a short distance toward the lake, came to a split and took the right fork, turning off his headlights so that he was driving by just his yellow parking lights. He came to a locked gate, turned the patrol unit off. We all jumped out.

"You still carry that megaphone?" I asked.

Diamond nodded, opened the rear hatch, pulled a small megaphone out of his supply box, and handed it to me.

"Follow me," Diamond said.

He ran around the gate, which blocked the drive but had no attached fence. Diamond would have disappeared into the darkness were it not for the moon, which was still fairly high in the sky even though it had been a few hours since it had illuminated Bosworth's hockey mask in the forest at my cabin.

Street held Evan's hand as we ran.

I held Spot's collar. Partly, to keep him from running ahead. Mostly, because, like all dogs, he reads the darkness with his nose and constantly makes mini-alerts if he senses a person or a dog or something more unusual in the dark. I'd learned his tells and his physical vocabulary. With my knuckles against his neck muscles, I could get a good idea if we were heading into dangerous territory.

Fifty yards down, Diamond turned right and angled off through the woods.

Diamond picked his way through the forest, heading north. There was just enough moonlight coming through the branches to give us a sense of where to go. The air was thick with the scents of pine needles and moist dirt and the herbal scents of nightshade plants. Every smell seemed to be made more pronounced by the dropping temperature, a crisp presence of cold that felt threatening. The cold flowed over us like an evil spirit, warning us away, letting us know that if things went wrong, they would do it with intensity and without forgiveness.

I felt Spot alert. He didn't express tension so much as awareness. I looked down at his head to see which way he was focused.

Ahead and toward the left. Toward the water.

To the right loomed a house lit by moonlight. It was down a slight slope. It consisted of two large boxes set at 30 degrees to each other, and it had a gabled roof that faced multiple directions. It was a large house, suitable for a rich rock band. The windows were black. No yard light that I could see.

Diamond made a soft shhh sound and held his arm up as he walked slowly forward. As we got closer, the house's garage came into view.

With a shift of pressure on Spot's collar, we angled out of the forest, toward the house. Parked in the drive was a black Audi wagon, invisible in the dark but for the reflection of moonlight off its shiny surface. I felt the hood. The heat was significant. The car had been driven recently.

I stopped and raised the megaphone with the small end of the cone not to my mouth, but to my ear. By pointing the large open end of the cone toward the house, I could listen to an amplified version of any sounds that might come. There was nothing beyond an airy whoosh, similar to what one hears when putting an empty conch seashell to one's ear.

With Spot as my guide, I took the lead and walked slowly and silently around to the lake side of the house. There was a large deck and a long expanse of floor-to-ceiling glass. I raised my hand, signalling the others to stay put. Then I moved over to the edge of the dark windows. I could see in the moonlight that there were open drapes gathered at the window edge near me. I carefully lifted up my megaphone, wide end toward the house, and eased it up against the glass. I made sure that I was positioned behind the bunched drapes. If anyone was in there, I didn't want them to see me or the megaphone.

Moving slowly so that I didn't rattle the cone against the glass, I leaned over so that my ear was at the megaphone.

I held my breath and listened.

There was nothing.

After a minute, I pulled the megaphone away from the glass, looking carefully, studious in my effort to not bump anything.

As I lowered the megaphone, something nagged at me from just below my level of consciousness.

I stopped, trying to grab the thought.

I turned back toward where I'd just been focusing, reenacting my previous movements. I brought the megaphone back up to the window glass, listened again to the age-old sea, turned it away from the glass. I was very deliberate, looking for whatever had nagged at me, going slowly, taking in every aspect of the night, the moon, the cold air, the humid smells, the sound of distant waves lapping at the shore.

And there it was.

Two things.

The first was that, as I'd brought the megaphone around, away from the house, I noticed that Spot was once again looking out to sea, staring at Tahoe's black plate of ice cold water ringed by snow-covered mountains. The other was that, as my megaphone made its arc away from the window, I did indeed hear sounds. Strange sounds. Possibly even human voices.

But they came not from the house where I'd come to listen.

They came from the lake.

FIFTY-NINE

Once again, I lifted my megaphone up and aimed the large open end out toward the lake. I heard waves. Wind. Water smacking rocks. A distant Canada Goose honking as he flew under the moonlight, trying to keep his family together as they wedged their V-formation north on a night trip toward the Arctic. Then came water slapping something more resonant. A boat hull, maybe. I stopped swinging my megaphone, brought it back a bit, waited, adjusted my position.

When I heard what might be the sound of water slapping a boat hull, I paused and waited. Maybe there was a different sound. Maybe not. I held still. Focused on maintaining a fixed, solid position. My shoulder muscles got sore. Started to quiver. But I kept the megaphone in place. And there it was. A human voice. Unintelligible. But human. Low in tone. Male. Tense.

I lowered the megaphone and whispered. "There's no one that I can sense inside the house. But there's a man out on a boat."

I stared out at the water. The moon reflection was to the south from where I'd pointed the megaphone. The area where the voice had come from was to the right, northwest. There was a stand of trees on the shore, blocking the view, nothing but blackness.

I whispered, "Let's walk down to the shore. Try to stay in the tree shadows. We'll come up behind the boathouse. We can probably see the boat from there."

I held Spot's collar and let him lead. The ground between the house and the shore appeared to be a rock garden, paths between boulders, cedar trees trimmed into sculptures, pools of water, and cascades down to the lake. The tree shadows fell to the side of the garden. The moonlight was bright. We were in full view, if anyone was watching. I bent down to minimize my profile and moved fast to the boathouse. The others followed my lead.

We came up behind the boathouse building. From that

position, I couldn't see the lake, which meant that anyone on a boat couldn't see me. The boathouse opened on a small harbor formed by an arcing breakwater of rocks that had been piled high. The best view would be from out on the breakwater, but that would put us in full moonlight, and I didn't want to take that risk. Diamond, Street, and Evan huddled with Spot and me in the shadow of the boathouse wall.

I said. "If we step out, we'll be in view and lit by the moon. So I'm going to peek around the corner."

I saw Diamond nod.

I kept my hand on Spot's collar, moved to the corner of the building, and looked out.

The trees that had earlier blocked the view were now off to our side. The lake was visible to the northwest. Floating about 50 yards offshore were several boats, all moored to buoys, all pointing west, into the wind, held in place by their buoy lines and the gentle force of the wind. The main boats I could see were motor cruisers with cabins. Two were in the 36-foot range, much larger than the boat that Jonas Montrop had been tied up in. One was closer to 40 feet. It had multiple cabins and a flying bridge. The sterns of each boat faced toward us on the shore. Beyond them were some other, smaller craft.

"Do you see anything?" Diamond whispered.

"Multiple boats, including three cabin cruisers, moored about fifty yards offshore. Because of their mooring arrangement, I can't tell which, if any, of the boats belong to this house or to neighboring houses. I also can't see any lights, so I can't tell which boat is the one with the person I heard."

"How would someone get to the boats?" Evan whispered.

"I can see a dinghy to the side of the biggest boat, so that's probably where the person is. The boat sterns are facing us, but their lights are off. Someone could be sitting there in the dark, looking right toward us, and we'd never know. Take a peek and see if either of you can tell?"

Evan looked out from behind the boathouse corner. After a half minute, she pulled back behind the corner and shook her head. "No movement, no lights, nothing," she said.

Street and Diamond leaned out next, but shook their heads

after they pulled back.

"I want to listen," I whispered. "But I worry the megaphone will catch the light. So let's move around the back of the boathouse to the other side. Maybe there's some cover there that will block the moonlight from shining on the megaphone."

I motioned for Street to take Spot's collar. Then I moved to the side, stepping carefully on stones and over shore bushes. The others followed. We had to step around an aluminum canoe that was propped upside down at the back wall of the boathouse.

"Careful," I whispered, pointing at the canoe. "If we bump this thing, it will make a boom that could be heard for a mile."

At the corner of the boathouse were some large boulders. I got down on my knees and positioned myself so that I could look between the boulders. I aimed the megaphone toward the boats, and put my ear to the small opening.

Again, there were wave sounds, water lapping at boat hulls, and some other sound I couldn't understand. It was like a small animal making little grunts. Or maybe the waves were causing two of the boats to rub up against each other.

I kept quiet, focusing on the sounds. They repeated. Waves and more waves and more squeaking grunts.

It almost sounded like whimpering.

Then came hushed words that stopped my breathing.

"Shut up, or I'll tape your nose, and you'll asphyxiate!"

I turned and whispered to Diamond and Evan. "There's at least two people aboard one of the boats. It sounds like one is holding another captive."

As soon as I said it, I realized that I'd made a mistake. Evan grabbed the megaphone from me, got down between the boulders, and pointed the megaphone at the boats. She put her ear to the small end.

I could hear her breathing, labored with worry and anticipation of the worst that she could imagine. There was nothing we could do but to wait. Evan was rigid with tension. She adjusted the angle of the megaphone a bit as if trying to hone in on a signal. She paused. Adjusted the angle again. Her breathing was still labored but regular.

Then she gasped.

SIXTY

Evan cried, a muffled shriek. She dropped the megaphone and turned her face to the ground, her hands in fists at the sides of her head. "No, no, no, no! It can't be!" she wailed in a panic.

"Quiet, Evan," I said in a loud whisper.

"He has Mia! I'd recognize that whimpering anywhere. You have to stop him! Mia is the only thing I care about in the world!" She stood up in full view of the boat.

I grabbed her and pulled her down as she cried out. I put my hand over her mouth, held her on the ground, and whispered into her ear.

"If you want to save Mia, you have to be quiet! We can figure this out, but only if you stay calm! If he hears us, he'll likely start his engine and race off across the lake. Do you understand me?! You have to be quiet and stay in control!"

Evan's body shook beneath me, tears dripping from her face.

"Nod if you can be quiet, and I'll let go of you."

She nodded.

I took my hand off her mouth. Evan curled up in a fetal position on the rocks and sobbed, her fist in her mouth to quiet the sound. Street bent down and put her hands on Evan, rubbing her back, talking in low tones in her ear.

"Okay, let's make a plan," I whispered. "Can you hear me, Evan?"

She nodded again but didn't move from where she lay on the rocks.

"There's that canoe behind the boathouse. The paddles are probably inside the boathouse. We can paddle out to the boats, figure out which one they're on, and board it."

"It'll never work," Diamond said. "Like you said, a canoe makes noise. If we're out there paddling around trying to figure out which boat they're on, he'll hear us for sure, and he'll escape."

Diamond peeked out at the boats. "If we can determine which boat they're on, we could paddle out and circle around so that we're approaching the bow. He's less likely to see us that way. We could make a fast approach to the occupied boat. Even if he heard us, we could maybe get aboard before he has a chance to start the engine and get away."

"How can we figure out which boat they're on?" I asked. "The voices could be coming from any of those three boats. We'd need something much more directional than this megaphone."

Evan pushed herself up into a sitting position. She ran the back of her hand across her wet cheeks. She was still breathing hard, but she seemed to be in control. Even in the moonshadow, I sensed a change on her face. Her expression had morphed from fear to something else.

Anger.

"I can go," she said in a low voice.

"What do you mean?" I asked.

"I can do a Night Swim. It might be too far to do it in one breath. But if I'm very careful, I can rise up slowly when I get halfway out. I'll take a second breath and submerge for the rest of the swim. If I quietly surface out past the boats, then I can swim up to each boat and listen. When I figure out which boat they're on, I can signal you somehow. Then you can paddle in fast, directly to the right boat."

"The water's too cold," Diamond said. "If anyone should go, it should be me. I've got more body mass. I could last longer before hypothermia sets in."

"Diamond, Evan's talking about a special type of swimming she's been practicing. Swimming underwater while holding her breath. She's part of a group that does this."

Diamond leaned to the side and glanced out toward the boats. "But those boats are too far to swim to underwater."

"No they're not," Evan said. Her voice sounded hardened almost as if she were speaking through clenched teeth. "I could probably do that distance in the pool in one breath. Out here, two breaths. They'll never know I'm coming up on them."

I wanted to ask about the nightmares. I wanted to talk to Evan about her incapacitating fear of the lake, how open water at night gave her terrors. But she didn't mention it, so I didn't. Maybe if she could make Diamond confident that she could do the swim, it would help give her the boost she would need to do what she'd never been able to do in the past.

"Are you sure you want to do this, Evan?" I said.

"I have to," she said.

I wanted to say, 'But you never completed the Night Swim.' I didn't want to lose Evan to a wild, misguided desire to rescue her sister. But I kept my mouth shut. There are times when a person is trained and practiced and finally ready to go into battle to fight for a heroic cause. Those are not the times to question their resolve.

Diamond said, "People have just a few minutes in water of this temperature before they lose all control of their muscles."

Street put her hand on Diamond's arm as if to stop him from verbalizing any more of his doubts.

Evan looked at him. "My sister Mia may have just a few minutes left before this psycho sticks a spear through her or worse. I'm going. How should I signal you?"

I remembered that I'd replaced my pocket penlight with one of the new key fob LED lights. I got it out, took it off my keys, and handed it to her. "I think it's waterproof. You can carry it in your hand or in your teeth. We'll circle around and come in from out in the lake. We'll watch the water near the bows of the boats. Try to get as close as possible to the boat with the man and Mia and then flash the light several times. If the light doesn't work, slap the water with your open palm. We'll hear that, and because the moon will be behind us, we should be able to see you. The man on the boat will think the slap is a fish jumping."

"Okay," Diamond said. "I'll call it in and tell my deputies to come with lights and sirens off."

Street said, "I'll run back to the locked gate and wait for them. I can bring them out here and show them where you are. Maybe they can find another dinghy to get out to those boats."

"Thanks, Street," I said. "Be careful."

Street squeezed my hand, turned to Evan and gave her a hug,

then ran off into the darkness. I held onto Spot so he wouldn't run after her.

Evan looked at Diamond and me. "I won't go until you find the paddles and are ready."

"Right." I was about to walk around to the boathouse door and see about breaking the lock to get the paddles when I stopped and looked under the canoe. There they were, a small gift against a world of despair.

"Diamond," I said, "let's carry this over to the water. Then we'll get you and Spot situated in the canoe and have the paddles ready before I get in and Evan begins her swim."

We walked bent over as we carried the canoe behind the boulders, minimizing our exposure to the view from the boats. We lowered the canoe down so that the bow was in the water and the stern rested on a sandy part of the beach.

"You want me in the bow?" Diamond whispered.

"Sure, unless you're good with a J-stroke."

"That sounds like something for maneuvering from the stern," he said. "I better take the bow."

"Okay. I'll hold the canoe as you climb in."

Diamond stepped from the beach sand into the stern, then, steadying himself with his hands on the gunnel, he walked forward, stepping over the thwarts, and settled himself into the front seat. There was a length of line tied to the canoe's bow ring. Diamond quietly coiled it and set it down at his feet.

Next was Spot. It took a little coaxing, but he'd been in lots of different watercraft. This was just another version. When he was lying down between the thwarts, I turned toward Evan.

"Once we get your signal and board the boat and make sure that Mia is safe, you can climb aboard. Or, if you're too cold, I'll haul you aboard. You'll want dry clothes."

"So I should give them to you," she said. Her voice wavered a bit as if she were already shivering.

"I think that would be best."

She put my LED light between her teeth, untied her shoes, and handed them and her socks to me. Next came her jacket, then her shirt. Last, were her pants. I took them all and stashed them under the stern seat in the canoe.

I walked back to Evan. Despite the fact that she was wearing her bra and underwear, I knew she felt naked, physically and emotionally. She was no doubt terrified by the prospect of the freezing water to come.

I put my hands on her bare shoulders. Her skin was already cold and blue-white in the moonlight. She was shivering in earnest.

"You can do this, Evan," I said. "When we're out there in that canoe, I know that when I look over toward those boats, I'll see you flash the light or slap the water with your hand." I gripped her shoulders harder. "I believe in you."

"No one but Mia has ever believed in me," she said, her eyes brimming with tears.

"Now I've joined the club. You can do this. You can save Mia. I'll be waiting for your signal."

I saw her jaw muscles clench tight.

I turned back to the canoe, leaned down with my hands on the gunnels, and pushed the canoe off into the lake as I stepped in and sat on the rear seat. I picked up my paddle. Diamond was turned sideways, watching. When he saw that I was ready to paddle on my right side, he raised his paddle on the left. As he lowered the blade and pulled back with a strong stroke, I matched his timing, and we quickly accelerated across the black water.

I looked back toward the boathouse. I saw Evan's tiny, lithe figure take two fast steps into the water. She made a silent, splashless dive, and disappeared beneath the icy, black waves.

SIXTY-ONE

To my knowledge, Diamond had never spent time in a canoe. But he was a learning machine, quickly realizing that, because I could see him and not the other way around, I would match his pace. So he set a brisk tempo. He always watched the blade of his paddle, making certain that it never bumped the canoe.

We headed south a bit to get some distance away from the boats that Evan was approaching from beneath. Then I steered us straight out into the lake. I knew we were visible, but the critical thing was silence. I assumed that the man on the boat wouldn't watch the shore full time. But if he heard us, it would alert him to look for us in the moonlight.

Soon, we turned north and raced up toward the boats. We were now broadside to the west wind, which meant the canoe teetered from wave top to wave trough, rocking dangerously. But by counter-leaning, we were able to keep from capsizing.

"You got a plan?" Diamond whispered, his head bent so that he was talking over his left shoulder on the windward side of the canoe.

"When Evan flashes the light, we race toward the boat's stern. You jump out first and take control of the man. My first priority is to get Evan onboard."

"Light flash near the boats," Diamond interrupted. He never paused in his paddling. "There it is again."

This time I saw it. I'd been expecting it to come from the bigger boat with the flying bridge. But the light flashed three times at the bow of one of the smaller boats.

"Let's make this tub get up and plane."

Diamond increased his stroke speed half again. He reached farther forward when he plunged his paddle into the water. Then he rocked his body back as he pulled, increasing both the power and the length of his stroke before he pulled the paddle out of the water to begin the cycle again. He wasn't smooth, he wasn't polished, but he was a machine, driving our canoe forward as if we were in an Olympic race.

I steered us to come alongside the target boat. When we were two boat lengths out, I whispered, "Stop paddling." We still rocketed forward across black water that showed no sign of Evan. I jammed my paddle down, doing a push stroke to slow us.

In one smooth motion, Diamond stood up, wrapped our bow line around a cleat on the cruiser as he leaped up to the cruiser's gunwale. He hit the rail with his hands and swung his legs up and over like a gymnast on the vault.

Diamond rushed into the pilothouse and disappeared from sight, as I focused on turning so that we came crosswise at the stern.

There was a swim platform. I got one foot on it and reached out. "C'mon Spot!"

He stood and jumped onto the swim platform. I reached down, grabbed his front legs and lifted his paws up onto the transom. "Up and over," I said.

He jumped over onto the aft deck. I followed and then took two fast steps to the pilothouse door, which was swinging open. Spot was at my side. Looking in, I could see that the companionway hatch was open to the main cabin below.

"Go help Diamond," I said as I smacked Spot on his rear. He wouldn't know exactly what I meant, but he would understand that I wanted him to move and be engaged. If he came to two men in a fight, he'd know he was on Diamond's side.

I stepped to the side of the boat and looked over. "Evan!" I shouted. "Evan, where are you?!"

There was no response.

From inside the boat, I heard Diamond's command, "Drop your weapon! Put it down, let go of the woman, and I won't shoot! Do it now!"

Holding the side rail, I trotted up the narrow deck along the side of the pilothouse and the main cabin, looking over the rail into the black water. Maybe Evan was hiding under the bow overhang. I leaned out and looked down. Nothing.

I stepped over to the other side. Nothing there, either. I started back along the other side of the boat. Then stopped.

When I had looked over, did I lean far enough out to see the waterline all along the hull? The boat hull had a substantial bow flare, so maybe not.

I ran back, held the railing hard and leaned way out. I could now see the entire waterline. No Evan. Just black liquid. My heart thumped.

I went back to the first side I'd inspected, and leaned as far out as possible.

There she was, a tiny person in the water next to the bow. She was almost hidden from my view by the flare of the bow.

She had one arm up out of the water. Her fingertips were hooked onto the tiny edge of a porthole.

"Evan," I shouted. "Evan can you hear me? Swim back to the stern and I'll lift you out."

She didn't respond. As I thought of lowering a line, her fingertips came off the edge of the porthole, and she slipped beneath the black water.

SIXTY-TWO

I didn't have time to take off any clothes. I leaped over the side railing, and dropped into the lake.

The water was so ice cold, it was like an electric shock. I knew Evan was stricken with hypothermia, unable to swim. She'd drop straight down into the depths. So I swam down. My eyes were open, but it was darker than the night above. I waved my arms back and forth hoping I might feel her as she sank. The cold, filtered moonlight coming down through the water put a sickly glow on my hands. I kicked hard, driving myself down deep. I sensed something pale below me. Pulled and kicked harder. Then my fingers touched hair.

I kicked again, felt her shoulder, got my hand on her arm. I turned around and swam toward the surface, kicking hard, pulling with my free arm, lifting her limp body.

When we broke the surface, we were 20 feet off the boat's port side. I turned Evan onto her back, wrapped one arm across her chest, and swam backward.

The canoe was still floating next to the swim platform, loosely held in place by the bow line draped over the aft deck where Diamond had thrown it. I swam around it to a small folding swim ladder. I stepped up and lifted Evan out of the water. She was a dead weight, limp and cold. Then she suddenly coughed. Water sprayed from her mouth, and my sense of relief was huge. But she was unconscious, her body chilled to a dangerous point.

The night air was very cold, and I wanted to carry Evan into the cabin to begin warming her. I was already shivering violently, and I knew that she was far past that, suffering hypothermia so significant that the shivering reflex had stopped.

I looked over toward the open pilothouse door. The interior of the pilothouse was dark. Light came out of the companionway that went down to the cabin. Diamond was silhouetted in the opening, holding his gun up with both hands. Whatever the situation was, I didn't want to bring Evan into that. But I could get her into the pilothouse and out of the weather.

I carried Evan into the darkened pilothouse and lay her down on a padded bench to the starboard side. Then I hustled back out to the canoe to get her clothes.

But before I dressed her, I needed to dry her off. I opened the various stowage lockers, putting my hand into the dark spaces to feel for any fabric I could use as a towel. There were none. Near the doorway was a tall chart table. Below the angled top were drawers. I pulled them each open in succession. The third one down had rags, neatly folded.

I pulled them out and used them to dry Evan off as best I could. Her skin was too cold and clammy and moist to pull on her clothes. So I draped her clothes over her body.

I pulled open more lockers and found several raincoats, yellow slickers with hoods. I draped them over Evan, tucking them in around her like blankets.

Whether she would survive her hypothermia or not was still in question. She needed a source of heat, another human body next to her, and a warm room. But this was the best I had at the moment.

Still shivering and soaking wet myself, I left Evan on the bench, went through the companionway and stepped down into the main cabin, which was lit with a ghostly glow from recessed lights under the galley cupboards.

"We can make this turn out okay," Diamond was saying in the smooth reassuring tones of a hostage negotiator. His gun was up, both hands wrapped around the grip. His gun was pointing at a man I'd expected to be Kang. But it was the man I recognized as Flynn from the photo of Flynn and Evan in the yearbook. Flynn was holding Mia in front of him, a little to his side. He had a foot-long ski pole spear pointed at Mia's throat, the tip pushing into her soft skin near her windpipe. Mia was rigid with terror. She had duct tape across her mouth. Her eyes were shut tight, tears streaming down her cheeks. Her body looked wooden, it was so stiff.

"I can help you," Diamond said. "If you drop your spear,

you won't get hurt." He sounded more like a shrink than a cop. "We can make this go easy. We can get you help. I'm willing to put in a good word for you and explain that you never intended things to go this far. You just wanted the money. Isn't that right? The murders were crimes of passion. Manslaughter. The other robbers tried to take the money away from you. You don't want to turn this into first degree murder. All you have to do is drop the spear on the floor and kick it toward me."

"If I drop it, you'll shoot me!" Flynn's Australian accent was pronounced. His voice shook with desperation.

"No I won't," Diamond said. "If I wanted to shoot you, I would have already done it."

Flynn made a half glance over his shoulder as if to see exactly what his position was. Behind him, a bit to his side, was the little door that led to the forward sleeping berth. The door was made of thin wooden slats. Flynn shifted closer to the door, his body language suggesting that he was going to drag Mia back into the sleeping berth. I didn't like that at all.

I could see that Flynn was reluctant to take his eyes off Diamond and his gun. He made a brief glance toward me.

"You're the guy who ruined it all," he said. "If you hadn't screwed everything up, I would've had more cash than I could ever spend."

I said, "You could have taken your share of the armored truck money and the kidnapping money. You could have been rich. Instead, you got greedy and wanted it all."

Flynn made a snort. "There wasn't money from any kidnapping," he said. "The only money was from the truck robbery. But then you started asking questions about Wilson High School. It was you digging up old pictures that destroyed everything I've worked for."

"But that's what you wanted," I said. "That was part of framing Evan for the murder. Once I saw the yearbook pictures of the men who raped her, I discovered that those were the men who were killed. That rape gave her a perfect motive, and it was the main reason she was almost tried as a murderer. Getting her sent up for murder would have been the perfect frame, Flynn. But then you committed the third murder while she was in custody. So we knew she was innocent." I thought that if he were convinced that Evan could no longer be framed for the murder, he might relent in some way.

Flynn's eyes were wild. "You've got it all wrong!" It was a desperate line from someone who was trapped.

"Then Gavin Pellman came to your garage apartment and challenged you," I said. "He knew you had the money."

"No!" Flynn looked confused but angry, and ready to explode. The spear he held at Mia's throat shook, the sharp point jerking the woman's skin back and forth. A bright red drop of blood started to run down the spear's point. Mia still had her eyes shut hard. A moaning cry came from her throat. I knew that Diamond would take the shot the moment he got an opportunity. But Flynn kept maneuvering Mia between him and Diamond.

I had to calm Flynn down. I had to get him thinking about something else. I suddenly thought about what Flynn had said, that there was no money from any kidnapping.

"I saw the woomera at your garage apartment," I said. "An ancient weapon like that can still be useful in the modern world? We were wondering how someone could get such power with a ski pole spear. But we didn't realize that a tennis racket could make a good woomera. You notched the ski poles at the end, so the flared edges would fit around the racket's rim."

Without turning away from Flynn, I said, "Diamond, what did you say that notched shape reminded you of?"

In my peripheral vision, I sensed Diamond make a slow shake of his head as if he thought that I was losing my senses.

"I thought it looked like the staff of Hades," he said, "his two-pronged pitchfork."

"That's right," I said. "You said Hades was a god, the god of death, right?"

Flynn was frowning at me. Maybe I was succeeding in distracting him.

"Right," Diamond said. "The god of the underworld. He was one of the three Olympian gods who were brothers. The others were Poseidon, the god of the sea, and Zeus, the god of the air."

"And what culture worshipped those gods?"

"The ancient Greeks," Diamond said. "Classical Greece."

As Diamond said it, all of what I thought I knew was shifting, the pieces of information resorting into different categories.

I realized that I'd missed the obvious about the killings. The misdirection. Even the motive for murder was probably not what we'd thought. Flynn was a sociopath as Dr. Morrell had described. He was the kind of person who committed crimes of passion. Not someone who was a planner.

The real killer was a true psychopath. A careful planner. An actor with no empathy. A Machiavellian manipulator. A narcissist who would plan the ultimate revenge and never have a second thought about morality.

I said to Flynn, "I now realize that the whole point of framing Evan was so that, when I realized that she'd been framed, I would turn my focus on you as the killer."

"You're not making sense, man. I don't know what you're saying." His spear gouged deeper into Mia's throat flesh.

In my peripheral vision, I saw Diamond tensing, his gun becoming more rigid in his hands. He was close to shooting. But I hoped he would sense that I was in the process of discovering something important, something that might be lost if he killed Flynn.

I said, "When I first thought that Evan had been framed, it seemed obvious that you were the likely perpetrator. You knew her from way back in Reno. You could have easily discovered where she lived and worked. You could have stolen her car and gotten it stuck near Montrop's house. One of the dead robbers had a shirt button in his hand, a button like those on Evan's shirt in the picture of you and Evan. It would have been so easy for you to get into her apartment, get one of the buttons and put it there in the dead man's hand. You'd be thinking that someone like me would eventually see those same buttons on Evan's shirt in the yearbook photo. And while you were in the apartment, you could have put one of the spears in her closet."

I paused to breathe.

"Believing that Evan was framed by you made you the perfect suspect. After all, you owned a woomera. You would be the one person to know how to file the ski poles so they fit a tennis racket. That made it look like she had the murder weapon. You knew all of the truck robbers from way back. You had the history with Jonas Montrop. You knew that his father had money and could be extorted by kidnapping Jonas. You'd probably met the gardener Kang. There was a decent chance that he told you about Reno Armored and their cash runs. The evidence that pointed at you blinded me to the truth that you weren't the killer, either. I never even considered that you might have been framed, too."

Flynn was frowning and shaking his head as if he couldn't track what I was saying.

"You never had the money, did you Flynn?" I asked, raising my voice. "You were set up to believe you'd get it, but it isn't going to happen! Don't you see, Flynn? The plan all along was that you're going to die, and you will still look like the killer. Meanwhile, the real killer will escape with the knowledge that he exacted the ultimate punishment on the people who wronged him. He gets to keep the money, too. If Diamond kills you now, you make the perfect murderer. You're holding a spear against Mia's throat."

"No! That can't be!"

"If Diamond doesn't kill you now, the plan was probably for you to die in an accident. We'd find your body and more evidence of your guilt. We'd all assume that you were the killer from the beginning. And we'd assume that you stashed the money, but we'd never find it. It's a perfect frame, Flynn. Look at you, holding a spear to Mia's throat! How'd the real killer manipulate you into that?"

Flynn yelled back, "The only person who…"

Flynn jerked and he made a little choking cough accompanied by a strange noise I didn't recognize, a noise like the snap of breaking twigs. Flynn's face showed wide-eyed shock, and he looked down as a bloody ski pole point suddenly protruded from the base of his neck, poking out and up, the point just in front of his chin. Flynn's face didn't lose its shock as he dropped his little spear.

I leaped forward and grabbed Mia, pulling her back as Flynn fell face first to the floor of the boat, the Hades-flared end of the shiny, oiled ski pole sticking up into the air.

SIXTY-THREE

Mia screamed through her nose and fought me, but I held her hard and close, backing the two of us up and then sitting her down on the settee. Diamond fired his gun at the little door with the angled slats, two of which had broken as the ski pole had been thrust through. He shot four times. The booming explosions were like bombs going off in the enclosed space.

I visualized another dead body in the sleeping berth, wondering if it was Kang.

But intruding into my thoughts were other things I'd seen, things I hadn't made sense of until now.

I remembered that even petite, well-meaning Evan Rosen had said that she and others had picked on the nerds when they were in high school. Such common harassment can be humiliating. And that might have put Evan and the robbers on someone's revenge list.

In that thought came the realization of what this case was really about.

It wasn't about money at all. It was about bullying.

Kids had done what kids do. They'd picked on a kid who was probably younger, smaller, and weaker.

What they never could have imagined in their youth was that the kid they picked on, the nerd they thought was so uncool, was smarter. And he grew up to be a psychopath who convinced the guys who bullied him to participate in a robbery to get a huge amount of money. Then he killed them off in the most violent, punishing way possible. It was all done in a manner to make the motive look like money, and pin the crime on someone else by using a double frame.

Pick on the wrong kid, and you might suffer a payback beyond anything you can imagine.

As Diamond was reaching to open the broken door, we heard movement. Thuds and bumps. Then came footsteps on the roof above us. The killer was still alive. He'd scrambled up through the sleeping berth hatch and clambered onto the deck above the main cabin, the deck that was our roof.

I called out in a loud voice. "You don't have to do this, Jonas. You've demonstrated that you are superior to all these dirtballs who tormented you as a kid. You've proven it to me, to everyone."

As I spoke, Diamond opened the broken door to the sleeping berth, leaned in and looked up.

There was another grunt. Then came the explosive sound of crunching material as a ski pole spear plunged down through the roof above my head. The pointy spear missed my shoulder by a foot. As it stopped, held in place by the grip of the roofing material above, its point was an inch above Mia's head.

Diamond ran up out of the main cabin and through the pilothouse out to the aft deck.

I pulled Mia off the settee, and we followed Diamond up through the companionway into the pilothouse. Spot joined us. The roof over the pilothouse was taller, giving a bit more room in case Jonas thrust more ski pole spears down from above.

Mia squirmed in my arms as I forced her down onto the bench where Evan lay beneath the mound of yellow rain slickers. I realized that she still had tape over her mouth. I pulled it off in a single, fast jerk. She cried in pain and shock.

"Evan is here!" I said at Mia's ear. "She's frozen, and I need you to warm her up." I lifted up on the pile of coats. Evan was still unconscious, and I still couldn't detect any shivering, a very bad sign. "Do you see, Mia? Evan is very cold, and she needs you to warm her up."

Mia realized it was Evan and began shrieking. Her cries were both joyful and fearful.

I gently pushed her down next to Evan. "Hold her, Mia. Warm her up. I'll put these raincoats over both of you."

Mia draped herself over Evan and held her hard, and I covered them both with raincoats. "Don't move until I come back," I said.

Spot looked toward the door where Diamond had run out, then looked down at where Evan and Mia lay under the pile of raincoats.

"Spot!" I said. I took his collar and pulled him over next to the heaped pile of yellow raincoats. I pointed at Evan and Mia and said, "GUARD THEM." I lifted the pile of coats to expose Evan and Mia's heads and directed Spot's nose to them. When I was certain he'd gotten a good whiff of them, I said, "GUARD THEM!" once again.

I shut the door down to the cabin, then ran out of the pilothouse, shutting the door behind me so that Spot wouldn't be tempted to abandon his station. With the doors shut, Spot would stay better focused. If the killer should attempt to enter the pilothouse, Spot would be on guard.

I found Diamond on the port side of the pilothouse. He had his gun up, pointing toward the bow. Standing on the foredeck at the tip of the bow was a figure in the darkness. He was wearing dark pants and hoodie with the hood pulled up. So the only easy thing to see was the bright white hockey mask, an angry, scary design that looked like Hades himself. It was made of hard plastic and had angular, menacing eye openings. There was a pointy nose with narrow slit nostrils. The mouth was a vertical grill of dark stripes that gave it a Hannibal Lecter look.

Perched over his shoulder was a large tube, a quiver for ski pole spears. In the opposite hand was a tennis racket. Because the rest of his body was dark, the mask and racket and quiver seemed to float in space.

"You're trapped, Jonas," I called out.

"That's what you think."

"Psychopaths like you are tripped up by your arrogance."

"Is that what you think? That I've been tripped up? Oh, but I have lots more surprises."

"Too late," I said. "You went too far, carried on a charade that was too elaborate and involved too many people."

"McKenna, you don't have a clue."

"Your singular achievement was to fake your own kidnapping before the other crimes took place. You couldn't be considered a suspect when you were supposedly strung up in the boat, right?

That took impressive planning, killing your stepfather with his paddle board and then leaving the forged note about me on his desk. You knew that it would draw me into the case, and you hoped I'd find you tied up in your boat, thereby cementing your alibi."

"And you fell for it all the way," he said, laughing.

"What was your stepdad's phrase? Obfuscation is fortification. The dirt decoy bag was obfuscation, right? If Kang had arrived earlier than normal to garden, he might have seen you in disguise. You would have shouted something about finding dirt instead of ransom money. Kang would never have thought it was you. And the cops would never think there was a connection between you and some strange sequence of events that left dirt in your stepdad's car. A son would simply steal money or simply kill a father. The obfuscation made it look like something else.

"Then you created the rope burns on your wrists and urinated in your underwear to set up the timeline that convinced us that you were tied up for days, while you were actually out killing your stepdad and robbing the Reno Armored truck and then murdering your fellow robbers. Spearing them with ski poles using your tennis racket as a woomera to connect with Flynn's Australian background was another brilliant move. It's too bad I untied the ropes that bound you. If I'd simply cut the lines, that would have preserved the knots. We would have been able to see what kind of clever slip knot you'd used so that you could put your hands through loops of line and tighten them after you'd waded out to your boat.

"If I hadn't found you, you would have released yourself and claimed you finally undid the ropes that tied you."

Jonas laughed again, a cackle of delight as if I were admiring his genius.

"We never found any other clothes. Did you walk all the way from your house wearing nothing but underwear? Probably not. You must have had another boat to use for transportation. So much obfuscation. Well done."

Several yards beyond Jonas, moored to the same buoy that held the pilothouse boat, was an aluminum fishing boat with an outboard motor. It was probably how he arrived from the South

Shore, and it was his intended escape vehicle after he left a boat full of dead bodies.

"You're demonstrating how little you know," Jonas shouted. "You and the cop and the women will die, and Flynn will disappear at the bottom of Lake Tahoe. And it will be obvious to the world that Flynn was the killer and chief robber. You want obfuscation, just go through Flynn's things. You'll find the receipt for the purchase of a bunch of hockey masks. I showed them to Flynn, and he got his prints on them. People will think he was the source for all of them. There's even one hidden in Randy Bosworth's house and another one at my stepdad's house. No one will be able to figure it all out."

"We know that your stepfather didn't buy his current house in Incline Village until five years ago. I'm guessing you didn't really live in Incline before that," I said. "You knew Flynn and the other kids at Wilson High in Reno. You referred to Flynn living in the projects. But it wasn't a joke about some building in Incline Village. It was a poor neighborhood in Reno where you lived, too. Right, Jonas? You went to the same schools, getting bullied by the older kids, right? You faked everything about this case, the ransom phone call, all the suspects. You probably used stories of potential riches to shape the behavior of the gardener Kang."

Jonas started to say something, then stopped.

I wanted him to confess to the murders, so I kept pushing.

"I bet you loved getting revenge on those jerks who pushed you around as a kid. They probably beat you up and humiliated you. So the only reasonable thing was to kill them, wasn't it? It was an amazing strategy to get them all involved as actual robbers. How delighted they must have been to have you come to them with this opportunity for riches. Then, at the end, you made sure they saw you as you speared each one of them to death. That was the ultimate goal, to be certain they understood it was revenge." I let the statement hang.

"But Evan didn't torment you, did she? I've met her, Jonas. I can imagine that she might have been rude and brusque and even dismissive of you back in high school. But did she go beyond that? From what I know of her, I doubt it. Yet you were willing to let her take the blame for the murders."

Jonas didn't reply.

I waited, wanting to charge forward and grab him but not wanting him to leap into the water, where I'd have to swim after him as he raced to the the small powerboat.

After ten long seconds came his voice, a high, wrenching tenor, garbled behind the hockey mask, and choked with tears. "I was just a little kid in elementary school, eleven years old, when the Three Gs came after me. That's short for Three Geniuses. That's what those scum called themselves. They were so stupid, they thought that was clever. They trapped me in the corner of the school playground and put dog shit down my shirt.

"So I threw the dog shit at them. The teacher didn't see what they did, but she did see me. I got suspended! They called the apartment where I lived. But of course my stepfather wasn't around. He was off in San Francisco putting together another one of his scams. I was living with neighbors in the same building as the Three Gs. And the neighbor lady was too busy to come to school and sign the form for them to let me back in. Because of that, I had to spend ten days stuck at home before they let me back in school."

Jonas backed up against the rail at the bow of the boat. His body leaned out over the water below, but he was held in place by his boot heel, which he hooked on the lower railing.

"The second time the Three Gs did it, I ran to the teacher and showed her. She thought I'd faked it and said I was disgusting. Later, because I'd told the teacher, the Three Gs beat me up, slamming my head onto the ground. I had to go to the doctor and get thirteen stitches in my head. The entire year was like that. I had to endure some kind of torture at least once a week." Jonas stopped for a moment. I could hear him crying.

"Every new school year, they came up with a new torture. Even after they dropped out of school, they would hold me down and cut off my hair in weird patterns. They poured urine down the front of my pants so that it looked like I urinated on myself. They stole my books, partially burned them, then left them on the principal's doorstep so he could find them with my name inside. And you know why? They said it was the toll that brainiacs had to pay to make the world fair.

"I was fourteen when my plan for revenge began to take shape. There was nothing I could conceive of that would be sufficient for the years of torture they put me through. But I made sure they could see me during their last moments. That was sweet, sweet, revenge."

"But why put Evan through such revenge?"

"They were looking for me after school one day. I hid inside the apartment maintenance shed. It was the best hiding place. They never would have found me. But Evan saw me as I went in. She told them where I was. They gave me the worst beating of my life."

"Evan was just a kid, too, right?" I said. "Most kids do crappy things at some point. But she didn't participate in beating you, did she? Maybe she was forced to tell them where you were. Later, they raped her, Jonas. They committed a worse crime against her than they ever did against you."

"Telling them where to find me was still a crime! It was terrible to be sold out!" He was panting hard, his enraged breaths making a shrill noise as the air rushed through the slots in the hockey mask. Gradually, his breathing slowed. When he resumed talking, his voice was a low hiss.

"They committed hate crimes against me. For that, they had to pay. Even my evil stepdad got his punishment. He ridiculed me from the time I was a little kid, saying that my acne was my fault and that I would never get a girl if I acted so nerdy. He was clever, and he knew how to dupe people, but he was stupid and mean. Just like the rest of them. He pretended to be a caretaker for the three big bands that kept houses on the lake. He skimmed their accounts by making up fake charges for fake repairs. What a small-timer! Padding the maintenance bills! He wrote the alarm codes in his book. It was so easy to look at his booking calendar and see when the bands were out of town. For years, I've had access to their houses and cars and boats."

Jonas reached his left hand up and drew a ski pole spear from the quiver.

"Don't do it, Jonas. Sergeant Martinez has you in his sights. He's an excellent marksman."

"Look, I'm turning myself in. I just thought you'd want to see how it works. The tennis racket woomera. The ski pole spear. I used ancient aboriginal principles, but I've created a new weapon. Much more efficient. And because it's a tennis racket, it's completely disguised."

Diamond said, "Raise that racket above your shoulder, you're dead."

"See," Jonas continued as if he hadn't heard Diamond speak, "you just nock the back end of the spear into the upper rim of the tennis racket, like this." He placed the notched end of ski pole spear against the outer end of the racket as he spoke. The spear seemed to click into place. "Kind of like nocking an arrow onto a bowstring. But instead of an arrow lying against the bow for support, the spear lies against the racket. Your fingertips hold the spear next to the racket handle so you can easily carry it. The spear is longer than the racket, but the extra length is hidden behind your forearm. It's a brilliant design. When it comes time to hurl the spear, you release your fingertips as you begin your swing. The spear tip swings out and up while the end of the racket propels the spear to a very high speed by pushing against the end of the spear, the same way a bowstring propels an arrow from its end. After a little practice, you can get the spear to go wherever you like, not unlike the way you can direct a tennis ball. It's very powerful as you've already seen." He began to raise the racket out from his waist as if to show us.

"Drop your weapon!" Diamond said. "Drop it now!"

"Okay, okay! Don't get so tense. I'll set it down on the deck."

Diamond was rock steady aiming his gun as Jonas slowly stepped forward across the foredeck above the sleeping berth. When Jonas was a few feet from Diamond, he bent over and laid the racket with its nocked spear down on the roof deck above the main cabin.

Diamond made a little head movement toward me even though he kept his gun and his eyes on Jonas. I leaned over, reached across the deck, picked up the racket and spear, and stepped away.

"Now your quiver," Diamond said. His gun was just four feet

from Jonas's chest.

"I have to reach my hands above my shoulder to get it off."

"Move very slowly."

Jonas reached up to the quiver strap and slipped it off his shoulder. He used his other hand to grab the quiver by its open end.

"I'm going to put it down where I set the racket," he said.

Diamond didn't move.

Gripping the quiver across its open end, Jonas bent over and gently lowered the quiver to the deck. "There. All safe. You can now…" He flipped the quiver toward Diamond, making Diamond jerk his gun out of the way.

Like a sprinter just out of the starting blocks, Jonas exploded forward. He took two steps and leaped up onto the roof of the pilothouse. He took another step and then jumped up into the air.

Diamond swung his gun around and fired.

Jonas landed with both feet on the hatch in the pilothouse roof.

I saw that he'd grabbed one of the ski pole spears as he'd tossed the quiver. He held the spear next to him, its oily sheen catching the light, as he crashed through the shattered hatch and dropped out of sight down into the space where Evan and Mia lay.

SIXTY-FOUR

I ran along the narrow deck at the side of the pilothouse while Diamond ran down the opposite side. I heard the crank of the engine starter motor. The engine rumbled, then roared. The boat moved forward with a sudden jerk, nearly sending me running off the stern into the lake.

I caught myself by grabbing the side rail.

The boat accelerated fast, the bow rising into the air. I realized that Jonas must have detached the mooring line when he was at the bow. The big boat rumbled at full throttle, heading west into the lake.

I got to the rear pilothouse door just before Diamond. I was wondering if Spot was standing guard over Mia and Evan when his growl roared from within. Then came a scream.

The boat jerked into a left turn as I pulled open the pilothouse door.

All I could see in the dark was the pile of yellow raincoats, a tussle of movement in the center of the space, and the scary hockey mask appearing to float in the darkness. Spot's deep growl mixed with Jonas's high-pitched cry. It seemed as if Spot was shaking Jonas. There was a thrashing motion that moved toward the doorway.

Diamond was to one side of the door, his gun up, but not aimed. He knew that the two women and Spot were both in the way.

Then Spot appeared. He had his jaws around Jonas's right thigh and was dragging him backward toward the doorway, away from Evan and Mia. His growl was ferocious.

I couldn't see the spear. I reached in past Spot, and grabbed Jonas by his left arm, one hand around his bicep, the other hooking into his belt. Diamond appeared next to me, still holding his gun. With his left hand, he grabbed the spear which Jonas held in his right hand. Diamond jerked the spear away from Jonas's grasp and tossed it toward the stern of the boat where it clattered toward the stowage bins.

"Okay, Spot, you can let go," I shouted.

He released Jonas's thigh.

I jerked Jonas out through the door onto the aft deck. Despite my hold on him, he was as strong as a wild animal, writhing and jerking in unpredictable ways. Spot stayed next to Jonas, snapping and growling. Diamond raised his gun with both hands but hesitated.

I pulled on Jonas, dragging him away from the pilothouse. He grabbed a support rail. I pulled his hand free. My feet were slipping on the wet deck. The boat was leaning hard to port as it arced around in a sharp left turn. Behind the boat, the canoe was bouncing violently on the waves of the wake, its bow line still hooked on the cleat where Diamond had tossed it. As the big boat turned, it looked like it might ram into one of the other boats that was moored not far away.

I reached to grab the stern rail for support. Once I could force Jonas down on the deck, Diamond could cuff him.

But Jonas looked past me toward the following canoe as if thinking that it represented a potential avenue of escape. Like a cornered animal that fights to the death, he lunged again, this time surprising me by leaping toward me using my pull to accelerate himself. Jonas twisted in a way I didn't expect, and my hand came off his arm.

Jonas might have succeeded in leaping right past me and into the water. But before I could react, Spot reached out and caught Jonas's ankle. Spot's grip was firm and he arrested Jonas's leap, jerking him back out of the air.

Jonas crashed backward down onto the edge of the boat, his lungs making a loud whomping exhalation as he hit, his body bending backward over the gunwale. His feet were on the aft deck surface, the small of his back on the boat's gunwale edge, and his head bending back and down toward the rushing black water just below. The hockey mask flew off and fell toward the canoe behind us.

Jonas had his wind knocked out of him. He opened his mouth

but could not find air to speak. With great apparent effort, he raised up his head. The look on his face was astonishment. But he wasn't looking at Diamond or me or even Spot. He was looking at the point of the bloody ski pole spear protruding from his abdomen just below the base of his sternum. He stared at it, trying to comprehend how the ski pole that Diamond had tossed could have fallen into the stowage bin and lodged with the deadly end pointing up.

Jonas's eyes didn't lose their surprise. But even in the dark, we could tell that they lost their seeing. I gave Spot the okay to let go of his leg.

The racing boat had come full circle and was about to crash into the largest of the moored cruisers.

Diamond holstered his gun, and we rushed into the pilothouse.

Diamond jerked back on the shifter, pulling it from Forward to Neutral. He spun the wheel to starboard.

The big boat straightened out as it slowed. I saw the larger cruiser out the port windows. Diamond continued to turn the wheel. The boat made a glancing blow against the side of the cruiser, then headed away toward open water as we coasted to a stop.

The mound of yellow raincoats hadn't moved.

"Can you find a light?" I said.

I heard Diamond move. A reading light flipped on at the chart table. It was enough to see.

I sat on the edge of the bench.

"Can you hear me, Mia?" I said in a soft voice. "It's Owen. Everything is okay. The bad men are gone. I'm going to lift off these raincoats. I need to make sure you and Evan are warm. Okay?"

I peeled back the layers and got down to Mia, who was still draped over Evan. Mia had her arms around Evan. She was crying. She lifted her head and looked up at me. In the dim light, I could see that her eyes were swollen and red, her face wet with tears.

"Is Evan okay?" Mia asked, her voice cracking with fear and worry. "It's dark," she sobbed. "I can't see if she's okay. It's too dark. I'm afraid."

"Let me look, Mia." I pulled back the edge of the hood that was still around Evan's face. Diamond had found another light switch, and turned it on. The light was another task light at the cockpit, but it cast indirect light toward Evan. Her cheeks had gone from white and cold to red and hot. She was shivering violently.

"Yes, Mia, Evan is okay. She's going to be okay."

Mia's face remained concerned, but she made a teary, worried grin and lay back down over Evan and hugged her, squeezing her sister as if she were hugging the essence of life itself.

EPILOGUE

A week later, we had an early evening picnic at the Wingfield Park island in the Truckee River in downtown Reno. The river gushed, the combination of outflow from Lake Tahoe 2000 feet above and the snow melt from the mountains near Donner Pass. We walked along the river rapids and found a comfortable place to spread out blankets on the grass. Street pulled out a gourmet dinner of roasted, skinless chicken and a salad of spinach, beet-leaves, and asparagus drizzled with olive oil and fresh lemon. Spot and Blondie lay dutifully to one side. Blondie watched the evening kayakers practicing their moves in the white water park. Spot stared at the food.

"Your hound is as focused as an eagle watching a bunny rabbit," Diamond said as he munched chicken wings. "Strange he's not drooling."

"That's because he understands this to be a human-only dinner."

As soon as I said it, Street reached into her carrier and pulled out two rolls of waxed paper. "Chicken burritos for His Largeness and Blondie," she said. She unwrapped one and held it up in front of Spot. Street was wearing her metamorphosis necklace. The small amber gem dangled at the base of her neck, catching the light and making the butterfly within sparkle.

"Now he's drooling," I said, as Spot watched Street hold out the burrito.

"Drool ain't the word," Diamond said. "More like Yosemite Falls."

Street tossed the burrito, and Spot grabbed it out of the air. Saliva flew. Next, she fed a smaller buritto to Blondie who was much more controlled with her enthusiasm. Blondie chewed with a sense of decorum. Spot, who'd already finished his, watched Blondie.

"Heard Mallory's boys found the money in the kid's boat," Diamond said.

"Yeah. Like everything in this case, the story that Jonas sold the boat to Flynn was more obfuscation, a ruse to direct suspicion at Flynn. All Jonas did was loosen the drain valve until the boat filled partway with water. That way no one would look in the bilge and see that the second fuel tank was actually filled with money. When the murders were pinned on Flynn, and the interest in the case died down, Jonas probably would have pumped out the boat and figured out how to launder the money. Or he could have just dipped into his fuel tank stash now and then to enjoy his untraceable cash in amounts small enough to avoid notice."

"A couple grand a month fun money for the next twenty years," Diamond said.

Evan was eating salad. She leaned over toward Street. "This is how you stay so thin. Spinach has no calories."

"Yes. And every time I make dinner for Owen, I worry that he stops for a chocolate shake on his way home. Anyway, you're lean, too."

"But not because of my diet," Evan said. "I have a terrible thing for chips. But it turns out that you can't eat chips while you clean houses. I know, because I've tried. If I ever get into law school, I'll be in big trouble."

"No wonder you get along with Owen. You have the same impulses."

"Speaking of law school," I said. "I saw Deputy DA Steve Ditmars yesterday. He asked if I had your address. I told him no but that I was seeing you tonight. So he asked me to give you a note."

Evan frowned as I reached into my jacket pocket and pulled out a folded envelope. I handed it to her. "Sorry, it got kind of munched."

Evan opened the envelope and pulled out two pieces of paper. She skimmed over the first page, then looked at the second, reading it carefully. She turned back to the first.

"Everything okay?" I said when I saw tears well up in her eyes.

She nodded. "Yeah. This is… I don't know what to say. He

says he's sorry that he misjudged me and underestimated me. He's written me a letter of recommendation to law school and says he'll send it to whatever schools I decide to apply to. He also says that when I get out of law school, I should give him a call if I want a job."

"Wow, Evan, that's fantastic!" Street leaned over and hugged her. Then Street turned to Mia. "Mia, your sister is going to go to law school! She's going to be a lawyer!" Mia's grin was wide.

"Owen told me you're going to follow in the Arabella Mansfield tradition," Diamond said. "You're going to be the first college graduate in your family. And soon, house cleaner turned lawyer."

"Thanks, but we don't know that, yet," Evan said. "Law school is very hard. Who knows if I can get in, and who knows if I can ever pass the bar exam."

"I know," I said. "I believe in you."

"Me, too," Street said.

"Count me in," Diamond said. "Whole lotta belief in you going around here. And besides, ain't no way law school and the bar exam is as hard as that night swim. Takes more time, maybe, and there's more stuff to know and remember. But not harder. You kicked butt, and that saved your sister."

"Me," Mia said. "Evan saved me."

After we ate, we walked back to where we had parked the Jeep and Diamond's ancient pickup. Blondie and Spot got into the Jeep, where they could snooze away their dinner while we headed out for the rest of our evening. While we walked, Evan and Mia held hands, and I realized that their relationship was something that most people never experience.

Street and I had a moment to ourselves. We held hands, too.

"Remember how you asked me to tell you if I wanted help protecting myself from my father?" Street asked.

"Did you make a decision?"

"I think so. I don't want to go all Rambo in preparing for something that may never happen. But I also don't want to ignore the threat. If he comes to punish me for all those years he spent in prison, I want to be ready."

"You want the middle ground approach?" I said.

"Yes."

"Okay, we'll begin tomorrow and follow whatever schedule suits you. Alarm system, awareness training, fitness regimen, self-defense practice. You're already very fit. But in a month, you will be a new woman, not fixated and constantly focused on a potential threat, but ready. In two months, you'll be primed and practiced. And if he comes for you, the thin, petite, bug scientist will be ready. He will get the surprise of a lifetime."

Street nodded. "Thanks. That's what I want."

The five of us walked to the Pioneer Center theater on Virginia in downtown Reno, where they were playing a revival of the musical Peter Pan. The performance had been sold out, but I'd requested that the box office call if they had a cancellation. The next day they called to say a patron had canceled his seats, freeing up seven expensive seats in the center of the orchestra section. I immediately took five of the seats without checking with my proposed theater companions. But when I called them, they all said yes.

In the lobby before the show, I introduced myself to a distinguished-looking woman whose name tag said she was Alison Brechtel, House Manager. We talked a bit and agreed to meet after the show.

Mia sat in the center of our block of five seats, with Street to her left and Diamond on Street's far side. Evan sat to Mia's right, and I sat next to Evan on the far right.

I've never been a big fan of musicals, but there was no denying the professional level of the singing and dancing and, in the case of Peter, flying.

The show was based on the 1954 version that starred Mary Martin, the same show as the TV version that Mia had seen dozens of times.

"Has Mia been to see lots of musicals?" I whispered to Evan.

"Just on TV. This is her first live theater of any kind."

"So this is a kind of big deal for her."

"You have no idea how big a deal this is."

Mia beamed through the entire show.

After the show, as the crowd worked their way up the aisles, the manager Alison Brechtel met us in the lobby. She introduced herself to Mia. "Owen McKenna tells me you're a big fan of Peter Pan and Neverland. I thought you might like to meet Peter and Captain Hook. They're backstage in the green room. Would you like that?"

Mia was speechless. She turned and gave Evan a questioning look.

"Yes, of course, Mia. How exciting!" Evan said. "Let's go!"

So Brechtel led the five of us back along a side corridor, through two doors, and into the green room. The actors were still in costume, talking to fans. Street and Diamond and I stayed back as Ms. Brechtel brought Mia and Evan over to Peter Pan and Captain Hook. From our distance, it appeared that Mia was bouncing on her toes. Both of the actors stayed in character as they shook Mia's hand. Mia was clearly awestruck, her grin was as high-wattage as grins get. Peter Pan reached out and handed Mia something, and then Evan coaxed Mia away.

As they returned to us, they both seemed like different people than the women we thought we knew. Mia glowed as if she'd been transported to another world. She held out her hand and showed us a clear vial of what looked like iridescent gold dust.

"Peter gave me fairy dust!" She shook the vial.

Evan also beamed, and it wouldn't be an exaggeration to say that I saw in her face something very much like excitement and anticipation of a new life.

We all walked out into the desert night, the stars as brilliant as the lights of Reno and Sparks.

Mia was ahead of us, talking to both Street and Diamond at once, gesturing with her jar of fairy dust. I pointed toward Mia as I bent down and whispered in Evan's ear, "I don't think I've ever seen anyone happier."

"You haven't," she said. "And I've never been happier, either."

Evan reached for my hand and squeezed it hard.

About The Author

Todd Borg and his wife live in Lake Tahoe, where they write and paint. To contact Todd or learn more about the Owen McKenna mysteries, please visit toddborg.com.

A message from the author:

Dear Reader,

If you enjoyed this novel, please consider posting a short review on Amazon or the book site of your choice. Reviews help authors a great deal, and that in turn allows us to write more stories for you.
Thank you very much for your interest and support!

Todd

Made in the USA
Monee, IL
29 September 2024